THE DISLOYAL CORONER

THE DISLOYAL CORONER

THE FENWAY STEVENSON MYSTERIES
BOOK 11

PAUL AUSTIN ARDOIN

For my kids,
Emma and Felix,
two of the bravest people I know

My high charms work
And these mine enemies are all knit up
In their distractions;
they now are in my power.

—William Shakespeare
The Tempest, Act 3, Scene 3

PART 1

MONDAY

CHAPTER ONE

Fenway Stevenson's phone buzzed in her purse a few seconds after the cashier at Dos Milagros gave her the receipt with 25 circled on the top. She handed the receipt to McVie with her left hand and pulled the phone out of her purse with her right, glancing at the screen.

Fenway tapped *Answer.* "Hi, Rachel!"

McVie pointed to a high-top table in the middle of the taquería, and Fenway nodded.

"Hi, Fenway."

A sad note in Rachel's voice; perhaps the saddest she'd sounded since being promoted from Fenway's assistant to press secretary in the sheriff's office. "Everything okay? Craig and I livestreamed your press conference from the road. Very commanding. Your delivery was great."

"Thanks." Rachel's tone was flat, almost depressed.

"What's wrong? Did someone complain?" The someone, in this case, being Sheriff Gretchen Donnelly; something had been off with her since before Fenway had helped McVie with his aborted move to Colorado. "Did they say you went too far in saying the cartel's gone?"

"That was no exaggeration," Rachel said. "All signs point to the Venn Cartel leaving the county. And besides, Donnelly told me to say that."

Of course, Rachel hadn't given the press the *reason* for the cartel's departure: the murders of Seth Cahill and Mathis Jericho two weeks before.

Cahill and Jericho had been critical in moving the raw morpheranyl—*Nyllie* on the street—driving the drugs from the boats landing north of Estancia to a storage unit at Cahill's facility, then storing it until the packaging and distribution centers were ready. But they had both been killed, and the murderer Fenway arrested had nothing to do with the cartel.

But those murders contained details the sheriff's office probably didn't want to make public.

"If the cartel's gone, that's great, isn't it?"

"Yes."

"Makes you look good too, right?"

"Right."

Fenway paused.

Rachel cleared her throat. "Listen, I know you and McVie got back from Colorado, like, two hours ago."

Maybe the fatigue in Fenway's tone was as evident as the sadness in Rachel's. "It's fine. We're taking a break from unpacking. Having dinner."

"If you're back in Estancia, that means you went to Dos Milagros, right?"

Fenway smiled at McVie; he hadn't even had to ask where she wanted to eat. The little things. "Guilty as charged."

"Anyway, the county hired a new deputy. Andrew Zellman. Working swing shift in the evidence room right now."

"Good experience, I guess."

Rachel chuckled. "Good experience, terrible hours. Anyway, he came to me and asked who I trusted in the department."

"He trusted you enough to ask you that?"

"I interviewed him before he was hired. We wound up talking for a while. He seemed worried, and I told him he could trust *you*."

"Me?"

"I trust you more than anyone in the sheriff's office."

Fenway had gotten Rachel through some terrible times, although hearing Rachel say she trusted Fenway so much still surprised her. "Oh. Thanks."

"So you should expect a call from him."

"Any idea what he's worried about?"

"No."

"And he can't go to Sheriff Donnelly?"

"I got the feeling he asked me about who to talk to specifically because he *doesn't* trust her. Not yet, anyway."

Fenway rubbed her forehead. The text from Donnelly almost two weeks ago—*Congratulations on solving the two murders*—still seemed weird, though Fenway couldn't put her finger on exactly why. Fenway *had* arrested the murderer, but Donnelly's text still sounded either passive-aggressive or like there was something secret between them.

"You're not too busy to take a call from a new deputy, are you?" Rachel asked.

"Uh—no. I guess not." Fenway paused. "Is he going to call me at work tomorrow?"

Rachel was silent.

"Oh—you gave him my cell phone number?"

"Well, yeah." Rachel cleared her throat. "This is his first job out of the academy. So it could be he doesn't yet know the unspoken rules." Rachel paused for a moment. "And who better to talk to him about that than you?"

"Than me?"

"You came in totally green. You hadn't even gone to the academy. But you read between the lines, right? And you got stuff done. And now look where you are."

"Unpaid therapist for new deputies?"

Rachel laughed, but her voice wavered.

"Okay, I'll ask you again: What's wrong?"

"Uh... what?"

"And no changing the subject this time. You should be proud of yourself. I figured you'd be bouncing off the walls. You held a press conference where you announced a big win for the county. I thought the Channel 12 reporter was about to volunteer to be president of your fan club. But you sound like you're about to put on your pajamas, eat a pint of ice cream, and watch a bad rom-com."

"Veinticinco," called the woman behind the counter. Twenty-five; that was their order.

"Go get that," Fenway said, elbowing McVie gently in the ribs, then going to the high bar table and plonking herself down on a stool.

"You can tell from my voice?" Rachel asked.

"Of course I can."

"I should never play poker."

"Not true. You should play with me. For money." Fenway shifted in her seat. "Now—what's the matter?"

Rachel was quiet.

An itch in Fenway's brain. "Oh. Trouble in paradise. Is it Brian?"

"I, uh..."

"It *is*. Something happened with Brian."

"I don't want to tell you. He reports to you now."

That much was true. Callahan had been a distant second choice for the open detective position in the Coroner's Office, and today had been his official first day as a detective reporting directly to Fenway.

"I thought things were going so well." Fenway glanced up when McVie placed the basket of two lengua tacos in front of her. She mouthed her thanks to McVie. "Brian got a promotion, and you're kicking ass in your job. Last month, weren't you talking about moving in together?"

Rachel sighed. "That's where I thought we were headed. In fact, that's what I thought he wanted to talk about late last week."

"So what happened?"

Rachel choked for a moment, then spat out the words. "He broke up with me."

"He—he what?"

"I know. I can't believe it either."

Fenway pressed her lips together. "He's an idiot."

Rachel sniffled. "Sure. That goes without saying."

"Was there any trouble? I mean—"

"I don't know. Maybe it was something stupid, like I make more money than he does. But we never talked about money." She sniffled again. "Maybe he felt like with his promotion he could get—he could get someone better than me."

"He cannot get anyone better than you."

"With his new title and everything, maybe he *thinks* he can."

"Did he give you a reason?"

"Typical stuff. 'It's not you, it's me.'"

"If he means that you're not an idiot and he is, then I agree." Fenway paused. "I'm so sorry, Rachel. I know you liked him."

Rachel scoffed, though her voice broke a little. "He was supposed to be my rebound guy after Dylan, anyway. Not supposed to be serious."

"Well, sometimes these things happen."

"I swear to God, Fenway, if you say 'the heart wants what the heart wants'—"

Fenway made a retching noise, then glanced around and realized she was in a restaurant. She lowered her voice. "I wouldn't *ever* say that. But I'm sorry you're going through this."

"It's fine. I'll get over it." Rachel gave a short laugh. "And you're a great detective."

"Why do you say that?"

"Because I'm in my sweats and I bought a pint of salted caramel ice cream. It'll be my dinner. The mouth wants what the mouth wants."

Fenway almost asked Rachel if she was still seeing her therapist, but it wasn't any of her business. And right now, maybe Rachel needed a friend. "Do you want me to come over?"

"I'd love nothing more than a distraction," Rachel said. "But you have too much going on. You said you're taking a break from unpacking. I bet you have hours more to go." She exhaled.

Fenway hesitated, glancing up at McVie.

"Don't worry about it," Rachel said quickly. "I'll put on a karaoke app and sing breakup songs at the top of my lungs, using my ice cream spoon as a microphone."

"That sounds healthy."

Rachel snickered.

They said their goodbyes and Fenway ended the call. "Sorry about that, Craig."

"Did I catch that right? Callahan broke up with Rachel?"

"Can you believe it?"

McVie took a bite of his burrito, then thoughtfully chewed and swallowed. "What's she doing tonight?"

"Sitting at home with a pint of ice cream, feeling sorry for herself, singing karaoke on an app."

"Did she say she wanted to be alone?"

"Well—no. She said she wanted a distraction."

"And what are *you* doing tonight?"

"Moving boxes into your storage unit with you."

McVie shook his head. "No way. This is *my* problem, not yours. You're letting me stay with you, which I can't tell you how much I appreciate. Right now, your friend needs you. She just broke up with her boyfriend of what, a year?"

"More like nine months."

"And it's her first boyfriend since Dylan died, right?"

Fenway said nothing.

"So go over to her house. Or have a night out with her. Invite Piper and Dez and Sarah."

"Dez won't want to come out—"

"I don't care who you invite, Fenway. The point is, you need to go over to Rachel's and help her feel better. Make mojitos or play Scrabble or swap terrible-man stories. Hell, screw the karaoke app —go out and find a karaoke place."

In Seattle, Fenway hadn't had many friends who were women; only her mom. She'd had classmates and co-workers here and there, but no one who ever came over and took care of her after a breakup with her boyfriend. She wasn't sure what she was supposed to do.

"Is that okay?"

"Of course it's okay. We got all the big stuff into my storage unit, and I can leave the rest of the two-person stuff for later. Or maybe I'll call one of my friends and see if they can help me."

"Not Brian."

"No, it won't be Callahan. And don't worry about me. Worry about Rachel."

Fenway blinked. "Thanks, Craig. That's—that's really nice. I appreciate it."

McVie frowned. "It's the least I can do. If I had an extra fifty bucks, I'd tell you the first round is on me."

Fenway pointed at her tacos. "You won't object if I eat my dinner first?"

They had almost finished when the phone rang in her purse again. Unknown number, but an 805 area code—local.

"This is Fenway Stevenson."

"Coroner Stevenson." A tenor male voice, not one she recognized. "This is Andrew Zellman."

"Of course," Fenway said. "I was expecting your call. And call me Fenway."

A hesitation, then a sigh. "Ms. Richards told you I might phone you?"

"She did."

"Yeah, so listen, I'm the new deputy, and I work in the evidence room. I don't want to bother you, but I don't really know what else to do." A note of panic crept into his voice.

"Okay, Deputy Zellman, tell me what's going on."

"Right," Andrew said. "Well, earlier this week, when I—"

Silence.

"Deputy?"

His voice changed from low and secretive to confident and professional. "No, I'm not sure how you got my number, but if you call the main line for the sheriff's office, they can direct you to the proper person."

"You can't talk now? Did someone show up in the evidence room?"

"That's correct. The main line."

"Do you want to call me back?"

"Certainly. Glad to help."

Then the line went dead.

Fenway looked up at McVie. "That was Andrew Zellman. New hire, works second shift in the evidence room."

"Zellman?"

"The sheriff's office is moving on without you, Craig." A smile touched the corner of Fenway's mouth. "First Mark retires, then Celeste quits. Soon, you'll look at the sheriff's office and won't know anyone here."

"This is the thanks I get? I suggest you go on a girls' night out, and you call me old?"

"If the orthopedic shoe fits—"

McVie laughed.

"Seriously, though," Fenway said, "Zellman has something to say that he isn't comfortable sharing with Sheriff Donnelly."

"Which is?"

"He started to tell me, but he got interrupted. Someone came into the evidence room."

"He was calling you from work? Do you have any idea what he wanted to say?"

"I'd be guessing, but if he isn't comfortable telling the sheriff, maybe he's worried about reporting something another deputy did."

McVie nodded. "Right. He wouldn't want to be thought of as a snitch."

"Cops have each other's backs." Fenway had broken through "the blue wall" a couple of times in the last year or two. It hadn't been easy. "I'm the last person to talk to about how to correct an error without holding people accountable."

McVie frowned. "He probably should talk to me."

"Because you're the former sheriff?" Fenway scoffed. "I don't know, Craig. You're such a rule-follower—"

"I might follow the rules, but I don't rat out my fellow officers when they don't. Everyone makes honest mistakes. I like teachable moments, not punishment."

Fenway tried hard not to roll her eyes and mostly succeeded. "He said he'd call me back. I assume it'll be when whoever is in the evidence room gets out of there."

McVie tapped the watch on his wrist. "Didn't you need to organize an impromptu *Make Rachel Feel Better* night?"

"If *someone* would finish their burrito, then I could," Fenway said.

McVie popped the last bite into his mouth.

CHAPTER TWO

Fenway called Piper on the way home. She was glad to be invited, as Migs was watching the Dodgers game with his friends.

"Okay, so we'll shoot for eight," Fenway said.

Piper paused.

"What is it?"

"I—uh, I can't thank you enough for getting me out of jail in Ruby Dunes. I can't believe—"

"Please, Piper, you'd have done the same for me. You helped my dad out of a similar situation. So maybe call it even."

Sarah was Fenway's next call.

"You sure she wants to go out?" Sarah asked. "I hate it when my friends pressure me to go out when I want to be left alone."

"She said she wanted a distraction. Said she'd be singing karaoke into her ice cream spoon." Fenway paused. "Do you know any places that have karaoke tonight?"

"We're not going to any stupid karaoke night at a barbecue restaurant with peanut shells on the floor." Sarah thought for a moment then squeaked with delight. "Oh, of course. I know just the place. Private karaoke rooms at this new place in Japantown. I'll get us a reservation."

As expected, Dez wanted no part of a private karaoke room. "No offense, Fenway, but that sounds like Dante's fourth ring of Hell to me."

"It's a private room. No one else will see you but us. You can bring Michi."

"Absolutely not," Dez said in a low voice. Was that the sound of a door closing behind her? "I will not subject myself to another lecture about how superior Japanese karaoke culture is. And, if prior experience has taught me anything, Michi will sing, bring the house down, then you won't get the mike away from her."

"That sounds like a hoot."

"Maybe for you. *I* want to get to sleep before eleven o'clock."

Sarah called back. "Reservation for two hours tonight. Rachel will feel so much better after she sings *Bad at Loving Me* at the top of her lungs."

Fenway found a black dress in the back of her closet. After a quick shower, she tamed her hair and did her makeup. She hadn't gotten dressed up in—well, a long time. Maybe not since her election-night acceptance speech. Surely, though, she'd had a night out dancing with Piper or Rachel? But she couldn't remember one for at least six months.

McVie had already left to drop some boxes off before the storage place closed. The black dress was definitely more for the evening, but by the time they got to the karaoke place, the late July sun would have set and the world would be slipping into the energy of the night.

Fenway had volunteered to be designated driver; after the events of the weekend east of Las Vegas, the last thing she wanted to do was drink. She drove to Sarah's apartment, took the stairs, and knocked on the door.

Sarah answered in a floor-length fire-engine red dress.

"Jeez," Fenway said. "Fancy."

"What, this old thing?" Sarah jutted a hip and posed.

Fenway also picked up Piper from the apartment she and Migs shared in the Terrace Rose neighborhood. Piper wore a vintage green pantsuit with flared bellbottoms that would have been at home in a 1970s rock documentary.

"Girl," Sarah said, "didn't I tell you to call me next time you went thrifting?"

Piper batted her eyes, slid into the backseat, and connected her phone to Fenway's car stereo. Fenway was mortified to discover she didn't know any songs on Piper's party mix playlist, while Piper and Sarah sang along. Yikes—all the women were four or five years younger than her. She'd never felt so old—and she wasn't even thirty yet.

She parked in a visitor's space in the parking lot of Rachel's townhouse complex a few minutes before eight. It took three door-bell rings before Rachel answered the door, true to form in olive green pajama bottoms with cartoon drawings of fried eggs, and an oversized T-shirt. She gaped at the three women for a moment, then a grin spread over her face.

"You came to kidnap me and help me forget about Brian?"

"Whatever gave you that idea?" Sarah said, holding a palm theatrically to her chest. "We were in the neighborhood, thought we'd head over to All Access Burger. Their five-dollar value menu is good for another hour."

"Or, you know, a private karaoke room," Fenway said.

"And drinks," Piper chirped.

"You guys," Rachel said, "that's so sweet. But I don't know if I have anything to wear."

"That's the salted caramel ice cream talking," said Fenway.

Piper squeezed past Fenway and went inside, then ran up the stairs. "I know *exactly* the outfit for you tonight."

Twenty minutes later, Rachel was in a chocolate brown wrap dress that managed to be both youthful and sophisticated. Rachel grabbed her purse, and they went out to Fenway's Accord.

"Listen," Sarah said, "I don't know if you're all about country or pop or hair metal, but I have a few screw-you breakup songs in mind."

"Only if they have swearing in them," Rachel said.

"Or if they're songs about destroying his pickup truck," Piper added.

Rachel scoffed. "His new, loud, obnoxious black pickup truck."

"That must have been quite an insurance payout," Sarah said.

"Insurance payout?" Fenway asked.

"A drunk driver totaled Brian's car a few months ago."

Fenway nodded. Rachel's former husband, Dylan, also had owned a big black pickup. After he'd been killed, Rachel couldn't sell the truck fast enough.

Sarah cleared her throat. "Just *sing* about destroying his truck, okay? I don't think we have enough money to bail you out if you actually cause property damage."

"You're assuming I'd get caught," Rachel said slyly.

VR Karaoke was in the two-block stretch of 17th Street between Ramblas and Las Estrellas that served as Estancia's pitiful excuse for a Japantown. A Japanese market, two sushi restaurants, an antiques shop, and VR Karaoke were all interspersed between produce stands and entrances to walk-up apartments. Fenway turned down 17th.

"Where are you going?" Sarah asked from the backseat of Fenway's Accord.

"Uh... VR Karaoke. Isn't that where you made reservations?"

"For nine o'clock. We can't show up there forty-five minutes early."

Piper pointed down a side street. "Ice Mountain. It's over a few blocks." She grinned at Sarah. "Ladies drink for half price on Mondays."

Rachel scrunched up her face as Fenway parked. "Well, I *do* like a good French 75. Two for the price of one are even better."

The parking lot was a block away from Ice Mountain, and

Fenway blinked as her eyes adjusted to the low levels of cool blue light and the pulsing beat of electronic music. The bar itself was translucent, lit up in azure with shapes of mountains. All the bartenders were gorgeous, wearing white fur hats and white cuffs with bare arms and white fur shorts. The male bartenders wore white vests, open to expose their muscular chests and abs; the women wore white fake-fur bikini tops.

"I love it," Sarah said. "It's so over the top." She turned to the bartender, a woman whose olive skin glowed in the blue light of the bar. A few minutes later, the bartender returned with three French 75s and a cola.

Sarah handed the cola to Fenway, and Rachel reached behind her to grab one of the French 75s.

"As my dad used to say," Piper said, "good riddance to bad rubbish."

They all clinked glasses, then drank.

"Woo," Rachel said. "That cocktail is better than salted caramel ice cream." She grinned at Sarah and clinked glasses with her again.

The other three stepped closer to the bar and ordered another round of French 75s before Fenway was half-done with her cola.

"One day you're young and fun," Fenway muttered to herself, "and the next day you're the designated driver, wondering why all the bartenders are wearing fur bikinis." She looked around. The bar area was fairly full of people, but the rest of the space wasn't crowded. And at a table in the corner, a man sat stirring his drink.

Fenway looked closer. Was that the head of Dominguez County's vice program?

It was. Fenway blinked again, trying to remember his name.

Steve. That was it. Steve Alvídrez.

At least a friendly face. Fenway walked over to his table. "Captain Alvídrez, right?"

He glanced up at her, then narrowed his eyes. "Uh, yes, that's me."

Fenway pointed to herself. "Fenway. Fenway Stevenson."

He stared at her in confusion.

"The coroner."

Recognition dawned in his eyes. "Oh, of course. I'm so sorry—I didn't recognize you. And in this bar."

"I get it. Kind of like when you're a kid and you see your teacher in the grocery store."

Alvídrez nodded. "Right, right." He half-stood, the table and the booth making it difficult. "I stick out like a sore thumb here. Would you like to join me?"

"Maybe for a minute." Fenway hooked her thumb over her shoulder. "I'm with those three by the bar. We're trying to make one of them feel better about her boyfriend breaking up with her."

Alvídrez followed the line of Fenway's thumb over to the bar. "Is it working?"

"We'll see. Karaoke's next."

His gaze returned to Fenway. Fortunately, to her eyes, not to the little black dress. "And on a school night, too."

"Don't worry, I'll have her home before curfew."

Alvídrez laughed.

Fenway looked around. "So this isn't really my scene."

"Mine either. I was here on a first date."

"Ah. How did it go?"

"Fine." Alvídrez paused. "No. She was... terrible."

"Oh." Nice to hear that others had as much trouble connecting as she did. Misery loves company, right? "Not as advertised in her photos?"

"Not as advertised in her *bio*. Her photo was the only real thing about her. Not interested in anything she listed in her bio. Not the same movies, not the same music. Lied about her major in college." He looked around. "This bar was her suggestion. Turns out she hasn't read a book since high school."

A note of sadness in his chuckle. "To be honest, I'm not quite sure why she agreed to go on a date with me."

Fenway glanced at Alvídrez; he was handsome, and he obviously took care of himself. Maybe his date had been looking for a hookup. She'd had a few dates like that in Seattle. A couple of promising evenings ruined when her date opened his mouth.

She turned to look at the bar, where Sarah, Rachel, and Piper clinked another set of French 75s. That was three, right? She turned to Alvídrez. Maybe she could get his mind off his terrible date. "So, uh, you heard Rachel's press conference, right? The Venn Cartel is out of the county?"

Alvídrez scoffed. "They might be gone for the time being with all the media attention around the Cahill and Jericho murders." He spun his glass on his cardboard coaster. "But they'll be back. Too many rich people with too much money here."

"And how long will the cartel be gone?"

Alvídrez smiled sadly. "Six months, tops."

Oof, Fenway couldn't stop talking about work, even when she was supposed to be having fun with her friends. She looked up as Sarah, the vision in red, walked toward the table. "Max says he can make a *killer* virgin Lemon Drop."

A Lemon Drop? Fenway hadn't had one of those in years. Maybe not since she graduated from Western Washington.

Sarah held her hand out to Alvídrez. "Sarah Summerhill. I'm the executive assistant in Fenway's office."

He shook her hand. "Steve Alvídrez. I head up Vice." He narrowed his eyes. "And Rachel is Fenway's former assistant, right?"

"Ex-assistants getting along and going out for an evening of karaoke?" Sarah said, feigning horror.

"Dogs and cats, living together," Fenway deadpanned. "Mass hysteria."

Sarah looked at Fenway blankly.

Oh no. A movie reference older than Fenway. Maybe even older than Alvídrez. No wonder Fenway felt so old tonight.

"Fenway and I worked together on the Cahill case," Alvídrez said.

"I thought you looked familiar." Sarah sighed. "It's my fault for not implementing a no-work-talk policy on our night out. Come on, Fenway, our karaoke room is almost ready. Let's get a virgin in you before we leave."

Fenway crinkled her nose, and Alvídrez laughed. "You ladies have a good night."

Fenway got up and walked back to the bar, where the abs-of-steel bartender had a martini glass full of a virgin Lemon Drop on the bar.

"What shall we drink to?" Piper asked, holding up her coupe glass.

"To terrible singing," Sarah said, clinking Fenway's glass first, then Rachel's, then Piper's. "May we live, laugh, and warble off-key."

Fenway took a sip of her virgin Lemon Drop—sweet sparkling lemonade with a sugar rim—then looked over at the table where she'd been sitting with Steve Alvídrez. The empty glass was on the table, and he had left.

———

VR Karaoke's private room was all neon greens and dark purples, with two low couches, a coffee table with a tablet, and a large video monitor on the wall facing the couches. Figuring out how to pick songs took about five minutes, even with Sarah showing them the way, and then Piper insisted on Rachel picking the first song. Bonnie Magnificent's *You Wanted Me to Catch You in a Lie* came up on the screen; the song was a little dangerous with its high notes, but a good, fun, screw-you tune.

Sarah had a strong contralto and obviously loved showing it off. She sang more than anyone else: pop songs, show tunes, classic rock. Fenway sang an old jazz standard from Georgette Miller, *Under My Skin,* that her father used to play after the Red Sox won. She found herself getting into it—almost not wanting the song to be over.

Rachel's stomach growled after Sarah's fourth song ended. They ordered spicy fried chicken, vegetable gyoza, ginger tofu udon. The food was surprisingly not-terrible, and she even felt slightly annoyed that she had to put down her chicken when it was her turn to sing again.

VR Karaoke also had a full bar, and although the French 75s were pricey, they were sizable.

Fenway was having such a good time she jumped when the fifteen-minute warning came onscreen. Rachel sang her second Bonnie Magnificent song, *End It Before I End You*, but instead of being fun and petty, this was dark and brooding. After the last lyric faded away, she was obviously in a funk.

Except for Fenway, they'd all had six or seven drinks over the course of three hours, and Rachel was especially wobbly. Fenway drove them all home, dropping Rachel off last.

"You doing okay?" Fenway said, pulling into Rachel's apartment complex parking lot. Her lips were still burning slightly from the spicy fried chicken.

"I guess," Rachel said. "I got a ton of work to finish this week. I need to focus on that. And I knew Brian was a rebound when we started dating. Maybe I'd gotten used to being married to Dylan." She hiccupped, then covered her eyes with her right hand. "I don't know what I'm doing."

"Oh, Rachel," Fenway said, hoping Rachel wouldn't throw up as she navigated the Accord into Rachel's parking space. "When it comes to love and grief and breakups, none of us know what we're doing. Look at my dad. He's almost sixty, and he has no idea what he's doing."

"He's rich, and he married a beauty queen."

"Dad lucked into both. Believe me, he doesn't know anything."

Rachel opened the door and Fenway turned off the engine.

"What are you doing?"

"Making sure you get in okay."

"I'll be fine. If you want, you can watch me until I open the door, like you're my mom."

"Tell you what—let's grab lunch tomorrow. My treat."

"Oh, a pity lunch?"

Fenway grinned. "Can you imagine how much Brian will lose his mind when he hears his new boss is going to lunch with the woman he broke up with?"

Rachel laughed. "If I'm not feeling too hungover, it's a deal."

Rachel opened the door and stepped out, a little unsteady on her feet, but otherwise okay.

Fenway backed out of the space, but didn't drive out of the lot until Rachel had gone inside and closed the door behind her.

———

Fenway opened the door to her apartment—and thought she'd stepped into the wrong unit. Her counters were spotless, her dining table was gleaming, and the carpet in the living room had vacuum lines. While Fenway had been at karaoke, McVie had been busy cleaning. Only a few stacks of boxes remained.

McVie walked out from the bedroom in boxers and a T-shirt, tight across his chest and biceps. He smelled of sandalwood and soap, freshly showered. "Hey, how was it? Rachel okay?"

"Sarah has an *excellent* singing voice," Fenway said.

"Really?"

"Yes. I'm surprised I haven't heard it before."

"You know, I don't do too bad at karaoke."

Fenway looked sideways at McVie. "You sing James Brown? Really?"

"The music I listen to and the music I perform at karaoke can be two different things."

Fenway arched an eyebrow.

"I sing dark goth music from the eighties. I've got the angst down pat. And hardly any of those singers could carry a tune, so I hold my own."

Fenway turned her head to look around the apartment. "You put in a lot of work when I was gone."

"Yeah. Didn't get everything out of the moving truck before they closed at nine, but Migs said he'd help me out tomorrow."

"That was nice of him." Fenway stared at how clean everything was. Had anyone ever done anything like this for her before?

She'd never been in this situation—moving in with a boyfriend. McVie seemed determined to disrupt as little of Fenway's life as possible, which was definitely not the case with the horror stories she'd heard from other women when their boyfriends moved in.

She took a few steps toward McVie and took his hand. "Thank you for cleaning the apartment." The words were out of her mouth, but they sounded inadequate.

"Thank you for letting me stay here."

"No problem." Kind of a lie; it *was* a problem. Fenway had to disrupt her life in a big, scary way to drive the moving truck halfway there and back. She had to take unplanned vacation days, move meetings—

Oh no. Move meetings.

McVie read Fenway's expression. "What? Did I do—"

"No, no," Fenway said. "I forgot. When I thought I'd be flying back to Estancia from Vegas yesterday, I told ADA Pondicherry I'd be in his office first thing this morning."

"Oh."

"But we drove, and we stayed in Palm Desert last night. And I obviously didn't show up in his office earlier." She paused. "I'll make sure to see him first thing tomorrow."

"What did he want?"

Fenway wanted McVie's take on the Mathis Jericho case, but he wasn't sheriff anymore. "Info on open case, that's all."

A whopping understatement: Jericho had been found dead in his boss's Corvette, eighteen bags of Nyllie surrounding him. It had all been entered into evidence, and Fenway thought she'd caught the killer. But while George Pope admitted to the murder of Jericho's boss, Seth Cahill, he'd pleaded not guilty to the Jericho murder. It was possible that the two deaths were less closely related than Fenway thought.

McVie stood for a moment, and Fenway looked into his eyes: a flash of concern.

"What is it, Craig?"

He hesitated.

"What?"

"You've been fantastic about letting me stay here, especially with this being so last minute."

"I'm not the one who had their life blown up in the last seventy-two hours."

"Yeah… but, look, I know I've stayed over here before, and I've got a toothbrush in the holder on the bathroom counter and a 2-in-1 shampoo in the shower."

Oh. Fenway had been so worried about McVie intruding into her life and her apartment, she didn't even think about giving McVie space of his own. Or making him feel at home. The decision had been sudden, of course, but that was no excuse. "You need a place to put your stuff."

"Not right away," McVie said hurriedly. "There's a corner of your bedroom where I can put a suitcase for now, and I've got a couple of boxes against the wall in the living room—"

"Don't be silly," Fenway said, although her chest tightened. "I'm sure I can clean out a couple of drawers in my dresser, and I can give you a drawer in the bathroom and a shelf in the medicine cabinet."

"I don't want to put you out."

Fenway felt her pulse quicken and her shoulders tense, but counted to ten, squeezed McVie's hand, and with effort relaxed her shoulders. "No, no, no. Of course I want to you to feel welcome here. This was so sudden that I haven't had any time to plan—or even think about what you'd need." And thinking about what to plan felt exhausting.

"You're busy. I understand."

"Tomorrow," Fenway said. Time heals all wounds, right? "It's late and I need to go to bed."

"Yeah. You must be tired."

Fenway took a step back. McVie had been working for the last several hours, but he was freshly showered and smelled like sandalwood and soap.

Maybe something good could come from this sudden life-altering change of plans after all. Fenway ran her hand over McVie's chest. "Well, I'm not *that* tired."

PART 2

TUESDAY

CHAPTER THREE

FENWAY WOKE UP, HER STOMACH CRAMPING. THE FRIED CHICKEN had been decent but heavy, and between the spices and the sugar in the mocktails—oof.

McVie was next to her, his arm draped around her shoulder, and she extricated herself quickly and padded to the bathroom. Modesty fan on high, door closed.

She blinked, her eyes adjusting to the light of the bathroom—she'd only put on the light above the tub, not the brighter ones above the sink—and tried to quell the rising panic in her head. What drawers would she need to empty? Would she need to clear out part of the closet? Should she go to the furniture store to find an armoire that might work in her small apartment? How could she let McVie know he was welcome there, without revealing she was freaking out?

Maybe the money she'd been able to save the last few months was enough to put a down payment on a condo. Home ownership—after she'd had to sell her mother's house in Seattle, she never thought she'd be able to buy a place to live again.

Did she even *want* to live with McVie? She loved him, yes, but she also hadn't made this decision because she *wanted* to move in with him. Moving in together seemed convenient—well, no. Offering her apartment was literally the only option. McVie might have been able to cobble some money together, go into credit card debt or something to get back to Estancia. But without a place to live in Colorado, McVie had had to move back. And he wouldn't be able to get an apartment without a visible source of income. Fenway's offer was something McVie couldn't refuse, even if he wanted to.

Maybe her father had another open one-bedroom and would be okay giving McVie a break on rent for the first couple of months. Fenway could lend him some money for the security deposit.

Then a hundred options and a thousand questions opened in Fenway's head. If she lent McVie money, would that cause trouble in their relationship? How much would she feel comfortable with? Would he accept it? How much would her father be willing to help McVie out? Would his application for rental be approved anywhere *but* the apartment complexes her father owned? Did she even want her father to know that she and McVie needed help?

Fenway shook her head. Yikes. Her brain wouldn't shut up.

And now wasn't the time to bring any of this up. Surely Fenway could bite her tongue for the next few weeks. Until McVie got a steady run of clients again—which might only take a month or two. Then he could move out and they could go back to seriously dating with the goal of maybe sort of one day seeing if this might lead to something like a commitment.

Fenway exhaled and put her head in her hands. Her pulse raced, and she took a deep breath. What was she worried about? McVie had *cleaned the apartment*. He obviously knew what the score was. He wanted to be with Fenway, and he was doing his best not to freak her out. She was lucky to have him.

After a few more deep breaths, her pulse calmed down. She flushed, washed her hands, and opened the two drawers, one on either side of the sink. The left drawer held nothing she used regularly: cotton pads for her makeup, three extra hair wraps, spray sunblock. She grabbed the items, then opened the cabinet under the sink, pulled out a square plastic container with an open top holding a few half-used tubes of travel toothpaste, and put the items inside.

There. Now McVie had his very own drawer in Fenway's bathroom.

Really, he'd been over at her apartment so much before his Colorado adventure that a drawer for him was long overdue. Right?

Fenway went back to bed. McVie had turned so that his back was facing her. She pulled the sheet up to her neck and stared at the ceiling for a long time.

————

Fenway finally fell back asleep, and it seemed like as soon as she closed her eyes, McVie elbowed her in the ribs. "That's yours."

Fenway sat up. Her phone on the bedside table was ringing. Dez. She turned and picked up. "Hey, Dez," she croaked.

"Sorry for calling early," Dez said, "but there's a hit-and-run over in Morongo Heights."

Ah. A neighborhood that Fenway knew as "up-and-coming," although according to Dez, Morongo Heights had been up-and-coming for about fifteen years.

"You need me on this one?"

"I'm afraid so. The pedestrian was struck and killed. Looks like it's been a few hours."

"Can't you contact Callahan?"

"No," Dez said. "The decedent is a Dominguez County Sheriff's Deputy."

Fenway's heart lurched. "A deputy? Who?"

"Andrew Zellman," Dez said. "A new—"

"Yeah, yeah, a new officer. Works in the evidence room. Second shift."

Dez let out a low whistle. "And here I thought you were bad at names."

"Text me the location," Fenway said, getting out of bed and going to her dresser. "I'll be right there."

———

The yellow police tape crossed Morongo Avenue. Fenway pulled the Accord to the curb about two blocks away and parked behind a police cruiser. She briskly walked down Morongo, her flats clicking on the asphalt. Even at six fifteen in the morning, the sunlight was brightening the mist that sat heavily over the road. Her blazer provided decent protection against the foggy Estancia July morning; the mist would probably burn off by midday.

She got out her ID and nodded to an officer who held the police tape up so she could duck underneath it. A prone body lay next to a white Mazda 6. The body was male, about five-ten, and wore a yellow windbreaker.

Fenway stared at the body for a moment. She'd seen almost as many corpses in this job as she had in her forensic nursing program. But a body lying in the street was different from a body in a teaching lab. She hadn't even met Andrew—and had barely talked to him on the phone—but she felt a lump rise in her throat and forced it back down.

Dez stepped out from behind the Mazda and waved a latex-gloved hand at Fenway. "Morning."

"Morning, Dez."

"Waiting for Michi to send the CSI team here, but from what I can tell, it's a hit-and-run. Looks like Mr. Zellman here went over the hood, then hit his head on the asphalt." She pointed to his head. "Cracked skull, I think."

"Tire marks?"

"Nothing that would signify hard braking."

"Are you thinking foul play?"

"Or someone who was so drunk or high they didn't realize they hit a pedestrian."

Fenway knelt down beside Zellman's corpse, snapping on a pair of blue nitrile gloves she'd taken from her purse. She lifted Zellman's arm, then his leg. Rigor had set in enough where she figured he'd been lying here most of the night. Maybe he was hit around midnight or one in the morning. CSI would be able to tell for sure.

"He called me last night," Fenway said.

"Who? Zellman? What for?"

"He asked Rachel who he could trust."

Dez paused. "What does that mean?"

"I'm not sure. He called me from work—from the evidence room—but then it became clear someone had walked in, and he didn't feel comfortable enough to talk."

"He asked Rachel who he could trust, but he didn't tell *her*?"

Fenway tapped her chin. "Possibly because Rachel's the PR person—she doesn't have any law enforcement ability. She can't start an investigation or anything."

"Yeah, but she could have pointed him in the right direction."

Fenway shrugged. "Maybe he thought the fewer people who knew, the better. Or maybe he panicked at the last minute and decided he didn't trust me, either."

"Maybe." Dez pointed at the Mazda 6. "That's Zellman's car. I think Zellman had parked and was crossing the street when he was hit." She pointed at a duplex across the street. "Zellman lives in 3310."

"Roommate or partner?"

"No, he lived alone. Just moved here from P.Q. First job after the academy. Just started his lease last month." Dez stared at the duplex for a moment. "Did he give you any idea what he was concerned about?"

Fenway squeezed her eyes shut. "He was a little surprised that I was expecting his call. And then he said he wasn't sure what to do.

After that, he said that something happened—uh, last week, I think. Then he shut up."

"Something happened last week, then. And he works in the evidence room." Dez paused. "And someone ran him over."

"If it wasn't an accident, then someone had motive," Fenway said. "I can start making inquiries into anything that might have happened in the evidence room. Maybe he noticed missing evidence, or maybe someone is making inappropriate inquiries."

"But it might be something else. He might have had something to hide. Or a jealous lover, or he owed the wrong people money."

"All options are open." Fenway knelt next to the dead man's hip. His end was violent—and Fenway could tell that even if the weight of the car hadn't killed him, he had a lot of internal injuries. He might not have lasted ten minutes—someone had hit him hard and at a high rate of speed.

She started to rise when something caught her eye underneath the Mazda. Gray plastic with a slightly curved side, and orange-yellow glass—no, translucent plastic.

"What is it?" Dez asked.

"I don't know. Maybe nothing." Fenway stepped over the body, then knelt next to the Mazda. Reaching a gloved hand under the car, she pulled the multicolored hunk of plastic out.

"Broken corner turning light," Dez said. She held out her gloved hand. Fenway handed her the plastic.

Dez peered closely at the molded plastic. "There's a number," she said.

Fenway peeled off a glove, got her phone out, and brought up a browser. "On the plastic? What is it?"

"Five seven three seven, Bravo Tango Tango, six zero zero dash eight Foxtrot."

Fenway typed the character string into her browser search window. The search came up with database strings that made little sense. She went back to the search bar and added "corner turning light."

The first three links were all lighting modules for BMW 3-series sedans, coupes, and convertibles. Gray plastic and beige plastic. She clicked and scrolled a little more. The gray plastic was for cars painted black, silver, charcoal, and red. The beige plastic was for other colors.

"We're looking for a BMW 3-series," Fenway reported. "Black, silver, charcoal, or red." She looked at the model years. "Three to six years old."

"Might be a hundred of those in Dominguez County," Dez said, "but if we get the deputies to canvass Estancia, we could narrow it down to a handful by this afternoon. If the driver didn't cover their tracks, maybe we'll even find who did this."

Fenway looked for other detritus in the road but found nothing. Deputies were knocking on doors, seeing if anyone had seen or heard anything, though this early in the morning, very few people answered.

One who did groggily reported a commotion in the street a little after midnight, and Dez told Fenway as she was scouring the street for additional clues.

"For now, we should assume that was the time of the hit-and-run," Fenway said, arching her back with a satisfying crack. "You'll be here to meet the CSI team?"

"Sure."

"What's Brian working on?"

Dez shook her head. "I don't know. He didn't pick up his phone."

"Maybe he's so mad at himself for breaking up with Rachel that he tied one on last night."

"Yeah, well, if he wants to get paid like a detective, he'll have to keep his phone on and answer when we call him."

Fenway felt a bubble of annoyance rise toward Callahan but took a deep breath. "I wasn't here for Brian's first day, though, so maybe I should give him the benefit of the doubt."

Dez laughed. "Look at you being all grown up about it. Can't call you 'rookie' anymore."

"Now you can make fun of Brian for being green instead."

Dez guffawed. "I wouldn't dare. Callahan would take it personally."

"*I* took it personally."

"No, you didn't," Dez said—playfulness and sharpness in equal measure. "When I called you out on your mistakes, you fixed them. If I call Brian out, he'll deny it and get all pissed off."

Fenway paused. "Really? He's that fragile?" Would she regret hiring him?

Dez folded her arms and gave Fenway a sardonic smile. "Why did Brian break up with Rachel?"

"You'd have to ask him."

"Yeah, but what do *you* think it was? You ask me, he's been nothing but a jackass after he bought that huge black pickup a few months ago. That truck costs more than I make in a year, so I know it costs more than *he* makes in a year. He's trying to impress someone, and it sure ain't Rachel."

"So you think he's with someone else."

"Or trying to be, anyway." Dez shot Fenway a sidelong glance. "And you know what they say about men who own big black pickups."

"I dunno, Dez. Sometimes a big black truck is just a big black truck." Fenway grinned. "See you in the office later?"

"If you're lucky."

———

Fenway got back in the Accord and started the engine, guilt gnawing her stomach. Maybe the hit-and-run had nothing to do with Andrew Zellman's call the previous night. She'd been so busy with organizing the karaoke night and getting ready that she'd forgotten he planned to call back.

Zellman didn't necessarily mean he'd call last night, though. He could have planned to call Fenway today, maybe before his shift started.

She should check out the evidence room, give it a full inventory. Make sure nothing was missing that might have given someone a reason to kill Andrew Zellman.

She put the car into gear when her phone rang. Rachel.

"Morning, sunshine," she said. "Hung over, or feeling okay?"

"Where's my car?"

Fenway paused. "What?"

"My car, my car. When you picked me up, it was in my spot."

Space number 19. Only twenty yards away from the front door of Rachel's townhouse.

"I went out there this morning to go to work, and it's gone. Then I remembered, when you dropped me off last night, it wasn't there, was it?"

"Uh—no. I pulled into your space."

"Okay, well, when you picked me up it *was* there. Someone stole my BMW."

Fenway paused, then frowned. "Your BMW is a 3-series, right?"

When Rachel mumbled assent, Fenway got a sinking feeling in the pit of her stomach. She'd dropped Rachel off well past eleven, hadn't she?

"Report your car stolen, Rachel." Then she bit her lip. "Anyone have access to it?"

"Uh—I don't think so."

"What about Brian? He ever borrow your car? He doesn't have an extra set of your keys?"

"No. He drove my BMW home a couple of times when I'd had too much to drink. That's it."

"He couldn't have—"

"He broke up with me, Fenway, but he wouldn't steal my car." Rachel grunted in displeasure. "I mean, he's a cop."

"Well, yeah, I know."

"McVie trusts him. Just because it didn't work out between us—"

"I get it," Fenway said. "Okay, where do you keep your BMW key?"

"The fob is always with me. In my purse."

"You have a second key fob?"

"Sure."

"Where do you keep it?"

"In the top drawer of my dresser."

"Not in your safe?"

"In my gun safe? No. I keep my gun in there."

So—anyone who came into Rachel's townhouse would have had access to the BMW key, too. "Anyone have an extra house key?"

"Um," Rachel said. "I gave a spare key to my neighbor. You know, in case I lock myself out."

"Which neighbor?"

"Mandy, next door. Number 18."

"How well do you know her?"

"Well enough. We wave hi to each other, and I have her spare key, too." Rachel paused. "She's out of town this week, though. Business trip to... uh, Phoenix, I think."

"Anyone else?" Fenway asked. "How about Brian?"

A scoff from Rachel. "No, Brian doesn't have a key. He didn't—"

"I'd ask you about your boyfriend no matter who he was," Fenway said. "Or who *you* were. Has Brian *ever* had a key?"

"No." Rachel said sharply. "I get that you're mad at him for breaking up with me—"

"I'm trying to figure out what happened. Listen, we need to find your car right away. And it's very important that you call the police to report your car as stolen immediately."

"Why?"

"Just do it, Rachel. In fact, I'm on my way over to your place."

"I have to get to work."

"The police will probably want you to make a statement. I'll come there."

"What are *you* going to do?"

I'll make sure you don't get blamed for this mess. But Fenway didn't say that. "I'll make sure this gets filed properly. You know, a lot of times the police don't take stolen car reports seriously."

"I would think, given where I work, they'd take it seriously."

"Probably," Fenway said. "But I'm coming over anyway."

CHAPTER FOUR

When Fenway pulled into the parking lot of Rachel's complex, two cruisers were already parked in visitor spaces. She looked toward Rachel's apartment; the front door of Apartment 19 was open, and Rachel was talking to an officer in a black Sheriff's Department uniform.

Fenway looked down the street. Two deputies, one on each side of the road, were purposefully striding down the sidewalks. Fenway shook her head. If the BMW had been stolen, and if it had been used to kill Andrew Zellman, it would be miles away from here by now.

After locking the Accord, Fenway walked toward Rachel's front door. Rachel was dressed in a navy business suit with bone-colored flats. Her long hair was in a ponytail, and her makeup was light—lipstick and maybe a touch of mascara.

Fenway had planned to go up to the officer interviewing Rachel, but Rachel caught her eye and frowned, so Fenway hung back. After two or three minutes, the officer turned around. Oh—he had a star-shaped badge on his left chest, not a shield shaped badge. This wasn't a deputy.

"Coroner Stevenson," he said, a smile crossing his face, friendly enough but still serious about the stolen car. He stuck out his hand. "Pleasure to meet you."

"Likewise," Fenway said.

"Lieutenant Satchel Brookline."

Fenway nodded. Brookline was straight-postured, hair cropped close to his head, so fine that Fenway couldn't tell if his hair was a dark blond or a brown color. His brown eyes were intense, and his grip was strong.

"Transferred from P.Q., right?"

"Just a couple of weeks ago. Learning the ropes, as they say."

"Wait—are you the backfill for Celeste Salvador? She wasn't a lieutenant."

"Don't ask me. I applied for the transfer, and I got it."

"Right." Fenway narrowed her eyes. "So you report directly to Sheriff Donnelly."

"That's right. Six years on the force in P.Q."

"Did you know Donnelly over there?" Maybe Brookline reported directly to her before she was elected Sheriff.

Brookline hesitated.

Fenway nodded. Whatever Brookline's past with Sheriff Donnelly, she was in no position to judge; she'd only been appointed coroner because of her rich father. Since then, Fenway had been duly elected, but she never would have had the opportunity if it weren't for nepotism. She changed the subject. "So what do you think, Lieutenant Brookline? APB on the BMW?"

Brookline's radio buzzed. "Hey, Lieu, we found it."

Brookline grabbed the radio. "The BMW?"

The deputy on the other end answered affirmatively; the BMW was on the side street, less than two blocks away.

"My BMW?" Rachel asked.

"There's damage," the deputy said over the radio. "You better see it for yourself."

"Someone took it for a joyride and crashed it?" Rachel said. "Oh, man, this sucks."

Lieutenant Brookline got back on the radio and walked toward the side street. Rachel started to follow, but Fenway stepped next to her.

"What?" Rachel asked.

"Stop talking," Fenway said. "If you've got a lawyer, call them. If what I think happened has happened, you'll need representation."

The color drained from Rachel's face, but she scrolled through her phone with one hand as she followed Brookline at a distance of about twenty paces back.

Fenway followed too, and they walked through the trees and concrete walkways between the townhouses. Soon the walkway emptied out onto a sidewalk, and they turned left. Crossing a street, Rachel's BMW came into view.

The front hood was dented. Blood on the bumper and on the passenger-side headlight. And the passenger-side corner light housing was completely missing.

Well, not exactly missing. The housing was being entered into evidence in the hit-and-run death of Andrew Zellman.

Rachel stopped in her tracks. "Is that—is that blood?" she whispered to Fenway.

"Remember, say nothing."

Rachel held the phone to her face. "The law office isn't open yet. It's not even seven thirty."

"Leave a message. Tell them what's going on. And give me their contact information."

"Why?"

"In case you…"

Rachel paled. "Get arrested?"

"I dealt with this in Vegas with Piper," Fenway said. "She had a good lawyer. Hopefully, you have a good lawyer, too."

"And in Vegas, you found the real killer."

"Maybe I can do it again. Besides, this time I have jurisdiction."

Lieutenant Brookline directed his team to take pictures of Rachel's BMW—lots of pictures from different angles. He asked Rachel to open the car, and his deputies snapped on their latex gloves and went over the car.

Fenway left Rachel's side for a moment and stepped forward next to Brookline, who was examining the area of the floor at the driver's feet. "Lieutenant, when I picked up Rachel yesterday, her BMW was in its parking space. When I dropped her off later that night, it wasn't there."

Brookline cocked his head. "Are you sure?"

"I'm sure."

"Sure enough to testify in court?"

Fenway had seen the BMW there when she'd picked up Rachel, right? She would have pulled into Rachel's parking space if it had been free.

Or maybe not; she was in a big hurry to get to the karaoke place, not realizing that Sarah had made the reservations for later. But Rachel would *never* have done this. Not in a million years.

"Yes, sure enough to testify in court."

The lieutenant shook his head. "I don't like that hesitation, Coroner."

"I was running over last night—uh, I was *reviewing* last night in my mind to make sure."

"This BMW matches the description of the car used to kill a Dominguez County sheriff's deputy. I don't take these things lightly."

Fenway crossed her arms. "And I don't, either. But Rachel Richards was with me last night. I picked her up at eight o'clock, and we were out until almost midnight."

"I know you're friends with—" He stopped, choosing his words carefully. "With Ms. Richards," he finally said. "But please let us collect evidence."

He turned, then stood. "Ms. Richards, would you be so kind as to open your trunk?"

Rachel hesitated. "I'm not sure my fourth amendment rights—"

Fenway held up a hand. "Rachel, your car is covered in blood, and they have reasonable suspicion to search."

"I can look for the trunk release if you prefer," Brookline said. "I'm sure it's around here somewhere."

Rachel held up the key fob, pushed a button, and the trunk clicked open.

Lieutenant Brookline walked around the corner of the BMW to the trunk, then lifted it open. He looked inside, then clicked his tongue. "Well, well, well."

Fenway stepped toward the rear of the trunk and peered inside.

Two plastic bags, the shape and size of two-pound flour sacks. Full of a nearly white powder.

The clear bags were the size and shape of the bags of morpheranyl they'd found with the dead body of Mathis Jericho two weeks before.

***

Rachel stood in blinking disbelief as she was handcuffed and placed under arrest. Fenway kept insisting to Lieutenant Brookline that Rachel was innocent—that the car had been in the parking space when she'd picked Rachel up and missing when she'd dropped Rachel off. Fenway hadn't had time to get the lawyer's information from Rachel; probably the same law firm that had dealt with Dylan, Rachel's now-deceased husband, when he'd gotten arrested over a year before.

But Fenway's protestations fell on deaf ears. Brookline put Rachel in the back seat of his cruiser, then closed the door and turned to Fenway.

"If you don't have hard exculpatory evidence," Brookline said, "I'm arresting her and taking her in."

"But she didn't do this." Fenway's mind raced. "The BMW has a key fob. Didn't I read that these key fobs are prone to—uh…" She searched her brain for the right term.

"Keyless relay theft?" Brookline said. "Or are you talking about OBD port hacking?"

"Either," Fenway said lamely.

Brookline shook his head. "The OBD wasn't broken into. Locked up tight. The housing around the steering column is solid, too—this car wasn't hot-wired. And as for keyless relay, I called in the VIN. Six weeks ago, the dealership updated the car's security system to prevent relay attacks."

"Those anti-theft measures aren't foolproof, are they?"

"No, but only organized car theft rings have the knowledge and equipment to bypass the updated systems. Not someone who'd want to steal a car for a hit-and-run. In my professional opinion, anyone who wanted to run over Andrew Zellman wouldn't have gone through the trouble and expense of bypassing the keyless relay anti-theft system to steal this BMW."

"If they wanted to frame Rachel, maybe they would." Reasonable doubt, after all. Something to tell Rachel's lawyer.

"No," Brookline said, gently but firmly. "Whoever stole this car had the key fob in their possession." He pointed to the front seat. "Ms. Richards is five-foot-two. The seats and the mirrors were all adjusted for someone around that height. If someone without the key had stolen the car, they would have adjusted the seats and mirrors to fit themselves."

"They could have adjusted it back."

Brookline shook his head. "It's a possibility, but I've never heard of a car thief putting the seats and mirrors back the way they found them." He paused. "Or returning the stolen car less than two blocks from where they stole it."

"Someone could have stolen Rachel's key. Or copied it."

Brookline sighed with a note of exasperation.

Yeah, Brookline was right to be skeptical. Local key copy places had safeguards in place for car key fobs. Not likely that anyone copied the key fob. "Okay, Lieutenant," Fenway said, "what do *you* think happened?"

"I think you dropped Rachel Richards off yesterday, then she drove her BMW to Andrew Zellman's apartment, where she ran him over, and then drove back here, parked, and went to bed."

"That's ridiculous."

"You dropped her off, right? Was she inebriated?"

"She wasn't driving."

"But she could have gotten in her car and driven to Zellman's house. Maybe it was to talk about evidence, or maybe Rachel stole the drugs from evidence earlier. Maybe Andrew stole the drugs and Rachel wanted them all to herself. I don't know her motive—we found a significant amount of drugs in her trunk and blood all over her hood and bumper." He pursed his lips. "Put yourself in my shoes, Coroner. How do I justify *not* making an arrest here?"

"Because I'm telling you her BMW was gone when I dropped her off."

"Tell it to ADA Pondicherry," Brookline said. "Maybe he'll agree with you and drop the charges. But there's no way I can go to Sheriff Donnelly and explain why I *didn't* arrest Rachel Richards for this murder."

Fenway put her hands on her hips—but she couldn't fault the lieutenant.

"And now," Brookline said, "I have to drive the suspect to the sheriff's office for processing."

"Gotcha."

Fenway stood on the sidewalk as Brookline drove Rachel away in the back of his cruiser. She trudged back to Rachel's complex parking lot and walked toward her Accord. She reached out to grab the door handle—

Hang on.

Fenway shut her eyes. Had Rachel locked the door behind her

when she and Piper and Sarah had pulled her out of her apartment and out for the evening?

Maybe not.

Maybe someone had broken into Rachel's condo, grabbed the extra key fob, and stolen the BMW—then returned the fob.

She shut her eyes and remembered the BMW in space 19 when she drove up in the Accord.

Was someone framing Rachel for Zellman's murder?

Fenway walked back to Rachel's front door, digging another blue nitrile glove out of her purse. She put it on her right hand and turned the front doorknob.

Unlocked. The door opened and swung into the hallway.

She stepped inside. Had someone been in Rachel's townhouse? And had they left any trace of themselves behind?

She closed the door softly. She needed to check the top drawer in Rachel's bedroom. Perhaps the extra BMW key fob was missing —it could have been stolen.

Fenway walked upstairs, taking care not to put her left hand on anything. Rachel's bedroom was directly ahead of the top of the stairs, and Fenway walked inside.

A high school yearbook was open on the dresser. Oof, Rachel must have had a rough night if she was going through past memories. She glanced at the open page: the Estancia High baseball team. Dylan—Rachel's former husband, may he rest in peace—was featured in the middle of a windup. Also in the team picture were Dylan's brother Parker and a few familiar faces: a man she often saw in Java Jim's; a downstairs neighbor she sometimes waved hi to. Oh —and Brian Callahan. A double whammy: Rachel's dead husband and her recent ex-boyfriend were on the same yearbook page. Maybe Rachel had been flipping through the yearbook after she'd gotten home, drunk.

But Fenway wasn't here to look at yearbook photos: she was searching for Rachel's second BMW key fob. The walnut dresser under the yearbook had three top drawers: left, middle, right. She opened the middle one—nothing. Then the left one.

The BMW key sat right on top.

That was unfortunate. It would be hard to believe that someone had broken in, taken the key, taken the BMW, killed Officer Zellman, then returned the key fob.

In any other situation, Fenway would immediately ask Rachel's boyfriend his whereabouts. Even a cop. Yes, it was more complicated that Callahan reported to Fenway, but she couldn't ignore protocol—or her gut—because the prime suspect had dated her detective.

She could sense an uncomfortable conversation with Callahan in the near future and shook her head to clear her thoughts. What else was in this drawer?

Odds-and-ends, mostly: a couple of scarves—not that there was much of a need for that in Estancia—a few handkerchiefs, two pairs of gloves. And below that, a key. Fenway picked it up; this one looked like it could be a house key.

Fenway set her jaw. Rachel might have been insistent that no one had access to her keys, but someone had gone through a lot of trouble to pin the hit-and-run murder on her. True, BMW key fobs were tricky to copy, taking a few hours or even overnight, but it could happen.

Fenway rubbed her chin. This was getting complicated. Occam's Razor: the simplest solution is usually the correct one. And Occam would agree: Rachel getting in her car and mowing down Andrew Zellman was the simplest solution.

Fenway would testify that the BMW was in Rachel's parking space when she arrived to pick Rachel up, and missing when she dropped Rachel off later that night. But she was only one person, and she was good friends with Rachel. Had Fenway been in the prosecution's shoes, she would have arrested Rachel too.

She walked down the stairs, out the front door, and tried the key in the lock. It fit perfectly, and Fenway turned the deadbolt behind her.

CHAPTER FIVE

Fenway parked in the structure next to the coroner's office and looked at the clock on her dashboard. 7:42 AM. Almost twenty minutes before the official start of her day. It would be her first day with Brian Callahan reporting to her, too; he'd been a deputy who had applied for detective in Fenway's office when Mark Trevino retired. Callahan's first official day had been Monday, and Fenway hadn't been in, as she was on the road back from Vegas.

Callahan hadn't been Fenway's first choice; another deputy, Celeste Salvador, had been a better officer, and when Fenway had worked with her, Celeste had impressed her with not only her intelligence, but her observational skills and her ability to put clues together.

But Fenway had dragged her feet. Well, not exactly dragged her feet, but she'd been in the middle of a murder investigation, and she hadn't filled out the right HR form, and—well, it was her own damn fault Celeste had taken another detective position in another county. At least Fenway assumed the position was in another county; she hadn't heard from Celeste since she'd gone.

Fenway got out of her car and walked toward the office, then stopped at Java Jim's and got a large latte. She hadn't had time for coffee before she'd gone to the crime scene.

There were four people ahead of her in line, and as she waited, she got angrier and angrier at Callahan. First, he'd broken up with Rachel—a close friend of Fenway's—days before starting this job. He'd also messed up badly two weeks before, driving by the house where Mathis Jericho's body sat in the front seat of Seth Cahill's missing Corvette, but not stopping.

Sloppy police work *and* a bad personal situation. Little wonder she was wary of Callahan, no matter how good of a deputy he'd been before.

She ordered her latte, so distracted that she gave her name as "Fenway" instead of the usual "Joanne," and had to endure the "order for Farley?" when the barista announced her latte was ready.

She walked back through the misty morning fog to her office. Sarah wasn't in yet, and Fenway opened her office door and plopped down in her leather chair behind her desk. She woke up her PC and glanced at the clock. Five to eight.

A few minutes later, Sarah came into the office, said good morning, then, catching Fenway's mood, scurried to her desk.

At a quarter after eight, Callahan hadn't come in. Fenway went through her email, clearing out the junk, replying to some requests for clarification.

Fenway looked down again. Twenty to nine. Still no Callahan.

She looked through her email and found an email from HR to Callahan, with Fenway copied, congratulating him on his promotion and specifying a starting time of eight o'clock on Monday morning. Sure, this was Tuesday, but the assumption should have been to start at the same time.

She pushed herself to her feet and went out to talk to Sarah.

"Hi, Fenway," Sarah said. "Did you have fun last night?"

Fenway smiled, though it felt a little forced. "I did. That private room was a good idea." She paused.

Sarah sucked in a breath. "There was something you didn't like.

Lots of swearing in the last song I sang, I know, I wasn't even thinking—"

"No, no, nothing about karaoke." Fenway started again. "The new deputy who's on second shift in the evidence room—"

"Andrew! Yes, he's nice."

"He was killed in a hit-and-run last night."

Sarah's hand flew to her mouth. "Oh *no*. And he just moved here. How awful."

"But that's not—" Fenway almost said *the worst of it*. But of course, that *was* the worst of it. "That's not all."

Sarah's eyes widened.

"Rachel's BMW looks like the car that—that killed him."

"What?"

"I saw Rachel's BMW. Missing the same front side light housing that was found at the scene. Blood on the hood and the bumper. I don't think there's any question about it."

Sarah blinked.

"They've arrested Rachel, but there's no way she did it. Her BMW was there when I picked her up, but it was missing last night when I dropped her off."

"What did you do when you saw her BMW was missing last night?"

Fenway paused. "Well—nothing. I didn't realize it was missing."

"And what about Rachel? Oh, Rachel was pretty drunk."

"Right."

"They've got to have cameras *somewhere* showing the BMW being driven around when we were all at the karaoke bar."

"I should think so. Maybe you can start looking for footage?"

"Uh—well, I can ask the folks in IT."

"Right. Do that." Fenway paused. "Also, I'm interested in who else might have had access to Rachel's keys. She says her next-door neighbor had a spare key but is on a business trip. Can you look into that?"

Sarah cocked an eyebrow. "That's not much to go on."

"The neighbor goes by *Mandy*. Unit 18. Otherwise, same address as Rachel." She paused. "That should be enough, right?"

Sarah nodded.

"One more thing, Sarah."

She looked up at Fenway expectantly.

"I expected Brian in by now."

"Dez, too," Sarah said.

"Dez is at the crime scene."

"Oh, of course."

"But Brian should be in by now."

Sarah was quiet.

"What is it?"

"Well—his first day was yesterday, and you weren't in, so we had him go through the handbook, the training videos, stuff like that."

"Yes, all the boring stuff I had to do on my first day."

"He called someone in the mid-afternoon, and then he left. Maybe four o'clock."

"Who did he call?"

"I don't know."

Fenway frowned. "You know all the phone calls here get logged, right?"

"I do."

"Can you see who he called?"

"He used his cell phone." Sarah paused. "You could have kept the job req open if you didn't want him, you know."

Fenway shook her head. "Not if I wanted to stay on good terms with Donnelly."

Sarah cocked an eyebrow. "You and Donnelly *aren't* on good terms. Hiring Brian won't fix that."

Sarah took a breath, like she was going to speak, then stopped.

"What?"

"Well—I know you and Rachel are close friends. Will you have a problem supervising someone who dumped her?"

"I sure hope not. But I'll definitely have a problem supervising someone who's late on their second day." Fenway tapped Sarah's counter lightly. "Let me know if I need to sign anything to get IT to obtain video footage faster. As soon as we prove Rachel didn't do this, the easier things will be."

Fenway went back into her office and tackled some quarterly spreadsheets.

A while later, the door to the suite opened, and Callahan came in, a large coffee in one hand and a leather bag slung around one shoulder. Fenway looked at the clock on her PC monitor: 9:23.

She closed her eyes and took a deep breath. This wasn't the way she wanted her first day with Callahan to start: with him being late. 9:23 was not a reasonable start time for his first day when the job offer email said eight o'clock. Well, second day, but first day with Fenway. And with him breaking up with Rachel, things would already be awkward.

Fenway tapped her fingers on her desk. How did she want to handle this?

She sighed, stood, and walked over to the door of her office. Sticking her head out, she turned toward Mark's old desk, where Callahan was setting up shop. "Brian?"

He raised his head from his PC monitor.

"Can you come to my office, please?"

"Sure."

Fenway went back to her desk and sat. What would she say first? Maybe she should lead with the murder like she had with Sarah. If she weren't feeling awkward with Brian, that's what she'd talk about first.

She sat.

She readjusted herself in her chair, steepled her hands, then folded them.

Then she furrowed her brow and looked at the clock. 9:34. She'd told him to come to her office almost ten minutes ago.

Fenway got up, went back to the threshold of her office door, and stared at Callahan, who was still sitting at his desk.

"Brian?"

"I'll be right there."

Fenway nodded, went back and sat.

But still no Callahan. Now it was 9:38. She stood from her desk, then Callahan appeared at the threshold of Fenway's office.

"Close the door behind you, would you?"

He gave Fenway a lopsided grin as he stepped inside. "Our first day together, and I'm already in trouble." He closed the door, then sat down in the guest chair in front of Fenway's desk.

A pattering sound. Fenway looked across her desk at Callahan; his knee was bouncing slightly, and his shoe was rattling against the plastic chair mat under Fenway's desk. *Tap tap tap tap tap.*

Fenway steepled her fingers. "I have some news—bad news, I'm afraid. We haven't even talked about the job and expectations, but I'm afraid this comes first."

"I don't like the sound of that." Callahan sped up his foot-tapping.

"Do you know Andrew Zellman?"

Callahan slowly nodded. "He's the new guy in the evidence room, right?"

"He was killed in a hit-and-run late last night."

Callahan dropped his chin to his chest, although the foot-tapping didn't cease. "Oh—oh no. I'm so sorry to hear that." He frowned. "Did we catch the guy who did it?"

Fenway studied Callahan's face. He looked tired. No, scratch that: he looked exhausted, but lack-of-sleep exhausted, not drunk or hungover. "They arrested Rachel."

"Rachel who?" Callahan raised his head.

"Rachel Richards. Your ex-girlfriend."

Callahan blinked. "Oh. You heard Rachel and I broke up." *Tap tap tap tap tap.*

Fenway furrowed her brow. "Did you hear me? The sheriff's office arrested Rachel. And you're more concerned that I found out you dumped her?"

Callahan rose from his chair and the tapping thankfully ceased. "Of course—of course. It—wait. She actually got arrested?"

"That's right."

"Who's lead on the case?"

"Well, it's not you, that's for sure. You didn't answer your phone when Dez called you this morning."

"I didn't—"

Fenway raised her hand. "I don't want to hear it. But, even if you *had* answered, you'd be removed, since you were the prime suspect's boyfriend until yesterday."

"The day before yesterday."

"Doesn't matter. You're not getting anywhere near this case."

"Of course not. Can I—can I go see her?"

"I don't think she's been processed yet." Although enough time had passed that maybe Rachel had gone through processing; if Fenway had had this conversation with Callahan at eight o'clock like she'd originally intended, Rachel would still be waiting in holding. But Callahan had taken his sweet time getting to the office.

"Is there anything else?"

Fenway hesitated. She wanted to talk to him about his tardiness, but she needed to be sure he had been nowhere near Rachel's BMW last night. She closed her eyes, steeled herself, then opened them again. "Where were—" She stopped, looked down at her desk. That would be too forward, especially on their first shift together. She took a deep breath and returned her eyes to Callahan. "In these kinds of investigations, we have to be thorough."

Callahan tilted his head. "You don't think Rachel did it?" He sounded almost surprised.

Fenway pressed her lips together, then spoke. "Do you believe Rachel is capable of running someone down in cold blood?" Oof—no. She was getting off track.

Callahan gave a slight shrug. "People hide their true selves all the time. You've arrested a lot of people I never suspected would be able to kill someone."

"Fair enough," Fenway said. "Even though we've made an arrest, we need to keep looking at other avenues."

His brow furrowed, then relaxed. "Oh, I get it. You need to interview everyone who might have had access to Rachel's BMW."

"I'm trying to get ahead of this, Brian." Fenway held up her hands, palms out. "If I don't ask these questions, the defense could suggest that we stopped looking once Rachel was arrested. Whenever a car is used in a hit-and-run, we always ask who had access to the car."

"No, I get it." He cleared his throat. "Rachel never gave me a key. Not to her car, not to her house, nothing." He chuckled. "I was actually a little miffed she wouldn't, but maybe she needed to take things slow."

"You never took her keys?"

"Nope." Callahan rubbed his chin. "You said this happened last night? If Deputy Zellman was run over before one in the morning, I have an alibi."

Fenway leaned forward. "That's good."

Callahan hesitated. "I didn't want to tell you, because it doesn't look great. For my job, I mean." He sank back into the chair. *Tap tap tap tap tap.* Yeesh.

"How about I be the judge of that?"

"I'm sorry," Callahan said with visible effort. "Yesterday, you weren't here, and I went through my onboarding videos, and Lieutenant Brookline took me with him on a private security gig in the evening out near Fresno."

Ah, the four o'clock call yesterday. Probably Lieutenant Brookline.

"I needed…" Callahan began, then screwed up his face. "Uh, I wanted something challenging, not watching videos all day, so I went. The event ran late."

"You said one in the morning earlier. Is that the time you got home?"

"More or less. I didn't check the exact time."

If Brookline confirmed the time, that would clear Callahan—at least if the time of death matched with the commotion heard in the street near Andrew Zellman's apartment. If Brookline and Callahan had arrived from Fresno at one in the morning, they would have been at least fifty miles away when Zellman was killed. No way Callahan could have been behind the wheel of Rachel's car. Fenway's shoulders slumped in relief; at least her new hire wasn't the killer.

"And," Callahan said quickly, "that's why I struggled to get moving this morning."

"Lieutenant Brookline can vouch for your whereabouts?"

"Yes."

"You know," Fenway said carefully, "Brookline didn't struggle this morning. He was at Rachel's a little after seven. His team is the one who found her car, parked two blocks away, the front end covered in blood."

"What?"

"I know she didn't do it, for what it's worth. Her car was parked in her space when I picked her up last night, and it was gone when I dropped her off after our night out."

Callahan blinked. "Night out?"

Fenway rolled her eyes. "Yes. Night out. I know you—" Oof. Fenway was about to say *I know you thought she'd be home crying her eyes out*—but that was not an appropriate thing for her to say to her employee. "I'll figure out how I can prove she wasn't at the crime scene. Someone must have footage of her BMW during the time we were out. A gas station, an ATM the car drove by, maybe a red-light camera."

"I can do some of Dez's paperwork on the case," Callahan said.

"No, you can't," Fenway said. "Anyone hears you're anywhere near this case, you could get fired. Romantic involvement with a suspect means you stay as far away from this as possible."

Callahan took a deep breath and nodded.

"Do you know anyone else who had access to Rachel's keys?"

"Why would I know that?"

"You were her boyfriend for several months. She ever talk about one of her friends, or her landlord getting her keys, anything like that?"

"I don't think so."

Fenway didn't think Rachel would harm anyone—and Rachel couldn't have been driving the BMW. *Someone* took the car. Brookline himself had said the car hadn't been hot-wired or stolen with the keyless relay attack. Someone had the key in their possession, so they'd probably been close enough to take the key to clone it—or borrow it.

She'd have to figure out who and how, or Rachel would be in jail for a lot longer.

———

After dismissing Callahan—she was too distracted to walk him through the procedural checklist, so she assigned him two more HR videos—Fenway walked outside to the plaza. Sure enough, the fog was burning off. Pockets of mist still hung in the air, almost ethereal, and Fenway shivered. Maybe she should have another large latte.

But with the conflict of interest in her department—which meant Callahan couldn't work on the case at all—her first order of business should be to inform the sheriff.

Ugh. Her last conversation with Sheriff Gretchen Donnelly had been so incredibly awkward—what had Donnelly texted her?

Congratulations on solving the two murders.

And now that the murder of Mathis Jericho had slid back into the "unsolved" column, Fenway's next interaction with Donnelly might be equally awkward.

She stood outside for a moment, feeling her body warm slightly in the dissipating fog.

She'd feel a lot better if Callahan's alibi checked out.

Fenway took out her phone, then scrolled through her office contacts. There he was: Satchel Brookline. She tapped his name.

"This is Brookline."

"Good morning, Lieutenant. Coroner Stevenson."

"What can I do for you?"

"I understand you and Detective Brian Callahan worked private security for an event last night."

"Yes, ma'am. We left right after work. A fundraiser out near Fresno. Paid well, too. I hope you don't mind me taking Brian along."

Fenway paused, trying to figure out how to respond.

"Is there a problem?"

"Callahan was almost an hour and a half late this morning."

"I see." Brookline cleared his throat. "We'll take steps to assure it doesn't happen again."

Fenway paused. Brookline's private security gig—and his inclusion of Callahan—would be an ongoing thing, not a one-off. Callahan hadn't mentioned his side hustle in their interviews. "Thanks, Lieutenant. Oh—"

"Yes, Coroner?"

"Please don't mention our conversation to Detective Callahan. While I'd like to reset our expectations, I don't want to seem like I'm hovering over him."

"Of course."

They ended the call, and Fenway sighed.

Another café latte sounded less like a good idea and more like procrastination. She trudged toward the sheriff's office building across the street.

———

She paced in the hallway about ten feet from Sheriff Donnelly's office before striding up and knocking on the open door. Donnelly looked up from the report she was reading.

"Fenway, hello. Are you here about the Zellman case?"

"I am," Fenway said. "You might have heard by now that Rachel Richards was arrested."

"Her car was found with the victim's blood on it, and a missing piece of the car was discovered at the scene of the crime." Donnelly leaned forward. "You're the one who discovered the corner light housing, if I'm not mistaken."

"Yeah, you're right," Fenway said. "But Rachel didn't do it."

Donnelly raised her eyebrows.

"I picked Rachel up at about eight o'clock," Fenway said. "And her BMW was parked in her space in front of her apartment. When I dropped her off at eleven, no BMW. I parked in her space."

"And you didn't report the missing car then?"

"Well, no. I was more concerned with getting her home safely. I didn't put two and two together until this morning."

"And Ms. Richards didn't notice either?"

Fenway didn't like Donnelly's inflection. Like there were air quotes around *notice*.

"She did not."

"Are you certain? The BMW wasn't parked in another spot or on the street?"

"No. When I picked her up, her BMW was in its assigned spot." She was *almost* positive, anyway. The conversation wasn't going well. Maybe she should have a chat with ADA Pondicherry instead.

Oh no. ADA Pondicherry. Fenway was supposed to have met him on Monday morning, and here it was, ten thirty on Tuesday, and she hadn't even called him yet.

"That also doesn't explain the two bags of morpheranyl we confiscated from her trunk."

"If her car was stolen," Fenway said, "it means someone else could have put them there."

Donnelly folded her hands and glared at Fenway. "I appreciate your insight, but—"

"I came in here," Fenway interrupted, "because we have a conflict of interest in the department."

"I'll say," Donnelly said. "Your new detective is dating Rachel Richards."

Fenway bit her tongue; Donnelly didn't need to know that they'd broken up. "That's correct. So Dez is taking the lead on this."

"And for the duration of this investigation, she'll report directly to me."

"What?"

Donnelly pressed her lips together. "You and Ms. Richards are good friends, are you not? I don't trust you to be any more objective than Detective Callahan."

"I can be objective."

"We have an optics problem, Coroner. No rational observer would believe you'd be able to be unswayed by your friendship with Ms. Richards."

A fair point. "But you and Rachel have been working together since your election," Fenway said. "Won't you have the same optics problem I do?"

Donnelly narrowed her eyes at Fenway. "I haven't been in social gatherings with Ms. Richards. You were at a bar last night with her, along with the assistant from your office and a former co-worker from the IT department."

Fenway took a step back. How did Donnelly know that?

Oh, of course. Steve Alvídrez. He'd seen them at Ice Mountain, and if Donnelly had mentioned the circumstances around Zellman's death and Rachel's arrest—well, of course Alvídrez would have said something.

If she trusted Donnelly, she probably wouldn't have an issue with having Dez report to the sheriff. But somehow, a chill ran down Fenway's back.

"Was there anything else?"

Fenway couldn't very well say something felt off. "No. Glad we could get on the same page."

"Anytime," Donnelly said, picking up the report again. "Oh, by the way, how was your trip to Colorado?"

"You wouldn't believe me if I told you."

CHAPTER SIX

Fenway texted Dez to let her know that she'd be reporting to Donnelly for the duration of the case. The text was fully professional, with no reference to the weird feeling she had about the sheriff.

Fenway walked to the front door of her building and reached out a hand to open it. Then she stopped.

She didn't want to go back into the office and see Callahan. Their interaction had been forced and uncomfortable, and he hadn't respected her authority.

Yuck. *Respected her authority.* That sounded terrible, even in her head. No wonder they'd gotten off on the wrong foot.

If Fenway was the decent manager she wanted to be, she'd have to work to get Callahan motivated and doing the right thing on his own. Avoiding him wouldn't help the situation.

She sighed, opened the door, and went into the coroner's suite. Fenway looked across to Mark's old desk. Callahan slouched in his chair, arms folded, staring glassy-eyed at the monitor.

"Callahan?" Fenway said.

He looked up.

"I'm headed over to the harbor. Try to locate some witnesses. You want to join me?"

Callahan rose and grabbed his light jacket from the back of his chair. "Absolutely."

———

Fenway turned her Accord onto Cypress Street. Estancia Harbor had only been a ten-minute drive from the coroner's office. Callahan sat in the passenger seat, looking out the window like an excited golden retriever. At least he wasn't nervously tapping his foot anymore. She glanced over at him before turning her attention back to the road.

"You haven't asked what case we're working on."

Callahan broke his gaze from the window. "I figured this trip was so I could shadow you, right?"

"More or less," Fenway said. "Most people learn more by doing than by watching videos."

"Definitely true with me."

"So we'll do some doing."

"What's the case?"

"Mathis Jericho."

Callahan flinched.

Yes, he was probably touchy about his lack of follow through because he'd driven right by the cabin with the Corvette holding Jericho's dead body.

"I thought," Callahan said carefully, "we caught the killer."

"Of Seth Cahill. Not of Mathis Jericho. We're reopening the case." How would Callahan react to this? Hopefully, he'd jump at the opportunity to fix his past mistakes, to prove his value.

"Ah." Callahan frowned and stared at the dashboard in front of him.

"Something wrong?"

A pause, then Callahan drummed his fingers on his knee. "No. Nothing's wrong."

Fenway debated whether to say something. Maybe Callahan would see this as a chance for redemption. Or maybe he'd think Fenway was rubbing his nose in his failure.

"We've all made mistakes," she finally said. "We rarely get the chance to correct them."

Callahan sat up straight. "I see. And you're giving me the opportunity to solve this murder?"

"Wouldn't be a bad first win for you." Fenway turned into the Estancia Harbor parking lot and pulled into a spot near the exit, far away from the other cars, then killed the engine.

"You like baseball, Brian?"

Callahan's eyes flicked toward Fenway. "Sure."

"No surprise that my dad's a big Red Sox fan, right?"

He gave her a weak smile. "McVie says your dad named you after their stadium."

"Right." Fenway drummed her fingers on the steering wheel. "When I was little, I had a hard time learning to ride my bike. I was doing okay at first, making it ten or fifteen seconds after my father let the bike go, but then I started overthinking it, and I was falling earlier and earlier."

Callahan cocked his head. "What does this have to do with the Red Sox?"

"Because my dad gave me advice that he heard from one of the Red Sox's pitching coaches. One of their big hitters was mired in a slump. The coach said, 'the more you think about the slump, the worse it gets.' You're putting pressure on yourself to take a big swing and get a home run to erase the slump."

Callahan nodded, lips pursed.

"The batting coach said to simplify things. Take a good at-bat and wait for the right pitch."

He furrowed his brow. "Take a good at-bat? How am I supposed to do that?"

"Slow things down," Fenway said. "Sit back. Be more passive. Don't force anything. The more you struggle, the more you'll change from the foundation you've built, and the worse things will get." Fenway leaned forward. "Don't try to solve the case on the first swing. Gather information first. See the whole picture. Be patient."

"Gather information," Callahan repeated.

"A homicide detective doesn't run around shooting up the bad guys. You need to put the puzzle together—and before you can start putting the puzzle together, you need as many pieces as possible."

Callahan nodded. "And we're here to get the puzzle pieces."

"That's right." Fenway raised her head and thrust her chin at the leftmost bank of boats in the harbor. "The *Ariel* is a whale-watching boat docked in Estancia. But it's been used to smuggle morpheranyl, and two weeks ago, Mathis Jericho drove the last shipment from the boat to the storage unit. So let's go."

"What's the plan?" Callahan asked, as he and Fenway exited the cruiser.

"Interview the captain of the *Ariel*," Fenway replied as they walked toward the boat slips. "Guy by the name of Stephan Butler."

"You didn't interview him before?"

"I did. But that's when we were investigating Seth Cahill's murder. Mathis Jericho was still alive."

"Did Butler give up any information?"

"He confirmed that Cahill and Jericho would take the Nyllie from his boat to the storage facility. He also confirmed that a British national named Calvin Banning accompanied the drugs to the storage unit."

"Who's Calvin Banning?"

"You read the reports on the Cahill murder, didn't you, Brian?"

"Of course."

"So for every morpheranyl shipment that landed in Estancia, Banning traveled on the *Ariel* with Stephan Butler."

"Oh, that's right. The report said Banning likely spent the night in the storage unit with the drugs." He paused. "So does that mean he's still running Nyllie?"

Fenway shook her head. "I think the drug runs were initiated by Anton Venn's cartel."

"And Venn is no longer in the county."

"According to—" Fenway almost said *Sheriff Donnelly,* but then realized she was talking to Callahan, who was probably on Donnelly's side. "According to the county, anyway."

She stepped onto the wooden pier and shaded her eyes. She'd seen the *Ariel* before—but in the middle of the night in the dark two weeks ago, and she wasn't sure she'd recognize it.

"You think this Butler guy killed Jericho?" Callahan asked.

"It's possible, though I don't see how Jericho's death helps him out. Butler must have made a lot of money smuggling. Jericho's death shined a light on Venn, and now Butler probably makes a lot less money whale watching."

Callahan rubbed his chin. "Money isn't always a motive."

Fenway stopped at the edge of the parking lot, about thirty yards from the Estancia Yacht Club, and studied Callahan's face. "You have another idea?"

"You said you interviewed Butler? Did you threaten him?"

"Not physically—"

"With prosecution," Callahan said. "Or ratting him out to Anton Venn. Like, if you suggested he was taking money off the top—"

"I see. Yeah, we threatened him with prosecution." Fenway scratched her temple. "Actually, we threatened to have the Coast Guard impound his boat."

Callahan nodded. "People's priorities change a lot when their livelihood is threatened. Maybe he figured it was time to deprioritize his illegal gravy train." He gazed out over the water. "He could be one of the smart ones who saved his drug-running money for a rainy day. Or even if he didn't, maybe he preferred a big pay cut to the risk of getting his boat confiscated or getting on Venn's bad side."

"I don't think Venn lets people off so easily."

Callahan turned to Fenway. "With all the police activity on the Cahill and Jericho cases," he said, "Venn's packed up shop. Yeah, maybe it's only for six months, three months, whatever, but this gives Butler an out. A chance to escape the drug-smuggling life he couldn't leave. And maybe that doesn't happen without Jericho's body turning up in that Corvette with eighteen bags of morpheranyl in the passenger footwell." He cleared his throat. "If you're looking for suspects, we should bear in mind that money doesn't *always* make the world go 'round."

"Good point, Brian."

So Stephan Butler shouldn't be ruled out as a suspect even though he was in a worse financial position after Jericho's death.

Not bad for Callahan's second day as detective.

———

The mist was almost entirely gone, although as she turned her head southwest toward the ocean, a line of clouds still hung over the water.

The harbor was beautiful: clean boats, shimmering water. She and Callahan walked toward the Estancia Yacht Club—overpriced, bland food, but a nice view, the one time her father had taken her—and walked around the building.

They walked past two-thirds of the boat slips, then passed an empty slip that could accommodate a boat as big as the *Ariel*. A metal gate and a small ticket booth sat in front of the slip. Fenway peered at the sign; the screws that affixed the sign to the post were slightly brown with rust, but the sign itself was new. A logo of a cartoon whale with a life preserver around its middle was at the top, and below that, in large block letters:

Butler Cruises LLC

Then, in smaller lettering below that:

Whale Watching Tours
Wine & Cheese Sunset Cruises
Corporate Events & More
Capt. Stephan Butler

"We're in the right place," said Callahan, "but where's the boat?"

Fenway studied the sign; it looked not only new, but professional. Curious.

A voice from behind them: "Just missed 'em."

Fenway whirled around. A young man stood to the side of the gate. He was maybe in his late teens, with deeply tanned skin, board shorts, and a floppy hat, with a length of thick rope looped around his shoulder, resting on his hip.

"Sorry," he said. "Didn't mean to startle you. The whale watching tour left about ten minutes ago."

Fenway nodded. "I actually wanted to speak to Mr. Butler. You know him?"

The boy shrugged. "He asks me to help him out every so often."

"You work for him?" asked Callahan, pulling out his badge.

The boy's eyes widened. "Hey, listen, I don't want any trouble. I don't know him very well."

"What's your name?" Callahan said.

"We had a few questions for the owner of the *Ariel*," Fenway interjected, trying to sound gentle. "No one's in trouble."

The boy's eyes narrowed, and his grip on the rope tightened.

"You know when he'll be back?" Fenway continued.

"I don't work for the guy," the boy said warily. "I work for the harbor. Kind of a jack of all trades. Help out where I can, make sure things are running smoothly, make sure boats are secured properly, that kind of thing."

"Sure," Fenway said casually. "And you keep an eye on everything, right?"

"I guess."

Fenway pointed to the sign. "You know when Mr. Butler put this sign up?"

He frowned. "Uh—sometime last week."

"Something change in the days before he installed the sign?"

The boy looked down at his feet and kicked the slats of the pier with his boat shoes. "I only started here in April. Before last week, he was gone pretty much all the time."

Fenway nodded. "And now?"

"The guy's been in and out of the harbor every day. The other whale watching tours fill up a month ahead of time, so when he started offering his tours, a ton of tourists signed up."

Hmm. A change in his business model. Maybe Callahan was right, and Butler had taken the opportunity of the Venn Cartel leaving to get out of the game. Or maybe he was making ends meet until the cartel came back.

At any rate, the tourist season was in full swing, so maybe Butler's pay cut wasn't that extreme.

"Have you seen anyone else hang out with Butler?" Callahan asked. More casual, less demanding. He was learning.

"Uh—well, there's that skinny English guy."

The kid was likely referring to Calvin Banning, the British national who had accompanied the morpheranyl from Butler's boat to the storage facility.

"Lately? Like in the last week?"

"Uh... I'm not sure."

Fenway thanked the young man, who nodded and walked away.

"We didn't even get his name," Callahan grumbled.

"But we got information," Fenway said. "And the kid clearly doesn't trust cops." She turned to Callahan. "You ever watch Craig interview a suspect?"

Callahan was quiet.

"He talked to every interviewee like he was their best friend in the world. Totally disarming. Sometimes they'd talk sports or their favorite songs or restaurants. Didn't always work, but sometimes they'd divulge a lot more than anyone expected."

"More flies with honey than with vinegar," Callahan mumbled.

"Exactly."

Fenway and Callahan walked along the slips. They asked a few more people if they knew Butler.

"This is taking forever," Callahan said.

"This is the job, Brian," Fenway replied. "A lot of research, a lot of interviews, a lot of grinding."

"You've shown me the ropes. I can take the east side. It'll go faster."

Fenway didn't want to let Callahan go by himself after only an hour of working together, but maybe showing she trusted him—even if she didn't—would be good for their working relationship.

"Yeah, definitely faster," Fenway admitted. "Okay, fine, I'll take the west slips."

None of the boats were occupied in the first set of slips. Fenway looked up and the boy they'd talked to earlier walked back to her.

"Hello again," Fenway said. She paused, then held out her hand. "I'm Fenway, by the way."

"Hi." He stared at her hand for a moment, then shook it. "I'm Logan." Friendlier now that Callahan wasn't with her.

"Pleased to meet you, Logan." She grinned. "Look at us—you named after Boston's airport, and me named after their ballpark."

"Airport?" Logan asked.

"Never mind," Fenway said quickly. "Did you have a question?"

"Well, I remembered something."

"Oh—that's great." Then Fenway shut her mouth.

An awkward pause, but Logan finally spoke. "A few days ago, Mr. Butler asked me about transportation. I told him about Flash-Ride, but he didn't want anything with an app."

Probably didn't want to be tracked.

"Anyway," Logan continued, "we've got a guy who runs a bike taxi tour of the shore and of downtown Estancia. Butler talked to him, and the bike tour guy took him away in his bike taxi. Came back maybe an hour later."

Interesting. Changing his business strategy, making a new business sign, and now taking a bike taxi for a trip. Where had Butler gone?

"Where's the pickup location for the bike taxi tour?"

"On the other side of the parking lot from the yacht club." Logan glanced at his watch. "Tours usually begin on the half hour, so you might catch the guy between tours."

Fenway hurried past the boats, climbing the steps back to the Yacht Club. Her Accord was visible in the parking lot, and a few feet on the other side of the gate was a hand-painted sign reading *Estancia Tour—historic downtown and shoreline.* But no bike taxi.

She glanced at the clock on her phone: 11:23. She'd probably have to wait a few minutes for the bike to return from the tour.

Hmm. If Stephan Butler didn't want to take a FlashRide, he probably would have paid the bike taxi in cash and not given his name. She scrolled her photos until she found the picture of Butler she had taken on the beach two weeks before. Kind of dark, and not a flattering picture, but his features were visible.

A bicycle carriage, all four seats taken, came closer and finally to a stop. The tour guide had a speaker clipped to his belt, and Fenway could hear his amplified voice from across the parking lot.

She rushed across the parking lot as the tourists were disembarking, handing the tour guide tips.

The guide, dressed in khaki shorts, canvas boat shoes, and a T-shirt that said *Estancia Bike Taxi Tours,* glanced up at Fenway as the last of the tourists walked away. "Sorry, ma'am, I'm taking my lunch break now. Next departure at twelve thirty."

"I only have one or two questions." Fenway took out her identification.

The tour guide glanced at Fenway's badge, then plastered on a customer-service smile. "That I can do."

"Stephan Butler. You know him?"

He frowned. "Doesn't ring a bell."

Fenway turned her phone to the tour guide, Butler's picture filling the screen.

"Oh, that guy. Yeah. Wanted to go to Dominguez First National Bank. I told him I do tours, not taxi services, but he offered me a hundred bucks. I didn't have anyone waiting for the next tour, so I figured what the hell."

"When was this?"

"Uh, three, four days ago. I don't remember exactly."

After he'd posted the new whale watching sign. "You sure it was the Dominguez First National Bank?"

"Positive. On Fourteenth Street and Las Canoas."

"He tell you why he wanted to go to the bank?"

"I don't get paid to ask questions. He had me take him there, then I waited for about twenty minutes. Good thing, too, because I was out of breath from the climb. It was good to rest. After he comes out, he has me take him back to the harbor. Tipped me forty bucks. A hundred forty bucks? That's more than I make on a full load of tourists."

"Did he have anything with him?"

"Like what?"

"A tote bag, or a suitcase, maybe?"

"Uh…" The man rubbed his chin. "A backpack. Gray, or maybe beige. Looked pretty ordinary to me. Medium size."

Fenway nodded.

"You gonna be much longer? I gotta get some lunch."

She shook her head. "Sorry to keep you. Good luck with your business."

He gave her an easy salute with two fingers at his forehead, then walked toward the yacht club.

Fenway looked up and back through the parking lot, then

spotted a white man with a mustache in a black security officer's uniform, walking between the cars, looking at the license plates and scribbling in a small notebook. She walked toward him, and he looked up at her suspiciously.

Fenway took her ID out of her purse. "Morning," she said loudly, when she was about fifty feet away from him.

"Can I ask what you're doing here?"

Fenway held her badge out for the man to see. "Investigating a homicide."

He motioned to her. "Let me see that."

She walked closer and held the badge out.

"Closer."

"You can see it fine from there. I'm the county coroner."

He glared at the badge, then up at her face. The man's lips were in the starting stages of a snarl.

Fenway pulled her phone out of her purse, then tapped until the photo of Stephan Butler. "Have you seen him around?"

The security officer nodded, crossing his arms.

"Where?"

The security officer shrugged.

Fenway started to say something else, then closed her mouth. Callahan was a hundred yards away, canvassing the boats on the east slips.

"Thanks for your time."

Fenway turned away as the man's eyes burned into her back. She walked toward the edge of the parking lot, took out her phone, and called Callahan.

"Detective Brian Callahan."

Fenway almost burst out laughing. He sounded so *serious*. "Hey —there's a security guard wandering around the parking lot. Can you come here and ask him about Butler?"

"Uh, sure, if you want." Hanging in the conversation was the unasked question: *Why can't you do it?*

"Great. He's not very forthcoming with me. I think he might want to talk to someone, uh, who he can relate to a little better."

"What? Relate to a little better?"

Fenway gritted her teeth. She was loath to spell it out for him, but she probably had to. "I suspect he'll talk to you, a white man, and will not talk to me, a Black woman."

Callahan was silent.

"Did I lose you?"

"No, no," Callahan said quickly. "I'll be right there."

"I'm not hanging out here," Fenway said. "I'll keep canvassing the west slips."

"How will I recognize him?"

"He's the only security guard wandering in the parking lot."

"Gotcha."

Fenway ended the call and walked around the edge of the parking lot to the boat slips on the west side of the harbor, saw Callahan crossing the parking lot, and breathed a sigh of relief.

She found two boats with people, but neither of them had heard of Stephan Butler, nor did either see anything unusual in the last week. Fenway wondered if she should head to the Yacht Club for a cold drink when Callahan walked toward her. Fenway glanced around the parking lot; no sign of the security guard.

"You get anything?"

Callahan pursed his lips and was silent until he was only a few feet away. "Yes." He glanced over his shoulder. "The guard probably took his lunch break. Even so—" He pulled his phone out of his pocket.

"You didn't record the conversation, did you? California is a two-party consent state." He should have known that.

"A parking lot is a public space where the guard has no reasonable expectation of privacy." Callahan swiped and tapped on the screen.

Callahan tapped the Play button and the muffled voice of the security guard came on.

"If you're with that woman—"

"Look, Terry, there are two ways this can go." Callahan's voice, also slightly muffled but louder; he must have put the phone into his pants pocket. "I can put a good word for you at the sheriff's office. Maybe get you a ride-along. More than that, I can't promise anything, but criminal justice classes at Estancia Community College are a good start."

"That's—that's nice of you, man."

"I know. I'm feeling generous." The sound of footfalls. "So answer my questions."

"What about that—" The guard paused, then said, "That *woman* I saw earlier."

"Don't worry about her."

A moment of silence.

"Or," Callahan said on the recording, "I can go to the security office with a warrant. Pull all the footage. Tell your bosses you were uncooperative. Say you were uncooperative because you told me 'we don't get many Blacks here.' You don't want me to do that, Terry. You might not even get a ride-along."

A wet, throaty sound. Had the security officer spat on the ground? "Fine, fine. Yeah, he reported a break-in on his boat. Whoever it was ransacked his sleeping quarters, but nothing was broken, and nothing was missing."

"Did you file a police report?"

"Like I said, nothing was broken and nothing was missing. He didn't want to make a big deal out of it."

"When did the boat get broken into?"

The security officer coughed. "Over the weekend."

So after Butler's bike taxi escapade.

"Any other incidents?" Callahan asked.

More silence.

"You have a good afternoon, sir," Callahan said.

The recording ended.

"Good work." Savvy, even—a far cry from the disorganized,

foot-dragging shlep he'd been in the office. And with the kid who worked at the harbor. Maybe Callahan needed experience in the field to become a decent detective.

"Thanks," he said. "Did you get what you need?"

"I'd like to get a copy of the incident report."

"No can do today. The security supervisor is gone until tomorrow morning. Hopefully, he'll be more cooperative than the security guard."

·

———

Even though Callahan was in the passenger seat, and she didn't know his musical tastes, Fenway put on some funk music at full volume when she turned out of the harbor parking lot. She needed to get the interaction with the security officer out of her system, and a filthy beat with a horn section would help.

McVie would like this bass line.

After the first song was over, though, with Callahan sitting stiffly in his seat, she turned the volume down. While she had questions about who broke into Butler's boat, she was more bothered by the two blocks of morpheranyl left in the trunk of Rachel's car.

"Everything okay?" Callahan asked.

"Just need to think."

Callahan nodded and was quiet for a moment, then said: "About what?"

Fenway sighed. "Well, look, I'm not supposed to be working on the Zellman case."

"No one can stop you from *thinking* about the Zellman case, though, right?"

Fenway paused. That much was true. And maybe Callahan felt guilty about Rachel, dumping her right before she was wrongly arrested, and wanted to think about the Zellman case too.

"I assume," Fenway said carefully, "that whoever stole Rachel's car in the evening—between eight and eleven thirty P.M. last night —also put two bricks of Nyllie in the trunk."

Callahan nodded. "I saw the police report."

Fenway hadn't asked him to review the report, but since his ex-girlfriend had been arrested, she wasn't surprised. "So whoever took Rachel's car would have to be someone who had access to the drugs."

"Doesn't narrow it down much," Callahan said. "I mean, those key fobs can be cloned pretty easily. Anyone from the cartel could have done it."

"Right," Fenway said, searching her brain until she found the terms. "Keyless relay theft. And OBD port hacking. But Brookline said the OBD panel wasn't broken into, and the BMW had the security upgrade to prevent relay theft. So whoever stole Rachel's car had the key."

Callahan was quiet.

"We have to figure out who had access to Rachel's key *and* to bricks of Nyllie."

"That's why you questioned me," Callahan said.

"For the key, anyway," Fenway said. "But Brookline told me you were with him until one in the morning."

Callahan threw Fenway a sharp look. "You checked out my alibi?"

"Of course I did. Not that I didn't believe you, but if we don't perform our due diligence, we get eaten alive by defense attorneys."

"So," Callahan said, "who are you thinking?"

Fenway scratched her scalp. "Stephan Butler had access to the drugs—or used to, anyway. I spoke to Steve—Captain Alvídrez— and he said Butler had gotten out of the business, at least for the time being."

"Maybe his whale-watching business is legit."

"Plus," Fenway said. "I can't connect him to Rachel. Not yet, anyway."

"The press conference," Callahan said. "I mean, saying the cartel is out of the county? That isn't smart. Maybe Butler heard Rachel say the cartel was gone, and he stole her car to teach her a lesson."

"I don't think so," Fenway said. "Not out of the realm of possibility, but not very likely. But whoever broke into Butler's boat?"

"You think that person stole the drugs?"

"It's a possible scenario. Maybe Butler had a few bricks of Nyllie left over, or maybe he was skimming off the top, and maybe that had gotten stolen from the boat."

"That's true. Besides, Butler wouldn't have reported anything missing to the security office if the only things missing were some bricks of illegal drugs."

Callahan was on a roll, now, reminding Fenway of the good quick-on-his-feet answers he'd given in the interview.

Then, suddenly, he went quiet.

"Everything okay?"

"I—" Then he lapsed into silence again.

"What is it?"

Callahan shook his head. "I don't want to think that way."

"We need to consider all possibilities, Brian. Even if—or maybe *especially* if those possibilities make us uncomfortable."

He hesitated, then spoke quietly. "What about Andrew Zellman?"

"What do you mean?"

"He'd been in charge of the evidence room during the second shift. What do we know about him? He's new. Maybe he stole the bricks of Nyllie in evidence that had been taken from Seth Cahill's Corvette when Mathis Jericho was found dead. Maybe this whole drug trafficking thing was why he applied to the Estancia sheriff's office in the first place."

Fenway thought back to the conversation she and Dez had had at the crime scene. Did Zellman owe the wrong people money? But the speculation was premature.

"Before we jump to conclusion, let's get some evidence." Fenway couldn't believe *she* was the one saying it.

"Yeah, yeah," Callahan said. "No harm in spitballing, right?"

"Well—"

"There should be eighteen bricks of Nyllie still in the evidence room, right?"

"From the Corvette? Yes."

"Are they still there?"

Fenway paused. "As far as I know."

"We should check," Callahan said. "If the Nyllie is still in evidence, then my wild speculation is flat-out wrong. But if the drugs are gone, then someone with access to the evidence room took it, right?"

Why would Zellman have called Fenway if he'd been the one to take the morpheranyl out of the evidence room? That made no sense.

And as for others: Deputy Donald Huke was in charge of the evidence room during the day shift. He was a rule-follower who made McVie look like a scofflaw.

No way did she believe Zellman or Huke had taken the drugs. But she'd said it herself: due diligence. And Fenway could make the excuse that reopening the Mathis Jericho case required a review of the evidence.

"Why," Fenway mused, "would someone kill Mathis Jericho and place eighteen bricks of morpheranyl around his body in the first place?"

Callahan thought for a moment. "Someone was trying to send a message."

"Possibly," Fenway continued. "Or the killer had gotten ahold of the bricks of drugs and used them to throw us off. To make it look like the killing was drug-related."

"Ah, I see."

"And when we arrested George Pope, we thought he'd murdered both Seth Cahill *and* Mathis Jericho. But he only murdered Cahill."

"And he's the one who drove Cahill's Corvette to the cabin," Callahan said.

"Yeah—not a big stretch to conclude that the same person who stole Cahill's Corvette killed Jericho and put his body in the car. But that didn't happen."

"So you—" Callahan started, then snapped his mouth shut.

"Yes," Fenway said. "Yes, I make mistakes too. We're not infallible. So let's get this reopened case re-solved."

Callahan nodded. "So now what?"

"We're back at square one. With the Jericho murder, anyway. We've got to follow the possibility that Jericho's murder *was* drug-related, after all."

"Are you looking at the Venn Cartel?"

"And people who did business with them." A thought popped into Fenway's head: Captain Alvídrez had been taking point on the morpheranyl cases. Fenway should loop Alvídrez into the investigation before looking into the morpheranyl bricks.

However, given that she had a weird, suspicious feeling about Sheriff Gretchen Donnelly, maybe it would be a good idea to perform due diligence on Alvídrez, too.

"Callahan, what do you know about Captain Alvídrez?"

"The head of Vice?" Callahan shrugged. "I don't really know. I don't have any friends in Vice."

She could ask McVie too—Alvídrez had worked for the county for a couple of years. But McVie recommended Gretchen Donnelly to succeed him as sheriff, so maybe McVie's optimism came with blinders.

"Hey," Callahan said, "are we getting lunch soon?"

Fenway glanced at the clock on the dash: 12:26. She must be distracted—she hardly ever went this long without at least *thinking* of lunch.

"Of course. We're pretty close to Dos Milagros, if that works for you."

"I actually went there last night. Maybe All Access Burger?"

Fenway had eaten there last night, too, but that made no difference to her taste buds. "Tell you what—we can hit Salt & Flame." If she was going to forgo Dos Milagros for a burger, it would need to be decent, not the slop at All Access.

Callahan's eyes widened. "I know I got a promotion, but I can't afford that."

"My treat." The words were out of her mouth quickly, almost before she realized it. The place was expensive. Still, her offer to pay would get them working together more amicably. She hoped.

Five minutes later, they pulled into the half-full Salt & Flame parking lot. Fenway parked the Accord, and Callahan opened the door, then paused. "You coming in?"

"You get us a table. I need to make a quick phone call."

"Sure."

When the restaurant's front door closed behind Callahan, Fenway dialed Piper's number.

"Fenway!"

"Hi, Piper." Fenway cleared her throat. "I need a favor."

"Name it."

"You know how there was a lot of weirdness in the last case, right? Seth Cahill, dead in a storage unit, and then his underling found dead in Seth's Corvette?"

"Right." Piper lowered her voice. "And the sheriff was acting weird, right?"

"Yeah." Had Fenway mentioned that to Piper? Well, she'd mentioned it to McVie, anyway, and they worked closely together. "So there's a whole drug thing around the investigation."

"Morpheranyl. Yep, I'm aware."

"I want to know if I can trust the head of Dominguez County's vice squad. His name is Steve Alvídrez."

"Really? You suspect him, too?"

"I think we have a fox in the henhouse, and I don't know who it is. Sheriff Donnelly is acting strangely, but I don't want to have blinders on."

"Yeah, okay. I can dig into his background."

"And be careful. I don't want the wrong person to find out that we're sniffing around. We've already had our evidence person killed."

"I heard." Piper drew in her breath sharply. "Are you okay?"

"I never met him in person. But my point is, I don't want to put any of my staff—or you, or myself—in danger."

"You don't have to worry about me. If there's one thing I do better than anyone, it's covering my online tracks."

"Let me know how much this'll cost me." Maybe she'd call her father, who might cover part of it.

"Nonsense. I'm not taking your money. I'll let you know as soon as I find something."

Fenway said nothing, but she'd figure out how to pay. The more clients McVie got, the sooner things could get back to normal.

When Fenway ended the call, it hit her: she *still* hadn't been to see ADA Val Pondicherry yet.

She was thoroughly annoyed at herself. She hadn't gone to his office on Monday morning, and it was already midday on Tuesday.

Plus, stopping at a high-end burger place wouldn't help.

Oh well. Better late than never.

<h1 style="text-align:center">CHAPTER SEVEN</h1>

AFTER SPENDING A HUNDRED DOLLARS ON TWO BURGERS AND duck-fat fries, then dropping a sated Callahan back at the office, Fenway walked up the stairs in the City Hall building to see ADA Pondicherry.

His office was a dimly lit, quiet oasis from the fluorescent glare and the bustle of the rest of the building. Two walls were covered floor-to-ceiling with walnut bookshelves, hardbound tomes in neat rows. The room reminded her of every law library she'd seen in movies.

Pondicherry's admin was new: a tall, thin, Black man in his sixties who had a reputation for eschewing business casual for three-piece suits. He looked up at her. "May I help you?" Today's suit was a light gray seersucker. Appropriate for a California summer day, Fenway thought.

"Hi, yes. Uh, Mister—"

"Morgan Crane," the admin said. How could someone sound like they had a British accent, and yet not have a British accent?

"Mr. Crane," Fenway said, "I'm Coroner Stevenson."

"Yes, I know who you are, Miss Stevenson."

"ADA Pondicherry asked me to come in yesterday at eight in the morning, but I was in Nevada over the weekend, and I drove back yesterday instead of flying."

Crane raised his right eyebrow.

Yeah—she'd mentioned Nevada. She sounded like she was partying all weekend. Probably not a good look in front of Mr. Crane. But whatever.

"Mr. Pondicherry is in a meeting."

"He asked me to meet him as soon as I returned to town. Does he have an opening later today?"

Crane cleared his throat. "I believe he was asking if you were in this morning. Terrible what happened with the deputy in the evidence room."

"Yes," Fenway said. "I had to tend to the investigation of the hit-and-run. That's why I didn't come in first thing this morning." A little white lie, but she was here now.

Mr. Crane motioned to a straight-backed wooden chair in the corner opposite his desk. "Have a seat, Coroner Stevenson, and I'll see if Mr. Pondicherry has some availability."

The chair was more comfortable than it looked, but that wasn't saying much.

Her phone buzzed—a text. She looked at the screen.

Salt & Flame was asking her to fill out a survey. She sighed. Wasn't the hundred bucks enough? She supposed their social media specialist had a job to do. Fenway tapped the screen and deleted the text, then she started cleaning up the junk from her email.

Another text, but this one was from Piper.

Alvídrez is clean so far

Divorced last year, but commendations from every job he's been in

No record of complaints or anything

His finances aren't great

> Since his divorce

> Some credit card debt, borrowed money
> from his retirement

Right—he'd been divorced somewhat recently. And divorce often caused financial strain. Was it enough for him to accept bribes from the cartel? Probably not, but it depended on the extent of the credit card debt. Piper had typed "some credit card debt," not "massive credit card debt." Then Fenway had a thought.

> Can you do Sheriff Donnelly next?

Three dots in response, then they disappeared, then they appeared again. Finally:

> I'll see what I can do

"Coroner Stevenson?" said Crane, hanging up the phone.

"Yes?"

"Assistant District Attorney Pondicherry can see you now."

"Thank you, Mr. Crane."

Fenway got up and headed into the back office.

Vel Pondicherry rose from his seat when Fenway walked in. A similar vibe: dark walnut and full bookcases in the back office, too. At least Pondicherry didn't have on a tie; probably not due in court today.

"I'm so sorry, Vel," Fenway said. "I ended up driving home instead of flying, and I didn't get home until last night."

Pondicherry nodded soberly. "And I assume you were are the scene of the Andrew Zellman hit-and-run early this morning."

"Yes."

Pondicherry bowed his head for a moment. Fenway couldn't tell if he was being serious or performative. But then he looked up, a gleam in his eye.

"I can't prove anything," Pondicherry said, "but I'm certain the Mathis Jericho murder is tied to the murder of Andrew Zellman."

"And you heard Rachel Richards was arrested for Zellman's murder earlier today."

Pondicherry nodded, then pointed at Fenway. "I read the report. You're giving her an alibi."

"Not an alibi, exactly. I picked Rachel up at eight o'clock. Her BMW was in its parking space. When I came back a little before midnight, it was gone." She frowned. "I didn't really notice then—I was concerned about getting Rachel in the door safely. But I should have noticed it was gone."

"If I were to bring charges against Ms. Richards, your testimony would likely supply enough reasonable doubt to sway the jury," Pondicherry said. "Nevertheless, I have to do my due diligence. I'm afraid Ms. Richards will be a guest of the county for at least a day or two."

Good. Pondicherry seemed unwilling to hold Rachel for long.

"But given your statement that Rachel's car was there when you left and missing when you returned," Pondicherry said, "I draw one unsavory conclusion."

Fenway pursed her lips. "Someone tried to frame Rachel. Why would someone want to do that?"

Pondicherry tapped his finger on his desk. "I rather hoped you could provide some insight."

Fenway folded her arms and stared at the top of Pondicherry's desk.

"The physical evidence points to Rachel's car being the murder weapon."

Pondicherry was silent for a moment.

"What is it?" Fenway asked.

"Are we sure that the hit-and-run was intentional?" Pondicherry rubbed his chin. "This wasn't a bunch of joyriding kids who were speeding through Zellman's neighborhood after midnight?"

Fenway pursed her lips. "I can't say for sure. I'm not on the case.

I'm providing the alibi—or whatever it is—for the prime suspect. I can't be on it."

"Of course," Pondicherry said. "Who is the lead investigator?"

"Detective Dez Roubideaux is taking lead and reporting directly to Gretchen."

Pondicherry flinched. "She's reporting to Sheriff Donnelly?"

"That's right." Fenway tilted her head. "Does something bother you about that?"

Pondicherry was quiet.

"Something doesn't sit right with me, either," Fenway said. "I don't know what it is, but Donnelly's acting weird."

He took a deep breath. "I'm glad you said something. I thought it was just me."

Fenway took out her phone and brought up the map application. "Rachel lives in the Scarlet Oaks Townhomes. That's across town from Morongo Heights, where Zellman was killed."

Pondicherry nodded.

"About a half-mile from Scarlet Oaks, there's a long straightaway on Mariposa Boulevard east of Ocean Highway. Popular spot for drag racing. Kids would drool over Rachel's BMW 3-series. Instead, the BMW runs over our victim ten miles away, then *returned* two blocks from Rachel's apartment complex."

Pondicherry rubbed his forehead. "Here's what I don't understand. If they were joyriding kids, you're saying they'd have stayed closer?"

"I'm saying that joyriding kids would take the car for a *joyride*. Morongo Heights is nowhere near the popular joyriding places. It's so far off the beaten path, I can't imagine anyone would go there if they *weren't* looking to run over Andrew Zellman."

"But," Pondicherry said, "if this were the Venn Cartel, the entire crime would have been orchestrated more believably. The BMW would have been back in Rachel's parking space, not parked on the street."

Fenway was quiet for a moment. "If I hadn't told the police that

I saw Rachel's car in the space when I picked her up, and didn't see it when I returned, though..."

Pondicherry thought for a moment. "We'd have a pretty solid case against Rachel. Especially if she'd stayed home all night."

"Does her apartment complex have cameras?"

Pondicherry shook his head. "You should know that better than anyone—when Rachel's former husband was accused of driving his truck through the coroner's office building, there was no footage of his truck at the apartment building to confirm or rebut his assertion that he hadn't taken his truck out that night."

Fenway wrapped her arms around herself.

Pondicherry leaned forward. "You just thought of something, Miss Stevenson."

Fenway cleared her throat. "Who knows Rachel's building parking lot doesn't have cameras?"

"You mean besides the police?"

Fenway raised her head and looked straight into Pondicherry's eyes.

Pondicherry's eyes widened. "You think a member of law enforcement is involved?"

"I don't *want* to think that," Fenway said. "But whoever committed the crime had to know the building didn't have cameras, had to know Rachel's schedule, had to know where to grab Rachel's key."

"That includes people in law enforcement and City Hall workers, but doesn't limit it to them. The City Hall building isn't so locked-down that a member of the public couldn't come in." Pondicherry frowned. "Whoever did it also had to have access to two bricks of morpheranyl."

Fenway nodded. "True. And we've accounted for all the confiscated bricks of Nyllie in evidence, right?"

Pondicherry hesitated. "Well, no. There are sixteen bags in evidence, not the eighteen we originally had."

Fenway frowned. "And no one's raised the alarm about this?"

"Sheriff Donnelly assured me she was looking into it. But we believe the two bricks in Rachel's trunk are the two missing bags."

Fenway scratched her scalp. "So someone took two bricks of Nyllie from evidence and planted them in Rachel's trunk."

Pondicherry ran a hand over his face. "Was Rachel Richards with you all night?"

"Until I dropped her off around midnight."

"You were at a bar?"

"Ice Mountain. And afterward we went to VR Karaoke."

"Rachel didn't leave at any point? Not even to use the facilities?"

Fenway thought for a moment. "I suppose she went to the bathroom when we were at karaoke."

"And how long was she gone?"

Fenway pursed her lips. "I didn't pay attention, but I can't imagine it was more than five or ten minutes."

Pondicherry nodded. "She could have taken a FlashRide or a taxi to her house and moved her BMW to the street, then gotten back to karaoke before anyone noticed she was gone."

"That would have been way more than ten minutes." Fenway crossed her arms. "Highly unlikely. And why?"

"To establish an alibi with you."

"I've gotta think there are more effective alibis." Fenway tapped her chin. "Could the two bricks still be at the lab in San Miguelito for testing?"

"I'm not sure."

"If so, maybe the bricks were from somewhere else." Fenway thought about the break-in on Stephan Butler's boat.

"Like where?"

"Well—maybe they were stolen."

"Stealing drugs from the Venn Cartel? I don't think anyone has that kind of death wish."

"I'll ask Dez to look into it more." Fenway furrowed her brow. "And—why target Rachel? There are easier cars to steal, and other parking lots don't have cameras. So why target her? What do they get out of putting her in jail?"

"My thoughts exactly."

Fenway popped her head up. "The press conference."

"The press conference Rachel gave yesterday?"

"That's right. Rachel said the Venn Cartel had vacated Dominguez County, right? So she's caught killing the guy guarding the evidence and two bricks of drugs are in her car. Now Rachel looks like she's on the take, doesn't she?"

"To the untrained eye, perhaps." Pondicherry scratched his temple. "Surely no jury would believe Rachel is the mastermind behind the drug-smuggling operation."

Fenway nodded somberly. "But arresting Rachel undermines the integrity of the entire department, doesn't it? So maybe it *wasn't* someone in law enforcement."

Pondicherry shook his head. "Unless that was a risk the perpetrators were willing to take."

"A cover-up," Fenway blurted.

Pondicherry nodded. "But this is all conjecture," he said. "We may find another bad actor whose presence explains everything."

Fenway thought for a moment. "So, about the two bricks of morpheranyl found in Rachel's trunk. I bet you didn't find any fingerprints on them."

Pondicherry smiled. "Wiped clean."

"Just like the eighteen bricks of morpheranyl we found with Mathis Jericho's body."

"And that's one reason the Jericho case is officially reopened," Pondicherry said. "I spoke with George Pope. Not only did he plead not guilty—even when we floated the idea of concurrent sentences—but I don't believe he did it. He didn't know Mathis Jericho. We thought perhaps Jericho had seen Pope commit the Seth Cahill murder, but that's not a reasonable conclusion."

"All right," Fenway said. "Then there's no time like the present. Let's go to the evidence room."

"What do you hope to find?"

"Anything that will explain why Andrew Zellman was killed."

Pondicherry glanced at his watch. "I have to interview a witness for a deposition in another case, and I'm afraid that will take all afternoon. Can you check with me tomorrow?"

Fenway didn't want to wait that long. "Someone has already killed the evidence deputy. There's another deputy in charge during the day shift. I don't want him compromised."

"We'll put extra security on the evidence room," Pondicherry said. "And I'll ask for protective details for him." He rifled through a few papers on his desk. "Donald Huke?"

"That's him." Fenway smiled. "He'll *love* the protection detail."

Pondicherry pushed a button on his desk. "Mr. Crane, see if you can reschedule my meetings for tomorrow morning."

"Right away, sir," Crane's voice said through the intercom.

Pondicherry glanced up at Fenway.

"Where'd you find Mr. Crane?"

"He's something, isn't he?" Pondicherry chuckled. "Just started a couple of weeks ago. The formality puts some defense lawyers— and defendants—off. I hated it at first, too, but everyone behaves a little better when Mr. Crane convinces them they're in the middle of a *Pride and Prejudice* miniseries."

She would go discuss the morpheranyl distribution with Captain Alvídrez. If she didn't know what she was looking for, she might not find anything to help her figure out who really killed Mathis Jericho —or who ran over Andrew Zellman.

After her meeting with Pondicherry, though, she was more certain than ever that Donnelly was hiding something. She was glad she'd asked Piper to look into Donnelly's background and finances, although she'd probably have to ask Piper for a deeper dive.

She gritted her teeth. Piper might have said she wouldn't take Fenway's money, but this would be a sizeable amount of work. She couldn't pay for this out of the county's budget—and while she had savings, she certainly couldn't afford the kind of deep-dive she needed from Piper.

She didn't have a choice. She took her phone out as she walked through the corridor and tapped *Nathaniel Ferris* in her contacts.

Hmm. She'd have to change that to *Dad* now that they were actually getting along.

"Fenway! Great to hear from you."

"Hi, Dad."

"I haven't heard from you in a few weeks."

Really? Had it been that long? Oh, and now she was calling and asking him for money. Not a great look. "I've been busy. I know that sounds like a lame excuse, but I actually *have* been really busy."

Nathaniel Ferris chuckled. "I heard you kept my favorite white-hat hacker out of jail in Las Vegas."

"Word travels fast."

"It would travel faster if you called more—" Ferris paused, then coughed. Probably thinking better of giving his until-recently-estranged daughter a guilt trip. "I mean, I'm proud of you. I knew you could do the job when I proposed that Craig appoint you coroner a year ago, but honestly, I never dreamed you'd be *so* good at it."

"Uh, thanks."

"I hope you're proud of yourself, too. Not only catching the bad guys, but keeping innocent people out of jail."

Fenway said nothing. She enjoyed the job, enjoyed the challenge. And yes, making sure justice was served was a big part of the draw.

"Don't forget about ferreting out corruption," she said, tongue firmly in cheek.

"Right," Ferris said, then his tone grew serious. "You get Craig's stuff out to Colorado okay?"

Oh no. He might have known about her keeping Piper out of jail and catching the real killer, but he didn't know that his daughter had moved in with McVie.

But Ferris misread her hesitation. "Look, I know the long-distance romance thing can be hard. Some people make it work, though."

"No, that's not it," Fenway said quickly. "Craig's job didn't work out. He moved back to Estancia."

A pause. "Oh. Well, I..." He hesitated. "Is that a good thing?"

"In the long run? I know he hated his job there, and he'll probably be happier here." Maybe this was an opening to ask for money without sounding like this was the reason for her call. "McVie's trying to get his old clients back on board."

"Good. I hope he can get most of them back."

"Right. Well, listen, Dad, I—"

"I thought he gave up his apartment, too. Is he staying in a hotel somewhere?"

Fenway bit her lip.

"Fenway? Did I lose you?"

"He's staying with me," Fenway said.

"Oh."

She couldn't read anything into that response. Her father hadn't hesitated, but neither did he sound particularly enthused, or unhappy, or anything.

"It's temporary," Fenway said, "until he gets the business back on its feet."

"Your lease doesn't permit someone to move in without informing the landlord," Ferris said, a light touch in his voice—but was it forced?

"Luckily," Fenway replied, "I know the building owner. And I'm informing him now."

Ferris laughed. "It's no problem, of course." Then another pause. "I can get something over to you in writing if you're worried—"

"I don't think it's necessary, but that's probably smart," Fenway said.

"I'm late for an appointment," Ferris said. "Charlotte says hello. I like talking with you, Fenway. Call again soon, okay?"

———

Fenway entered the coroner's suite and stopped in her tracks. She'd intended to walk to Vice to talk with Steve Alvídrez, but she went on autopilot when she was talking with her dad.

Callahan stared intently at his computer screen, typing with his index fingers. Notes from their interviews at the harbor, Fenway hoped. If Callahan had started typing the notes without a nudge from Fenway, that was a good sign.

Dez still wasn't at her desk—not surprising. While Fenway wanted to know what Dez was working on and whether she'd found any exculpatory evidence for Rachel, she knew Dez wasn't allowed to talk to her about the Zellman case.

Fenway ducked into her office and sat at her desk. She'd call Captain Steve Alvídrez and see if they could have a strategy session. Maybe at Java Jim's. But first, one more call to Piper to see if she found anything. She picked up the office phone and dialed McVie Investigations.

"McVie Investigations."

"Craig? I thought you'd still be at my—at home."

"Just came in to drop a few things off. I see you already have Piper hard at work on something that doesn't bring in any revenue. You must want me to be your kept man."

Fenway rolled her eyes. "Send me the bill," she said.

"No, no, of course I won't."

"I need Piper to do a deep dive into Donnelly's background. And I know what that's worth." She took a deep breath. Why was it so hard for her to ask her father for money to cover this?

Did she want to mention her conversation with her father? That he knew she and Craig were now cohabitating? Maybe not quite yet.

McVie paused. "You know, after my terrible experience with Payback Systems, suddenly my cheating-spouse work doesn't seem half bad."

"It's all about perspective." Fenway cleared her throat. "Listen, I'm about to ask Steve Alvídrez to coffee."

McVie was silent.

"Not like that," Fenway said, feeling heat rise to her face. "We re-opened a case where drug distribution is involved, and I need to figure out what type of evidence I should look for. But I asked Piper if Steve Alvídrez was clean. I don't want to work with someone who's in bed with the—" She almost said *Venn Cartel*, then stopped herself—McVie was a civilian now. "With the bad guys."

"You're working on the Mathis Jericho murder," McVie said.

"You know I'm not at liberty to discuss this with people outside the department."

"Yes, I know. Sorry. Can't help the sheriff in me sometimes— gotta get my grubby little mitts into everything."

A flash of panic as Fenway pictured McVie throwing his clothes all over her apartment, then took a deep breath and banished the thought from her head. "Did Piper find anything out about our, uh, other subject yet?"

"Other subject?"

Fenway was silent.

"Ah. Donnelly. No. Hasn't had time. I've got her doing some background checks for a client."

"Okay."

"And paying clients come first, even if you did get Piper out of jail. But she'll be back on it this afternoon."

"I get it." A pause. She wanted to ask Piper to look into what Stephan Butler was doing at the bank, but she'd already asked enough of her. Besides, Fenway could go herself. And it wouldn't be tied to the Andrew Zellman case—this was specifically regarding the Jericho murder.

"You coming home on time tonight?" McVie asked.

"I don't know—you did such a good job cleaning the house yesterday. My closet could use organizing."

"Hilarious. No, I was wondering if I was on my own for dinner."

"I don't think I'll be late—I'm not on this case, since Rachel was arrested."

"Did you hear how that's going?"

"I'm not allowed to hear how that's going."

McVie paused. "The reason you're not on the case is because you're friends with her, right?"

"Yeah."

"So be her friend. Go visit her in jail. See if she needs anything, or if you can call anyone for her. She might tell you something specific that could exonerate her—maybe she walked to the grocery store or All Access Burger after you dropped her off. Or maybe she was watching a show on Skysense—the Supreme Court said their usage records can be used to establish a defendant's alibi."

Fenway nodded. Why hadn't she thought of that? "You're a good man, Craig McVie."

He harrumphed. "Well, I try."

After hanging up, Fenway popped her head out of her office. Callahan was still gazing at his computer screen, hunting-and-pecking on the computer keyboard, and Dez still hadn't returned.

"Brian?"

He glanced up.

"I've got to head to Dominguez First National over on Four-teenth. Checking out where Butler went a few days ago. Want to come?"

Callahan jumped to his feet. "Love to."

"You type up the notes from this morning?"

"I'm, uh, about half-done."

Fenway turned the options over in her mind. If Callahan hadn't been on his first week, and if she hadn't wanted to make up for not being in the office on his first day, she'd make him stay and finish the notes.

She tilted her head. "Did you call the security office at Estancia Harbor?"

Callahan knotted his eyebrows.

"To get the report of the break-in filed by Stephan Butler."

"The manager won't be back until tomorrow morning."

Fenway pursed her lips. "Right, sorry, I forgot." She wanted him to see a case through and get engaged with the process, but was she being too hard on him because he wasn't her first choice?

"How long will it take you to finish typing up your notes?"

"Maybe another ten minutes."

"Let's go as soon as that's done."

Callahan visibly sighed.

"Or I can go to the bank myself."

"No, no," he blurted. "I'll finish right now."

Fenway nodded and stepped away from Callahan's desk. Sarah waved her hand.

"Yes?"

"Did I hear you say you're going to a bank?" Sarah asked.

"That's right. The guy who captained the boat? Remember him?"

"I do. Steven Butler, right?"

"Stephan," Fenway said, emphasizing the hard *F* in the middle of the name. "But close enough. We need to figure out what Butler was doing there. He brought a backpack with him, so I think he might have had a bunch of cash to deposit."

Sarah tilted her head. "Or something to put in a safe-deposit box."

"That's a good thought."

"If Butler accessed a safe-deposit box, do you want me to get a warrant application ready to go?"

"Thanks, Sarah, but let's wait until we find out if he *has* a safe-deposit box." Fenway walked into her office, then turned around. "Hey, can you call Captain Alvídrez's office?"

"Uh, sure."

"Check with his assistant and see if he's available this afternoon. I want to set up a strategy session with him to deal with the new leads we're getting on the Jericho case."

Sarah nodded and Fenway shut the door to her office, then sat heavily in her chair. She could research Butler and his revived whale-watching business for a few minutes. But she got nowhere; his LLC looked clean.

Ten minutes later, Fenway stood, stretched, and stepped out of her office.

"Callahan, you have your notes done yet?"

"Just finished." He stood.

Sarah leaned forward. "Alvídrez has meetings and asked if you'd meet him for a late lunch. 2:45?"

"I've already eaten, but sure, I'll meet him."

"He suggested Dos Milagros."

Fenway grimaced. Could she go into Dos Milagros without ordering a lengua taco?

It was a challenge she'd have to accept.

———

Ten minutes later, Fenway pulled the Accord into a *Visitors Only* space at the bank. She and Callahan went in—the line for a teller had only two people in it.

As she and Callahan walked to the back of the queue, another teller, her dark hair in an updo, walked up. "Next, please." Fenway pulled out her badge and her phone, and the teller's face dropped.

"Good afternoon." Fenway tapped her phone and Stephan Butler's photo appeared. "I need to talk to the teller who worked with this man. His name is Stephan Butler."

The teller pressed her lips together. "I'm sorry—let me talk with my manager."

"Of course."

The teller stepped back, and a woman behind another counter

ten feet away looked up. She and the teller conversed for about fifteen seconds, then the woman glanced toward Fenway and Callahan. Fenway held up her badge so the woman could see it. The woman turned and spoke to the teller.

Callahan leaned toward Fenway. "Why won't they talk to you?"

"Privacy laws, bank policy, something like that. Gray areas and fine lines. But don't get confrontational, even if they say they can't confirm anything."

"More flies with honey?" asked Callahan.

"You got it."

The two women spoke in hushed tones, then the manager nodded. The teller turned and walked back to the window.

"I apologize for the delay," the teller said. "I wasn't sure what bank protocol is, or what the law is. I can't tell you everything about our interaction with Mr. Butler, but I can answer *some* questions."

"Such as?"

"I was the teller who waited on him. He came in last week; I can't recall if it was Thursday or Friday. He acted nervous, and he was holding a backpack. If I'm honest, I thought he was going to rob us, but instead he opened an account and rented a safe-deposit box. Per bank policy, I cannot tell you how much he deposited or allow you to see the safe-deposit box."

Fenway blinked. That was easier than she thought.

"I understand. Mr. Butler is part of an investigation." Fenway put her badge back in her purse. "I know we need a warrant to see the contents of his safe-deposit box, so I won't ask to see it. Just one more question: can you tell me if Mr. Butler has returned to the bank after his initial visit?"

The teller frowned. "Not when I was working, but I'm not here every day. And he might have used our ATM."

"Thank you." Fenway set her jaw; she would try to extend the warrant to cover their security footage as well. She walked out of the bank, a spring in her step—that could have hardly gone better. She went back to the car and turned the engine on. 2:31.

"Should we get started on a warrant for the safe-deposit box?" Callahan asked.

Fenway shook her head. "We don't have enough for a warrant yet."

"Back to the office?"

"I'll drop you off," Fenway said. "I've got barely enough time to get to Dos Milagros to meet Captain Alvídrez."

Callahan chuckled. "Sarah said you liked that place. I didn't know you liked it enough to have a second lunch there."

CHAPTER EIGHT

After dropping Callahan off, Fenway found a parking spot on Fourth Street directly across from Dos Milagros, looked both ways, and hurried to the taquería. Alvídrez was already in line when Fenway walked in, and she tapped his shoulder as she walked up. "Hey, Captain Alvídrez."

He grinned. "Call me Steve, please." He shook Fenway's hand, firmly but gently—and was it for a beat too long?

Fenway cleared her throat. "Glad you suggested this place. This is probably my favorite restaurant in all of Estancia. Maybe even the whole West Coast."

"I've never been, but it came, uh, highly recommended. And they've got lengua, which is always a good sign."

Fenway nodded, surprised to find another culinary adventurer who wasn't grossed out by the idea of eating cow tongue. "I couldn't agree more. Some people I know get a boring burrito every time."

Fenway couldn't resist ordering a single taco and a small horchata, and Alvídrez ordered three tacos and a large horchata, then pulled his card out before Fenway could object. After paying, Alvídrez stepped to the side, holding his arm out, and Fenway chose a high-top table on the side, a few feet away from where she and McVie usually sat. Alvídrez grabbed their drinks and sat across from Fenway.

"So," Fenway said, "I assume by now you've heard that the police arrested Rachel Richards in the hit-and-run death of Andrew Zellman."

Alvídrez was quiet for a moment. "I didn't know Zellman," he said slowly. "He hadn't been here very long. I know Rachel, though. I'd never have suspected."

"It was her car," Fenway said. "But Rachel wasn't behind the wheel."

"You know this for a fact?"

"I'll testify to it in court if I have to."

"So who was driving?"

"I don't know," Fenway said. "Dez is the lead investigator. And I've been, uh, encouraged to recuse myself from the case. But I think someone who's involved in the morpheranyl trade is setting Rachel up."

"What makes you think that?"

Fenway cocked her head. "Lieutenant Brookline pulled two bricks of Nyllie out of the trunk of Rachel's car."

Alvídrez widened his eyes. "No!"

Fenway paused. Both ADA Pondicherry and Lieutenant Brookline had known. "Why wouldn't the investigators have told you?"

"I don't—" Alvídrez folded his arms and sat back on the stool. "I suppose it's only been a few hours since Rachel was arrested. Maybe it hasn't..." He trailed off.

"As head of the Dominguez County Vice division, wouldn't you be the first one informed when drugs are found?"

"I'll bring this up with Gretchen," Alvídrez murmured.

For a brief moment, Fenway wondered if the sheriff hadn't told Alvídrez because she suspected him; with his unstable finances from his divorce, maybe she couldn't trust him with information. But that was a stretch.

"I think Rachel's being framed," Fenway said. "Someone wants to tell the story that Andrew Zellman stole two bricks of Nyllie from evidence and Rachel killed Andrew and took it back."

"I can't believe no one told me about the drugs in the BMW's trunk."

"I was hoping you already knew about it and could give me more information," Fenway said, "but I might as well ask anyway: why two bricks of morpheranyl?"

"What do you mean?"

"Two bricks, sitting in the trunk. What story are the police putting together for Rachel? Will they say she was running drugs from the harbor to L.A. for the Venn Cartel?"

"Two bricks? That's not enough for a shipment anywhere—not even to a local dealer."

"Skimming off the top, then? A trunk full of drugs, and the cartel will never care about two bricks missing?"

"That makes no sense," Alvídrez mused. "Plus, she leaves the bricks lying in the trunk? Doesn't hide them in a wheel well or under the seat out of view?"

Fenway took a sip of horchata. "So you can see why I think she was set up."

Alvídrez nodded. "If they'd brought this to me this morning, I would have flagged it right away—this is exactly how you'd frame someone."

The woman behind the counter called their number, and Fenway jumped up to grab their order. As she came back to the table, Alvídrez was staring at the wall behind Fenway's stool, his eyes glazed over.

"What is it?"

"This is exactly how you'd frame someone—*if you didn't know what you were doing*," Alvídrez said.

"Oh. So we shouldn't look at the cartel."

Alvídrez snapped back to the present, then pulled his basket in front of him. "Not unless they're purposely trying misdirection.

Arranging everything in a way that wouldn't look like the cartel set it all up." He shook his head. "But what would be the point of that? Does the cartel really want the police to think that someone's framing Rachel? Why not frame Rachel a better way?" He picked up a taco. "I don't know what to think."

A trio of young white women, probably seventeen or eighteen years old, walked in, phones in their hands and laughing. They were all talking over each other, then walked to the counter and gave their order. One of them glanced at Fenway as she walked past, although Fenway didn't recognize her.

Fenway picked up her lengua taco and took a bite. It was as delicious as always; the meat melt-in-your-mouth tender, the spiciness of the salsa flavorful without too much heat, the cheese melty enough without getting gooey. She sighed, wishing she wasn't so full so she could savor the meal more.

"Oh, wow," Alvídrez said with his mouth full.

"I know. They don't mess around." Fenway smiled. "You've got a little salsa on the corner of your mouth."

Alvídrez picked up a napkin and swiped it across the wrong side of his face. "Did I get it?"

Fenway lifted a hand and pointed to the correct side of his mouth. He wiped it off.

Fenway nodded and took another bite.

"So," Alvídrez said, an easy, light tone in his voice, "I heard Craig McVie moved to Colorado."

"Well, his daughter moved there," Fenway began.

"Are you two still dating?" His voice was casual, no eye contact, like he was making conversation. But Fenway recognized a man fishing for an opening.

Fenway shifted in her seat. She needed Alvídrez on her side, but she'd need to play this carefully. "Yes," Fenway said, "And—"

"Long distance?" Alvídrez asked. "That's gotta be rough."

"It didn't work out," Fenway said.

"You and McVie?" Alvídrez's tone was less casual, so optimistic as to be ambitious.

"McVie's move to Colorado," Fenway said quickly. She almost mentioned how McVie's job and apartment disappeared from under him, but simply said, "Things got complicated, so he's back in Estancia."

"Oh," Alvídrez said, then paused and took another bite. He chewed carefully and swallowed. "Excellent. He's a good private investigator. And one of the few who actually have a moral compass. The county can use people like him."

"Even if the Venn Cartel didn't set Rachel up, are *they* still here?" Fenway asked, changing the subject. "Rachel gave a press conference that they'd exited the county, but that could be wishful thinking."

Alvídrez took a sip of horchata. "They're not gone. They've hit pause until everything dies down. No chatter, no tips, no nothing. Like I said before, six months, tops."

The three young women went to a table on the other side of the taquería, now talking about the classes they'd take when school went back into session. The same young woman glanced at Fenway again.

Fenway turned away and continued eating. Did Fenway know the teenager from somewhere? She didn't think so.

"What are our next steps?" Fenway asked Alvídrez.

"I suppose we should go to the evidence room," Alvídrez replied, then took a bite of his last taco.

"I'm hoping to meet ADA Pondicherry in the evidence room tomorrow," Fenway said. "Operating under the assumption that those two bricks of Nyllie were originally found with Mathis Jericho's corpse, so I'm not there to work on the Zellman case."

"Ah, that's right. Your forced recusal."

Fenway tapped the tip of her nose.

"No one's forced *me* to recuse myself," Alvídrez said. "Perhaps

I'll call Detective Roubideaux and see if she'd like my assistance. We could meet there this afternoon." His eyes twinkled.

"As long as I maintain adequate distance from the Zellman case," Fenway said. "Investigating Mathis Jericho's death gives me a good reason to be there."

"Noted." Then he set his drink down. "Hold on—Mathis Jericho? Wasn't his murder solved?"

"We've reopened the case. The guy we arrested for it says he killed Seth Cahill, but not Mathis Jericho. The ADA believes him." Fenway paused. "And so do I."

"I thought the same person killed them both."

"That was our assumption, too," Fenway said, "but now that we know that's not true, we'll look at the evidence in a new light."

Alvídrez wiped his mouth with his napkin, then threw it in the taco basket with a satisfied grunt. "Best tacos I've had in a long time. You sure you've only been here a year? Usually people have to live here a decade before they find gems like Dos Milagros."

Fenway laughed, grabbing both food baskets and walking to the trash. "Maybe I'll see you in the evidence room later?" But why hadn't he been told of the drugs before?

Alvídrez, following Fenway, nodded. "Now I have an excuse to push back my afternoon meetings."

How could she ask about Alvídrez's finances without making him think Fenway suspected him? And did she *really* think credit card debt and alimony were enough for him to risk his job?

They walked out of Dos Milagros into the sun, which had finally burned off the fog. The afternoon was growing warm, but a gentle breeze blew off the ocean. A perfect Central Coast summer day.

Surely Alvídrez would understand the concept of due diligence. Fenway steeled herself and took a deep breath. "Since law enforcement might be involved, we took a look at your—"

A woman tapped Fenway on the shoulder and Fenway turned. The woman was about twenty years old, Black, and looked familiar.

"You dropped your phone," the woman said, pressing a black clamshell phone into Fenway's hand.

"What? No, that's not my—"

But the woman was gone, hurrying away down Fourth Street.

"Wait!" Fenway said, holding up the phone. "This isn't mine!"

Alvídrez nodded. "I'll catch up with her." And he sprinted after the woman.

Fenway clicked her tongue. He hadn't even taken the phone.

She took another step to cross the street—

A compact car screeched down the block, and Fenway looked up. The car wasn't stopping. It was accelerating.

Fenway dove onto the sidewalk.

She lay prone on the concrete for a moment, getting her bearings. She wiggled her feet and moved her legs. The car had missed her, but not by much. She took a deep breath in and out.

Footsteps. "Fenway!" Alvídrez's voice. "Are you okay?"

She jumped to her feet—ow, a shooting pain in her knee, but nothing that would stop her from walking—and ran into the street. Maybe the car was still speeding away, and she could get a license plate.

The car was a small white hatchback, maybe a Dokko. What was that model called? Some sort of music thing—Concerto? Sinfonietta? No—the Toccata, that was it. But she couldn't read the license plate from this distance.

She looked down at herself, the adrenaline subsiding. Mild pain in her elbow; she'd skinned it. And a big scuff in her trousers at her right knee—maybe all the way through the cloth.

"Are you okay?" Alvídrez repeated.

"Fine," Fenway said gruffly. "I think these pants are ruined, but I've only got a couple scratches." She brushed off the top of her trousers, dirty from the sidewalk. The hole in her knee wasn't too noticeable.

"I got the license plate."

Fenway's head snapped up. "You did?"

"I know, I know, I should have seen if you were okay first, but you can't take the cop out of me."

"What is it?" Fenway asked—oh, wait. She was still holding the clamshell phone. Was the phone related to her almost being run over? She blinked at the phone, then picked up her purse off the ground. From inside, a buzz.

"I texted you the license plate number," Alvídrez said, his phone in his hand. "As soon as I get back to the office, I'll run the plates."

"Thank you."

"You sure you're okay? I can take you to the hospital."

"No. I'm fine. More shocked than anything."

"You think that was intentional?" Alvídrez asked.

The car had accelerated as soon as the driver had seen her in the street, right? "Yeah. I'm pretty sure it was intentional." Fenway took a deep breath.

A tiny little car, too. Bigger than she was, but a massive SUV would have *really* meant business. She almost chuckled in spite of herself.

"Who would try to run you over?"

Fenway thought for a moment. "Maybe it's someone who thinks I'm on the Zellman case and doesn't want the truth coming out."

"Don't you think it's more likely someone who doesn't want you digging into the Mathis Jericho murder?"

Fenway shook her head. "No one outside the coroner's office— except for you and ADA Pondicherry—knows the case has even been reopened. Dez doesn't even know."

"And Sheriff Donnelly."

"Right." Fenway tapped her chin. "Unless..."

"Unless what?"

"Two weeks ago, on the Seth Cahill case, we investigated a boat that had smuggled morpheranyl in from Mexico. You remember that?"

Alvídrez squinted in thought. "The *Ariel,* if I'm not mistaken."

"Captained by a man named Stephan Butler. And today, working on Mathis Jericho's murder, I went to the harbor."

"The *Ariel* is still docked there?" Alvídrez asked.

"Maybe a legitimate tourist boat now. Anyway, I was asking questions around the harbor, and I found out Butler went to physically visit a bank."

Alvídrez tilted his head. "Lots of people go to the bank."

"Yes, but he rented a safe-deposit box, and a day or two later, someone broke into the *Ariel*. Didn't file a police report, though. Said nothing was stolen."

"So you're thinking whatever Butler put in the safe-deposit box, that's what the intruder was after?"

"I think it's a possibility."

"And you think Butler tried to run you over because you might force him to reveal what he put in the safe-deposit box?"

"Maybe." Fenway squinted in the direction the Dokko Toccata had gone, as if she could remember it better. "The only thing I can think of is that someone believes I'm getting too close to the truth. Could be Butler and his mystery safe-deposit box. Could be someone from the Venn Cartel."

Then she stopped. Sheriff Gretchen Donnelly's cryptic message after she'd arrested George Pope for both the Seth Cahill and Mathis Jericho murders—*Congratulations on solving the two murders.*

Perhaps Donnelly didn't want the truth about the second murder to come out. Did she want the Mathis Jericho murder swept under the rug, with George Pope as the guilty party and the case closed?

Maybe Donnelly was behind the wheel of the Dokko Toccata.

No. That was ridiculous—Donnelly was the sheriff. Fenway glanced at Alvídrez, who was busy tapping on his phone screen.

Maybe she couldn't trust him, either. He was in Donnelly's inner circle, and he'd been with Fenway seconds before the car almost ran her over. He could have easily sent a text to the driver as they were leaving the taquería. All that flirting could have been a misdirection.

If the car had been stolen, and if they couldn't get a lead on the driver, it wouldn't matter that Alvídrez had gotten the license plate. But it would make him seem like a good guy, like someone Fenway could trust.

Fenway smiled at Alvídrez and hoped she faked it well enough. "Thank you, Steve. I'll see you back at the sheriff's office."

"We need to make a police report," Alvídrez said, holding up his phone. "Are you okay? Do you want me to drive you back?"

Fenway opened her mouth to argue—but Alvídrez was right. Making a police report was policy, even if it gave the driver more time to get away.

And even if it gave Gretchen information about Fenway knowing that someone was after her.

"I'll meet you in your office," Fenway said.

"You sure?"

"I'm fine. I've dealt with worse." She managed a weak smile.

Alvídrez tried to get Fenway to go back with him, but Fenway's hackles were up, and she firmly declined. She turned and walked to her Accord. In the driver's seat, she took a deep breath and looked at herself in the sun visor's mirror.

Her hair was disheveled. Lines around her eyes and the edges of her mouth. She had to stop being on high alert all the time. Although apparently her messy looks weren't dissuading Steve Alvídrez from making an awkward pass at her. Or whatever that was.

Her phone rang. She grabbed her purse—

Wait, no, that wasn't her phone. That was the phone the somewhat-familiar stranger shoved in her hand earlier.

Fenway needed to figure out who the second phone belonged to —and what it had to do with her almost getting run over. She looked at the screen: the caller was from the 805 area code—good, someone local, or relatively local. She opened the clamshell phone and pushed the *Answer* button. "Hello?"

"Hello, Fenway."

CHAPTER NINE

Fenway's jaw dropped open. "Who is this?"

"Hold on." The sound of rustling, background noise—was that a TV in the background? Finally, another voice.

"Hi, Fenway."

"Dez?"

"You got it."

"How—what did you—" And then it came to her: the young woman who'd shoved the phone in her hand was Dez's niece, the one who went to community college and was studying accounting.

"The question you're looking for is *why,*" Dez said. "But you haven't seen me in a few hours."

"You aren't the one who tried to run me over, are you?"

"What?"

"Someone tried to run me over right outside Dos Milagros. Driving a Dokko Toccata."

"Wasn't me. Or my niece. Are you okay?"

"Tore the knee of my trousers, hurt my pride. Why aren't you calling me on *my* phone?"

"Because something is going on," Dez said, "and I don't know who to trust."

"What—you think our phones are being tapped?"

Dez paused. "You can call it an overreaction, but you know that quote: 'Just because you're paranoid doesn't mean they aren't after you.'"

"Who's after you?"

"I don't know yet, but someone tried to run you over. You've had your phone tracked before, Fenway. You should know the feeling better than most. Now listen—did you get back to the office yet?"

"No. I'm in my car. About a block from Dos Milagros."

"Good," Dez said. "Now, listen, they made me lead on this case, and I'm reporting to Donnelly."

"She told me before she told you. Donnelly kicked me off the case pretty quickly."

"And if I know you, you didn't pay much attention to her directive."

Fenway cackled. "Hey, I can follow the letter of the law."

"I didn't say you couldn't," Dez said sweetly.

"Besides, ADA Pondicherry said he wouldn't be pursuing charges against Rachel."

"Not if Donnelly has anything to say about it."

"What do you mean?"

"Donnelly had me pull Rachel's financials. Nothing suspicious in her regular checking or savings accounts, no weird credit card activity. But she has some accounts at a different bank, one that hasn't had any activity since April of last year. In the last two weeks, she's been getting payments. Big payments—a few bucks under the ten-thousand-dollar reporting limit. Three times over the last two weeks."

Fenway was quiet.

"Did I lose you?"

"No, I'm still here."

"So Gretchen wants this to be an open-and-shut case. Her theory is that Rachel took the BMW out after you dropped her off, ran over Zellman, took the two bags of morpheranyl from his car, and went back home."

"That—that makes no sense."

"She's got the whole means-motive-opportunity thing mapped out. Hasn't even authorized overtime for me to work on it because she says we've caught the killer."

"And you don't like it."

"No, I absolutely don't like it. Gretchen's got the idea in her head that once Cahill and Jericho were killed, Rachel took over the distribution of the morpheranyl."

"Wait—what? Where would she store it? Cahill Warehouse Storage is no longer an option, and neither is the cabin in the hills."

"I don't have the storage answer yet, but Gretchen found a U-Move-It facility on Carlsbad Avenue that rented a truck to Rachel. Or an account with her name, anyway."

Fenway thought for a moment. "Why bring attention to the drug trade with the press release that the Venn Cartel was out of the county?"

"According to Gretchen? Misdirection."

"But Rachel wasn't the source of information for the press conference. In fact—Sheriff Donnelly was."

"I'm not the one saying it makes sense, Fenway. I'm the one saying something's not right in the sheriff's department."

Fenway closed her eyes. If someone had created an overarching plan to distribute morpheranyl and frame Rachel, then Fenway coming to get Rachel last night had thrown a wrench into their plans—whoever *they* were. But Fenway figured Donnelly was involved. "And you think someone is listening to our conversations?"

"I can't rule it out," Dez replied. "I don't know if it's Donnelly or someone who works for the cartel."

"But Rachel *doesn't* work for the cartel." She asked the same question of Dez she had of Alvídrez and Pondicherry: "If someone else is behind this, why frame Rachel? She's one of the least believable people as the new head of the cartel in Estancia."

"I think someone wants Rachel out of the way. Maybe the same people wanted Andrew Zellman out of the way."

"Zellman called me yesterday," Fenway murmured.

"You told me. Right as you and Craig were finishing dinner, right?"

"Right." Fenway closed her eyes and thought. "He said something had happened earlier this week. But he had to go before he gave me any information." She scratched her temple. "Maybe the person who tried to run me over can shed some light on this."

Dez harrumphed. "How are we going to find—"

"California plates."

"You got the license plate number?"

"Captain Alvídrez did. He texted it to me."

"Well, let me have it."

"You're in the office?"

"I'm outside Michi's building. I can access the DMV database from here."

Fenway tapped on her screen until Alvídrez's text came up. She gave Dez the license plate number. Dez muttered to herself.

"That can't be right," Dez said.

"What?"

"Give me the license plate again."

Fenway repeated it.

"Dokko Toccata?"

"Correct."

Dez clicked her tongue. "The car belongs to Deputy Donald Huke."

———

The evidence room was down the hall from Sheriff Donnelly's office, and Fenway walked the long way around the hallway to avoid running into her. Coming around the corner, Fenway nearly ran into a low sofa sticking out a few inches into the hallway from a window nook.

"They've gotta do something about that," Fenway said after she'd regained her balance.

The evidence room was open, and Deputy Donald Huke sat on a stool behind the gate. "Hey, Coroner," he said.

Fenway nodded. "Deputy Huke."

He studied her face. "Is—is something wrong?"

"You been here all afternoon?"

"Yes. I—uh, I had a bathroom break about an hour ago, but I was back in under five minutes. Pretty sure, anyway. I didn't time myself."

Fenway nodded. "What kind of vehicle do you drive?"

Huke brightened. "I bought a new car. One of those little econoboxes. I know, I know, a big guy like me in a tiny vehicle. I've heard the clown car jokes." He put his hands on his hips. "It gets great gas mileage, and I don't need anything fancy. Since I'm commuting in from San Miguelito now, I needed something that didn't put me in debt every time I had to fill up."

"A Dokko Toccata?"

Huke blinked. "Yes. How did you know?"

Fenway paused. "You're sure you were here all afternoon?"

"Positive."

"Someone driving your car," Fenway said, "tried to run me over about twenty minutes ago."

Huke blinked. "*My* car?"

"Yes."

Huke jumped off the stool. "No." He opened the cage, closed it behind him in a rush, then pulled the heavy door closed in front of the cage. He fumbled with his keys, then locked the door. "I—I need—"

He turned and hurried down the hallway toward the rear of the sheriff's office. Fenway followed as Huke went from a fast walk to a trot, then as he pushed the rear exit door open, he broke into a run. Fenway kept up with him.

Huke dug in his pocket as he crossed the parking lot, pulling out a key fob. The Dokko Toccata was parked on the right side of the lot, and it chirped.

Huke stopped, then bent halfway, resting his hands on his knees. "It's still here." He coughed, then stood upright. "I had an appointment to upgrade the security next week."

"So we need to take fingerprints," Fenway said. Someone had stolen Rachel's BMW and killed Andrew Zellman; now someone had stolen Donald's Dokko and tried to kill Fenway.

What did Fenway know that could get her killed? And what did Zellman know that got him run over?

Huke walked toward his car. "That's not the space I parked in this morning."

"Don't touch anything," Fenway said sharply.

"I won't," he said, his voice dazed. "I want to see..." He stepped gingerly to the side of his economy car and peered through the driver's side window. "The driver's seat," he said.

"What about it?"

"It's all the way back—exactly like I'd have it. If someone took this car..." He walked around to the front of the car and placed his hand over the hood.

Fenway had to bite her tongue to stop from telling him not to touch the car—but he kept his hand an inch from the hood.

"Still warm," he said. "Someone drove this car in the last ten minutes."

"File a police report?" Fenway asked.

Huke stared at his car. "That's the protocol. I don't know what I'll say, though."

"Cameras everywhere in this lot," Fenway replied. "Hopefully, something was caught on video."

Huke looked up into the near edge of the parking lot. A black camera mounted on a pole. He swung his head around; another camera on the other side of the lot.

"I don't like this," Huke said. "First Zellman is killed, then Rachel is arrested, then you almost get run over—and I was obviously the person they thought would be arrested for it."

"You were in the cage all afternoon."

"Of course I was, but I can't prove it," he said. "They're doing an audit of the video monitoring after Zellman's death. The video was off yesterday, and no one knows why. IT said they'd look into it. They came in and dismantled the cameras before lunch."

Fenway blinked. "I didn't hear anything about that. You heard about the video glitch from Jordan and Patrick?"

"No, some contractor from Hackson Square. Came in here with a hard case full of equipment."

Fenway furrowed her brow and pulled out her phone, then tapped on the screen. She turned the speakerphone on.

"Dominguez County IT, Jordan Daniels speaking."

"Hey, Jordan, it's Fenway. You had contractors come in and take the cameras down in the evidence room?"

"What? No—in fact, we were about to pull the footage from last night."

"So as far as you know, the cameras in the evidence room were in working condition?"

"Did someone say they weren't?"

"The contractors who came into the evidence room this morning."

Jordan let out an exasperated sigh. "No contractors that I know of."

Huke's face fell. "Well, who was it, then? He had a work order from the county. Your signature on it, too, Mr. Daniels."

"I didn't sign any work orders—not for the last month. Hold on —I'll be right over. You're in the evidence room?"

"No, we're in the parking lot. Someone stole Huke's car and tried to run me over this afternoon."

Jordan paused. "Did I hear you right?"

"Yes."

"Are there still cameras in the parking lot?"

"Yes—we're looking right at them."

"Give me five minutes."

They ended the call, and Fenway turned to Huke, who looked crestfallen.

"I swear, Fenway, everything looked in order. He told me he had to repair the wiring. Said they had strict orders to update the equipment and make sure everything was in working order."

"The contractors went into the evidence room?"

"Just one guy."

Fenway pressed her lips together.

"As far as I know, the evidence is safe. We've got everything boxed up, and a lot of the boxes are in their own cages. Not within arm's length of the cameras, either."

"So you're sure he didn't take anything?"

Huke paused. "I was sure he was from Hackson Square, and if he wasn't, then I'm not sure of anything."

"What did he look like?"

"Medium height, white. Brown hair. A full beard. Glasses with thick black frames—they call those Buddy Holly glasses, right?"

Fenway cracked a smile. "Some people do. Why were you sure he was from Hackson Square?"

"Those hot-pink-and-black bowling shirts they all have with the logo on the back. You can see those coming a mile away."

"Tattoos? Piercings?"

"Not that I could see."

Fenway folded her arms. "Let's check with the sheriff's office about any recent thefts at Hackson Square. Maybe someone stole a uniform."

———

Huke and Fenway entered the property theft unit's bullpen in the sheriff's office, and Fenway stopped in front of Brookline's desk. "Long time, no see, Lieutenant."

Brookline looked up from his computer. "Ah, Coroner. And Deputy Huke. To what do I owe the pleasure?"

"We have had several crimes in the last twenty-four hours targeting law enforcement in Dominguez County. Then, this morning, a man pretending to be from Hackson Square took all the cameras out of the evidence room."

Brookline stood from his chair. "What?"

"And someone stole Deputy Huke's car this afternoon and attempted to run me over."

Brookline's eyes widened.

"That sounds awfully familiar," Fenway said. "Sounds like someone is stealing the cars of county employees and running over *other* county employees. And your prime suspect for the Zellman murder was in jail when I jumped out of the way of the car."

"I assume you say you weren't driving," Brookline said, looking at Huke and crossing his arms.

"I was in the evidence room all afternoon," Huke replied.

Brookline looked at Fenway. "And you believe him?"

After everything Huke had done for Fenway—helping her clear her name when she'd been accused of murder, gathering evidence to keep her father's wife out of prison—Fenway knew Huke would never have tried to run Fenway over. He was such a cautious driver, he'd never have driven so recklessly down Fourth Street, either. Even if murder had been on his mind. "I believe him," Fenway said.

"This doesn't exonerate Rachel Richards," Brookline said.

"That's not what I came in here to ask," Fenway said. "I want to know if you've had any reports of burglaries or break-ins at any of the Hackson Squares in the county."

Brookline frowned. "I don't have a running catalog of every

property theft in my head, but I haven't heard of any. What are you thinking?"

"That someone stole a pink-and-black uniform shirt and wore it into the county offices, then stole our cameras."

"Is anything else gone?"

"We're figuring that out right now."

Brookline sat back down and pulled the keyboard toward himself. He tapped the keys. "Hackson—that's a C-K-S, right? Not an X?"

"Correct."

Brookline blew out through his mouth, his lips flapping slightly. "I don't see any burglaries at any of their locations in the county. Not in the last year, anyway." He squinted at the screen.

Fenway thought for a moment. "If someone from the Venn Cartel stole the cameras—"

"What?" Brookline's mouth dropped open. "The Venn Cartel?"

"Then," continued Fenway, "the uniforms might have been stolen outside the county. Maybe L.A."

"It's more likely that the uniform was bought at a thrift store."

"Or bought from a former employee," Huke said.

She leaned toward Huke. "Maybe we should put you with a sketch artist. See if the local Hackson Square employees recognize him."

Fenway's phone buzzed in her purse. She dug around for it and pulled it out. "It's Jordan." She tapped the screen, then turned the speakerphone on. "Jordan, thanks for calling back. I've got Deputy Huke and Lieutenant Brookline with me."

"Our cameras have all been compromised," Jordan said.

"What? All of them?"

"Our footage for at least the last two weeks. The footage and the backups have all been overwritten."

Brookline broke in. "But surely you've got offsite backups—or everything is backed up to the cloud, right?"

Jordan was quiet. "The county supervisors voted last year to keep law enforcement footage off public clouds. We can't guarantee the footage stays on U.S. servers. We get offline backup daily, and we move physical storage every month. But it looks like the offline backup has been compromised, too. Someone knew what they were doing."

Brookline's eyes darted to Fenway. "A disgruntled former employee?"

Jordan was quiet. Of course, Brookline was probably referring to Piper Patten. Piper had been fired after she'd uncovered too much evidence against a crooked ADA. But Piper had no beard, and disguising herself and sneaking around was only something she was good at in the virtual world.

"Have you been able to find out when the footage was deleted and overwritten?"

"The snapshots from the last two weeks all have a modified date of this morning. Between about two a.m. and eleven."

"Who has access and authorization to do that?" Fenway asked.

"Well—me," Jordan said. "And Patrick, of course. Anyone else in the IT department needs authorization from me. And I didn't give anyone authorization." He hesitated. "But there's no way to send deletion commands remotely. We set those commands with least-privilege access. You have to be in the office to access those files, period."

"Unless someone opened a back door into the system," Huke said.

Fenway shot a glance at Huke. "You know anyone who could do that?"

Huke shifted his weight uncomfortably. "Well—if someone wanted to break through the firewall, with enough resources and knowledge, they could do it."

Jordan sighed. "Deputy Huke is correct. We're running a skeleton crew in the IT department. Patrick's terrific, but he's one person. We've done a lot with automation in the last year, but keeping our systems patched would be a full-time job for three people." He cleared his throat. "We'll do a full analysis of the system today," he said. "Maybe we'll have to take down parts of the system."

"If our email being down for a few hours is the worst that happens, I'm okay with that."

"I'll give you more information as soon as I get it," Jordan said.

"Send the information to me," Brookline said. "Coroner Stevenson is in charge of suspicious deaths in the county, and I'm in charge of property theft. As far as I know, these stolen cameras haven't resulted in any murders, right, Mr. Daniels?"

"Uh, not that I'm aware of."

"Thank you." Brookline shot a glance at Fenway.

Jordan Daniels ended the call, and Fenway stared at the phone. Brookline was correct in one respect: Fenway was in charge of investigating suspicious deaths—but the theft of the cameras and the destruction of the footage seemed like a cover-up of a murder—and that squarely placed all the activities within Fenway's purview.

Except Fenway had been kicked off the Zellman murder investigation.

Brookline glanced at Fenway. "I know you don't want to hear this, but Piper Patten had the knowledge to hack the system. And after she was let go last year, she had the motive to do it, too."

Fenway furrowed her brow. "There's no way. Piper's been through a terrible ordeal over the weekend—"

"Wrongfully arrested for a murder she didn't commit," Brookline said. "It's all over the precinct. And how you found the actual killer and got her out."

"So you know she wouldn't have been able to plan anything like this over the weekend." Fenway crossed her arms. "This kind of hack takes planning, right? And coordination? Unless you think Piper is such a master of disguise, she fooled Huke into thinking she was a man. You've heard her elfin voice, right?"

Brookline was quiet.

"What is it, Lieutenant?"

"From what I understand," Brookline said carefully, "Piper Patten is close friends with Rachel. You, too, right?"

Fenway pursed her lips.

"No one thinks Rachel acted alone in this murder," he continued. "If the idea was to take over distribution for the Venn Cartel in the county, all she had to do was get rid of the evidence we had. The bricks of Nyllie and the eyewitnesses. Mathis Jericho and Seth Cahill were already dead. Rachel needed to get the bricks out of the evidence room."

"Keep going," Fenway said.

"Pretty girl like Rachel," Brookline said. "Andrew's a single guy, new to town, right? Rachel starts sweet-talking him, laughing at his jokes. Pretty soon, he agrees that she can come see him at work—or maybe she shows up unannounced. And when she thinks he's not looking, she takes the drugs out of evidence, a couple bricks at a time. A big purse could hold one or two bricks."

Fenway didn't like this at all.

Brookline leaned forward, putting his arms on the desk. "But—" Then he stopped and blinked twice. "I shouldn't be telling you this."

Fenway shrugged. "You're telling me a scenario that's running through your head. You're not telling me about the evidence you found, or the strategy the prosecution's using." And at least a small part of Brookline must not believe in Rachel's guilt; that was why he wanted to tell Fenway.

Brookline screwed up his mouth. "It seems to me a likely turn of events."

"Sure."

"I think Andrew caught her. Maybe the night before last. Could be she talked her way out of it, convinced him she wasn't *really* stealing the Nyllie bricks. But after that conversation, she knew he suspected her, and so she had to get rid of him. And that meant covering her tracks."

"I'm not hearing Piper's name yet."

Brookline shrugged. "Your friend Rachel visited the evidence room Monday afternoon. We have footage."

"No, you don't," Fenway said. "Jordan just said all the footage from the last two weeks was erased." Fenway dropped her hands to her sides. "Why are you lying, Lieutenant? Treating me like a suspect you're interrogating?"

"Well, that's what a good interrogator would tell Rachel." Brookline rolled his eyes. "Plus, I know the reputation Piper had when she worked here. Maybe Rachel convinced her to install some malware—maybe she says she was trying to get back at an old boyfriend or something like that. Brian told me he and Rachel broke up, right?"

"Right."

"So the malware Piper gave Rachel opened up a backdoor in the firewall, then Rachel went in and overwrote all the video footage. The perfect crime." He straightened and cleared his throat.

"You have nothing to back up your assertions." Fenway tapped her foot. "And you still haven't explained the man who pretended to be a Hackson Square employee."

"Let's call it a working theory," Brookline said. "But it explains everything about the murder," Brookline said. "It explains the two bricks in the BMW's trunk—"

"How so?"

"Those are the two bricks she got out of the evidence room without Andrew noticing."

Fenway said nothing.

"It explains why Andrew Zellman was targeted. It explains how Rachel covered her tracks. Plus, there's hard evidence that her car ran Zellman over. No evidence she wasn't behind the wheel."

"Except for my testimony."

"A good prosecutor," Brookline said carefully, "would point out that you didn't report her BMW as missing when you dropped Rachel off. I'm no district attorney, but I don't think your testimony establishes reasonable doubt."

Fenway pressed her lips together. Not what Pondicherry told her. But maybe Donnelly's team members—including Brookline, from the sound of it—were convincing him otherwise.

"Rachel didn't break out of jail, steal Deputy Huke's car, and try to run me over. You have a story for that, too?"

"Thanks for reminding me," Brookline said. "Deputy, if your car was stolen, we'll need a report."

"You'll need to take fingerprints, too," Huke said.

Brookline nodded at Fenway. "Anyone else see the car almost run you over?"

Ah, now he was throwing shade at Fenway: the only person who contradicted the Rachel-as-killer story, now also the only person who saw Huke's car outside the police parking lot.

Oh, wait. "Captain Steve Alvídrez," Fenway said. "He's the one who got the license plate number."

"And my engine was warm," Huke interjected, "in a different parking space than where I left it this morning."

"Ah," Brookline said. "Always good to get a corroborating story."

"Not that you don't believe me," Fenway said dryly.

"Cops aren't infallible," Brookline said.

"Don't I know it," Fenway said, taking a step back. "I'll see you after you file the police report, Deputy Huke. I'm getting out of here before Brookline tells me Rachel is a reincarnation of Jack the Ripper."

CHAPTER TEN

THE JAIL STOOD NEXT DOOR. FENWAY WOULD HAVE LIKED A longer walk to calm herself down, but she needed to visit Rachel and show her support—and ask if Rachel had seen or heard anything suspicious in the last couple of days.

She was in a daze as she signed in and went through the metal detector. The guard led her to a private room down the hallway. A metal table, two metal chairs: the same chairs in which she'd interviewed several suspects before. But she wasn't here as an investigator, she was here as a friend.

The far door opened, and Rachel entered.

Even though it had been only about eight hours since Rachel's arrest, the young woman looked exhausted, as if she hadn't slept the night before. But she saw Fenway and her face brightened.

"Hey, you," Fenway said. "They treating you okay in here?"

"I'm in a private cell," Rachel said. "The one they keep for prisoners with a high risk of getting attacked. Standing behind a podium talking about how great the police are must make me as much of a target as if I were a cop." She tilted her head. "You have an update on my case?"

"I'm testifying in your defense—or at least I will if asked. That means I'm not on the investigation."

Rachel's face fell.

"The ADA says my testimony will provide enough reasonable doubt, but I believe there are other forces at play keeping you here."

"Like what?"

Fenway shook her head. "Your car was the murder weapon," she said. "That'll take some undoing." She pulled a chair out and sat. "I know someone framed you for this, but I don't know why."

"Or who, obviously."

"Can you think of anything you learned over the last week that would make you a target?"

"Me? A target?"

"Someone wanted both you and Andrew Zellman out of the way —and they figured they'd kill him and frame you. So what do you know?"

Rachel blinked. "I—Nothing. Only what I read in the press reports."

"You don't write the press releases?"

"With direction from the county offices, sure. But I didn't do my own research into the Venn Cartel. Gretchen handled most of that."

Fenway tapped her chin. "Any newsworthy items come across your desk lately? About the Venn Cartel or the Mathis Jericho murder, maybe from an anonymous source?"

Rachel frowned. "My job isn't that exciting."

Maybe Fenway could try a different tack. "In the last week, what did you do that was different?"

Rachel scoffed. "Brian broke up with me. That was different. And Andrew asked me who he could trust. That was about it."

Fenway sat back in the chair and scratched her scalp through her curly hair. "Where did he do that? In the evidence room? Your office? The break room?"

"Oh, in my office, right around four o'clock on Friday. You'd already left for Colorado."

"And you mentioned me."

"Yes, I said you'd be back on Monday. Since he works the second shift, I figured he'd stop by at about the same time."

But Fenway had gotten delayed by the murder investigation near Las Vegas and hadn't been in the office on Monday. A sinking feeling in her stomach: if Fenway *had* been at her desk on Monday afternoon, would he have told her what the issue was? More importantly, would he still be alive? Instead, he'd called her in the middle of his shift, gotten interrupted, and been run over an hour after he left work.

Of course, had Andrew told Fenway first, she might have been targeted too—although, with the mystery driver trying to run Fenway over, she *was* a target.

She tightened her jaw. Why hadn't she filed a police report yet? If the media knew Fenway was being targeted by someone, the publicity might dissuade the potential killer from acting. She promised herself she'd file the report as soon as she could.

"They've uncovered additional evidence against you," Fenway said.

Rachel's mouth dropped open. "For what?"

"Hidden accounts with thousands in payments over the last two weeks."

Rachel's brow knotted. "I think I'd know if I had a hidden account. Dylan's retirement account and his old checking and savings accounts got transferred into my name after his death." Rachel swallowed hard, then continued. "But aside from my IRA and my regular checking and savings accounts, no, I don't have anything."

"Dylan's old bank accounts," Fenway said. "Do you pay attention to them?"

Rachel looked down at the table and shook her head. "I didn't think Dylan had other accounts. Maybe I should give all this info to my lawyer."

"Yeah." Fenway nodded enthusiastically. "That's a great idea. He can get a financial specialist to look at those deposits."

Rachel was silent for a moment. "So they're really framing me. Secret payments to an account I forgot about, payments I didn't know about, stealing my car."

"Have you thought more about who might have had access to your keys?"

"I told you, no one has an extra BMW key. Dylan had one, of course, but I got it back with his effects. I keep that at home in my dresser." Rachel crossed her arms. "Dylan's brother had a copy of our house key. But after Dylan died, I got the house key back from him. And I never lent Parker my BMW key."

Fenway nodded. She'd talked to Parker Richards over the course of her investigations. He'd pointed her to a low-level dealer named Zoso, who was often very helpful at getting Fenway information—even telling her what he knew about the morpheranyl trade, though he wasn't involved.

No proof that Parker had done anything with Rachel's key, but as he was a recreational drug user—always one bender away from screwing up his life—he might know *something*.

"After the whole thing with"—Rachel shuddered—"that RAT software last year, I don't trust anyone. If I lock myself out, or if I lose my key, I call Mandy. And if she's out of town, it's a call to a locksmith and a couple hundred bucks. I'm okay with that."

Fenway pursed her lips. "Think, Rachel. *Someone* must have—"

"I don't know anyone who would steal my BMW," Rachel interrupted. "Who goes around stealing cars and running people over on purpose?"

"A murderer, that's who. And twice in twenty-four hours? Can't be a coincidence."

Rachel's eyes widened. "*Twice?* Who else was run over?"

"Me." She cleared her throat. "A close call. The driver missed me."

"You? Are you okay?" Rachel's eyes narrowed. "Wait—is that what happened to your pants? Did you rip a hole in them jumping out of the way?"

"That's right."

"And the car that ran you over was stolen?"

"Not just stolen. It was Deputy Huke's new car. Stolen out of the police parking lot."

Rachel jumped in her chair. "Someone stole his car out of the sheriff's office parking lot, and they're still insisting that I drove the BMW myself?"

"Makes no sense," Fenway said. "Sheriff Donnelly must want this case closed so badly she's willing to ignore exculpatory evidence."

"Unless..." Rachel said.

Fenway looked into Rachel's eyes. "Unless someone on the inside is involved, and Donnelly's trying to cover it up."

"I didn't want to say it."

Fenway leaned back in the chair. "You leave your purse in your office, right? With your house key and your car key inside?"

"Well—yes."

"If you didn't give a key to your neighbors or to Brian, then maybe someone came into your office and took a key out of your purse when you didn't notice."

Rachel looked skeptical. "It's not like I have it sitting out on the desk—" Then she stopped.

"What is it?"

"I got in Monday morning and got pulled into a meeting with Sheriff Donnelly," Rachel said. "Usually, I put my purse in the bottom drawer of my desk, but I left it on top of the desk that day. I didn't have time to put it away."

"How long was it there?"

"Uh... maybe a few hours? The sheriff and I worked on the press release together, then I went down to see Vice to see if there was any chatter about the Venn Cartel."

"You went to see Vice?"

"Yes. Captain Alvídrez, in fact. He thought we were poking the bear by mentioning the Venn Cartel leaving the county. Apparently, he'd heard about the announcement and thought it was a mistake. He said he'd come to my office to see me, but I wasn't there."

"What about your assistant?"

"She had to run errands. Alvídrez said he'd wait for me."

"And she left him alone in your office?"

"It's not like..." Rachel cleared her throat, then folded her hands in front of her. "It's not like we don't trust him."

Fenway grimaced. Alvídrez was the one who'd gotten the license plate number of the Dokko Toccata that had almost run Fenway over. An uneasy feeling crept over Fenway. Being in charge of Vice, Alvídrez was in the *perfect* position to cover things up. His team regularly transported captured drugs to the evidence room. He had authority on all drug cases, in fact. Andrew had his call with Fenway interrupted by a law enforcement representative; Captain Steve Alvídrez commanded that kind of instant shift in attention.

"Did you talk with Captain Alvídrez about Andrew Zellman?"

Rachel rubbed her temples. "He asked if I'd met Zellman yet, and I told him he and I had a conversation on Friday."

"Did you mention that Zellman asked who he could trust?"

"Uh—no. I mean, definitely not."

Fenway furrowed her brow.

"I mean, sure, I wanted Andrew to feel like we were a welcoming team, you know? So I told Alvídrez to make it clear to Andrew that the lines of communication were open." Then her face crumpled. "I just heard that come out of my mouth. Not that far from saying Andrew was looking for someone to trust."

Fenway sat back in the chair again and stared up at the ceiling.

Alvídrez wasn't behind the wheel of Huke's car, but he was with

Fenway at Dos Milagros. He knew that was her favorite place—he'd even suggested it. He could have easily texted someone that he was exiting the taquería with her.

Then Fenway flinched.

"What?" Rachel asked.

"Alvídrez saw us," she said. "He saw you, me, Sarah, and Piper in that bar around the corner from VR Karaoke. I even told him that's where we were going."

Rachel tilted her head.

"Alvídrez knew, Rachel. I told him I was designated driver, so he knew your BMW was at your apartment, unattended. He knew we'd be out for a few hours. He saw the rest of you doing shots and probably realized you'd be too out of it to have a solid alibi at midnight."

"That's a stretch, Fenway. We could have still been out at midnight."

"Maybe," Fenway conceded. "But was he alone in your office before?"

Rachel considered for a moment. "He could have been there long enough to take my house key and made a copy."

"He could have, yes. The story fits."

"But why? Just in case he had an opportunity to steal my car? That doesn't make any sense. Lots of unproven allegations."

"Just as many as the story the sheriff is telling to charge *you* with the murder of Andrew Zellman," Fenway said. "And I know you didn't do it."

"Okay," Rachel said, "but you said they've got a money trail leading to me. That's supposed to be my motive, I suppose. What have you got for Alvídrez?"

"His divorce put him in debt. I'm having Piper look into his finances." Fenway paused. "He was with me when I was almost run over. He could have signaled to an accomplice to pancake me with Huke's Dokko."

"Wait—Huke has a Dokko?"

"A Dokko Toccata."

Rachel screwed up her mouth. "Someone could have taken my key to steal my car. When you said someone stole Huke's car, I wondered how. Now I know. The Dokko Toccata."

Fenway looked blankly at Rachel.

"The Dokko Gangz? You've heard of them."

Fenway shook her head.

"Gangz with a Z."

"Still no. Who are they?"

A line formed in the middle of Rachel's forehead. "Dokko. Cheap but reliable, right?"

Fenway grunted. "Didn't Dokko get in trouble a few years ago for tricking the gas mileage testing systems? Got fined hundreds of millions."

"Yeah, well, turns out they cut corners on their manufacturing, too," Rachel said. "A few months ago, a bunch of Photoxio videos came out about how amateurs can hot-wire Dokkos in thirty seconds. The company didn't install proper security measures in their ignition systems. A bunch of users calling themselves the Dokko Gangz made videos of them stealing the cars and going joyriding. They went viral because people are terrible."

"There's really a thirty-second hotwire hack?"

Rachel smiled. "I did my own research for this press release. The rise of Dokko thefts in Dominguez County." She held up her index finger. "Just pop the automatic door lock with an app you can download from any of a dozen hacker sites. Pretty easy to find." With a flourish, she held up a second finger. "Then two Phillips-head screws get the steering column cover off. There's a standard USB port under the cover." A third finger joined the other two. "Then you take any USB cable and plug it in. That bypasses the immobilizer for the 'turn-key-to-start' system."

"Wow."

"I was so freaked out, I took my BMW to the dealer and had them install a bunch of security upgrades."

Ah, that would explain why Rachel's BMW had been upgraded to prevent the keyless relay attacks.

"So," Rachel continued, "anyone with a smartphone, a USB cable, and a screwdriver can steal a Dokko Toccata in about thirty seconds."

"This is a known issue?"

"You'd know about it too, if you were on Photoxio more."

"That doesn't narrow down the pool of suspects at all."

Rachel nodded. "The sheriff's office did a training on it last week. Thursday, I think. What to look for, how to prevent it. Informational campaign to contact Dokko to get the fix."

"And everyone took the training?"

"Mandatory for the property crime team and the deputies."

Right. Huke would have taken the class, and that's probably why he made the appointment to upgrade his car's security.

Fenway dropped her arms to her sides, then looked at the hole in the knee of her trousers. It was more noticeable than she'd thought. Maybe she could go home to change.

She was more sure than ever of Rachel's innocence. But she needed to figure out where Alvídrez had been at many times in the previous two or three weeks. And she needed to do it without alerting him that she suspected anything.

———

After visiting her apartment to change into a pair of dark jeans, she drove to the business park where McVie Investigations was located and walked up the staircase to the second floor.

She opened the door to McVie's office, and Piper looked up from her desk. "Hey, Fenway. Let me finish one thing up and I'll show you what I've found."

"No rush. I was on my way back to the office and figured I'd stop in. McVie here?"

She shook her head. "Client visit, but he'll be back soon."

Fenway took a seat in front of Piper's desk and tapped on her phone screen to bring up her email. No updates. She put the phone to sleep and tapped her chin with it. Maybe going public wasn't such a bad idea—it might make the sheriff's office take action. Or at least pretend to care.

Piper tapped the *Enter* key with finality, then turned to Fenway.

"Interesting stuff," Piper said.

"I'm all ears."

"Dylan Richards had a bank account at Bank of the Bay when he was alive. Rachel was the beneficiary. She hasn't touched it since the bank switched the account into her name—no activity until a few weeks ago. Those payments you told me about? That's the account where they went."

"How come Rachel doesn't know about them?"

"Because a few weeks ago," Piper said, "someone changed the contact information for the account. Instead of going to her apartment, the statements go to a mailbox at OvernightExpress office in Paso Querido."

Fenway knotted her brow. "Someone?"

"Whoever it was logged in through the *Forgot My Password* functionality."

"But there should be two-factor authentication, right? Sending a one-time passcode to Rachel's phone or her email, right?"

Piper nodded. "Two-factor authentication works great until it doesn't. Remember, this wasn't Rachel's account, it was Dylan's."

Fenway's eyes went wide. "And someone has Dylan's old phone."

Piper shook her head. "Not old phone. Old number."

"Do you have the number?"

"Yeah. Want me to send it to you?"

"Please." Fenway bit her bottom lip in thought. "Can you locate where the person logged into Dylan's old account? Somewhere in Estancia? You can pinpoint that, right?"

Piper shook her head. "They used a VPN to obfuscate their location. I can try, but I wouldn't hold my breath."

"Still, all this information is enough for reasonable doubt, right? That Rachel isn't the one who deposited these payments?"

"ACH payments from a bank on St. Augustine Island," Piper said. "Easy to set up, hard to track. I'm working on it, but I'm not sure I'll be able to prove who the account belongs to."

"But you have an idea who's behind this, right?"

"This kind of financial obfuscation is something the Venn Cartel is good at."

"You think it's the Venn Cartel?"

"I don't know," Piper admitted. "I've also got a blurry photo of a silver BMW coupe on Morongo Heights Road at ten minutes to midnight." Piper turned her monitor toward Fenway. "But that doesn't match any prior activity of the Venn Cartel. They don't steal cars and run people over."

Fenway squinted at the screen. "That photo was taken *before* I dropped Rachel off. You can barely make out the make and model. If you told me that was Rachel's BMW 3-series, I'd believe it, but you can't read the license plate."

"Right. It's not much. Wouldn't be enough to convict anyone, but if you testify that Rachel was with you at the time—"

"You could testify too."

Piper shook her head. "I checked my doorbell camera. You and Rachel dropped me off at 11:41. Nine minutes between the time the two of you left my house and her BMW drove in front of that ATM camera. She'd have to hurry to be the one behind the wheel, but it could be done."

Fenway frowned. "So everything still hinges on my testimony. That Rachel was with me, and that her car wasn't in her parking space when I dropped her off."

"Right." Piper turned the monitor back in front of her. "One more thing. Someone rented a U-Move-It van on Sunday in Rachel Richards' name."

"In person?"

"Online. The van was picked up at the U-Move-It on Carlsbad

and 17th. Paid with a debit card attached to Dylan's old account—the one where the contact info was changed."

"Someone's making Rachel look like the guilty party," Fenway said. "And I know the sheriff doesn't believe me."

Piper nodded. "And the U-Move-It van hasn't been returned, either."

Fenway rubbed her chin. "So where is the van?"

Piper grinned. "I wish I knew someone who had the hacking skills to get into U-Move-It's GPS tracking system to find the van."

"You can do that?"

Piper feigned shock, placing a delicate hand below her collarbones. "I'm sure I don't know what you're talking about, Miss Stevenson. I would *never* condone anything illegal."

Fenway chuckled but shook her head. "Tell that to Lieutenant Brookline. He thinks you and Rachel are in cahoots."

"Nah, I work alone," Piper said, a smile playing on her lips.

The door opened and McVie entered.

"Hey, Craig," Fenway said. "How's the job hunt?"

"Another former McVie Investigations client returns to the fold," he said, and grinned. "More work than before, too. We're almost back to where we were before I left."

"That's great."

"As terrible as Payback Systems was, the silver lining is that it gave me a new appreciation for private eye work."

"And I appreciate the added job security," Piper said.

"What do you have going on now?" asked Fenway.

"No work yet. I have to return the moving truck."

"To the U-Move-It on Carlsbad and 17th?"

"Right."

"I have to investigate a rental agreement there. Want to drive with your favorite client?"

"My favorite client?" McVie turned in a circle. "I don't see Bob Quinlan in here—"

Fenway smacked McVie playfully on the bicep. "I don't think Mr. Quinlan does for you what *I* do for you."

McVie elbowed her lightly in the ribs. "I know he pays me."

"Sick burn," Piper said. "I'll send you the vehicle info on Rachel's van."

"My dad's good for it," Fenway said to McVie. "I might even pay for dinner later."

CHAPTER ELEVEN

THE BELL ON THE DOOR CHIMED AS FENWAY AND MCVIE WALKED into the U-Move-It. Flat cardboard boxes, stacked vertically against the walls, lined both sides of the aisle between the front door and the counter.

"Evening, folks," the man behind the point-of-sale system said, his tattered U-Move-It cap showing an outdated logo on the front. "How can I help you?"

"Returning a truck," McVie said, putting the key fob on the counter.

As McVie went through the return process with the U-Move-It employee, Fenway wandered around the small shop. Besides the moving boxes, the shelves were full of packing materials, from kitchen dish packs to moving blankets.

Fenway stared at one of the kitchen kits. This kit had no dish packs, but instead bags and small boxes for spices, flour, sugar—

She squinted. Something about that looked familiar.

The clear bag in the product photo on the box.

Were these the same type of bags full of morpheranyl as Fenway saw in Rachel's trunk? Yes, it was a plain, clear bag, but the sharply angled corners looked the same.

She picked up a package. Less than ten bucks. She wasn't sure if she could get them analyzed, but maybe she could compare them to the bags of drugs from Rachel's trunk.

A beep from the point-of-sale system drew Fenway back to the counter.

"All right, Mr. McVie, you're all set," the man in the old cap said. "You need anything else?"

"This," Fenway said, handing the package of bags to the man.

McVie's eyes cut to Fenway briefly.

"I'll pay you back."

McVie signed on the machine's screen.

"One more thing," Fenway said, pulling out her badge, "I'm looking for information on a truck that was rented a few days ago."

The man's eyes took Fenway in, then he said carefully, "We'll be happy to provide any customer information with a warrant or a court order."

Fenway shook her head, pulling her phone out and bringing up Piper's email with the van info. "Not looking for customer information," she said. "Wondered if you had pickup times, and when the return date is."

"I'll need the—"

"Reference number 3276 Delta Delta Tango X-Ray 4343."

The man looked up and blinked, then turned to the keyboard on the counter. "Come again?"

Fenway repeated the number.

"Reserved Sunday morning. Picked up that afternoon."

"What time?"

The man bent toward the monitor and squinted. "3:47 P.M."

"Did you speak with the person who picked up the rental?"

"Picked it up using the app. I never saw who got it."

"You have cameras covering the parking lot?"

"Have 'em in the drop-off area. A couple other places, too, but those vans you're asking about are usually parked in one of the blind areas." He shrugged. "The cameras are intended to view drop-off, not pickup. Management is more concerned with the shape of the vehicles when they come back than with who picks them up."

And, Fenway thought, without cameras to show any dings or damage when the vehicles got picked up, renters would have less evidence to dispute the company for conflicts.

"How do you know who picked up the car?"

The man stared at the screen. "Everything was done through the app. Miss Rich—uh, the renter created their profile online, uploaded their driver's license and payment information, then had to pick up the van."

"So no one ever *saw* Rachel Richards drive the vehicle," Fenway said. "In fact, no one ever saw her at all."

The man shifted uncomfortably. "It's all according to company policy. You have an issue with it, take it up with U-Move-It management."

Fenway pointed at McVie. "What do you have to do to log into that app?"

"Me?" McVie said.

"Yeah. Could you rent a van with *your* ID, but on *my* phone?"

"I don't know."

Fenway pulled her phone out of her purse, tapped on the screen, and went to the App Store. "Guess there's one way to find out." Searching for *U-Move-It*, she soon started the app downloading to her phone.

She set the phone down and opened the package of plastic bags, then pulled one out. Oh, these weren't clear. This one was had a white stripe, about a half-inch wide, around the upper third of the bag. She held it up to the man behind the counter. "The picture shows a completely clear bag on the package."

He nodded. "That's the latest batch we got in."

"This batch has a white stripe—but you sold clear ones before?"

The man shrugged. "No one cares if there's a stripe on the bag. Maybe it makes it easier to label with a Sharpie."

Fenway tapped on the newly downloaded app and handed her phone to McVie. "Log in."

McVie took the phone uncertainly, but typed in his username and password.

Fenway glanced at the screen. "Welcome, Craig McVie," she read out loud. "So no two-factor authentication?"

McVie shook his head. "I didn't get any security messages on my phone, either."

Fenway looked up at the man behind the counter. "So anyone with Rachel's username and password could have rented the van."

McVie tapped. "Oh, wow," he said. "My driver's license is even in here." He tapped again. "Oh—it's asking for a credit card. My payment info didn't come over into the app."

Fenway rubbed her forehead. "That explains why there's activity on Dylan Richards' old debit card, but not on Rachel's."

McVie logged out.

Fenway gave McVie a crooked smile. "What, you don't trust me?"

"Fine, call me paranoid, but I don't want my driver's license on *anyone's* phone." He turned his head to look at the man behind the counter. "And this app has *privacy violation* written all over it. I won't use it anymore."

"Doesn't matter," Fenway said. "If U-Move-It gets hit with a password breach, someone else can still download the app to their phone, log in as you, rent a van, and drive it to L.A. with millions in illegal drugs."

"What?" the man behind the counter said.

"Got a phone number for your corporate office?" Fenway said. "Maybe the cybersecurity division?"

———

After ten minutes on the phone with U-Move-It's cybersecurity director, who grew more panicked by the second, Fenway had a promise from the company to provide more information about the phone that had used the app—but Fenway wasn't holding her breath. The company had outsourced the app development to a third party who wasn't based in the United States and therefore not under obligation to provide information that could have proven Rachel didn't make the reservation.

The man behind the counter didn't wish them a nice day as they left the facility.

"Think we're blackballed from renting a truck ever again?" McVie said.

"I hope not," Fenway said. "But they better close their security loopholes. If they had their user passwords stolen and people are using stolen payment information to rent trucks and run drugs to other states and counties, I can't imagine that will go over too well with law enforcement. Not to mention the legal liability."

"You won't mention this to Gretchen?"

Fenway shook her head. "No way. She told me to stay away from Rachel's case."

"Maybe I could tell her. Say I noticed it when I returned the truck."

"Oh, please, McVie, if you tell Sheriff Donnelly, she'll definitely know I'm involved."

"She can't fire you."

"No, but she can make my life hell. Not something I need right now."

They got into Fenway's car and drove in silence to the freeway.

"Something's bothering you, Fenway."

Fenway shook her head. "You remember the boat captain?"

"The one you interviewed after you found the dead guy in the storage locker?"

"Right."

"Yeah. Evan Butler or something like that."

"*Stephan* Butler."

"Right. Figured he'd be long gone."

Fenway shook her head. "He seems to have gone legit. Whale watching tours."

"Wasn't that his cover story for drug running?"

Fenway shrugged. "He'd taken a group out on a tour when I visited the harbor today. Captain Alvídrez even said Butler's cover story might now be his *real* story." She glanced at McVie, then back at the road. "Butler had a break-in on his boat over the weekend."

"Can't say I'm surprised. Guy gets involved running drugs for the Venn Cartel, he'll attract some trouble. And the harbor's not exactly a crime-free zone in Estancia."

"And," Fenway said, "I found out he rented a safe-deposit box a day or two before the break-in."

McVie nodded. "You think Butler put something in that safe-deposit box, so the person who broke in didn't find what they were looking for."

Fenway bobbed her head. "Maybe. I suppose it could all be a coincidence."

"But you don't like coincidences."

"Neither did you when you were sheriff." Fenway got into the left lane to turn onto Ocean Highway and stopped at the red light.

McVie pointed to the right. "Instead of going back to the office," McVie said, "why don't you go to the harbor and see if Butler's around? It's past five. Maybe he's coming back by now."

Fenway frowned. "If you were still the sheriff, I would in a heartbeat. But you're a civilian now. I can't have you coming with me to interview possible suspects. Or witnesses."

McVie smiled. "You've been riding the line, Fenway."

"Sure I have, but I know where the line is. I can ask you for your opinion on the approach to a case, and I can ask you details on any case you used to work on. I can't tell you about the details of an open investigation."

"Sounds like you're stretching the limits of plausible deniability."

Fenway shrugged. "You're the Boy Scout, not me."

"If we're playing the game that way…" McVie pulled out his phone. "Look at that. Bob Quinlan's wife spent four hundred bucks on lunch at the Yacht Club at the harbor last week. And he doesn't think she was alone."

Fenway arched an eyebrow.

"Let's head over there," McVie continued. "You can go talk to Butler, and I'll go to the Yacht Club to get information." He grinned. "Maybe we can see if they have a table available for dinner. I don't know about you, but investigations work up my appetite."

Fenway checked over her shoulder, then pulled out of the left turn lane and made a right onto the on-ramp for Ocean Highway going toward the harbor. "Okay, Craig," she said. "But you're running interference for me if Sheriff Donnelly gives me any trouble."

"You think I have any sway with her?"

"She likes you. She doesn't like me."

Five minutes later, Fenway pulled the Accord into the parking lot of Estancia Harbor. As she killed the engine, Fenway looked through the windshield at where the *Ariel*'s dock was—and sure enough, the boat was docked.

McVie got out of the car and strode purposefully toward the Yacht Club. Fenway opened the driver's side door and got out, but didn't rush toward the dock. What would she say to Butler? She wanted to know what was in the safe-deposit box, what the would-be thief was looking for, or if anything was truly missing. How would Fenway approach this interview without scaring him off?

She walked toward the harbor, her mind churning, then stepped toward the *Ariel*.

And she saw Butler. He was moving a coil of rope from the dock onto the boat, and with a lithe, graceful movement more suited for a man of twenty-five than sixty—or however old Butler was—he nimbly jumped from the dock to the boat, never losing his grip on the large loop of rope over his left shoulder.

"Good evening, Mr. Butler," Fenway called. About twenty feet away—that seemed appropriate.

"Hey!" Butler shouted, dropping the coil of rope onto the deck. "The same rules govern this boat when it's docked as any other residence. You need a warrant to search—"

"I'm not looking to search your vessel," Fenway said. Apparently, the catch-more-flies-with-honey approach wouldn't work on Butler. "I have a few questions—"

"I'm not interested in answering," Butler said.

"Now come on," Fenway said—oh, that was close to a whine. She tempered her voice. "I'm a woman of my word. Coast Guard never touched your boat last week. You gave us the answers we wanted, and you helped us arrest Seth Cahill's killer."

"I'll be sure to put 'law enforcement consultant' on my résumé," Butler said warily.

Fenway laughed. Did that sound forced? Well, it was. At least Butler would think she was trying. "Only problem is, we thought the same person killed Mathis Jericho too."

"Who's Jericho?"

"You know who that is, Butler. The kid who drove with Cahill. The one who showed up alone at Portico Inlet. Dead in his boss's Corvette with a pile of drugs around him. Could've been a death scene in *Scarface*."

Slowly, Butler turned to face Fenway. "I told you all I know before," he said. "I don't know the kid. Thought he was in over his head. And if he died like that, I'd say I was right."

"I'm not here to ask you questions about what happened last week. I heard you had a break-in on the *Ariel*."

Butler's breath caught, but he continued looking evenly at Fenway. "True enough. But nothing was taken. So I didn't even file a police report."

"What happened?"

"Someone forced the lock to my living quarters. But the noise must have alerted someone—or maybe something scared off the intruder."

Fenway ran her tongue over her teeth and took a deep breath. "Or maybe they didn't find what they were looking for."

Butler pursed his lips and stared at Fenway. "You must think you know something."

Fenway nodded. "I know you took a backpack with you to First Dominguez Bank on Friday. I know you rented a safe-deposit box there."

Butler ran a hand over his face. "Last I checked, that's not a crime."

"I know your boat was broken into that weekend. And you say the intruder didn't take anything?"

Butler was quiet.

Fenway tapped her temple. "Did the intruder leave because the thing they were looking for was in the safe-deposit box, not the boat?"

"I don't know who broke in, and I don't know why they didn't take anything." Butler chuckled, turning to open a plastic box at his feet on his right. "For all I know, the intruder was a random drug addict looking for something to sell to get high. And there are a million possibilities why they might have gotten scared off."

Fenway put her hands on her hips. Did she want to lay her cards on the table? Butler was a suspect in the Jericho murder—Callahan had convinced her he might have had motive. She thought for a moment; maybe if she didn't go into too much detail.

"We think the person who broke into your boat might have been involved in some more serious crimes," she said.

"That doesn't sound like my problem."

"If we could identify the intruder—"

"I never saw him."

"But if you tell me what you put in the safe-deposit box—"

"I'm the victim here," Butler said sharply, turning to Fenway and glaring at her. "Nothing's missing, so I knew the cops wouldn't care. Then you show up, demanding to see the contents of my safe-deposit box." He crossed his arms. "You're getting dangerously close to harassment."

Fenway bristled and met his eyes. "You've been running Nyllie between here and Mexico for months, if not years."

"You don't have any proof—"

"We could get proof easily," Fenway said, though she wasn't sure if that were true. "But I care more about protecting people from murder. I don't work in Vice." Fenway leaned forward, although the side of the boat was between them. "Cops are getting killed, and I suspect it's over getting whatever it is you put in the safe-deposit box. I don't think the break-in was a total surprise to you."

Butler broke from the staring contest. "If I'd been expecting it, don't you think I would have put in some security measures? Maybe asked the security staff to make sure my boat was secure? Maybe bought an alarm system and installed it?"

"You don't have that already?"

Butler set his mouth in a line, and his eyes were restless, untrusting. "I bought a much sturdier lock and installed it myself, and I ordered a security system for the boat. I suppose I'm locking the barn door after the horse is stolen, but I'm not taking any more chances. The next intruder to break in might not get scared off so easily."

A light bulb flashed on in Fenway's head: the British national who was on the *Ariel* during all the morpheranyl shipments. "You think maybe the intruder was Calvin Banning?"

Butler swiveled his head to Fenway, then laughed. "I do not," Butler said.

"Because you trust that he wouldn't do it?"

"Well, he wouldn't, but that's beside the point. He's not here— he's doing a job on the East Coast. I haven't seen him for a week, maybe longer."

Fenway stared at Butler, saying nothing for a moment. The moment stretched out.

"So," Butler said, "if you don't mind, I've got work to do." He turned and began rummaging in the plastic box.

"Would you like us to investigate who broke in?" Fenway said, a little more gently. "We could dust for fingerprints—"

"No," Butler said.

"I thought you said you wanted us to catch the intruder."

He shook his head. "I said you didn't *offer* to catch the intruder. But the last thing I want is for you to plant fake evidence on my boat."

Fenway crossed her arms. "If you'd like us to investigate the break-in, you let us know."

Butler looked up. "I'm running a clean business now. I've seen enough of you in the last two weeks to last a lifetime. So I'd appreciate if you left me alone."

———

McVie was leaning against Fenway's Accord, staring out over the ocean, when Fenway walked back to the parking lot. Fenway looked back over her shoulder: the sun was low, and though the beach here faced mostly south, the light skittered over the water, with glittering sparkles across the surface.

Fenway stepped next to McVie. "I take it we're not eating dinner at the Yacht Club."

"Only if I want my food spat in. The waitstaff didn't exactly appreciate my questions."

"Get what you need?"

McVie kept his eyes on the water as he gave Fenway a distracted nod. "It's beautiful here," he murmured. "I've lived here so long, I took the ocean for granted. When was the last time I was at the beach? I can't remember."

"You went there a day or two before you left for Colorado."

He shook his head. "I took photos for a client then," he said. "I mean coming to the beach to relax. Hear the roar of the waves, feel the sand between my toes. When was the last time I did that?"

Fenway looked out over the water. The ocean *was* beautiful.

"I never took you to the monarch grove, did I?"

McVie looked at Fenway. "The monarch grove?"

"I used to go running out there. You know where my street dead ends?"

"Yeah."

"There's—" Fenway paused. This would take too long to explain. "I'll show you. Maybe tomorrow morning. Now that you live in the complex, you should know its best-kept secret."

McVie put his sunglasses on. "Ready to head back?"

"Sure."

The drive back was quiet, with McVie looking out the window. Fenway felt a gnawing in her gut. McVie was rarely contemplative, which sometimes bothered Fenway. Mostly, though, she was glad of his gregariousness, how he could talk to anyone, how his demeanor put everyone at ease. She could have been in Estancia like she'd been in Seattle: morose, distant, with few friends—none close. Instead, McVie had gotten her out of her shell, and while she didn't think he was responsible for the friends she'd made in Estancia— Rachel, Piper, and Sarah were closer friends than any she'd had in Seattle—she found it easy to be more open and friendly when she was around McVie, and hard to be morose and distant. Maybe that's why she hadn't wanted him to move to Colorado. And maybe that's why she was so scared of him moving in; there would be no respite from the openness and friendliness that she craved but also feared.

She should go back into therapy and talk this out.

McVie's phone dinged.

"Piper wants to talk to you when you drop me off," he said.

Fenway cleared her throat and ran her hand through her hair.

Five minutes later, they opened the door to McVie Investigations. Piper turned her head as they walked in. "I transcribed the interview with the maître-d'," she said to McVie. "Searched Karen Quinlan's social media, too. I have a couple of candidates for her affair partner."

"Thanks," McVie said. He pointed to his office. "In my email?"

"Yep."

McVie walked into his private office.

"Now, you," Piper said, turning to Fenway. "I wasn't getting anywhere with Alvídrez. He's either clean, or he's good at hiding stuff. Thought maybe a change of focus to Sheriff Donnelly would be good for an hour or two."

"Gotcha. What did you find?"

"You probably won't like it." Piper clicked on the PC and an electronic receipt appeared. "I know you suspect her, but if you think she's the one to steal Rachel's BMW and run over Andrew Zellman, she's got an alibi for Monday night."

Fenway took a step toward Piper's monitor and leaned forward, reading the top of the receipt on the screen. "Bixby's."

"Right—the bar and grill in P.Q. Twenty-one miles away from Morongo Heights."

Fenway rubbed her chin.

Piper pointed to the screen. "Time on the receipt is two minutes before the timestamp on the ATM camera that recorded Rachel's BMW. No way Gretchen was driving."

"All that proves is that her credit card was there, not necessarily her."

Piper raised her eyebrows.

"If she's involved in this, she just gave herself plausible deniability."

"I suppose it's not unheard of to pay with someone else's credit card." Piper shrugged. "You think she lent her credit card to someone so she could steal the BMW? Is she the mastermind? The big villain?"

Fenway paused. "It's possible. But I get the feeling the Venn

Cartel is behind this whole thing. The big media splash for how they're leaving the county. Maybe the cartel is bribing Sheriff Donnelly to look the other way or to cover up some crimes." Beyond her gut feeling that something was off, she had little to go on. What was the point of covering up Jericho's murder—and was Donnelly behind it, or Alvídrez, or Butler? Or was it the Venn Cartel?

"If you want evidence against her, then," Piper said, "we'll need to see if there's a money trail. But right now, the money trail points to Rachel's accounts, not Sheriff Donnelly's."

Fenway drooped her shoulders.

"If it helps," Piper said. "All the suspicious activity has been in Dylan Richards's old accounts and not in Rachel's main accounts. But Rachel did contact Bank of the Bay last week to cancel one of Dylan's credit cards that he'd had for a few years."

Fenway's phone dinged. A message from Sarah: Deputy Huke had sat with a sketch artist. Another ding: a drawing of the Hackson Square impostor. Fenway tapped the graphic, and it expanded to fill the screen. The man was white, a full beard that didn't quite hide his high cheekbones. His eyes weren't particularly large or small, but they were set close together, and his nose was slightly crooked. He had a mop of straight hair that almost looked fake.

McVie came out of his office. "Hey, Fenway, you ready for some dinner? I've got an idea."

Fenway turned her phone to McVie. "You know this guy?"

McVie peered closely at Fenway's screen. "His face kind of rings a bell, but I don't know from where."

"Was he involved in a previous case of yours?"

"Maybe."

Fenway opened her mouth, but her stomach rumbled.

McVie smiled. "Sounds like your stomach is officially telling you to take a break. And I think you should, too." He tilted his head. "You wanted to try that new Indonesian place on Santa Ana Street before I left for Colorado, but we never got the chance. How about tonight?"

"You're right. I *should* take a break. Besides, I always think better after a decent meal." She bit her lip. "But we might need reservations."

"Way ahead of you. Seven o'clock. Craig, party of two." McVie smiled as he held up the key to his Highlander.

CHAPTER TWELVE

Santa Ana Street was on the border of the industrial area of town. The Indonesian restaurant, Meja Ibuku, stood in a long storefront that looked like it was slowly being revitalized. Across the street, a construction site stood with wire fencing all around. A white wooden sign proudly proclaimed luxury condos opening in the fall. McVie pulled into the crowded parking lot and found a space in the middle of the third row of spaces.

Affixed to the window of Meja Ibuku were hand-drawn signs advertising rijsttafel, beef rendang, and gado-gado. Fenway didn't even know what those last two dishes were, but her mouth was watering before Craig even held the door open for her.

The restaurant was long and narrow, with tables for two on the side of an area that resembled a wide hallway more than anything else. An aroma of chilis and curry hung deliciously in the air, and—was that a hint of anise? The tables were almost all full, and the conversation was loud, mostly drowning out the Indo-pop playing through the sound system in the restaurant.

They sat at a low table off in the wide hallway, and Fenway took a few minutes reading about the concept of the rijsttafel—Dutch for *rice table*—on the menu. After a few minutes, McVie closed his menu and handed it to Fenway. "I'm leaving it up to you."

Fenway ordered for both of them: the minahasa rijsttafel was a sampling of eight dishes, with three that Fenway hoped would be spicy enough for her. She ordered mint tea for both of them, then sat back in her low chair and took in more of the sights and smells. Fenway didn't know much about Indonesia, but she'd gone down a rabbit hole on the internet when Meja Ibuku first announced its opening two months before.

McVie glanced around at the decor on the walls. "Am I crazy, or does a lot of this stuff look German?"

"Dutch," Fenway said. "Indonesia used to be a Dutch colony."

The server set down a small plate in front of them: krupuk, Indonesian prawn crackers. Fenway's eyes lit up, and she popped one in her mouth. Perfect. McVie picked up a cracker skeptically, then tentatively put it into his mouth, chewing carefully. Fenway couldn't tell if he liked it or not.

"I didn't even know Indonesian food was a thing," McVie said. Then he stopped, grabbing another prawn cracker. "That's not what I meant. I mean, I didn't know it was a thing in the U.S."

"I've read about Indonesian cuisine," Fenway said, "but I've never had it." A few months ago, her father had gushed about an Indonesian restaurant on Utrechtstraat when he'd talked about taking Charlotte to Amsterdam for their anniversary. The bile of jealousy that had risen in Fenway's throat didn't taste nearly as good as the prawn crackers.

McVie's jaw dropped open. "You suggested this place a couple weeks ago, and you don't even know if you like Indonesian food?"

Fenway smiled.

McVie often got Fenway out of her shell—like getting her to go out with Rachel to karaoke. Fenway liked to think she was equally good for him in getting him to try new things. Odd how they both could get stuck in their comfort zones, her with social situations and him with food. And the other one could get them unstuck.

One day, McVie would order a lengua taco. Then Fenway would know she'd won.

She thought about Andrew Zellman, moving to a new city, killed before he could settle in. McVie moved to a new city, and his ex-wife and daughter undercut him before he'd even finished his first week. Two cautionary tales of how things can go south when leaving comfort zones.

The server set down a wooden tray with eight small dishes, four of them steaming with heat. McVie's eyes widened. "That's what you ordered?"

"Yep. Try a little of everything. Figure out what I like." Fenway grabbed a chicken satay skewer and then spooned a bit of two vegetable dishes onto her plate.

McVie looked a little overwhelmed, so Fenway pointed out the less spicy dishes. He smiled at her—his face was almost pained—as he took a few pieces of coconut chicken and spooned some rice and vegetables onto his plate.

"I can't believe I'm trying this," McVie said, staring at his food skeptically. "It's a good thing you're so cute." He visibly steeled himself and took a bite of the coconut chicken. Then his eyes lit up.

"Pretty good?"

He chewed and nodded.

They ate in silence for a few minutes, McVie adding a little of everything onto his plate. He fanned his mouth after taking a bite of the beef with spicy peppers, which was Fenway's favorite.

"All right," McVie said a moment after taking a drink of mint tea. "You might turn me into a slightly more adventurous version of myself." He chuckled.

Then a thought struck her.

"Hypothetically," she said, "if someone were to set you up for the murder of Andrew Zellman, why would they do it?"

McVie's brow furrowed. "Me? Why would they want to frame me?"

"Humor me. You were sheriff for a long time. What kinds of things would you look for?"

McVie cocked an eyebrow. "You aren't behaving as though you're off the case."

"That surprises you? I'm asking Piper to do a background check on Gretchen."

"If the killer framed me, it would be because I saw something," McVie said. "As the former sheriff, I'd be too visible to kill, so framing me might be the best option."

"Wouldn't you tell the cops what you saw?"

"Not if I didn't know its significance."

"That's a possibility," Fenway said. "Maybe Andrew saw something. That could be why he asked for someone he could trust."

"And what about Rachel?" Maybe she had done something unexpected.

Oh—of course.

"She canceled one of Dylan's credit cards last week," Fenway said.

"So?"

"So—all those payments that establish a money trail to Rachel went through Dylan's old accounts."

McVie took another bite of the coconut chicken.

"Think about it. If you were messing around in Dylan's old accounts and Rachel cancelled Dylan's credit card, wouldn't you worry that she'd cancel his old debit cards next?"

McVie swallowed. "Or at least start reviewing the bank statements."

Fenway cocked her head. "Is Rachel the kind of person who doesn't review her bank statements?"

"Aren't we *all* the kind of people who don't review those statements?" McVie said.

Fenway bit her lip. "You're such a Boy Scout, I thought for sure you'd balance your checkbook every week."

"You're telling me you do?"

"Of course I do." She and her mother had been so poor in Seattle for so long, she always knew exactly how much money she had in her account. Some days it had meant she left early and walked to work. Some months it meant choosing between paying the electric bill and getting food.

McVie had obviously never been poor. He'd never wondered where his next meal was coming from. McVie's current situation might be the first time in his life he'd worried about money.

Fenway set her fork down.

"Rachel can't review her bank statements from prison," she mumbled.

"What?"

Fenway looked up. "Nothing. But I have other places I can look now."

McVie grunted, spooning the spicy beef dish onto his plate. "Always happy to help."

Fenway pointed to his plate. "That's the spicy one."

McVie glanced up at Fenway, a smile touching the corner of his mouth. "Yeah, I know."

————

They arrived back at Fenway's apartment. The hall light cast shadows around the room from a stack of McVie's boxes in the living room. Fenway took a deep breath—they'd barely been back from the trip for a full day, and Fenway couldn't expect McVie to have moved all the boxes out of her apartment yet.

McVie closed the door behind him and then pulled Fenway in for a kiss. His lips were soft, and he tasted of mint tea.

Fenway broke from the kiss, smiling, and held up the small

paper bag with the four small cartons of leftovers. "I'll be right back."

She crossed into the kitchen, took the cartons out of the bag as McVie's phone dinged. She had next to nothing in the fridge—she hadn't gone to the grocery store since coming back from her aborted trip to Colorado.

When she came back to the front room, she raised her arms to drape them around McVie's shoulders, but he was staring at his phone and frowning.

"What?" Fenway asked.

McVie's brows knotted, then he turned the phone around to show Fenway the screen.

Fenway and Captain Steve Alvídrez. At Dos Milagros. They were both smiling, and Fenway was leaning toward Alvídrez, her hand raised, an inch or two from his face. The photo looked like they were sharing a private moment, almost intimate. The gado-gado turned in Fenway's stomach.

You've got some salsa on your face.

Fenway blinked. A million thoughts went through her head. Where did he get that photo?

He was a private investigator with a telephoto lens on his camera, after all.

"Did you—" Fenway swallowed hard. "Did you follow me today?"

"What? No! I just got this."

Fenway tilted her head. "Someone sent you this photo?"

McVie looked at the screen again. "Yes."

Fenway almost demanded to know who it was, but stopped. An outburst would sound defensive, like she had something to hide. She took a step back. "Captain Alvídrez and I had lunch today, late, maybe two thirty. He hadn't eaten yet, and I needed to talk with him, so I met him there."

McVie looked from Fenway's face to the phone screen and back.

"Alvídrez had salsa on his face. I didn't touch him, I pointed it out. Someone must have…" Fenway's voice trailed off.

The three teenaged girls in the taquería. Ugh, she should have known.

"Megan sent you that photo," she said.

"Honestly," he said. "I thought the photo was fake. Photoshopped or maybe AI-created."

"You know she's trying to get you and Amy back together," Fenway said. "I bet there were two dozen pictures her friends took of me and Alvídrez. And I bet this is the only one where we look even vaguely…" Fenway cleared her throat. "Vaguely *chummy*."

Fenway looked at the phone screen picture again and noticed Alvídrez's eyes. Oh. He wasn't looking at Fenway in a chummy way. She recognized that look from ex-boyfriends, from guys who'd hit on her on the dance floor, from McVie when he was feeling amorous. And McVie could see it too.

"This picture is of two colleagues talking about the murder of Mathis Jericho." Fenway felt her pulse race. "He and I talked about visiting the evidence room later that afternoon." Fenway paused for a moment. "Which we did. And it was a good thing Steve was there, because—"

Fenway stopped. The afternoon had been so busy, she wasn't sure what she had told McVie.

"Because what?"

"Because he got the license plate number of the car that tried to run me over."

McVie snapped his head up.

Fenway closed her eyes, cursing under her breath. "I guess I didn't tell you about that."

McVie stared wide-eyed at Fenway. She saw the internal struggle on his face.

He spoke after half a second. "You're okay?"

"Of course I am. The car missed me." Fenway averted her eyes and focused on a moving box in the corner of the living room. "To be honest, I'm more pissed off that I got a hole in the knee of my trousers. I just bought them last month."

McVie pulled out a chair from the kitchen table. "How—" He started again. "Why didn't you..." Then he sat down heavily and took a deep breath. "I'm glad you're okay." A vein appeared on his forehead. "So Alvídrez got the license plate? They caught the person who tried to run you over?"

Fenway shifted her weight uncomfortably. "Well, no. The car was stolen." How much should she tell McVie? He was a civilian now, after all—not privy to the details of investigations, and Fenway knew this would dovetail with the Andrew Zellman murder. "Everything happened so fast, and then I've been running all around trying to—"

"You came to the office," McVie said. "We were in the car together, fifteen minutes to the U-Move-It place, another fifteen minutes to the harbor. We sat and stared at each other for an hour at dinner while you gave me a graduate-level seminar on the history of Indonesian cuisine in the Netherlands. It's not like you didn't have a million opportunities to tell me."

"I know, I know," Fenway said. "But honestly, once we found out that the car belonged to Deputy Huke—"

McVie's eyes grew even bigger.

"He wasn't behind the wheel," Fenway added hastily.

McVie turned, put his elbows on the table and rested his head in his hands.

"What is it, Craig?"

"I get that you're much more of a private person than I am," McVie said. "I know you haven't been in a lot of long-term relationships before." He took a breath. "And I'm so glad you weren't hurt —or worse."

Fenway crossed her arms.

"I love you, Fenway. I know I sometimes get too wrapped up in wanting to move our relationship forward." He put his palms flat on the table. "But this is important. When something like this happens..." He sighed. "I'm your boyfriend. I care about you. I think you care about me. And when you don't tell me this sort of thing..." He trailed off, his forehead creased.

"It's not like I was trying to hide it from you," Fenway said. "Maybe some people would say that they didn't want you to worry, but that's not why I didn't mention it."

Why hadn't she mentioned it?

Dez's niece had put the burner phone in her hand just before the car tried to run her over. And Fenway had to solve the Jericho murder quickly. She was running a million miles an hour.

"I know it seems like something I should have told you," Fenway said. "But—so much was happening. It's not like I didn't think you needed to know—I honestly forgot about it myself."

"You were almost run over, and you forgot about it?"

"Well, kind of, yeah." Fenway heard the wishy-washiness in her voice. "Maybe I had a trauma response," Fenway ventured. "You know, like denial is the first stage of grief? I might still be in denial that it happened."

McVie was quiet for a moment. Fenway stared at him, wondering how angry he was.

Finally he spoke; quiet, measured tones. "If it had been me," he said. "If I'd been almost run over by a car, wouldn't you want to know as soon as I could tell you?"

Fenway's stomach dropped.

McVie glanced at the clock on the microwave. "How much time has elapsed since you almost got killed? Eight hours?"

Closer to seven, but Fenway nodded anyway.

"I think I'd feel better if you *were* trying to hide it from me. If you were trying to spare me the worry. But you didn't think about telling me at all."

Maybe McVie was right.

But suddenly she saw herself at sixteen years old, in her homecoming date's kitchen, with his parents coming downstairs to meet her, and the flicker in their eyes when they saw she was Black. The days of searching thrift stores for the perfect dress, her mother sewing to fix a frayed hem, all that work gone. All the pride she had when she looked in the mirror and saw, for once, maybe what her date—a handsome white boy on the basketball team *and* the honor roll—saw in her. Replaced by a twisting, gnawing white heat in her gut. Like this awkward meeting was *her* fault.

She never wanted to feel like that again.

Fenway took a step forward. "I almost get run over, and *I'm* the bad guy?"

McVie flinched and blinked rapidly. Then he sucked in a breath. "You're absolutely right," he said. "You went through a traumatic experience. I'm sorry. It's not about me." He stood and turned to Fenway. "I'm really glad you weren't hurt," he repeated.

Part of Fenway wanted to go to McVie and embrace him. Yes, the stolen car had nearly struck her, but that hadn't crossed her mind in hours. And McVie had seen a photo with Fenway and another man—the kind of cheating-girlfriend photo his clients paid big money for.

But the white heat in her gut burned hotter. Fenway was right to be annoyed at McVie, wasn't she? She was the one who'd almost been run over, but he was pissed off that Fenway hadn't called him the minute it happened? Screw that.

Fenway looked at McVie's face. Sympathy and compassion tangled up with hurt and anger.

"I don't know why—" Fenway began. She stopped and stared at the floor, her stomach in a knot.

Had McVie kept his own apartment, maybe Fenway would have suggested they spend the night apart. But that was impossible.

She raised her chin and looked McVie in the eye.

"I don't know why I—" she repeated, then the white heat in her stomach sparked into a flame. "I don't know why I owe you an explanation."

McVie drew a sharp breath in.

As soon as it was out of Fenway's mouth, some part of her knew she'd crossed a line. She should apologize, try to backtrack.

But the look on McVie's face, so close to the expression of her homecoming date's parents—Fenway tightened her jaw and looked down. "Maybe you want to sleep on the sofa tonight."

"No."

Fenway arched an eyebrow.

"I'll sleep on the floor if you don't want me in your bed, but I'm not letting you out of my sight tonight."

Fenway furrowed her brow.

McVie pursed his lips. "Someone wants to kill you, Fenway. And that's not happening on my watch."

PART 3

WEDNESDAY

CHAPTER THIRTEEN

Fenway awoke with her back to McVie. She blinked. The room was almost completely dark, but the first rays of daylight filtered through the windows. Probably not quite six o'clock.

She pushed herself into a sitting position and looked over her shoulder at McVie. He usually slept without a shirt, but last night he'd put an old concert tee on. His sign that nothing romantic would happen—which she was more than fine with. She'd put on a ratty, unflattering set of pajamas. They pretty much both fell asleep in wary annoyance.

Sharing an apartment with a boy was stupid.

She tiptoed to her dresser and pulled out sweat shorts, a sports bra, half socks, and a T-shirt. A minor pang of guilt: she'd promised McVie that she'd show him the butterfly grove, but she was still full of—what? Anger? Resentment? Whatever they were, the feelings were negative.

She went to the bathroom, then washed her hands and pulled her clothes on, leaving her pajamas in a heap on the vinyl floor. McVie was more of a neat freak than Fenway was.

She grabbed her running shoes from the rack next to the front door, slipped them on without untying them, put her key in the hidden inside pocket in her running shorts, and left, pulling the door shut quietly behind her.

The morning was foggy, as many summer mornings were in Estancia, but the cool, damp air reminded her of Seattle. Fenway felt a pang of sadness at how much her mother would have loved to come back to see the California coast, and how proud she would have been of Fenway. She blinked hard as she walked across the parking lot.

She turned left, toward the *Not a Through Street* sign. A hundred yards further was the dead end, with new white paint on the wooden fence the width of the road. The red and yellow reflectors, spaced several feet apart, looked new as well. Or maybe it had been so long since Fenway had taken a run to the butterfly waystation that everything seemed new. One thing that was definitely new: posts on either side of the dirt path leading into the trees. And a small sign: *Monarch Waystation 1.1 mi.* Wouldn't be a well-kept secret much longer.

She broke into a jog and her knee barked its objection as she passed the fence. Hadn't been the same the last few months—and diving out of the way of the car hadn't helped. Fenway tightened her jaw; she should have exercised the knee, gotten it used to movement. She didn't want to be an old woman with creaky joints; she wanted to be the seventy-five-year-old who still ran half-marathons or hiked Half Dome.

After a few minutes, she passed a familiar grove of trees and followed the path through a small clearing. As it was almost every time she made this trek, the mist was thick, with a canopy of branches serving as a kind of umbrella for the fog. Further on, a new post and a new brown metal sign outside the next grove of trees: here was the monarch butterfly waystation.

The waystation only served the monarchs twice a year through their annual passages up and down the west coast. Only a few scattered butterflies—or maybe they were those moths that had evolved to look like monarchs—fluttered about. She was a few weeks too late for the mass explosion of butterflies, as well as the crowds of people who left their cars at the end of the road and made this same hike.

Aw, crap. McVie would *love* this. He would think it was cool.

Fenway replayed his words in her head from the night before. How, indeed, would she feel if it had been McVie whose life was in danger, and he hadn't told Fenway? Not during forty-five minutes of driving around town in near silence, not during dinner, not during not one but two different visits to his office?

She kept jogging, now through the white milkweed blossoms on either side of the path. In five more minutes of jogging, she should come upon the second grove.

The white heat in Fenway's stomach had dissipated. They'd get over this, right? Maybe she wouldn't even need to figure out why she hadn't told him about almost being run over. Time heals all wounds.

"So stupid," Fenway muttered as she jogged.

The trees ended at the edge of a grassy plain, and the mist hung in the lightening sky. She'd first seen this plain over a year ago, with fifty feet of uninterrupted grass from the edge of the trees to the end of the grass. Back then, the grass was tall and uninterrupted. But now, the matted grass created a meandering path to the end of the plain.

The view was beautiful. The crisp morning air, the smell of the salt from the ocean; this should have been exactly what she needed to stop thinking about her fight with McVie and get her focus back on the Jericho investigation. She took a deep breath as she jogged, willing herself to appreciate the scene in front of her, driving all the hurt and guilt and shame out of her head.

Wait. Shame?

She saw the evening through McVie's eyes. Before he'd found out Fenway had almost been run over, he'd had to wrap his head around Megan sending him a picture of Fenway and Alvídrez together. Megan sure knew how to push his buttons.

And this was a big button on the McVie Anxiety Machine: Amy had been unfaithful in their marriage—not only with Rachel's former husband, Dylan, but with other men. McVie tried not to let it bother him, but he wasn't his usual kind, easygoing self when that button got pushed.

She knew McVie trusted her. He'd even said he thought the photo had been fake—that was his first reaction, that his daughter was messing with him. The reaction was right: Megan *was* messing with him. But the photo had been real. Seeing it—and, probably, seeing the raw attraction toward Fenway in Alvídrez's eyes—hadn't exactly put McVie in a trusting emotional place.

Fenway slowed to a walk here, and a minute later stood on the edge, at the three-foot drop-off to the beach, a hundred yards of sand between her and the Pacific Ocean.

The painting still hung above her bed, signed by her mother: this might have been one of Joanne Stevenson's favorite spots. The rock outcropping, the windblown cypress trees.

Not just one of her *mother's* favorite spots; this was Fenway's favorite place in the world, too, and she lived less than two miles away, a fifteen-minute run.

She took in a deep breath of the misty, cool morning air, then suppressed a shiver. Not warm enough to be out in a T-shirt and shorts, although she hated how her body temperature had already adjusted from the damp chill of Seattle in the year-plus she'd been in Estancia.

She'd technically been correct: McVie shouldn't have focused on himself last night, but now with distance from the situation, seeing the live version of the painting above her bed, Fenway thought maybe she should give McVie a little more grace.

Fenway stood at the edge of the field, above the beach, and stared at the ocean for a few more minutes. The world was vast, the ocean infinite here, and yet problems were smaller, her goals clearer.

She turned and walked back across the field toward the butterfly grove.

As she entered the grove, footfalls, snapping twigs. Low in pitch: probably a man.

Fenway's pulse sped up, and she realized what an idiot she'd been. McVie's words echoed in her ears: *Someone wants to kill you, Fenway.*

And here she stood, in a grove of trees hidden from civilization, alone, unarmed, in the dim gray light before sunrise, before ninety percent of Estancia was even awake. If she'd been in a horror movie, the theater audience would have screamed at her to stay out of the butterfly grove.

The eucalyptus trees here served little cover, but to Fenway's left, off the path, lay three fallen logs in a tangle of underbrush on the ground. She couldn't see around the mishmash of wood and bushes, but it looked like the ground had a short drop-off of a foot or two. She glanced around: it was the only thing even close to a hiding place.

She darted over to the logs. Yes, the logs sat on a mound, and there *was* enough room for her to hide. The spot was muddy, but Fenway would rather be muddy than dead.

Fenway ducked behind the bushes and brought her knees close up to her body, and heard the low squish of her shoulder settling into the mud. This was one time she wished her five-eleven frame was smaller. She was breathing heavily and tried to slow her pulse, keep her breaths shallow and quiet. Her head spun with dizziness, but after a few seconds, her pulse slowed closer to normal.

The footfalls got closer.

Fenway blinked. Even from this distance, she found something recognizable in the breathing, in the gait.

Then, barely audible: "Dammit, Fenway."

She stuck her head up.

McVie.

Still wearing the T-shirt he'd fallen asleep in, and a pair of sweat shorts that Fenway thought he'd worn to bed as well.

She stood—mud sticking to her shoulder and hip—and hurried to the path. He saw her. His face changed from gritty determination to relief.

"Hi," she murmured.

He swallowed hard. "Hi."

"You were worried."

He pressed his lips together and put his hands on his hips, then kicked the ground with his shoe. "Someone's trying to kill you, and you were gone when I woke up."

"How did you know I was here?"

"Your car was still in its parking space. And I know you sometimes go out here when you need to think."

"Yeah."

He opened his mouth again, but after a moment, closed it. Probably realized that the last thing Fenway wanted to hear was a lecture.

"I was on my way back," Fenway said. A glop of mud slid off her shoulder down her arm. Ick.

McVie nodded, then turned and started back the way he'd come.

She followed several paces behind McVie. His breathing was ragged, more than if he'd been running on the trail. He was worried, maybe even coming down from panic.

This wasn't about him—but it wasn't all about Fenway, either.

"I didn't mean for you to worry," Fenway said.

"I know." More twigs crunching under his feet.

"I wasn't thinking," she said, more quietly. "I wanted to go for my morning run. It didn't even occur to me that coming out here might be dangerous." Even as that was out of her mouth, she knew how little sense that made. After all, she'd been attacked on this trail back in November. Why were the pieces not falling into place when it came to protecting herself? She swallowed hard. "Do you think I should go to work? Maybe I won't be safe there."

"You're probably safest at work. No one will try to kill you at the sheriff's office or in your building." McVie paused. "At least, I don't think so."

Fenway increased her pace, catching up with McVie.

"What did they say when you filed the report?"

Fenway paused. "The report?"

"The report that someone tried to run you over." McVie took a sharp breath in. "You didn't file the report yet?"

"Well—we filed a report for Huke's car being stolen. And we found that someone had entered the evidence room who faked being an IT contractor. We put that in the system."

McVie looked over his shoulder at Fenway. "But you didn't file a report for someone trying to kill you."

"I know, I know. I should have. Time got away from me."

McVie pressed his lips together. He wanted to say so much. A crinkle between his eyebrows. He rubbed his hands together, for warmth, sure, but maybe also to keep his hands from clenching into fists.

She felt like McVie wanted her to apologize, but if she said she was sorry now, she'd sound insincere.

"I've done a lot of work in therapy, Fenway," McVie said, still walking briskly. "We all do things to sabotage ourselves. But maybe you should look into why you're not prioritizing your physical safety." He stole a quick glance back at her. "Or mental safety."

Fenway couldn't figure out where to be angry or sad at that, but she kept quiet all the way back to her apartment. McVie opened the door with his key and walked into the kitchen, where he opened a cupboard and got a water glass. Fenway followed behind him and grabbed several paper towels off the roll, dabbing at the mud on her clothes. No, that wasn't working. She'd have to take them off before she got mud all over the apartment.

She glanced at McVie, downing his water. Oh, there was something else she hadn't mentioned. Had barely thought about.

"My dad knows you moved in with me," she said.

McVie filled up his water glass again. "Good. I'm glad he knows."

Fenway paused. Was that supposed to mean something? She changed the subject. "When do you need to be at work?" she asked. A flash in her head of the photo of Alvídrez and Fenway that Megan had sent to McVie.

He drank the glass of water, then waved his hand dismissively. "Later today. You go ahead and shower. I'll move some more of these boxes into my storage unit before I head into the office."

Fenway went into the shower, clothes still on, and the mud swirled down the drain. She took her clothes off and had to do her entire hair treatment—she'd been in the dirt, after all. It took almost forty-five minutes. When she got out, McVie wasn't in the apartment. The stack of boxes in the corner of the living room had disappeared.

———

Fenway was on edge. She put the burner phone in her purse before she left the apartment, and that reminded her how sketchy this entire investigation was.

She paused about two feet from her car.

Someone was trying to kill her.

Why wasn't that getting through to her?

She'd been targeted previously. About eight months ago, Fenway had been in the garage when a minivan exploded in front of her. Fenway had never seen a car bomb explode before—she thought car bombs were the stuff of spy movies, not of real life.

What did a car bomb look like, anyway? Fenway figured there'd be at least a telltale wire or two hanging down, maybe a flashing light. Something that stuck down from the bottom of the car that didn't look like it should be there—at the very least, a box or package that wasn't covered with road grime.

Nothing. No lights, no wires, no timer—and everything on the bottom of her car was dirty. She hadn't been to the car wash in a few weeks. She took a few steps back and unlocked her car with her key fob. No explosion. She got in the car, held her breath, and started the engine.

Again, no explosion.

She arrived at the office safely, and over a half hour early. She wanted to go to Java Jim's—but she always went to Java Jim's. Maybe someone would be waiting for her there.

She shook her head. First of all, she'd always gone to Java Jim's at least an hour later in the day. Second, it was in the plaza across from the sheriff's office. Probably one of the safest places in the city.

Fenway ordered a latte and a breakfast sandwich, but gave the barista the name *Rachel* instead of the usual *Joanne*. The barista looked askance at Fenway, but said nothing.

As soon as the barista wrote the name on the cup, Fenway had an idea: she'd go visit Rachel again. Fenway had asked her about finances and key fobs, but she hadn't asked about the U-Move-It truck rental. If Rachel had seen unusual activity on her U-Move-It account, or if she'd gotten a strange request for a login on her phone, Fenway might have something to go on.

After wolfing down her sandwich and bolting her latte, she walked across the street to the county jail building, showed her badge to the guard, and walked through the metal detector. Though it wasn't yet eight o'clock, the guard pointed Fenway to one of the interview rooms. She hadn't even waited five minutes before another guard brought Rachel in.

"Long time, no see," Rachel deadpanned. Bags under her eyes. Shoulders drooping. Still a spark of fire in her eyes, but dimmer than usual.

"You okay?"

Rachel tightened her jaw. "I'm stuck in a cell by myself, I don't know what's going on, and I can't do anything to help."

"Maybe you can," Fenway said. "We discovered that someone rented a moving truck in your name. Do you know anyone who had access to your app or your U-Move-It account?"

Rachel looked confused. "I've never rented from U-Move-It before."

Fenway sat back in the chair. Dammit. Someone had stolen Rachel's credentials and created an account without her knowledge. She thought for a moment. "You know, the payment card on the account is Dylan's. Did *he* have a U-Move-It account? Or could someone have used his information instead of yours?"

Rachel crossed her arms. "He rented a truck for his brother once, helped him move. Maybe three or four years ago. This was before Parker got his act together, when Dylan and I were still dating."

"And did Dylan use the U-Move-It app?" If Dylan already had the app, Fenway could look for someone who took over the account, rather than someone who created a new account with Rachel's stolen credentials.

Rachel scrunched up her face. "I don't know. Maybe? I don't remember." She dropped her arms to her sides. "But—you said the payment card was Dylan's? I never saw anything."

"A Bank of the Bay debit card."

Rachel scowled. "I cancelled Dylan's credit card there last week. I didn't think he had any other accounts there."

Ah. Now Fenway realized how Rachel had a U-Move-It account without knowing it. "Piper discovered recent activity on those Bank of the Bay accounts, and your name is on those accounts too. Checking, savings."

Rachel furrowed her brow. "Wait—these were Dylan's bank accounts? Why don't I know anything about them?"

"I wonder," Fenway continued, "if someone was using those bank accounts to launder drug money."

Rachel blinked. "Those payments—they look like they're going to me?"

"That's right."

The tendons in Rachel's neck tightened.

"You said you called Bank of the Bay to cancel one of Dylan's old credit cards, right?"

Rachel nodded. "Oh—yeah. I checked my credit report, and the card was on there. I hadn't heard of it before, but, you know, Dylan was like that. Wanted to have his own stuff that I didn't have visibility into." She pressed her lips together; hidden accounts and credit cards were part of how he'd been able to keep his affair with McVie's ex-wife from Rachel.

Fenway rubbed her chin. "We could be looking at identity theft. Someone gained access to those open accounts at Bank of the Bay."

"If I didn't know about it," Rachel said, "that means my address isn't on the old accounts, right?"

"Piper found that someone changed the address to one of those mailbox places in a strip mall."

Fenway stood and paced around the room. "If drugs were involved, maybe the Venn Cartel figured out how to hack your computer or the Bank of the Bay user information or something." She looked at Rachel. "Did you notice any..."

Rachel's eyes glazed over.

"Rachel?"

"If drugs were involved," Rachel said.

Of course. Fenway should have put the pieces together sooner. "Parker. Since Dylan helped him move, Parker might have had access to the U-Move-It account."

"Right." Rachel frowned. "And I bet Dylan let Parker use his bank account, too."

"Do you know where Parker is now?" Did Rachel still call him her brother-in-law?

"He hasn't exactly kept in touch with me since Dylan died."

Rachel blinked and cleared her throat. "Last I heard, he was living in an apartment on Querido Dunes and 47th."

"Then that's where I'll start."

———

Fenway walked across the street to her building, her head awash in possibilities. Parker was a user, not a dealer, but maybe he'd gotten behind on his payments, and someone at the Venn Cartel realized they could pin something on Rachel. She'd talked to Parker on the phone only two weeks before, when she had questions about Nyllie and he'd put her in touch with Zoso. But if Parker was the common denominator that connected Rachel's financial accounts to the mystery payments, he might have enough information to unstick the case.

She opened the door to the coroner's suite. "Morning, Sarah." Sarah Summerhill sat behind the desk, stiff and silent. Fenway shot her a look, and Sarah's eyes darted over to Fenway's private office.

Ah, crap.

Fenway walked in, and Sheriff Gretchen Donnelly was sitting behind Fenway's desk.

She paused in the doorway, Donnelly glaring at her.

"You're in my chair," Fenway said. Oof, she'd meant that to be playful, but her tone was caustic.

"And you're in my investigation," Donnelly said.

Fenway dropped her laptop bag in the guest chair. "I'm on the Mathis investigation, not the Zellman investigation."

"Bullshit," Donnelly said. "I checked the logs at the jail. You've gone to see Rachel twice in the last sixteen hours. You were there fifteen minutes ago."

Fenway cocked an eyebrow. "I need to stay out of the investigation because she's my friend. I can't offer her emotional support?"

"You were there outside of visiting hours."

Fenway was silent, turning possible responses over in her head.

"And," Donnelly said, "you failed to create a police report for the incident yesterday."

Oh, crap. This was *really* going to bite her if she didn't play this right. "What are you talking about?" Fenway said. "It was Deputy Huke's car that was stolen. I was standing next to him when he made the report."

"But nothing about you almost being run over. Why is that?"

"Part of the same crime, isn't it?" Fenway heard the sweet innocence in her own voice and hoped Donnelly would buy it. "When someone's car gets stolen, and we find out the car was used to commit property damage or whatever, it's part of the same crime."

"Attempted murder of a law enforcement officer *always* needs its own report."

"Oh."

"Surely you knew that, Coroner."

What could Fenway say? Did she fail to make a report because she didn't trust the sheriff's office? Or was she truly in denial that someone tried to kill her? Did she fail to make a report for the same reason she didn't say anything to McVie? "I'll file a report today."

Donnelly stood. "You know I don't have the power or the authority to fire you, but I could start a recall campaign."

Fenway nodded. She also knew she was visible and popular in the county, but that didn't mean it would be a pleasant—or inexpensive—battle to have.

"And," Donnelly said, "if I find out that you're interfering in the Zellman murder case, I'm not above arresting you for obstruction of justice."

Fenway almost retorted with a smart-ass comment, but she didn't need Donnelly up in her business.

Donnelly strode out of Fenway's office, shot Sarah a nasty look, and walked out of the suite.

As soon as the door shut behind Donnelly, Sarah got up and walked briskly to Fenway's door. "Sorry about that."

"Not your fault. The sheriff busts in and wants to wait in my office, you can't stop her."

"She tried to intimidate you."

"Yes."

"I don't like it."

"I don't either," Fenway said. "I'll be glad when this investigation is behind us."

"Has Dez gotten anywhere?" Sarah asked.

"I don't know." Fenway smiled. "I'm not supposed to talk with her, right?"

Sarah arched an eyebrow.

Fenway pointed her chin at Callahan's desk. "Brian's not in yet?"

"No."

"I wanted a copy of the incident report from Estancia Harbor." She scratched her temple. "When did he leave last night?"

Sarah was quiet.

Fenway nodded. "Sorry. Not a cool question. You're not going to tattle on him."

"I hope you understand. The detectives here need to trust me. You do too. If something affects a case, or affects safety, of course I'll say something. But I can't tell you if someone leaves a few minutes early."

"I don't care about a few minutes. I care about dozens of minutes. Oodles of minutes, even."

"Still."

Fenway nodded. "I respect that." She cleared her throat. "I've got to make a phone call. Would you close the door?"

Sarah hesitated, then nodded. "Of course."

After Sarah left, Fenway waited for a few beats, then took the burner phone out of her purse.

How secure was the office? Especially now that Gretchen had been in here—she could have easily planted a bug or other kind of listening device.

Ah—right. Fenway went around to her chair, then opened the

bottom drawer of her desk. There, underneath several notebooks and cables, was an electronic listening device detector. She'd used it before—maybe ten or eleven months previously, on another case when McVie was still sheriff.

Fenway pulled the bug detector out, switching it on with a beep and a flash of green lights.

Fenway carefully went all around her office and found nothing.

Kind of refreshing. She'd suspected Gretchen for so long that she'd thought for sure she'd find a recording device in her office.

She opened the burner phone and called Dez.

"Fenway?"

"Hey. Donnelly told me if she found me messing with the Zellman case, she'd arrest me for obstruction."

"I love how people think threatening you is a good idea," Dez said drily.

"So," Fenway said, mindful that the bug detector might not be foolproof, "I'll focus a hundred percent of my efforts on the Mathis Jericho case."

"You're somewhere you can't talk?"

"I probably can, but I figure better safe than sorry. I'll go take another look at Seth Cahill's Corvette." A pause. "We searched it already, but that's when we thought Cahill's killer also killed Mathis Jericho. Maybe we weren't looking for the right things."

"Seth Cahill's Corvette is in the impound yard," Dez said.

"That's right."

"And that's where Rachel's BMW is, too."

"Yep."

"Give me thirty minutes," Dez said. "I'll make sure no one follows me." A pause. "And you do the same."

CHAPTER FOURTEEN

Fenway drove her Accord down Fifth Street to Santa Magdalena Avenue, and after a half-mile, a high chain-link fence with barbed wire at the top appeared on the right-hand side. She turned into a gated driveway, slowing for the guard station.

"Morning, Coroner," the guard said.

Fenway wished she weren't so terrible with names—she'd been here before. After a brief hesitation, the name came to her.

"Morning, Pete. I'm here for the Corvette from the Cahill case. Well, it's the Jericho case now."

"Garage 3B," Pete said. "You remember the way?"

Fenway paused.

"Down to the third row. Make a left, and you'll see the garages."

"Thanks."

"You know the code?"

"Uh—no."

Pete nodded, then went into the guard station. Fenway narrowed her eyes. What was he doing in there? A moment later, her phone buzzed, and Pete appeared again.

"One-time passcode to get you into the garage, good for the

next fifteen minutes. Fill out the online form next time and I won't have to do that."

"Thanks."

Pete turned back to his guard station, pushed a button, and the orange-and-white gate arm raised. Fenway drove the Accord in over the fresh asphalt, then turned left. A set of garages, the same as she'd seen a few months before, appeared on the left. Fenway turned off the engine of the Accord. The impound yard smelled of engine oil and recently poured asphalt.

The fog of the early morning was burning off, though slowly. Fenway walked toward the garage, stepped up to a roll-up door marked 3B, and uncovered a keypad next to the door. She looked at her phone screen, punched in the one-time passcode, and with a click and the sound of gears turning, the door raised.

The red Corvette sat in the garage, still with the dust and dirt from Miranda Duchy's front yard caking the outside. Fenway crossed her arms and stared at the car.

Fenway tapped her chin. No one but Seth Cahill's murderer knew that the Corvette had been left at Miranda Duchy's cabin. So maybe Jericho's murder was a crime of opportunity.

Fenway frowned. The murder—and the disposal of Jericho's body—might have been opportunistic. But the killer had been at the cabin for a reason, and Fenway suspected the drugs were the reason. Jericho knew the morpheranyl was being stored at the cabin, and his killer had known it too.

So why was Jericho killed? Did he know too much? Was he getting in the way? Did he threaten to go to the police, or did he want too big of a cut of the pie?

Fenway pulled up the fingerprint report on her phone. No fingerprints anywhere—the car had been wiped clean.

A voice behind Fenway. "Howdy, stranger."

Fenway turned and smiled. "Hey, Dez."

"I see you're hard at work on the case you're *supposed* to be assigned to."

"You'll be shocked that I'm actually here for the Jericho murder." Fenway motioned her head to the Corvette. "The first time Celeste and I looked at this car, we thought whoever had driven the Corvette to the cabin had killed Jericho."

"Ah. So you were actually telling the truth on the phone, not misdirecting in case anyone was listening."

"Right." Fenway held her phone up. "None of Mathis Jericho's prints in the car; not on the steering wheel, the door handles, nothing."

"That makes sense," Dez said. "George Pope had already admitted to driving the Corvette to the cabin. He obviously wiped his fingerprints off the inside." She bent down and looked through the driver's side window. "Yeesh, this still stinks."

"A dead body was in there for about twelve hours," Fenway said. "On a summer day."

"You think CSI missed something?"

"Possible, but I doubt it. Maybe I'm not looking at what they found in the right light." Fenway stared at the Corvette for a moment until Dez cleared her throat.

"Sorry," Fenway said. "Did you want me to look at the BMW?"

"Far be it from me to go against Donnelly's orders," Dez dead-panned, "but if you *happen* to watch over my shoulder…"

"Right, sure."

"And I should examine the BMW before anyone sees us. Sheriff Donnelly will blow her top if she hears we were together."

Dez led Fenway two garages over to 3D.

"They've removed all the evidence from this too, right?"

"Right." Dez crossed her arms. "Also wiped clean."

Fenway furrowed her brow. "Why would Rachel wipe her own car clean?"

"If you asked Sheriff Donnelly, she'd probably answer that Rachel wanted it to look like someone had stolen her car." Dez glanced at Fenway. "So the lack of fingerprint evidence doesn't exonerate Rachel."

Fenway walked to the driver's-side door and looked inside. "The seat is definitely close enough that Rachel could drive." Fenway pointed at three buttons on the inside of the door, marked M, 1, and 2. "Memory seats, though. Whoever drove this would simply need to push one of these buttons, and the seat and mirrors would go back to how they were set up for Rachel."

"Hard to prove that."

"Yeah, I know."

"And I went over the ATM camera footage. A dark night like Monday, all we got were reflections off the BMW's side windows. No way to tell who was driving. Or what their seat position was."

Fenway furrowed her brow. "Hey, the Corvette has memory seat settings too, right?"

"Fancy car like that? I hope so."

Fenway walked out of the garage and back to the Corvette. She bent over into the driver's side, almost gagging on the smell, and sure enough, there were memory seat buttons on the Corvette too.

She looked at the seat position. Pretty far back.

Fenway pulled up her phone and looked at Seth Cahill's vital statistics, then Mathis Jericho's, and finally George Pope's.

"What is it?" Dez said.

"Seth, Mathis, and George. Seth was five-six, Mathis was five-eight, George was five-nine."

"So?"

"So the seat is set for someone at least six feet tall. Probably six-two, six-three."

"Like McVie." Dez chuckled.

"Well, yeah, as tall as McVie. Close, anyway." Fenway looked at Dez. "Someone drove the Corvette *after* George Pope. He wouldn't have had the seat this far back. And the memory seat would have been set for Seth Cahill. Maybe Tyra, but she's not six feet tall either."

"You're almost six feet."

Fenway opened the door, and despite the smell, sat in the

driver's seat. Her feet were a little too far from the pedals. "Not a short driver," she said, getting out as fast as she could. "Definitely at least a six footer."

"If not George Pope, who would drive the Corvette? And why?"

Fenway rubbed her forehead. "Maybe someone took it for a joyride?"

Dez cocked her head.

"Yeah, that's not it. Maybe someone had to make a run of Nyllie from the boat to the storage unit."

"Unlikely," Dez said. "We would have seen the Corvette on the tape from the storage place." She thought for a moment. "When Callahan drove by the cabin, he didn't see the Corvette?"

"Don't remind me." Fenway rolled her eyes.

"Point is, the Corvette must have already been in the carport. Maybe the killer wanted to hide the body. Or hide the Corvette. Could have been that George Pope left the Corvette in the driveway, and someone took the car and pulled it into the carport, where it couldn't be seen from the street."

"Someone had the key?"

Fenway shook her head. "I bet George Pope left the Corvette key in the car. Probably didn't care if it got stolen."

"So anyone could have driven it."

"Anyone who knew Cahill moved the Nyllie storage location to Miranda Duchy's cabin."

"Who would that be?" Dez asked.

"Lots of people could have known. The two guys who brought the Nyllie from Mexico—Stephan Butler and Calvin Banning, for sure."

"But Banning has an alibi for the murder, right?"

"He had an alibi for..." Fenway trailed off. "I'll have to check my notes."

"What about Stephan Butler?"

Fenway shook her head. "When I interviewed him before, he denied all knowledge. But late last week he took something to a safe-deposit box, and then a day or two later, someone broke into his boat. He says they didn't take anything—but I think the intruder was looking for whatever's in the safe-deposit box."

"That's hard to prove, too."

Fenway exhaled loudly. "I know. And it doesn't mean Butler's a suspect. But he knows *something* he isn't telling me." She scrolled through her phone. "When we brought Butler in for questioning, did we process him?"

"I don't think so."

"You remember how tall he was?"

"I had to look up at him. But I gotta look up at everybody. What about you? Look up or look down when you were talking to him?"

Fenway shut her eyes and tried to remember. He'd been on the boat when she talked to him last, so she didn't have a good idea of where he was relative to her height. And they were on the sandy beach near Portico Inlet the first time. Not exactly conducive to accurate height assessment, either.

Dez went back to the BMW while Fenway walked around the Corvette. She circled the sports car three times, looking at the dust, the seats. She popped the trunk release in the driver's door panel, leaned into the car, and opened the glove box. But she found nothing. CSI had taken everything that wasn't bolted down into evidence anyway.

The sound of an engine starting.

Fenway closed down the garage door of 3B and walked to the BMW garage. The BMW was running, Dez in the driver's seat. Fenway walked up next to the window.

"Rachel's shorter than I am," Dez said.

"Why did you start the car?"

Dez shrugged. "Wanted to see if something jumped out at me. Radio tuned to the country station, steering wheel in a weird position, maybe the murderer's name spelled out in LCD letters on the dashboard."

"No such luck?"

"Nothing jumps out at me, anyway. No warning lights, no low tire pressure, radio off, a quarter-tank of gas—nothing weird at all." Dez turned off the engine. "Sheriff Donnelly wants this case open and shut, and I'm running out of ideas to show her Rachel's innocent."

Fenway nodded. "I better head back. And we should definitely leave separately."

"I'll call you if I think of anything."

Fenway left the garage and got back in her Accord. As she was about to drive past the guardhouse, she braked and rolled down the window.

"Pete?"

The guard's head appeared.

"We've had a couple of vehicles stolen from law enforcement in the last couple of days. One right out of the sheriff's office parking lot. Anything suspicious happen here in the last few days?"

Pete thought for a moment. "Not that I know of."

The bowling shirt of Hackson Square appeared in her mind's eye. "Anyone come to service the cameras?"

Pete tilted his head. "The sheriff's had the cameras off for a few months now."

"Why?"

He shrugged. "She didn't tell me, but it came a couple weeks after the Wamsutta drug trial, so, you know."

Fenway looked at Pete blankly.

"That little town in northern Wisconsin—the one where they made the fentanyl raid about six months ago?"

Fenway blinked.

"It was all over the news."

"I must have missed the story."

"The cops found packages of fentanyl patches inside the fenders of two SUVs. Arrested everyone in the vehicles—including one of the drug cartel lieutenants."

"Sounds like a win."

"It would have been, but two deputies mishandled the vehicles in the Wamsutta impound yard. The defense got the recordings from the cameras in the impound yard, and the judge threw the whole case out. Two days later, one of the drivers who'd been arrested got high and slammed into a school bus." Pete set his jaw. "Sheriff called and said we'd be taking the impound yard cameras offline."

Fenway's mouth fell open. "That school bus accident was because deputies had screwed up? So instead of making sure impounded vehicles don't get mishandled, we're turning the cameras off?"

Pete shrugged again. "I don't make the rules, Coroner." He gave her a half-hearted salute. "You have a good day."

After a few blocks, Fenway pulled to the curb, put the car in Park, and closed her eyes. Though the Jericho murder had only occurred two weeks before, Fenway felt like a year had passed and she'd been a different person back then.

She needed to reorganize her thoughts; many of the assumptions she'd made about the Mathis Jericho murder simply weren't true.

Fenway had assumed that George Pope had killed Mathis, first of all. That was wrong. He'd driven the Corvette, but didn't have Mathis with him.

Fenway rubbed her forehead. Whoever had driven Mathis to Miranda Duchy's cabin had probably killed him, moved the Corvette from the driveway into the carport, and arranged Mathis's body.

Who was the last person to see Mathis Jericho?

Fenway had notes on the case.

A buzz in her purse. A moment of panic: did someone tell Donnelly that Fenway and Dez had met at the impound lot?

But no, it was another reminder text from Salt & Flame about taking their post-visit survey.

She deleted the text and drove back to the town center, trying to focus again. What had happened last Wednesday, two weeks ago exactly, the day of Mathis Jericho's death?

She walked into the building lost in thought, trying to piece together the events of Wednesday from two weeks ago. When she entered the coroner's suite, Sarah and Callahan were both at their desks. Callahan looked bored; Fenway needed to give him some direction beyond the training videos.

"Brian?"

Callahan looked up.

"Did you get the incident report from the security office at Estancia Harbor?"

"Left messages. Haven't heard back yet."

"Follow up on it. Go over there if you have to."

Fenway walked into her office and sat at her desk, bringing up the paperwork from the Seth Cahill case. Because she'd arrested George Pope for both murders, her notes from the day of Jericho's death would be in this set of documents.

Sure enough, she found her notes from Wednesday morning.

As she read her notes, the events of that morning came back to her. Dez had awakened her at three A.M. and dragged her to Puerto Avila beach, where they waited in the chilly night wind for the *Ariel*, which never came. Then Fenway realized the ship had probably come aground further north—and she'd been right. They got to Portico Inlet in time to talk with Stephan Butler, but not in time to catch the exchange of morpheranyl.

But she and Dez had suspected the drugs went back to Cahill Warehouse Storage, so that's where they went. Confirming their suspicions, Fenway had found traces of Nyllie in Mathis Jericho's trunk.

Fenway scrolled down: what had happened to Mathis Jericho's car? After finding the drugs, Mathis had agreed to come to the station for an interview. But Dez drove him to the station; he didn't take his own car. Someone had to drive him back to the storage facility, right?

She looked at the M.E.'s report. Time of death was somewhere between ten A.M. and three P.M. A long window, for sure, but with the body left in a car during a summer day, Michi's time of death estimate couldn't be as narrow as it usually was.

Fenway clicked back on the window with her notes. Had Jericho stayed? Had he walked out, maybe taken a FlashRide or the bus back to his workplace?

Ah—there it was. *Deputy Brian Callahan drove suspect Jericho back to his place of business.*

Maybe Callahan saw something when he dropped Jericho off.

Fenway rose and opened the door to her office. "Hey, Brian, can you come in here a minute?"

Callahan stood with a shocked look on his face.

"It's nothing bad," Fenway said quickly. Only his third day in his new position, and already he was acting anxious around her. First impressions were big, she reminded herself.

Fenway sat back at her desk as Callahan walked in and warily took a seat.

"Two weeks ago, Wednesday," she said.

Callahan pursed his lips. "What about it?"

"That's the day Mathis Jericho died."

Callahan flinched. Probably reminded him of driving by Miranda Duchy's cabin and not doing his due diligence to find the Corvette.

Fenway didn't want Callahan on the defensive, so she leaned forward. "You drove Jericho back to the storage facility that morning. Did you see anything unusual when you dropped him off?"

Callahan squinted. "Like what?"

"Someone waiting for him, maybe? Any signs of the Venn Cartel, perhaps. Or did you get followed from the sheriff's office?"

Callahan shifted in his chair uncomfortably. "I don't know. I wasn't exactly looking for someone tailing me."

"You didn't notice anything out of the ordinary?"

Callahan stared up at the ceiling for a moment. "Let me think."

Fenway waited.

"You know," Callahan began slowly, "I seem to remember a white sedan. Midsize, I think. I saw it a few cars behind me when we got on the freeway. And a car pulled up to the curb when I dropped Jericho off. I don't know if it was the same car that was following me." He paused. "I don't even know if the car was really following me."

"Would you recognize the car if you saw it?"

Callahan shook his head. "Honestly, I thought it was a different vehicle. I don't have anything to base that on. Just that there are probably a hundred thousand white domestic sedans in California."

"You didn't get a good look at the driver? Or maybe a license plate?"

Callahan shook his head, then glanced at his watch.

"Okay, I didn't expect anything. But never hurts to ask." Fenway put her elbows on her desk and steepled her fingers. "How was Jericho?"

"What do you mean?"

"Was he nervous about going back to the storage facility? Or maybe he was angry that we'd wasted his time?"

"He was quiet, mostly. I don't think he liked you interrogating him, but, uh, he wasn't acting like someone was about to kill him."

Fenway nodded.

"Aren't you looking at the boat owner? The *Ariel* guy?"

"He's one suspect."

"And do you have other suspects?"

"Maybe the guy who was with Butler all the time—Calvin Banning. He was sleeping in one of the storage units every time they made a drug run. Wanted to make sure no one made off with any of the morpheranyl. But he may not be in the county anymore—Butler said he left for the East Coast."

"No one else?"

Fenway paused; if she told Callahan she suspected Sheriff Donnelly, he'd probably tell her immediately. "Do you know any of the players in the Venn Cartel? It's possible one of them thought Jericho was skimming off the top or getting in the way of someone who should get a better cut of the drug sales."

Callahan frowned. "I wasn't too close with the guys in Vice. But I bet Captain Alvídrez knows most of the players. At least in Dominguez County."

Fenway sighed. "This is dangerously close to becoming a cold case if I can't get any more evidence."

"What kind of evidence are you looking for?"

"Beggars can't be choosers," Fenway said. "I'll take anything right now." She looked up at Callahan. "After you get the security incident report from the harbor, maybe find an eyewitness who saw Jericho with someone between the time you dropped him off and when he died. He had to get to the cabin somehow, but either he didn't take his car, or..."

Callahan narrowed his eyes.

Could it be that obvious? And had they overlooked Mathis's car with everything that had happened?

"You're thinking something, Coroner," Callahan said.

"Do you know what happened to Jericho's car?"

"What, that little blue econobox? No, I don't."

"We didn't take it for evidence?" Fenway hadn't been looking for Mathis Jericho's small blue sedan at the impound yard, but she didn't remember seeing anything there either.

"Not that I remember."

"What were you in charge of on that case?"

"On the Cahill murder? I was only in charge of driving Jericho's ass back to the storage unit." He paused. "And I was in charge of driving by Duchy's cabin, which I screwed up."

"Okay, Brian, stop beating yourself up over it. I'm not interested in you feeling guilty about it. We all screw up. Learn from it so you don't do it next time and move on."

Callahan nodded, then surreptitiously glanced at his watch again.

"You in a rush to get back to those training videos?"

He looked up, cheeks reddening. "Uh—I'm meeting a friend for lunch."

Fenway exhaled slowly. Were these the signs of a man meeting a new girlfriend? And while his ex was suffering in a jail cell, too. But Fenway didn't have the strength to call Callahan out on it. "Go enjoy your lunch. And get that incident report from the harbor."

CHAPTER FIFTEEN

ALONE IN HER OFFICE AFTER CALLAHAN LEFT, FENWAY PUT HER head in her hands. She wasn't getting anywhere with the Jericho murder.

She lifted her head and read over the suspect list from her computer screen. Yes, these were all suspects from Seth Cahill's murder, but any of them might have had a reason to want Jericho dead, too.

Tyra Cahill, Seth's widow and Jericho's boss. Isabella Chan, Jericho's co-worker. Miranda Duchy, Seth's mistress—or rather affair partner; a less bodice-ripping term, certainly. Stephan Butler and Calvin Banning, the two people who smuggled morpheranyl from Mexico.

And Jericho's body being found in Seth's Corvette—that needed an explanation, too.

Fenway perused her notes, but nothing jumped out at her. Of her suspect list, Butler and Banning were the only two who had dealings with the drug side of Jericho's life.

She blinked at the computer screen. Banning hadn't been with

Butler for a while, although the two of them were, or at least had been, morpheranyl partners in crime.

If Butler wanted to go straight-and-narrow and Banning wanted to stay in the game, Butler's assertion that Banning had left the state might have merit. A professional breakup.

Fenway stood, grabbed her purse, and walked out of her office to Sarah's desk. "Hey, Sarah, we had a guy in here for an interview two weeks ago. Calvin Banning."

"Thick Scottish accent, right?"

"Geordie," Fenway said. "North of England, not quite at the Scottish border. I haven't seen him around Estancia, but his partner in crime says he's on the East Coast. Can you work your magic and see where he is?"

Sarah gave Fenway a crooked smile. "Don't we have detectives for that?"

Fenway raised her head theatrically and looked around the empty office. "Detectives? What detectives?"

Sarah rolled her eyes. "I can see what's in the database. His info is in the Cahill case file?"

"Yep."

"I don't suppose you'll tell me where you're going either."

Fenway looked over her shoulder at the closed door to the coroner's suite. "Brian's meeting a friend for lunch," she mused.

Sarah crossed her arms. "He dumped Rachel for someone else?"

"I don't know anything about Brian's love life," said Fenway.

"Seems awfully quick, though, don't you think?"

A swarm of possible explanations fluttered through Fenway's head, but she wanted to focus on the task in front of her, so she shrugged. "I'm getting Mathis Jericho's car key from evidence, then I'm heading over to Cahill Warehouse Storage. I think Jericho's car is still there. And I've got to have more evidence to go on that what I've got now."

Fenway walked out the door of the office building, toward the sheriff's office. Then the gears in her head started turning.

She felt more strongly that Andrew Zellman's death might be connected to the drugs that Mathis Jericho helped traffic. If someone had pinned the murder on Rachel, that could mean Rachel knew something about the drugs: their location in the evidence room, the identity of another person who'd hired the *Ariel*, or footage that showed... something.

After all, Rachel was the one who'd announced that the Venn Cartel was out of the county.

She crossed the street, but instead of going to the sheriff's office, she turned right at the plaza and went toward the county jail.

If Rachel knew something, was she even aware that she knew it? Rachel had mentioned Parker, and maybe that had jogged her memory. Maybe she'd remembered something else in the last couple of hours.

Fenway opened the door and put her purse in the plastic bin to go through the metal detector. The guard looked thoroughly bored.

"Morning."

"Can I get into an interview room with Rachel Richards?"

"Twice in one day, huh?"

"That's right." Fenway stepped through the metal detector, and Quincy handed her purse back. "Room 2, on the right side."

She went into the second room on the right; this was a smaller room than the room she was usually in, and the table was smaller. There were only two chairs. She sat in one of them.

How could she ask Rachel what she knew? Especially if Rachel didn't know what it was?

Maybe Fenway could walk Rachel through the last few days, see if she remembered anything new. Rachel's job was to talk to the media, to the sheriff, to all kinds of law enforcement personnel. Surely one or two of those interactions were unusual. Or maybe Rachel would walk through her day, and something would jog her memory.

She ran through questions to get Rachel's mind going in the right direction. What had her interviewing class at Seattle University said? That was only a year and a half ago, but she remembered almost nothing. Her notes from that class were in a box at home in a closet. Probably next to one of McVie's boxes.

Fenway sighed. She'd ask what she could..

She looked at the clock on her phone. Fifteen minutes had passed since the guard directed her to this room.

The door opened behind Fenway. The guard stood in the doorway, the corners of his mouth turned down.

"Sorry, Coroner," he said. "Rachel Richards was moved about an hour ago."

"She was... she was moved? Where? Who moved her?"

"I'm trying to find out, but I don't have that information."

Fenway bristled. "She hasn't even been arraigned yet. She wasn't moved to the women's prison, was she?"

"Like I said, I don't know," the guard grumbled. "They didn't tell me, and the protocol is to let everyone know."

"Who requested the transfer?"

The guard shrugged. "An order like this usually comes from high up, but I don't have any more info."

Fenway stood. Had Donnelly given the order to move Rachel?

She grabbed her purse, walked out of the interview room, past the guard station, and out the front. Gretchen obviously didn't want Fenway talking to Rachel. Maybe she thought they'd align their stories before Rachel's arraignment.

Fenway took a deep breath and counted to ten. She wanted to storm into Donnelly's office and demand what was going on.

But if Donnelly was involved in the drug trafficking or the deaths of Jericho or Zellman, Fenway should keep her cards close to her chest. If Donnelly knew Fenway suspected something, she'd be more likely to cover her tracks.

And maybe Piper could uncover them.

She took out her phone and began pacing around the plaza. She tapped her contacts list.

"Fenway—wow, two days in a row!"

"Hi, Dad," Fenway said. "Listen, you still have contacts in the sheriff's department, yeah?"

Ferris exhaled. "Now that Craig isn't sheriff, not nearly as many as I used to. Besides, you have far more contacts now."

"Maybe you can talk to a few people who *won't* talk to me."

"Maybe one or two."

"Can you see if any of them know what happened to Rachel?"

He paused. "Rachel—Rob Stotsky's daughter?"

"That's right. She was arrested yesterday, and now she isn't in the county jail. No one seems to know what happened to her."

"I'll do what I can."

"Thanks." Fenway hesitated, then steeled herself. "And—Dad, I need a favor."

"Anything."

"I have to hire McVie Investigations to do a little, um, research."

"Oh, that's good."

"Well..." Fenway looked around the plaza. No one was within eavesdropping distance, but she lowered her voice anyway. "It's not the kind of research I can charge to the county."

"Oh," Ferris said. "Something from within the county office."

"Um, I'm not sure how much I can say, but yes, something like that." Fenway braced for the criticism: that maybe she was imagining things, that she could pull herself up by her bootstraps.

Instead, Ferris said, "You need me to cover it?"

Fenway blinked and nearly stumbled in her pace around the plaza. "I hate to ask—"

"After what Piper Patten did for me? I can never pay her *or* McVie back. And if it means getting Rachel out of danger—or whatever is happening—no price is too high. Have them send me the bill."

A wave of relief washed over Fenway.

"I'd love to catch up, but it sounds like you have a lot on your plate."

"I do. Thanks, Dad."

After saying their goodbyes, Fenway called Piper, asking her to look into where Rachel might have been moved. And asking for a more expensive deep dive into Donnelly's background.

"Send the bill to my dad," Fenway told Piper.

"I told you, your money's no good here—"

"My dad's money better be," Fenway said. "McVie needs to get the company back in the black, and my father is more than willing to help."

Piper hesitated. "Yes, okay. He'll get the bill."

Fenway walked toward the sheriff's office, taking more deep breaths to calm herself down.

———

Fenway visited Deputy Donald Huke in the evidence room. His eyes widened when he saw her.

"I'm so sorry, Coroner."

"For what?" Did Huke know something about where Rachel had gone?

"My car almost ran you over."

Ah. Nothing about Rachel, then. "We already talked about this, Deputy. You're not at fault."

He ran a hand through his hair. "I feel responsible."

"You weren't behind the wheel."

"I know, but if I'd been more careful—"

"How could you being more careful have changed anything? You parked in the sheriff's office lot. You'd think that would be the safest place in the city. Plus, it's not like Estancia is a hotbed of stolen car action."

"I know, but I could have had a steering wheel lock on the car."

"I blame the person who stole your vehicle, not you." She paused. "Is your car okay?"

Huke shrugged. "I haven't seen it since it was towed to impound for fingerprints." His cheeks grew red. "I need to open an insurance claim. My old car was starting to nickel-and-dime me, so I thought getting a new car would make my life easier."

Fenway shook her head. "If you want my take on it, I think they'd have stolen your car no matter what you drove. Something important happened in the evidence room, and whoever's targeting us wants that evidence gone, and everyone who knows about it out of the way."

The color drained from Huke's face. "What happened in the evidence room?"

Fenway shook her head. "I wish I knew. I'd like to get us all under a protective order, but the best protection would be to solve the Mathis Jericho case."

Huke crossed his arms. "You think they want to steal evidence in the Mathis Jericho case?"

"I've got a gut feeling, that's all." Fenway scratched the back of her neck. "And there's something we know—or they think we know, anyway. The Hackson Square impostor might have taken the evidence when he was here. But they're still after us."

Huke glanced past Fenway, up and down the corridor, then leaned forward and lowered his voice. "I can pull all the evidence from the Jericho case, put it somewhere else."

Fenway frowned. "Aren't there chain of custody requirements?"

"We have procedures for evidence when we think the evidence room might be compromised. If there's a case against a deputy, for example."

"I see." Fenway chewed her bottom lip. "Who do you have to inform?"

Huke paused. "I haven't memorized the procedure, but I think I have options. You remember when Jennifer Kim was arrested?"

How could she forget being locked in the courtroom with Kim —six of the most harrowing hours of Fenway's life? "Uh, yeah. I remember that."

"We had to pull the evidence from that case and put it somewhere else."

"Where?"

"I don't know. They didn't tell me. I know they wouldn't tell ADA Pondicherry, either." Huke tilted his head. "I got to meet the U.S. Attorney for Southern California."

"Yeah, if we can move the evidence, let's do it," Fenway said. "And be careful. Maybe you and Melissa should stay with friends for a few days."

"Unless the protective order comes through."

"Right."

Huke nodded. "Well, enough about me. You came here for something?"

"Speaking of the Mathis Jericho case," Fenway said, "I want to see Jericho's effects when his body was found."

"Sure thing. Come on back."

Huke buzzed Fenway behind the counter.

"Maybe we should have bulletproof glass," Huke mumbled.

"Bulletproof glass won't protect us from getting run over in the street," Fenway said.

Huke led Fenway over to a metal shelf, then bent down and pulled out a brown box about the size of a cardboard file. He picked it up, then walked to a table in the back of the evidence room.

Fenway followed him, then leaned over the box as Huke removed the cover. Not much: wallet, two keychains—

"Where's his phone?"

"CSI still has it."

"Did they check it out?"

Huke shook his head. "As far as I know, we never got it. I figured CSI was having trouble breaking the encryption on Jericho's phone or something."

"Have you talked to Melissa?"

Huke pursed his lips. "She and I don't talk shop at home. One of our relationship rules."

Fenway nodded. Maybe that would be a good rule for her and McVie, too. "Can I sign out the keys?"

"Which set?"

Fenway squinted: one set was clearly work keys. Cahill Warehouse Storage would want them back. The other keyring only held four keys. Three of them looked like house keys; the other was a key fob for, Fenway hoped, Mathis's sedan. She pointed at the smaller key set.

Back at the evidence desk, she filled out the form to sign out evidence.

"How strictly does this process get enforced?"

"When I'm here, every time." He paused. "Unless I get tricked, like the guy pretending to be from Hackson Square."

Fenway nodded. She shuddered to think how someone had waltzed into the evidence room with a fake work order and gotten so close to hundreds of evidence boxes. Defense lawyers would have a field day if they knew.

Huke took the completed form from Fenway. "Maybe the Hackson Square guy took something." He handed Fenway the keys.

"If he'd been casing you, he'd know you were a stickler for the rules."

"Everyone has a weakness," muttered Huke. "I don't *think* the guy took anything, but..." He sighed. "I better do a full inventory."

"Sorry, Deputy."

———

Twenty minutes later, Fenway parked in one of the two open parking spaces in front of the gates at Cahill Warehouse Storage. The bushes in the planters in between the building and the sidewalk looked in need of a trim, and a few stray weeds stood an inch or two tall in a thin strip between the planter and the driveway.

Either Tyra Cahill hadn't replaced Mathis Jericho yet, or the replacement didn't do a good job.

On the other side of the gate, four parking spaces were marked *Employees Only*—and Mathis Jericho's small blue sedan, now coated with a thin layer of dust, sat in the second space from the left.

Fenway got out of her Accord and stared at Jericho's blue sedan for a few minutes. Odd that Tyra Cahill hadn't asked the county to tow it off the property. Odd that the forensic team hadn't been proactive and brought it to the impound yard to be scoured for evidence.

Perhaps if she'd realized earlier that George Pope *hadn't* killed Mathis Jericho, she'd have requested the car be processed already. As it was, though, no one thought Jericho's car was relevant to his murder. His body had been found miles away, in his boss's Corvette, and about twenty-four hours later, Fenway had arrested the suspect. Oh—and there'd been the tropical storm to deal with, too; Jericho's car wouldn't have been towed with the storm raging.

Okay, so the confluence of events two weeks before convinced Fenway that the county wasn't incompetent. She went to her trunk and retrieved her fingerprint kit. Maybe taking evidence from Jericho's car was something Dr. Yasuda's team should manage, but since the little sedan had slipped through the cracks so far, Fenway figured she'd at least take fingerprints herself. Two weeks of the car sitting in this parking lot—through the tropical storm, no less— would be enough to cast shade on the chain of custody, anyway. But whatever clues she could find would be better than nothing.

The gate was locked, and she didn't have a code, so she walked into the office. A young Asian woman of medium height was walking out the door at the rear of the office into the parking lot. Fenway racked her brain—ah, right; Isabella Chan. She'd pointed Fenway to the location onsite where Seth Cahill had been killed.

In the office, Tyra Cahill stood behind the counter. She had her curly brown hair tied back in a ponytail, and her light brown skin had a slightly ashen quality to it. She wore a Howard University T-shirt and faded blue jeans with sandals. Not put together as she'd been when Fenway had first met her.

Tyra looked over at Fenway, and Fenway had to try not to flinch. Tyra's face was pallid, her eyes vacant, puffy, and red. The lines around her eyes and mouth were pronounced. She wore no makeup, and she slumped her shoulders. A flicker of recognition showed briefly in her eyes.

When Tyra had been told about Seth's death, she seemed to take it in stride. He'd been unfaithful, his affair partner had been the prime suspect, and Tyra seemed much better off without him. Besides, their divorce had been finalized not long before. But if Fenway was interpreting Tyra's behavior correctly, the grief was finally hitting her, and she may not have known how to deal with it effectively. Yes, Tyra might be better off without Seth, but they'd been together for over a decade, and the divorce didn't negate all the positive emotions.

Huh. If this coroner thing didn't work out, maybe Fenway could be a therapist. No, that would take more schooling. She snapped back to the present.

"Hi, Tyra," Fenway said. Oh—she'd called Tyra *Mrs. Cahill* before, but the waves of grief emanating from the other woman made her feel friendlier, more familiar. Fenway forced a smile onto her face, added the appropriate amount of head tilt for sympathy. "I'm sorry to bother you."

"Oh—you're Coroner Stevenson. Yes, what can I do for you?"

Fenway pointed at the far door that led to the parking lot behind the gate.

"You need to talk to Isabella?"

"No, no—I mean, maybe later, but I'm here to examine Mathis Jericho's car."

Tyra clenched her jaw. "You know, that car has been here gathering dust for a couple of weeks. I've called the county, but no one seemed to know what to do. Are you planning to take it?"

"I'll figure it out after I analyze the car," Fenway said. "Mathis didn't have any next of kin?"

"He listed his mother on his emergency contract form, but it's a North Carolina phone number and it was disconnected."

Fenway could feel the tangled red tape this would cause already. "I'll let you know when we'll get it off your property." She pointed again to the rear door. "In the meantime, can I examine his vehicle?"

Tyra shrugged. "If it'll get the car out of the lot faster, absolutely."

"Thanks," Fenway walked past the counter and through the rear door, into the parking spaces on the inside of the iron gate, and felt a bit of relief. If Tyra had wanted to, she could have made Fenway come back with a warrant.

The key fob opened the door, and Fenway snapped on a pair of blue nitrile gloves. She expected a mess of fingerprints inside. When she and Dez had the warrant two weeks ago to search his navy blue sedan, Jericho's trunk was a mess of fast-food packaging and dirty towels. He probably hasn't cleaned his car in years, and that was a good thing: if any evidence of Jericho's drug running had been in the car, chances are it was still there. So before she started coating the interior with fingerprint dust, she wanted to go through the glove compartment and trunk.

Two weeks ago, there had been two small patches of white powder on the trunk liner; probably spilled morpheranyl, which had erased all doubt in Fenway's mind that Jericho had been the one transporting the Nyllie from Stephan Butler's boat at Portico Inlet to Cahill Warehouse Storage. And Butler's partner in crime, Calvin Banning, had traveled with Jericho to make sure all the Nyllie got where it was supposed to go.

She hadn't tested the residue on the trunk mat for Nyllie, using its presence for leverage to convince Jericho to give up information at the sheriff's office. Fenway wasn't sure what she'd gain from testing the drug residue in the trunk, but with little else to go on, she didn't want to leave any stone unturned.

Hmm. So much for her preconceived notions of Jericho's sloppiness. The inside of the car was clean and tidy. Fenway thought for a moment. Jericho had been coerced to come for the interview because of the drug residue in the trunk, so maybe he'd done the smart thing and cleaned his car before Fenway could come back and find anything else in the car.

She reached down to the left of the driver's seat and popped the trunk.

Fenway walked around the back of the car, bracing herself for the stink of two-week-old fast food and sweaty gym clothes.

The trunk was completely empty.

CHAPTER SIXTEEN

Fenway couldn't believe it: the trunk was not only empty, but spotlessly clean. No white powder residue, no fast-food bags, no dirty towels. She looked in the nooks and crannies next to the wheel wells; those were empty as well. No first aid kit, no tire pressure gauges, no jumper cables. Disappointing. Someone had cleaned everything from the trunk—specifically to make sure no evidence remained.

Fenway closed the trunk, her glove leaving three marks in the grime. The outside of the car was dusty enough that Fenway was positive the vehicle hadn't moved in at least a week. But if Fenway had been Mathis, she would have cleaned the car as the first order of business after coming back from the sheriff's office. She opened the glove box: nothing but the car's registration, user manual, and insurance papers. The center console was, like the trunk, empty.

Fenway stood and paced around the car. Yes, Mathis would have been smart to clean his car after the interview. But he'd died the same day—in fact, two or three hours at most after returning to the storage place. Would Jericho have had time to clean the car?

If he'd taken it to a detailer, maybe. Usually getting one's car detailed required appointments, and Fenway didn't think Jericho was the kind of person who would spend one or two hundred dollars on getting his car detailed.

She opened the driver's door again and set the fingerprint kit on the ground. She took out the fingerprint dust and brushed it onto the steering wheel and the inside of the door's armrest where Mathis would have pulled the door shut after getting in.

Fenway blinked. Nothing. The fingerprint dust didn't stick to anything.

Even if Jericho had taken the car to a detailer and they completely cleaned the inside, he still would have left fingerprints driving it back to Cahill Warehouse Storage.

A few possible scenarios flitted through her head: perhaps a mobile detailer came out to clean Jericho's car, and Jericho didn't have a chance to drive the sedan again. Even though Jericho probably wouldn't spend that kind of money on detailing a car, he might have a friend who worked for a car detailing company; maybe he traded some Nyllie he'd skimmed off the top for a detail.

But still—two to three hours was a tight turnaround. Had a mobile unit come by? And if so, when? She wished that she'd had more of an exact time that Callahan had dropped off Mathis Jericho.

Ah, but wait: Cahill Warehouse Storage had cameras, right? Seth Cahill had turned them off when he received shipments of the morpheranyl, but the cameras should have been on the morning of Jericho's death. Fenway cleaned up the fingerprint dust, closed her plastic case, and locked up the car. She went back inside the office.

Tyra Cahill and Isabella Chan were both in the office; Isabella had several padlocks and keys in front of her and looked to be organizing something.

Tyra looked up from the computer. "All done?"

"With Mathis's car, yes. At least for now. But I'd like to look at your security footage from two weeks ago."

Tyra frowned. "Didn't you catch the guy who killed him?"

Isabella shifted her weight, then raised her head and glared at the two of them.

"Isabella, would you make sure the utility shed is locked? I think I left it open the last time I was out there."

Isabella gave them a curt nod and left through the rear door.

After the door closed behind her, Tyra turned back to Fenway. "Well?"

"Well, what?"

"I thought the man who killed Mathis is in jail."

Fenway shook her head. "He killed… he killed your ex-husband. But he didn't kill Mathis."

Tyra blanched. "Why was he murdered, then?"

"The investigation is ongoing," Fenway said. "And that's part of the reason I'd like to look at your security footage."

Tyra shrugged. "Be my guest. Give me a minute and I'll set you up at the computer in the back room." She cocked her head. "Was that the day of the big storm?"

"The day before—the storm hit Thursday evening." Fenway looked at the rear door and bobbed her head. "What was that about?"

"Isabella?" Tyra sighed. "I don't think she and Mathis were involved, but his death hit her hard. A lot harder than Seth's death hit her, anyway."

"She and Mathis were the only employees whose last name wasn't Cahill. Plus, they were close in age, right? Maybe she feels alone." Fenway thrust her chin at the window beyond which Mathis's car was visible. "Can't be easy walking past that every day." Who would Fenway even talk to about getting Mathis's car towed somewhere—maybe to CSI in San Miguelito?

"Yeah, well, unfortunately, no matter how alone she feels, Seth left me a business in the red. I can't afford to hire anyone to replace either Seth *or* Mathis. And it's not like new customers are lining up to rent storage from murder central." She glanced up at Fenway. "That's why getting Mathis's car out of here is so… uh, necessary."

She typed for another moment, then clicked the mouse with a flourish. "Okay, come with me."

She led Fenway down the hallway to the back office—the same PC that Fenway had viewed footage on two weeks before. Tyra sat down, setting the security footage program up, then rose from the task chair. "You got everything you need?"

"I think so."

"Microwave popcorn's in the vending machine if things get too boring." Tyra smiled and closed the door. Now that Tyra didn't think she was a suspect—as she'd been in Seth Cahill's murder—she was more amiable than she'd been before.

Fenway started the recording from the Wednesday morning two weeks before. She watched it at 5x speed—slow enough so she could see people coming and going.

She watched as Dez's Impala pulled into the parking lot— Fenway had been the passenger—and drove past Mathis's car. They drove around the corner. Ah, that's right; Mathis had been weeding along the main path that morning. A few minutes later, Dez's Impala appeared in the front lot, and a moment after that, Mathis appeared on foot, Fenway following a few paces behind. Fenway and Dez looked through his trunk, Fenway talked to Mathis, and after a few minutes, he followed them to the Impala and they all departed.

Her phone rang. She pulled it out of her purse—oh, not her regular phone. Her burner. She dug it out and answered the call.

"Dez?"

"Donnelly thinks we've got enough evidence against Rachel to officially charge her," Dez said. "Arraignment's tomorrow morning."

Fenway grunted. "Do you know where they've taken her?"

"What?"

"I went to see Rachel first thing this morning, and we talked about Dylan's old bank accounts." Oh, that's right—she still needed to talk to Parker. "But I went back a couple hours later, and the guards told me they'd moved her but wouldn't say where."

Dez was silent.

"So you don't know where they took her?"

"I don't," Dez said. "Somebody's keeping me in the dark."

"They already had her in her own cell. Why would they move her?"

"Maybe they don't want you talking to her." Dez harrumphed. "You know Donnelly's theory of the Zellman murder is that he found out Rachel was running drugs for the Venn Cartel after Seth Cahill died, then she rented a truck and drove the drugs to L.A. Maybe she doesn't want you trying to find exculpatory evidence."

"So glad our county sheriff cares so much about the truth." Fenway exhaled through her teeth. "Gretchen's story would explain *some* things. Not why Rachel had two bags of Nyllie in her trunk—"

"Skimming off the top."

"And isn't one of our theories that skimming off the top got Mathis Jericho killed? So why would Rachel do that?"

"Same reason everyone steals stuff. Money. Greed."

"I don't buy that."

"But you're only saying you don't buy it because you know Rachel. Take the average greedy bastard, you'd have come up with this theory yourself."

Fenway said nothing.

"Anyway, since Donnelly thinks Rachel was stealing drugs from the Venn Cartel, I think Donnelly will *also* suggest Rachel killed Mathis Jericho too."

Fenway put a hand over her eyes. "You've got to be kidding me. Wasn't she working two Wednesdays ago? In the morning? A dozen people must have seen her in the office."

"You want my take on it? I think Donnelly will say Rachel hired someone, or maybe had someone in the Venn Cartel do the actual deed."

"She have anything resembling evidence?"

"If she does, she hasn't told me." Dez cleared her throat. "But I'm calling you to let you know she could ask you to recuse yourself from the Jericho case at any minute. Especially if she concludes the Zellman murder is connected."

"So I have to close this fast," Fenway said. Honestly, she was shocked that Donnelly hadn't asked her to stop investigating the Jericho murder, especially since she'd acted like she was covering something up.

Maybe Donnelly thought Fenway would never find whatever she'd hidden—and that taking Fenway off the case would look suspicious. Better, perhaps, to have Fenway investigate where Donnelly could keep an eye on everything.

"Well, you're good at closing cases fast." Dez chuckled.

"Maybe you can help me out. I'm at Cahill Warehouse Storage, reviewing the video of you and me taking Mathis to the interrogation room. Sometime between then and noon—or maybe one o'clock at the latest, someone drove Mathis to Miranda Duchy's cabin, we assume under the guise of delivering or picking up bags of morpheranyl from her garage. Then they murdered him and dumped his body in Seth Cahill's Corvette."

"Ah, so you want to see where Mathis went after we dropped him off?"

"Here's the weird thing, Dez: someone cleaned Mathis's car after we interviewed him. Not a single fingerprint inside. And you know how we found some Nyllie residue in the trunk? Now the trunk liner is so clean you could eat off it."

"With your weird palate, you probably *would* eat off it."

Fenway ignored Dez's comment. "The car was dusty and dirty, so I know it's been sitting outside for at least a week, probably more. And if I'd been Mathis, the first thing I would have done is clean the car so you and I wouldn't have any reason to arrest him."

"So he did that?"

"Honestly, I kind of doubt it. He didn't have enough time to get it detailed and bring it back to the lot before he was killed."

"So someone else cleaned his car?"

"Unlike Donnelly, I don't jump to conclusions before I have evidence."

Dez barked a laugh. "Okay, Miss It's-Only-a-Theory."

Fenway felt the heat rise to her cheeks. "Okay, fine, maybe I get ahead of myself sometimes. But Mathis wasn't working by himself on transporting and storing the Nyllie. Not when Seth Cahill was alive, and not afterward. Calvin Banning drove with him from Portico Inlet to the storage facility at three in the morning, and Stephan Butler captained the boat. There must be other people to pick up the Nyllie and drive it to the Central Valley or to L.A."

"What have you found so far?"

"I got through the part of the video where you and I took him to the sheriff's office."

"Let me know what you find."

They said their goodbyes and Fenway turned back to the monitor. Very little happened after Mathis Jericho left with Dez and Fenway. At 10:03 AM, a pickup truck drove in, its bed piled with boxes. Three SUVs between ten fifteen and eleven thirty. The pickup left between the second and third SUVs. One U-Move-It truck arrived at 11:33 AM; looked like one of the smaller ones, maybe fifteen feet long. Fenway slowed the video to regular speed, then stared at the screen. She paused the video, then backed it up slowly, trying to see if she could recognize the driver. Maybe the driver was innocently moving their belongings into a storage unit, but if the driver was Stephan Butler or Calvin Banning, that truck might have been full of morpheranyl.

Unfortunately, the reflections off the driver's window muddied the image too much; she couldn't even tell the height of the driver or the length of their hair. At one point, the sun reflected off a piece of the chrome on the side of the truck and shone right into the camera. Fenway blinked. No wonder the reflections made the driver so difficult to see.

She noted the license plate, then sent a message to Sarah, asking her to check who had rented the truck.

The U-Move-It truck drove out at 12:17 PM, and Fenway still couldn't tell who was in the truck's cab. Mathis's car hadn't moved—and at this point, Mathis was probably dead. Or soon would be.

An itch in Fenway's brain. Something was wrong; what was it?

Calvin Banning was supposed to stay with the Nyllie; both Stephan Butler and Banning had more or less agreed that Banning staying with the Nyllie was part of their process. So where was he? Jericho had taken the Nyllie to Cahill Warehouse Storage with Banning in the passenger seat of his car. So where did Banning go?

Maybe Banning had left early that morning, before Fenway and Dez had gotten there.

She went to a different video file. This file started at midnight, turning Tuesday night into Wednesday morning.

At 2:24 AM, Mathis's car pulled in front of the storage facility. Mathis got out, opened the office, and the video ended at 2:29 AM.

Ah. So Mathis had learned from Seth Cahill to stop the camera recording when they'd taken a run to the beach to get the Nyllie and bring it back.

The recording started again at 6:37 AM. Mathis's navy blue sedan was already in its parking space.

Banning could have left with the Nyllie before the camera came back on. He could have been in the U-Move-It truck, too. Fenway went back to the first recording. The drivers of the pickup and SUVs all had their driver's-side windows down—they all had to punch in their codes. No one looked like Calvin Banning, but maybe she could check with Tyra's records to make sure none of the drivers had the slightest connection with the Venn Cartel.

So Jericho hadn't cleaned his own car. Had someone else done it?

Fenway kept watching until the video file ended. A few other cars came and went. She opened the file for Wednesday evening and sped up the video to 10x, but no one touched Mathis's car.

Thursday's files showed the same thing, but as the wind picked up with the storm coming in, the camera shifted slightly so the car was no longer completely in view. As the rain started coming down in sheets, the video recording ended. Power had been knocked out.

Friday morning, the video didn't come on again until 2:48 PM. Fenway halfway expected the parking lot to be full of standing water, but except for a few large puddles and a few small fallen branches, the lot was relatively unaffected.

Fenway sighed. The storm had provided cover for someone to clean Jericho's car thoroughly and put it back. Fenway had no idea if it had been a car detailer or the deluge that had washed all the old dirt off the navy blue sedan. She kept watching on 10x, but no one came near the car in either of the Friday video files, or all through the weekend. And the car grew dustier over Saturday and Sunday. Fenway doubted anyone had moved the car since; it would have had to be cleaned Friday morning.

A ping on Fenway's phone—her official phone this time. A message from Sarah.

SARAH

The Nidever U-Move-It confirms the van in question was in their lot a few weeks ago but won't tell me who rented it

Do you want me to ask them anything else

FENWAY

Send me their number please - I will talk with them

Fenway went back to the Wednesday morning file, scrubbed over to 11:33 AM, and zoomed in on the U-Move-It truck's license plate as her phone dinged with the phone number.

A moment later, Fenway dialed the U-Move-It two blocks from Nidever University.

"U-Move-It, this is Paige."

"This is Fenway Stevenson, the Dominguez County Coroner. I have a question regarding one of your moving trucks."

No response on the other end.

"I believe you spoke with my assistant, Sarah Summerhill?"

"Oh—yes. She said her boss would be calling."

"That's me."

"Right. Uh—so, like I told your assistant, I can't give you renter information without a warrant."

"But you can tell me where certain vehicles were, can't you?"

"We can tell you when they were rented and returned."

"Can you tell me their locations at specific times?"

Paige paused. "Not all our vehicles have GPS trackers. For the ones that do, I'll have to check if I can give you that info without a warrant."

"I see. Well, let's get started, and if I need a warrant—or you need to check—then we'll cross that bridge."

"Okay." Paige's voice was unsure, but Fenway heard the clacking of keyboard keys. "Do you have the vehicle ID number?"

"I have a license plate number."

"Okay."

Fenway gave Paige the plate number. More keyboard noises. "Okay, that sixteen-foot truck was rented four times from our facility in May."

"No, this would have been June seventeenth."

A pause. "Hold on."

More keyboard clicking. "That vehicle wasn't in our area in the month of June."

"What are you talking about? I'm looking at the license plate on the screen." Fenway glanced at the timestamp in the corner. 17-JUNE, 11:33:43.

Trepidation in Paige's voice. "The system is telling me that vehicle was rented from our facility on May twenty-sixth for a one-way trip. It was returned to our facility in Rock Creek, Texas, on June first. It's been rented for two more long-haul trips. On June seventeenth, the truck was in Chicago." A pause. "If you like, I can send you the toll receipts from the Illinois Tollway on that day."

Fenway blinked. How was this possible? "Thank you for your help."

"Is there anything else?"

"Not right now, thanks."

Fenway ended the call and stared at the wall above the monitor.

There was only one explanation: the security footage on June 17 had been replaced with footage from late May. And someone had modified the timestamps so it *looked* like it had been recorded June 17.

Fenway suspected they'd replaced the footage to cover up a crime.

She stood and walked into the front office.

"Tyra?"

Tyra Cahill turned. "Oh, hey. All done?"

"Who provides the services for your security cameras and footage?"

"Oh—let me see. Seth set all that up."

"One of the big national providers?"

"No, Seth wanted to give business to one of the local businesses. He bragged that they'd given him a good deal, too." Tyra scratched her head. "They do a lot with computer security, too. Our anti-virus stuff on our computers, that kind of stuff."

Fenway's stomach dropped. "Hackson Square."

CHAPTER SEVENTEEN

Tyra snapped her fingers. "Yes! That's it. Hackson Square."

Fenway tightened her jaw. "Did... did one of their technicians visit in the last couple of weeks?"

Tyra nodded. "After the storm. One of their technicians came by Friday morning and got all our cameras working again."

"On that Friday?"

"Yes. Great service. I didn't expect them out until the following week. I'm sure they have hundreds of businesses who were in the same boat. But hey, if they show up a few days early, I won't complain."

"Wait—they showed up early?"

"Sure did. I called on Friday morning when I saw the cameras were down, and they scheduled a visit the following Wednesday. But their technician showed up that afternoon. Said he was servicing one of the other businesses in the neighborhood, and he finished way earlier than he expected." Tyra leaned forward. "I know it's against Hackson Square's policy to tip the technicians, but I gave him fifty bucks. I wish I could have afforded more."

Fenway closed her eyes. She felt a headache starting.

"Coroner?"

She opened her eyes again. "Yes, sorry. Uh, listen…" Fenway pulled her phone out and popped her photos up until she found the police sketch of the Hackson Square impostor that Huke had seen.

"This guy?"

Tyra brightened. "Right, that's him—" Then her face clouded. "Hold on, that's a police sketch."

Fenway nodded.

"What did he do?"

Fenway shook her head. "I can't comment on an ongoing investigation." That sounded a lot better than *I'd like the answer to that, too.*

The front door opened, and Fenway heard two heavy footsteps—then they stopped.

"Coroner?"

Fenway turned. Detective Brian Callahan stood inside the office.

"Detective," Fenway said.

Callahan didn't move. Fenway furrowed her brow. "Did you need to speak with me?"

"Well—" Callahan tilted his head, then caught the look in Fenway's eyes. "Yes. Why—uh, why don't we step outside?"

"Good idea." Fenway strode across the office, past Callahan, and opened the door. Callahan walked through it and Fenway exited behind him.

Fenway took a few steps away from the door, almost to the sidewalk, then turned. "Okay, Brian, what are you doing here?"

"I'm following your lead."

"What?"

"We were working the Mathis Jericho case, right? Yesterday morning, you took me to Estancia Harbor."

"That's right."

"And you've been asking Sarah to research rental trucks."

Callahan crossed his arms. "You could ask me to do that, you know. I'm a detective. I should be detecting."

A pang of guilt—then a burst of indignation. "In one sense, you're right, Brian. You're a detective who reports to me. I should have you do the detective work." She tightened her jaw. "But you haven't been reliable. You showed up over an hour late yesterday, you've slacked off. I'm not inclined to give you important work to do."

Callahan tilted his head. "I'm sorry about that," he said. "But I also got the security guard at the harbor to cooperate with us."

Fenway nodded. "You did."

"Look, when I was a deputy, I wasn't expected to take initiative." He pointed at Fenway. "Your predecessor once told me I wasn't paid to think."

Maybe that's why Celeste Salvador no longer worked for the sheriff's office.

"So, look," Callahan continued, "I know I *am* paid to think now. But there'll be some growing pains. You not being here on Monday, well, it made me think this wasn't the job I thought it was."

"You know that's not true—"

"And I know I screwed up by not showing up on time yesterday." Callahan rubbed his forehead. "But that was one day. You saw my attendance record in the sheriff's office. You know I take my job seriously."

Yes, Fenway thought Callahan *did* take the job seriously—one of the biggest reasons she was okay giving him the job after Celeste Sandoval didn't work out. And he was a person McVie trusted to have his back.

Callahan hadn't seemed serious lately, though. Especially not in the last two days. But Fenway didn't want to argue—not in the middle of the investigation. She pressed her lips together and said nothing.

"Anyway." Callahan cleared his throat. "Sarah mentioned U-Move-It."

"Right."

"And I figured it has something to do with that van Rachel rented?"

For a moment, Fenway wanted to ask Callahan if he knew where Rachel had been moved. But he probably knew less than she did. "She didn't rent it, but her name is on the reservation."

"Yeah, that's what I meant." Callahan dropped his hands to his side and tried to appear casual, as if he were emulating McVie. "I was thinking: Seth Cahill's Corvette was parked in one of these storage spaces. And the Nyllie was stored in one, too."

"Right."

"And the van that Rachel—uh, that was rented a few days ago is still missing. What if it's here?"

Fenway raised her eyebrows. "What makes you think it's here?"

"Whoever rented it under Rachel's name took it to L.A., didn't they?"

Word traveled fast.

"So maybe they have another shipment to take," Callahan continued, "and they don't want to go through the hassle of renting another van. They could extend this rental, right?"

"That's certainly possible."

"So they'd have to have somewhere to put it, right? And where better than here?"

"Because the cops are crawling all over this place," Fenway said. "As evidenced by both of us being here."

Callahan frowned. "Well..." He sighed. "Yeah, that's true. Still, it can't hurt to look, right?"

"You have a warrant? Do you even know what storage space you think the van is in?"

"I figured we could start with units that are behind in payments."

Fenway crossed her arms. "Come on, Brian, you scored well enough on the detective exam to know that you can't gloss over search-and-seizure requirements."

"There's no expectation of privacy when the renter breaches their contract, right?"

Fenway was quiet. The courts had been divided on that question.

"Yeah," Callahan continued, "we need the permission of the facility. If we accidentally see something stored in a unit we don't have a warrant for, sure, we can't use it in court, but we'll know where to look. We can tailor a warrant for the unit, and the ADA can argue inevitability of discovery."

Fenway got a bad taste in her mouth. Callahan was technically correct, although navigating that strategy successfully was tricky, not to mention ethically gray. She thought for a moment before responding. "I have an excuse when I don't follow procedure to the letter," Fenway said. "I got appointed to this position because of my medical background. If I screw up on police procedure, everyone shakes their head and says the position should have required more law enforcement knowledge before I came here. But you, Brian, are the backstop for my ignorance. You've been through the academy. You passed your detective exam. You should know all this stuff backward and forward. It gets out that this is how we investigate, we lose the public's trust."

Callahan looked at the ground and kicked his foot. "Yeah."

"Besides, I've been through the video footage, and the U-Move-It van Rachel rented? Not on it. So we wouldn't have enough to apply for a warrant anyway."

"We could still ask the owners if we can look in the units behind on payments."

Ugh. He wouldn't take no for an answer. "Look," she said, "I appreciate your enthusiasm for this work, but we can't go on fishing expeditions, as much as I might like to."

Callahan kept staring at the ground.

"Did you have another reason you wanted to stay on the property?"

"Uh—no."

"That didn't *sound* like a no."

Callahan hesitated. "All right—well, I thought maybe I'd ask out Isabella while I was here."

Fenway pursed her lips and felt her blood pressure rise. "You—you were going to ask out a witness?"

"We got a confession out of George Pope, right? Isabella isn't a witness anymore." He paused. "Besides, I didn't even work on the Seth Cahill murder."

Fenway tried to keep her breaths slow and even as she dropped her hands to her side. "Brian—I can't even tell you how inappropriate it is for you to ask out someone who's involved in these cases."

"But she's not involved—"

"Are you kidding?" Oops, that was louder than Fenway wanted to be. "She's the co-worker of the victim in the case you're currently assigned to."

Callahan frowned. "I'm officially assigned to this case?"

"I—" Fenway clenched her hands into fists. "You interviewed people at the harbor. You're here with me. What case do you think you're investigating, if not this one?"

He rubbed his forehead. "See, I knew I didn't want to tell you."

"Because it's unethical?"

"Because you're friends with Rachel."

Fenway took a step forward. "That's not why I'm angry that you wanted to ask Isabella out."

A scoff from Callahan.

Fenway almost took another step forward, then stopped. No, a confrontation right now wouldn't do any good. All the ways she wanted to react were too much. Maybe not too much in a closed-door session with him in the office, but certainly too much for standing on the sidewalk in public a hundred feet from the victim's car. She took a deep breath and counted to ten. Then twenty.

"The reason it's inappropriate for you to ask out Isabella Chan,"

Fenway said evenly, "is that she's a person of interest in an active investigation."

"You and McVie dated."

"Neither of us were a person of interest," Fenway said. Although —maybe that wasn't true. At one point, Fenway had certainly suspected McVie of killing her predecessor. Although that was after they'd already…

Fenway came back to the present. "And someone in Isabella's position will *always* feel like they can't say no to a police detective."

Callahan bristled. "That's not my intention."

Fenway shook her head. "Maybe you need to go back and watch the sexual harassment awareness video again."

He shrugged.

She wanted to say so much more—like *We're here to collect evidence, not try to get laid*—but that would be unproductive. Instead, Fenway crossed her arms again. "Tell you what, Brian. Go to the sheriff's office and you get the sketch of the guy who pretended to be a Hackson Square employee. Huke sat with our sketch artist earlier."

"I need to go to the office for that?"

Fenway took another cleansing breath. True, Callahan could receive the sketch on his phone, but she wanted him out of her hair —and away from Isabella Chan. "I'd like you to figure out who he is. What his connection is to Hackson Square—former employee? Friend of a former employee? You can use the full resources available to you at the office."

Callahan opened his mouth to say something, but thought better of it. He closed his mouth, then turned and walked to his cruiser, parked in front of Fenway's Accord.

Fenway blinked after him. After he drove off, she swore under her breath. She'd been an idiot for not getting the red tape cut in time to hire Deputy Celeste Salvador as her detective. Firing Callahan was next to impossible with the police union, but surely there would be some ways to transfer him to another department.

She walked to her Accord. Kind of rude to leave without telling Tyra they were done, but she was so agitated because of the interaction with Callahan, she didn't trust herself to keep her cool.

Fenway started the engine and tapped her hands on the steering wheel. "You know what would make me feel better?" she asked aloud. Fenway pulled her phone out and tapped Favorites.

McVie answered. "Hey, Fenway."

"You free for lunch?"

A pause. "Dos Milagros?"

"Dos Milagros, and a bunch of questions about how the hell to handle Brian."

"Ah." McVie paused. "I can meet you there in twenty minutes. I may need a margarita or two to delve into that subject."

———

Twenty-five minutes later, Fenway walked down the sidewalk. She'd parked three blocks away, partially because street parking was nonexistent in front of Dos Milagros today, but also because she didn't want to be too visible to anyone who might wish her harm. She didn't *think* she'd been followed to Dos Milagros, and besides, she'd been almost-run-over in front of the same restaurant the day before, so the chances that the same perpetrator would make another attempt twenty-four hours later in the same place was unlikely.

McVie was waiting for her outside the entrance. His face fell when he saw her.

"Hey, are you okay?"

Fenway nodded. "Yes. I'm fine."

McVie looked at her out of the corner of his eye. "You sure?"

Then the realization hit her: they'd had an argument, and McVie wasn't happy with her keeping her near-miss from him. He must have thought they were still upset with each other.

Maybe talking about Callahan would help them move past their fight.

"I could kill Brian," Fenway said.

McVie tilted his head. "What happened?"

Fenway stepped forward and opened the door. "Food first."

After they ordered, Fenway walked to a booth in the corner—where they *never* sat—and plopped down. McVie walked up with drinks and set down her horchata.

"Okay," McVie said. "What's going on?"

"I don't know what to do with Callahan," Fenway said. "He—he came to Cahill Warehouse Storage to ask out one of the employees."

McVie arched an eyebrow.

"That's bad, Craig."

"I mean, dating someone cops meet through work isn't encouraged."

Fenway frowned. "I sense a *but* coming."

McVie ran a hand over his face. "Look, this isn't an excuse or anything, but at least half the guys in the sheriff's office have asked out people from the, uh, the job. A lot of guys in the force look at it like"—McVie bit his lip in thought, then the idea came—"jaywalking."

"Jaywalking?"

"Yeah. Jaywalking is illegal, but everyone does it. As long as you don't jump out in front of traffic, everyone will let it slide."

"I'm not talking about co-workers, or people who are sort of co-workers, like Rachel and Callahan, or you and me. I'm talking about persons of interest, witnesses, suspects."

McVie nodded. "Yeah, it happens pretty often." He leaned forward. "You know Mark and Randy met when Mark was a beat cop, and Randy got his motorcycle stolen?"

Fenway's jaw dropped open. "Mark? You're talking about Sergeant Trevino, recently retired paragon of excellence, whose shoes are too big for Callahan to fill? They started dating *during* the investigation?"

"Oh." McVie shook his head. "No, not during the investigation. After the case closed."

"Yeah, well, what about dating during active investigations? That's what we're talking about."

McVie furrowed his brow. "I thought you closed the Cahill case."

Fenway hesitated.

McVie held up his hands. "Sorry, I didn't realize that the Cahill storage employees are part of an active investigation. That's definitely against policy." McVie scratched his chin. "Although I'm sure cops have done it. Just not made it known until after the case closed."

The woman behind the counter shouted their number and McVie stood, leaving Fenway to mull things over.

McVie returned, placing the tray between them. He'd remembered to get a big spicy salsa container for her and a small green salsa container too. "But it's mostly the other way."

Fenway knotted her eyebrows. "What do you mean, 'the other way'?"

"Usually the people we meet during our investigations are hitting on us."

"Did you say 'we'?"

McVie nodded. "Oh, yeah." He pulled his burrito closer to himself. "You know I got hit on all the time when I was sheriff, right?"

Fenway paused. While that bit of information didn't surprise her, she'd never heard it explicitly. "I never thought about it."

McVie took a bite, then chewed and swallowed. "If you want to know what I think, Amy couldn't handle it. I'm pretty sure she was convinced I was cheating on her with a few of the women I met through my investigations."

"And you never cheated?" *Except with me,* Fenway thought, although that had been a gray area.

McVie shook his head, though the look in his eyes made it clear that he was purposely leaving out the first night he and Fenway had been together.

Fenway narrowed her eyes. "You don't jaywalk either, do you?"

McVie ignored the question and took a drink of his lemonade. He set the drink down. "Besides, I saw too many of my colleagues going through terrible divorces when they couldn't keep it in their pants. You remember Duke Tommasso?"

"No."

"Probably before your time. Anyway, he was on wife number five. Met every single one of them on the job."

Fenway was silent. "So I should let this go? If Callahan wants to date Isabella Chan, I just look the other way?"

McVie shook his head as he was chewing his next bite, then swallowed. "No. When the investigation is over, maybe, although things are different than fifteen years ago. There's a power dynamic he's got to respect. At least until your investigation's over. He can't ignore the policy."

Fenway nodded through a bite of her taco, then swallowed. "Then what do I say to him? I don't want to be a scold, but I want him to stop it."

"Then be a scold. That's the job. Your employees aren't all going to like you the way Dez and Sarah do. And that's not necessarily a bad thing."

Fenway took a bite in silence. The tacos didn't taste as good today. McVie looked out the window behind her. A minute or two ticked by.

No, that wasn't it. The taste of the tacos had nothing to do with the cook. She closed her eyes and steeled herself. "I'm sorry."

"For what?"

"For not telling you I almost got run over."

McVie set down his burrito. "Look, this is complicated. I know the circles of trauma. And I broke that rule."

Fenway cocked her head. "The circles of what?"

"Circles of trauma. Maybe you studied this concept when you got your nursing degree?" He grabbed the salsa containers and held the small green salsa above the big spicy salsa. "Concentric circles."

"Oh, I think I know where you're going with this," Fenway said. "I learned this as *ring theory* when dealing with cancer patients. The person in the green salsa, they're in the middle—they're the one with cancer. And they can say anything they want to *anyone* in the other circles. They can yell or cry or bitch or whatever. Everything is fair game."

McVie nodded. "And you almost got run over. So you're in the middle. And *I* can go to other people who are in circles outside mine and do the same thing: I can complain, I can say how upset I am that you didn't tell me, and how unfair it is. But I can't complain to someone in an inside circle." He raised his eyes from the salsa containers. "That's you. So even if I feel shitty about you not telling me you were almost run over, I need to complain to Dez or Piper or someone else. Not you. *Never* you."

"Right." Fenway stared at her uneaten taco. "I didn't think about me being on the inside ring."

McVie took another bite of his burrito. She stared at the middle of the table for a moment.

"I didn't forget to tell *you* I was nearly run over, Craig."

He glanced up, still chewing, eyes wary.

"I forgot about it *entirely*. I didn't mention it to anyone. Not Callahan, not ADA Pondicherry. I had to talk to Captain Alvídrez about it—he saw everything—and I had to tell Dez. Donnelly even yelled at me for not submitting the report, and I still haven't done it. It's not about you." She paused. "Is that fucked up?"

McVie chewed thoughtfully, then nodded.

Circles of trauma, indeed.

She needed to get back into therapy.

CHAPTER EIGHTEEN

FENWAY WALKED TO HER CAR, HYPER-AWARE OF HER surroundings. No issues, no one trying to run her over or shoot at her. She drove to the town center, and as she walked toward the coroner's office building, she got a sinking feeling in her stomach. She didn't want to discuss anything with Callahan. He might have seen some of his other deputy friends asking out witnesses or victims or even suspects, but he should know that wasn't okay. McVie had validated her feelings about it—even if he'd given Callahan a half-assed excuse for asking out Isabella Chan—but she hadn't asked McVie exactly how she should bring it up with him.

Still, McVie was right: she wasn't in this position to be buddies with Callahan; she was here to get results. To get cases solved. So she needed to have the conversation with Callahan.

Then she veered toward the sheriff's office.

She had expected the video footage from Cahill Warehouse Storage to be missing when Cahill or Jericho had turned off the recording, but she was surprised the videos were doctored.

So the question was: what footage had been replaced?

And another question: who had replaced the video—or more

accurately, who had pulled the strings to get the Hackson Square impostor to replace it?

Fenway walked across the street to the sheriff's office and once again took the long way around to the evidence room so she wouldn't have to walk past Donnelly's desk. Again she almost ran into the low sofa that stuck out into the hallway from the window nook.

She passed Lieutenant Brookline in the hallway about a hundred feet from the evidence room. He glanced at her quickly, averted his eyes, and didn't say hello as she passed. Had Donnelly said something to him?

She got to the evidence room, Huke standing behind the gate, shoulders slumped.

"Oh—did you forget something?" he asked.

Fenway shook her head. "I found some disturbing, uh, information about the video footage from Cahill Warehouse Storage."

Huke tilted his head.

"The facility where Mathis Jericho worked," Fenway said. "Looks like the same Hackson Square impostor who was in here also went to the storage facility and messed with their recordings."

Huke raised his shoulders. "Someone else got fooled, too?" The relief showed in his face: at least he wasn't alone in getting tricked.

Fenway nodded. "Hackson Square was hired to store the video footage. And the video footage from two weeks ago was replaced with old footage. So it wasn't only you and Cahill Warehouse Storage—I think Hackson Square was compromised, too."

Huke's expression went from depressed to serious. "Then—why aren't you at Hackson Square?"

"I want to make sure I know what I'm looking for," Fenway said.

"How can I help?"

"Let me see the boxes of evidence from both the Cahill murder and the Jericho case."

"The Cahill murder's closed," Huke replied, opening the gate and letting Fenway through. "We've got the evidence on that shelf to go back to the next of kin. Well—not the drugs, of course."

"The bags of Nyllie," Fenway said. "Are they here?"

"In a safe behind the back room," Huke said. "All illegal substances, weapons, other contraband—they all go back there."

"Did the guy from Hackson Square go back in the safe?"

"Only to check the cameras—" Huke paused.

"Did you open the safe?"

Huke hesitated.

"You did. While he was here?"

"He didn't go into the safe. At least..." Then Huke trailed off.

"What is it?"

"He was fixing the cameras, and—well, you remember on Monday when we got the anonymous tip on all those guns?"

Fenway shook her head. "I wasn't in on Monday."

"Oh. Well, Sheriff Donnelly took a call from an unknown number—turns out it was a burner phone—about a bunch of cheap handguns that got dumped in Santa Anita Park."

"And the call panned out?"

"Yes. Three boxes' worth. Most of the guns were in terrible shape—a lot of them weren't working."

"How do a hundred cheap handguns get dropped in Santa Anita Park?"

"We were all wondering the same thing. Anyway, I had to go back and forth a few times."

"Between the gate up in front and the safe in back?"

"Yes. And... well, before I got any of the gun boxes, I opened the safe."

"Right where the Hackson Square guy was working?"

"No, no," Huke said. "He'd already moved on. He was working on the cameras in the..." Huke paused, then put a hand over his eyes.

"What?"

"He was in the room with the cold case files. Or at least I

thought he was in there. But I couldn't see him—not when I went up to the front, nor when I dropped the boxes off—right inside the entrance to the safe."

"I think I need to see this safe."

Huke locked the gate, then pulled the main door closed. "I'm not taking any chances this time." He beckoned Fenway to follow him.

Fenway had been in the evidence room before, but she had no idea it was so large. It wasn't as big as the warehouse for evidence in Los Angeles, but it was still much bigger than she'd expected.

The main evidence room had rows and rows of shelving with boxes and files, but where Fenway thought the room ended was a half-wall, with another room behind it. A metal door to the right stood open.

"That's the cold case room," Huke said, pointing.

"And where's the safe?"

"Right around this corner."

Another steel door, but this one had a key for a deadbolt and a numeric keypad.

"You need both a key and the code to get in?"

"That's right."

"In my head, I pictured a big bank vault door with one of those ship-captain wheel things on the door."

Huke gave Fenway a tight smile. "We're not in a casino heist movie."

Fenway examined the door: nothing scratched around the lock. "So you left this door open?"

"For about three minutes while I carted the boxes of guns back and forth."

"And did you check if anyone was inside?"

Huke paused, then shook his head. "It locks from the outside. If anyone had gotten stuck in there, they'd be in there until the next time someone opened it." He leaned forward toward Fenway. "The walls have the same anti-cellphone service paint on the walls that they use in the courtrooms."

"So a potential thief can't work with anyone on the outside?"

"That's the idea. The paint is pricey, but they used what was left over from the courtroom remodel. I figured no one in their right mind would go in there—on the off-chance they'd get locked in."

"So what's in there from the Jericho case?"

Huke pulled out a set of keys, flicked through several, then unlocked the deadbolt. He held his left hand over the keypad and typed in his code with his right. A beep, a click, and the door opened an inch.

He pulled the door all the way open, then stepped inside with Fenway. He pointed at the third set of shelves on the right. "Second and third shelves."

Fenway stepped over to the shelves Huke had shown her. Five unmarked white cardboard boxes sat on the second shelf from the bottom.

"Those are the bags of morpheranyl CSI took out of Seth Cahill's Corvette." Huke hesitated. "Those bags were all around Jericho's dead body."

"You know I see a lot of dead bodies, right? Being next to a bag of drugs that was touching a dead guy doesn't exactly freak me out."

Huke nodded.

Fenway pulled a box out; it was fairly heavy, and she set it on the floor. She knelt next to the box and opened the lid. This box was on the wrong shelf; it contained evidence from Seth Cahill's office at Cahill Warehouse Storage. A few items from his desk, including the ledger that Fenway and Dez discovered the evening Cahill was found dead.

She moved that box to the shelf above, then considered for a moment. She should put the box back in the right place. There were the other boxes of Cahill evidence, two shelving units to the left. She made some room on the third shelf and placed the box there.

She returned to the Mathis Jericho shelf and pulled another box down. This box was heavy too, but felt like everything inside was more solid, like it couldn't shift around. She opened the lid. Four bags full of white powder, looking suspiciously like bread flour, but much more expensive.

She pulled the third box out. Same thing: four bags of white powder—

Hold on.

"Deputy Huke," Fenway said, "have you seen these bags of morpheranyl before?"

"When the Vice guys delivered them, of course—two weeks ago," Huke said.

"And do you remember what the bags looked like?"

"Uh, clear plastic."

"Was there a white stripe on each of the bags?"

Huke frowned. "Not that I remember. But I wouldn't swear to it in a court of law."

Fenway remembered the bags surrounding Mathis Jericho's dead body. Clear bags, mostly rectangular. Eighteen of them.

"Deputy," Fenway said, starting at the boxes, "didn't you say that the Hackson Square contractor brought in a case full of equipment?"

"That's right."

"Did you see any of the equipment?"

Huke thought for a moment. "He pulled out a—uh, I don't know what you call it. A handheld thing with red and black cords with metal spikes."

"A voltmeter? Maybe eight or ten inches long? Looked like a remote control on steroids, but with a big screen with numbers?"

"Could've been. He got up on the table and put the spikes somewhere on the camera, then it made a couple of beeps. Bad beeps, you know? Like when someone answers a game show question wrong."

"And then he took down the cameras, didn't he?"

Huke nodded.

"But you didn't see anything else he had in his case?"

"Uh... no." Huke rubbed his chin. "Now that I think about it, he closed the lid of his case right after pulling out the, uh, voltmeter."

"Like he didn't want anyone to see what was inside?"

"Well, I didn't think so at the time."

Fenway pulled the other boxes down and counted the bags. Sixteen. Two found in Rachel's trunk—that would be eighteen.

Hang on. What did Sheriff Donnelly think Rachel had done? Did Donnelly think Rachel had stolen the drugs from the evidence room and been caught by Andrew Zellman? Or did she think Rachel had picked up a new shipment of morpheranyl and stolen two bags and put them in her trunk?

If Rachel was supposed to have stolen drugs from the evidence room, why were there sixteen bags here? There were originally eighteen bags, and yes, the other two bags were found in her trunk. But the sheriff's story was that Rachel had coordinated taking a new shipment down to L.A. and taken the two bags from that shipment. In that scenario, there would still be eighteen bags in evidence. So what story was Donnelly peddling? Had Rachel taken two bags from the evidence room, or taken two bags from this mysterious U-Move-It van shipment?

"The left hand doesn't know what the right hand is doing," said Fenway.

"What?"

"Two bags are missing," Fenway said.

"What?" Huke repeated.

She stared at the four open boxes on the floor, all with four bags each of white powder. She squinted: a white stripe about a half-inch wide, difficult to see with the white powder in the otherwise clear bag, encircled every one of the plastic bags, about a third of the way down.

"Deputy, can you get Steve Alvídrez over here right away?"

"I'm in so much trouble," Huke muttered under his breath.

———

Ten minutes later, a knock on the evidence room door. Huke opened it and Captain Steve Alvídrez stood there. "I came as soon as I could."

Fenway nodded. "Captain Alvídrez, do you remember what the bags of morpheranyl looked like? The ones found in the Corvette with Jericho's dead body?"

Alvídrez frowned. "They looked like any other plastic bag. Clear. Rectangular. I didn't measure the size, but, I don't know, maybe nine inches high, five or six inches wide, maybe three inches deep."

"You remember a white stripe on any of the bags?"

Alvídrez frowned. "No."

"It would have been hard to see."

"We looked closely. I would have remembered that."

"Deputy," Fenway said, "you said earlier that the contractor brought in an equipment case."

"That's right," Huke replied.

"Hold on," Alvídrez said. "What contractor?"

"A person claiming to be from Hackson Square," Fenway replied. "Had a signed work order, had the uniform, but IT never contracted with anyone."

The color drained from Alvídrez's face.

Fenway addressed Huke again. "During the time you were moving the weapons from the gate to the safe, did you see where the contractor's case was?"

Huke furrowed his brow. "The *impostor* took the case with him into the cold case room."

"And you left him in there alone?"

Huke pressed his lips together. "I'm one person, Coroner. I could either leave the contractor—who had a signed work order, who I thought was licensed and bonded—in the cold case room alone, with files that are ten, twenty, sometimes fifty years old, that no ADA has touched since I started working here. Or I could leave several boxes of firearms unguarded in the hallway. What choice would you have made?"

Fenway held up her hands. "I apologize, Deputy Huke. I didn't mean to sound accusatory. I wanted to be sure of the order of events. Given the circumstances, it sounds like you followed procedure." She wasn't sure that was true, but Huke was often obsessed with following the rules, and she didn't want him to panic.

Huke mumbled, "Sorry," and his shoulders relaxed slightly.

Fenway turned to Alvídrez. "I think someone swapped these bags. And they did it recently."

"Swapped?" Alvídrez asked. "You mean—the bags all have white stripes now, but the bags were clear before?"

"Right." She motioned with her head to the evidence room. "We should probably have this conversation inside."

Huke opened the gate for Alvídrez, then all three of them went back to the safe. Fenway explained to Alvídrez how the U-Move-It on Carlsbad and 17th had bags that looked exactly like these, recently replacing the clear bags. Against a bag full of white powder, the white stripe was difficult—but not impossible—to see.

"Look," Fenway said. "That's not right. Those aren't the bags I saw in the car with Mathis Jericho's dead body."

Alvídrez turned to Huke. "So you think the Hackson Square contractor came in and messed with the evidence?"

"Impostor, not contractor," Fenway said, "but yes. I believe he came in and turned off the cameras, then replaced the bags of morpheranyl with these."

Alvídrez tightened his jaw, then pointed to the boxes. "Did you touch the bags inside these boxes?"

Fenway nodded. "I took two bags out of that first box."

"But not the rest?"

"No. And I counted only sixteen bags, not eighteen like we originally had."

"Where are the other two?" Alvídrez said. "Oh—that's right, they were supposedly found in Rachel Richards' trunk."

"I've got to get these bags all fingerprinted," Alvídrez said. "Again."

"And you should test the contents for morpheranyl," Fenway said.

Alvídrez narrowed his eyes. "You think someone stole all the Nyllie and replaced it with cornstarch?"

Fenway gave Alvídrez a small smile. "Well, I don't know if it's *cornstarch*, but yeah—the guy sneaked in here, stole the real drugs and replaced them with something else."

Alvídrez tightened his jaw. "Maybe the Venn Cartel aren't out of Dominguez County after all."

"Maybe not."

———

Fenway left the sheriff's office, her head swirling. Who had the Hackson Square impostor been?

Whoever it was, they'd been involved with a plot to kill Andrew Zellman and falsely imprison Rachel. The plan, Fenway thought, was also to kill her and blame Deputy Donald Huke for it.

Crowds filled the plaza this afternoon: city workers outside getting some sun now that the fog had burned off, a few deputies drinking sodas, and people in suits texting on their phones. Fenway glanced over her shoulder and saw ADA Pondicherry's assistant a few paces behind her. He looked out of place in his three-piece suit, like he'd stepped out of period drama. What was his name? Fenway searched her brain until it popped out: Morgan Crane.

She looked carefully before she crossed the street. No cars lying in wait. She hurried to the other sidewalk. Did she want an afternoon coffee? Well, yes. But she would be delaying the inevitable talk with Callahan. She knew she needed to have a serious conversation with him, but wasn't sure how to do it. Maybe she'd call her contact in HR to get some guidance. Ugh—her stomach dropped thinking about it.

She glanced up as she reached the glass front door of her building—and in the reflection, she saw Morgan Crane still following her.

Fenway had been followed before, once. But she'd been driving her car, and she'd outmaneuvered the vehicle following her. Could she—

No, she was being ridiculous. Crane was walking into a county office building, and as a county employee, he probably had business here. He could have been walking to the IT department down the hall to get a laptop upgrade. Vital Records was on the third floor; maybe he needed to get something there. Quite presumptuous of Fenway to think it was all about her.

A little voice in Fenway's head: someone tried to kill you, and the police still haven't caught the person who tried to run you over.

She took out her burner phone and called Dez. The phone rang once, then a prerecorded voice came on: "The person you are calling has not set up voicemail yet. Goodbye."

So much for that.

Wait. Did Fenway think that Morgan Chase would attack her in the coroner's office—with Sarah and Callahan both there?

Still, Fenway couldn't shake the chill that went up her spine. She took a deep breath and walked into the coroner's office. Sarah looked up from her computer and nodded at Fenway in greeting. Callahan was standing at the printer behind his desk.

At that moment, Fenway realized that she and Dez were the only ones who had connected the Mathis Jericho murder and the Andrew Zellman murder—and connected them both to the attempt on Fenway's life. Gretchen Donnelly *should* have connected them, too—Dez had even warned her that Donnelly's conclusion was imminent. The sheriff *should* have pieced everything together by now and released Rachel. Was Donnelly really that clueless?

No. Donnelly was one of the most intelligent people Fenway

had ever met. So why hadn't Donnelly kicked Fenway off the Jericho case too?

Fenway stepped toward Sarah's counter. "So you heard about the incident yesterday, right? How someone stole Huke's car and nearly ran me over?"

Sarah nodded. "And how the cameras at the sheriff's office—from the parking lot to the evidence room—have gone offline."

"We've removed the cameras at the impound lot, too," Fenway said, "although that might have been through design, not a, um, nefarious third-party."

Sarah coughed. "Okay, James Bond."

Fenway tried not to panic: at any moment, Morgan Crane would burst through the door of the coroner's suite. She gripped the edge of the counter.

"This might not be a spy movie, but someone's targeting me, Rachel, and Don."

Sarah's face scrunched up. "Uh... who's Don?"

"Deputy Huke."

Sarah's eyes widened. "Oh, Donny? Yeah. Crazy. He bought one of those steering wheel locks for the Dokko on his lunch break. Won't prevent anyone from breaking in, but at least no one else will use his car to run you over."

"No one else seems to think that someone targeted all four of us—Zellman, Huke, me, and Rachel. And no one's contacted me about protection, either. Donnelly knows I'm a target, yet hasn't even mentioned a security detail." Fenway knotted her brow. "I need to figure out who would want us out of the way. Do you have any ideas? What does someone think we know or thought we saw?"

Sarah shook her head. "That's a question for you, Rachel, and Donny."

Fenway hesitated.

"What is it?"

"At the risk of sounding stupid," Fenway said, "ADA Pondicherry's assistant followed me into the building."

Sarah tilted her head.

"I know, I know. He's a county employee, he probably had business in the building, and so far, he hasn't come in here and stabbed me. But I still got a weird feeling."

"Okay."

"And even though my gut is wrong half the time, that's a better track record than most things in my life. So—can you do a little research into him?"

"What's his name?"

"Morgan Crane."

"Oh, he's the dapper gentleman. Silky voice. Silver fox."

"He's dapper all right, but maybe something's off. So can you look into him?"

"Yes, but isn't this more Piper's area of expertise?"

"Tell you what. If you find anything that you think needs a deeper level of scrutiny, let me know. I already have Piper working on a few different things."

"At least you're keeping us all busy."

A buzz in Fenway's purse. She pulled her phone out. A text from Captain Alvídrez.

> Can you come to my office?

She wanted to jump at the chance to get out of discussing Callahan's missteps with him. But difficult conversations were part of the job.

> Need to take care of something

> Be there in 15

"Brian," Fenway said, walking to her office, "can I see you for a minute?"

Callahan grabbed a few papers out of the printer and hurried to Fenway's side.

"Hey," he said, closing the door behind him. "I thought I'd take a little initiative. I got an employee list from Hackson Square, then I ran the records of everyone who lives within a fifty-mile radius."

Fenway raised her eyebrows. "Well—that's good."

"Not as many as you'd think," Callahan said, "but there are about a dozen names. A couple of them are back in prison, though." He handed one of the printouts to Fenway. "I also got a list of all the employees who were let go over the last year. The company policy is to hand in the shirts, but because the company forces the employees to purchase the shirts using their own money, they can't legally force anyone to return them."

"So it could be literally any of these people."

Callahan bobbed his head noncommittally. "I called about ten of the people on the list. They all said they turned their shirts in."

"Of course they did. You're a cop, and they didn't want to get in trouble."

"Who'd want to keep a uniform shirt, anyway? They're hideous. It's not like you can wear them out for a nice dinner. And they're uncomfortable."

"Who knows?" Fenway said. "Maybe the employees want to keep them out of spite. Or to be a Hackson Square employee for Halloween." Fenway glanced through the list: at least a hundred names, but none that jumped out at her. "Or to impersonate an employee to steal a million dollars' worth of drugs from our evidence room."

"Right."

"Can you get a list of people from Hackson Square who returned their shirts? We could cross-reference with this list and narrow down the names."

"Uh—well, they said I couldn't have that without a warrant."

Fenway stared at the list of names again. "Everyone on the list has plenty of reasons to say they've given their shirts to Hackson Square, even if they haven't."

Callahan was silent.

"And Hackson Square was trying to enforce something illegal, so they've got no incentive to cooperate with us either."

"I could get a warrant."

Fenway nodded. "That's probably the only move we have." She scratched her scalp as she took the seat behind her desk. "See if you can get Judge Azurra. He's usually pro-business, so we won't get accused of judge shopping, but he's pro-privacy rights, too, and forcing employees to buy uniforms and then requiring them to be returned is something that might annoy him."

"Seems pretty cut-and-dried to me," Callahan said. "We need the list so we can narrow down the suspect pool."

"Don't phrase it like that. That sounds close to a fishing expedition, and Azurra *hates* fishing expeditions." Fenway shook her head. "Ask Sarah to look over the application before you submit it. She knows what Azurra looks for."

"Gotcha."

Fenway snapped her fingers. "Hey, did Lieutenant Brookline find anything?"

Callahan shook his head. "Satchel even reached out to the manufacturer. No missing shirts anywhere in the system. Besides, the shirts are made in Bangladesh."

Fenway scratched her chin. "What about the rejects?"

"Brookline asked that. They stay overseas." Callahan grinned. "So unless our impostor flew internationally to steal shirts, I think that line of questioning hit a dead end."

Fenway pointed at a blank line in the printout. "What was here?"

"Where?"

"There's a blank line." She flipped the page. "There are a bunch of blank lines."

"I said some people were incarcerated. I didn't include them in the printout. No use wasting time trying to chase them down."

Fenway nodded. "Send me the electronic copy, then fill out a warrant application. Once I review it, you can take it over to City

Hall." She handed the printouts back to Callahan. "Your initiative is good. It's what I like to see." She paused. "But I have to—"

Callahan raised his hand. "I apologize, Coroner. I was way out of line, going to see a potential witness to ask her out."

Fenway paused. "Do you really think you were out of line? I mean, I hear that kind of thing goes on all the time."

Callahan chewed his bottom lip.

"Do you think this is one of those situations where you apologize, and then you can do whatever you want if I don't find out?"

"No," Callahan said quickly.

"Your sergeants and lieutenants might have looked the other way for your co-workers," Fenway said, "but it's against policy."

"I know," he said. "Rachel and I started a relationship when we both worked here, but dating another county employee isn't the same thing as asking out a witness in an active investigation."

"Good to hear."

"And it was in the training videos," he continued. "I shouldn't have even entertained the thought."

Whew.

"Thanks, Brian." Fenway nodded. "And I appreciate your initiative."

After the door shut behind Callahan, Fenway sat back in her chair. The conversation hadn't been as difficult as she'd feared.

She was lucky that she'd never had to have a difficult management conversation with Dez or Mark; of course, they'd been on the job much longer than she had.

She wondered if she should document this and put it in Callahan's personnel file.

He'd only been officially reporting to her for three days, and already she'd dealt with a host of his—uh, challenges. That was the polite word.

Hopefully, Alvídrez had some information she could use. She wanted to distract herself from Brian Callahan—and maybe get some clues to solve this case.

CHAPTER NINETEEN

FENWAY AGAIN WALKED THE LONG WAY AROUND THE SHERIFF'S
office to avoid Donnelly. She went through the bullpen for the vice
detectives, then knocked on the blue door with Alvídrez's
nameplate.

"Come in."

Fenway opened the door. "Hi, Captain. You wanted to see me?"

"Jeez, so formal. You can call me Steve."

"Right." Fenway remembered he'd said that before. "Steve."

He leaned back in his chair and interlaced his fingers behind his
head. "I was half right."

Fenway narrowed her eyes. "With what?"

"Cornstarch. The powder in the bags is a mixture of Vitamin D
powder and cornstarch."

"You've analyzed it already? I thought the lab in San Miguelito
has at least a two-week turnaround."

"There are more ways to find out what's in a plastic bag besides
a lab."

Fenway raised her eyebrows. "Like what?"

"Like my tongue," Alvídrez said. "Most of these drugs taste bitter, so the good fake stuff uses a compound like vitamin powder that also tastes bitter. Fools a lot more people than flour or powdered sugar." He motioned toward the guest chairs in front of his desk.

Fenway sat. "So how do you know this was definitely vitamin D powder?"

"I've been doing this a long time." He tapped his nose. "I've gotten some vitamin D powder that's bitter, some other stuff that's flavorless. Hard to find the bitter stuff on the market now—people like the flavorless stuff better."

"So how can you tell the difference?"

"The bitterness of dark chocolate is a lot different from the bitterness of apple cider vinegar, right?"

Fenway smiled. "Right."

"And the bitterness of vitamin D powder is different from the bitterness of morpheranyl."

"I see."

"We could do a taste test sometime."

Fenway said nothing.

Alvídrez cleared his throat. "I mean, knowing how to determine cocaine and heroin from ketamine or vitamin powder—"

"Right," Fenway said, a tightness creeping into her shoulders. "Knowing all that would help me in my job."

"And you bringing this to our attention is helpful," Alvídrez said quickly. "Had you not suspected the switch, we'd have gone for months, maybe years, with sixteen bags of these half-and-half fake drugs."

"I appreciate that, Captain," Fenway said.

Alvídrez blinked—possibly because of Fenway using the honorific again. "Anyway," he said, "I have my team looking for large online orders of vitamin D powder. The stuff usually comes in ten-ounce packages for thirty bucks. A lot cheaper than morpheranyl, but someone had to order forty or fifty pounds of this."

"What about local stores?"

Alvídrez shook his head. "There are five stores in the county that sell it, and when they're fully stocked, they have maybe twenty ten-ounce packages in stock. Someone would have had to go to every single store in the area and buy them out. And we asked—no one bought more than three of the small packages in the last month."

"So they probably ordered online."

"Right. But tracking the sales could be almost impossible, especially if they split orders between multiple vendors."

Fenway paused. "Fingerprints?"

"We sent the packages to the lab in San Miguelito. They're backed up, but I hope to have results in the next few days."

Fenway pursed her lips. "Did anyone recognize the sketch of the impostor?"

Alvídrez furrowed his brow. "The sketch?"

Fenway pulled out her phone and brought up the sketch the police artist made from Huke's description.

A spark of recognition in Alvídrez's eyes.

"You know him."

"I arrested him before," Alvídrez said. "He's into pills. Low-level dealing. Did a six-month stint in jail rather than give up the name of his supplier." He rubbed his temple. "I can't put a name to the face."

"The name of his supplier," Fenway muttered. "We talking the Venn Cartel?"

Alvídrez shrugged. "We were never sure. We suspected as much. But there's only so much we can do. I wanted to tail the guy when he got out, but you know."

"Privacy laws," Fenway said. "Just because the guy was in jail doesn't give you probable cause to rake through his life."

"You sound like the judge," Alvídrez said, rising from his chair. "Hey, Jensen!"

A large Black man in a suit and tie appeared in Alvídrez's doorway.

"You met the coroner?"

"Met her? Hell, I voted for her," Jensen said.

"Show him the sketch," Alvídrez said, handing Fenway the phone.

Fenway turned the screen to Jensen, who leaned forward to look.

"We arrested this guy last year," Alvídrez said, "and I can't remember his name."

"Aw, man," Jensen said, "a white dude? You know they all look alike to me."

Fenway chuckled.

"No, all right." He blinked. "You know, if this guy didn't have a beard, he'd look like Frank Fantastic."

"Is that a cartoon character?"

"Name of a guy who we put away for selling pills. What was that, a year ago?"

Alvídrez nodded. "That's right. He looked different with a beard."

Fenway turned. "Frank Fantastic can't be his real name, though."

"Kind of a dumb street name, too, but everyone called him that because his stuff was top-notch." Jensen laughed. "People said we wanted the name of his supplier—not so we could arrest him, but so we could try his stuff and find out what all the fuss was about."

"Cop humor," Alvídrez said.

Jensen pinched the bridge of his nose. "Man, what was the guy's last name? I mean, once you hear *Frank Fantastic*, you forget about his real name."

"First name really Frank?"

"Yep. Old-school name for a young guy."

"Did his last name begin with F?"

"No, something fancy." He raised his head. "Kingman. That's it. Frank Kingman."

"And he got out of jail recently?"

Jensen looked at Alvídrez. "He did?"

"Six months flew by," Alvídrez said. "He got out in March."

"There you have it," Jensen said.

"Thanks, Jensen. I owe you a beer."

Jensen chuckled. "That makes it an even twelve-pack now."

"Get out of here," Alvídrez said, smiling.

Jensen walked back into the Vice bullpen.

"Is Mr. Fantastic on parole?" Fenway asked.

Alvídrez shook his head. "He was arrested for a misdemeanor. Six months and he was out, a free man. No ankle bracelet or anything, and no probation. That's one reason the judge wouldn't authorize a wiretap or us following him."

"Still don't have his supplier's name?"

"And we still haven't tried out his stuff for quality assurance."

Fenway chuckled. "Do you have an address?"

"I can get you his address and his arrest record. That was the first time he's done anything worse than 'drunk in public' with his friends." Alvídrez sat back down and turned the monitor slightly to the side. "Bring a chair over here and take a look."

Fenway hesitated. She didn't want to give any mixed signals to Alvídrez, who seemed determined to say flirtatious things to her. And he'd seemed so professional two weeks ago. Maybe hearing that her boyfriend was moving three states away had triggered something he'd kept under wraps.

She scooted her chair to the side of his desk so she could see the monitor. Alvídrez tapped the keyboard, and the photo of Frank Kingman appeared.

"Last known address," Alvídrez said, "was an apartment over past the industrial area."

"Can I see his arrest record?"

Alvídrez clicked on the screen and a list came up. He clicked on the first link. "This one was from about a year and a half ago, before he was caught selling pills."

Fenway squinted.

"Grand theft, pled down to petty theft." Alvídrez shook his head. "We should have known these three were on a downward trajectory."

"Wait—these three? Who are the other two?"

Alvídrez zoomed in.

Names of arrested:

Frank Kingman

Parker Richards

Alexander Woolford

Fenway jumped in her chair.

"What is it?" Alvídrez asked.

She pointed at the second name: Parker Richards. "That's Rachel's brother-in-law." And after visiting Rachel in jail, she was supposed to go see him. Fenway swore at herself silently.

Alvídrez paused. "That can't be a coincidence, can it?"

"I need details."

"Yeah, well, it turns out Frank Fantastic was stealing equipment from Parker's workplace. We figured it was to feed their drug habit."

"But Parker didn't go to jail."

"No, he flipped on Frank. Parker got probation and time served, and he lost his job."

"Where did he work?"

"Some computer firm in..." Alvídrez clicked on the screen again and furrowed his brow. "Well, we found the connection."

Fenway leaned toward the screen.

Parker had been fired from Hackson Square.

———

"Fenway?"

The woman's voice at the threshold to Alvídrez's office made Fenway jump.

Oh no. Sheriff Gretchen Donnelly.

"When you're done with Captain Alvídrez, please stop my office."

"Uh," Fenway said, "sure thing."

Donnelly left, striding across the bullpen.

"Uh oh." Alvídrez's gaze lingered on Fenway for a moment. "Called to the principal's office."

"Yeah. I've been—" She couldn't say she'd been avoiding her.

"You've been what?"

The gears in Fenway's head turned. "I didn't want to talk with her until I'd made more headway on the Jericho case."

"Now you can tell her we've found the Hackson Square impostor."

Fenway paused.

Alvídrez cocked his head, glanced up at the open office door, then leaned toward Fenway and lowered his voice. "You don't want to tell her?"

"It's not..." Fenway fumbled for words.

"You don't trust her." He nodded. "I thought it was just me. Something's not right with her, is it?"

"That's what Pondicherry said, too." Fenway let out a sigh of relief.

"She's acting like she has something to hide," Alvídrez said. "Ever since you solved the Cahill murder."

"She could have something personal going on. It might not be related to work."

"Maybe she thinks if Andrew Zellman can be mowed down in front of his building, then none of us are safe."

Fenway screwed up her mouth.

"Yeah, that doesn't feel right to me either," Alvídrez said.

"What do you think the issue is? I mean, I'm not imagining that she's being weird, right?" She pulled her phone out and scrolled to the text from Donnelly, then turned the screen to Alvídrez.

> Congratulations on solving the two murders

"This was when we thought George Pope had killed Jericho, too," Fenway said. "Weird message, right?"

Alvídrez frowned. "I don't see why it's weird. You thought you'd solved both murders, right?"

"Yes," Fenway said. Ugh, this was hard to explain. "It's the way she phrased it. Not *Congratulations on solving the case* or *Congratulations on pulling another killer behind bars.* She said, *solving the two murders.*"

Alvídrez stared blankly at Fenway's screen. "Sorry, you'll have to walk me through it."

Fenway exhaled. "Why make such a simple sentiment so stilted? I think Donnelly was hinting at subtext."

Alvídrez chewed his bottom lip. "Subtext like what?"

"Like—I think she *knew* that George Pope didn't kill Mathis Jericho, but she didn't want the real killer to be caught."

Alvídrez stared at Fenway.

Fenway shifted her weight. "Well, when I say that out loud, I sound like a conspiracy theorist."

"Sometimes, our gut feelings are all we have to go on."

"I guess."

"I'll get this information over to you right away," he said. "That way, you'll have something to distract you after Donnelly tells you whatever she's going to tell you." He grinned. "And look at the bright side—yours is an elected position, so she can't fire you."

"She could recommend a recall."

"She'd fail." Alvídrez smiled. "Now go rip off the band-aid. If you need me, you know where I am."

———

Fenway knocked on Donnelly's open door. "You wanted to see me?"

Sheriff Donnelly nodded and motioned to the seat in front of her. "Come in and close the door behind you."

Uh oh. This *was* like the principal's office.

Maybe Brian Callahan had complained to the sheriff about how Fenway had given him two talkings-to in the last three days.

Maybe she'd found out about Dez's burner phone.

Fenway sat.

Donnelly tapped on her computer for a moment, then stopped, turned her chair to face Fenway straight on, then put her elbows on the desk and steepled her fingers.

"How's the Jericho case going?" Donnelly asked.

"Not much headway," Fenway said. "Lots of pieces that don't fit, but no real leads. But now I—" Fenway paused. How much did Fenway want to reveal?

Frank Fantastic had messed with Cahill Warehouse Storage's recordings. Did Donnelly need to know that Frank had been the one to disable the evidence room cameras too? Especially if Fenway didn't trust her? Fenway promised herself she would tell Dez first thing.

Half the truth, then.

"Just now," Fenway said, "I was in Alvídrez's office, and we got an ID from someone who altered the recorded footage at Cahill Warehouse Storage."

Donnelly narrowed her eyes. "Didn't Seth Cahill mess with the cameras?"

"Not him—this was two weeks ago on Friday. When both Cahill and Jericho were dead."

Donnelly frowned.

"As we know, Callahan dropped Jericho off at the storage place in the mid-morning," Fenway continued, "and a few hours later,

Jericho was killed. I wanted to check the footage at the storage place to see if we could get any idea where Jericho had gone. Did someone pick him up? Did he meet anyone?"

"And what did you find?"

"That the video footage was replaced with other footage—at least a month old," Fenway said.

"A month old?"

"There's a truck in the footage that's been in Texas since late May. We believe he switched out the video so we can't see who cleaned Mathis Jericho's car."

"And you know who did it?"

Fenway shifted in her seat. She could give Donnelly half the information now, but she was certain Donnelly would find out that they'd identified Frank from the sketch—and she would wonder why Fenway hadn't given her the whole story. Ugh.

"The same guy who disabled the cameras in the evidence room on Monday," Fenway said. "His street name is Frank Fantastic. Real name is Frank Kingman."

Donnelly blinked.

"Arrested for a couple of misdemeanors, spent six months in jail. He wore a Hackson Square shirt to get into Cahill Warehouse Storage, too. Same as the evidence room."

Donnelly sat back in her chair and glared at Fenway. "So," she said, "where is this Frank Fantastic now?"

"We're getting his last known address."

"You're not supposed to be working the Zellman case," Donnelly said sharply.

"I'm not," Fenway said. Oof, her tone was more defensive than she wanted it to be. "We discovered that the person who disabled the cameras in the evidence room and the person who altered the footage at Cahill Warehouse Storage were the same person."

"Is this Frank Fantastic person connected to Cahill or Jericho? Or anyone on this case?"

Fenway opened her mouth to say that Frank Kingman *was*

connected to Parker Richards, Rachel's former brother-in-law. But then a chill went down her back.

The first thing that popped into Fenway's head: Donnelly would use this information to keep Rachel locked up—if, in fact, Rachel had been transferred to the women's prison.

The second thing: so much evidence was tangled up between the Mathis Jericho case and the Andrew Zellman case that the two *must* be linked. Frank Kingman using the same Hackson Square shirt to sneak his way into both Cahill Warehouse Storage and the evidence room confirmed that.

And third: the awkward-subtext text from Donnelly.

Fenway wanted to ask Donnelly where Rachel was, but knew Donnelly wouldn't tell her. Either she didn't know, or she'd *pretend* not to know.

Fenway suspected Donnelly had been doing something shady before, but with her line of questioning around Fenway—doing everything she could to keep Fenway away from the Zellman murder and keep Rachel in jail—now she was all but positive.

"We're trying to figure out the connection," Fenway said.

"We?"

"I'm working with Alvídrez. Jericho's body was found with bags of morpheranyl, after all."

Donnelly leaned back and looked at Fenway through narrowed eyes. "Eighteen bags."

"Right." That was... odd. Why was Donnelly specifying the number of bags? Should Fenway tell her there were only sixteen bags in evidence? Had Alvídrez already told her? As much as she didn't trust Donnelly, odds were that she either knew about the missing drugs already or would soon. Fenway opened her mouth, but Donnelly cut her off.

"The connection between Frank Fantastic and Mathis Jericho," Donnelly said.

"Do you have a theory? Or evidence?"

Donnelly studied Fenway's face. The sheriff had the perfect

opportunity to ask Fenway to recuse herself from the Jericho case now that Fenway had established a plausible connection to the Zellman murder. Fenway braced herself.

But instead, Donnelly said, "I wonder if you knew that your father is a big investor in commercial real estate."

"Yeah," Fenway said automatically. "Of course I know that."

"And did you know," Donnelly said, "that he owns four of the commercial properties where Hackson Square leases their locations?"

Fenway said nothing. This was news to her, but she didn't like where Donnelly was going with this. Donnelly had already kept Rachel in jail unnecessarily—against where the evidence pointed her. Was Donnelly trying to railroad Fenway, too?

Then a possibility popped into Fenway's head: she didn't trust Donnelly now, but was the sheriff behind the plan to run Fenway over? And since that didn't work, was Donnelly now trying to lock Fenway up to get her out of the way?

"My father owns half the commercial properties in the county," Fenway said carefully. "He retired from the oil company, but he still has *plenty* of business interests."

"I'm familiar with his investments," Donnelly said. "The legal ones, anyway. And I know he gave you over a hundred thousand dollars back in November."

"You think that was a payment for—what? Drugs?" Fenway glared at Donnelly. "That was to pay off my student loans."

"And he bought you a car."

"He's my father." A battery of explanations lined up in Fenway's head: they'd been estranged for years, and he was making up for lost time; his guilt was having him throw money at the issues—but Fenway didn't owe Donnelly an explanation. If one of her father's expensive lawyers were here, they would probably tell her to shut up.

Donnelly was about to accuse Fenway of something. Drug

running. Maybe Jericho's murder, or maybe even Zellman's. And she sat across from Fenway, sizing her up.

Fenway had options. She could force the issue and ask point-blank if Donnelly was accusing her of something. She could ask, less directly, about evidence she knew about. A good time, perhaps, to mention the missing drugs. And maybe turn the tables a bit on Donnelly.

"Sheriff," Fenway said, "don't you want to know what Frank Kingman did in the evidence room when he was supposedly fixing the cameras?"

"He stole the drugs we found with Jericho's body," Donnelly said calmly.

"Ah. Alvídrez already told you."

"The drugs *you* found with Jericho's body."

Fenway paused. "What does that have to do with anything?"

Donnelly exhaled and looked up at the ceiling, as if deciding a course of action, then lowered her head and looked at Fenway again. "You are disloyal to the sheriff's office, Coroner."

Fenway sucked in a breath. Whatever she thought Donnelly was going to say, that wasn't it. And—why did that hurt so much?

She'd been more-or-less pushed into the coroner position by her father, but she never did his bidding and had pissed him off on more than one occasion.

"If I could be accused of being disloyal to anyone," Fenway said, "it's my father."

Donnelly continued glaring at Fenway. "Maybe that was true a year ago. But it's not true now."

Ah. When McVie—a man Fenway had a romantic interest in—had been sheriff, she'd been loyal. But now that he had moved on, Donnelly was accusing Fenway of disloyalty to the job.

The last thing she wanted to do was bring her love life into the conversation, even if Donnelly was making nothing more than veiled references to it. But there was another way to steer this conversation.

"I work for the people of this county, Sheriff. I don't work for the sheriff's office." She leaned forward. "I don't report to you."

"Then let me rephrase." Donnelly leaned forward, eyes locked with Fenway's. "You are disloyal to the *law*."

Fenway gritted her teeth. "That's a load of bullshit, and you know it."

"Oh," Donnelly said, "you've done a lot to catch killers, no doubt. But maybe the black-and-white of the law has more gray areas for you."

Fenway raised her eyebrows, and a line from her counseling sessions with Dr. Tassajera flashed in her mind: *With abusers, every accusation is a confession.* Was Donnelly about to accuse Fenway of masterminding these murders?

"You found Mathis Jericho's body," Donnelly said.

"I was with Deputy Celeste Salvador."

"Who you were interviewing for the open detective job," Donnelly said. "And who has conveniently disappeared."

Fenway could see where this was headed. Donnelly's theory had Fenway masterminding the morpheranyl trade after Seth Cahill's death, maybe at her father's behest.

"How did you know Jericho would be at Miranda Duchy's cabin?" Donnelly said. "Especially after Deputy Callahan went there and reported nothing out of the ordinary. You were the only one who insisted on going back. What had he done, Fenway? Did he get in the way of you taking over the Nyllie distribution in the county?"

Fenway almost laughed at Donnelly's ridiculous accusation, but she stayed quiet.

"And when you arrested George Pope for Cahill's murder, you threw the Jericho murder in."

"We've all made incorrect assumptions." Fenway wanted to get up and storm out, but she needed to see what she was up against.

"I probably shouldn't say this," Donnelly continued, "but I'm stumped how you involved Celeste in this mess. I kept delaying her transfer to your office. Figured she might roll on you if she didn't report to you. Or if she thought you'd betrayed her by promising the promotion, then not delivering."

"What?" Fenway said. "You're the one who stopped her transfer? HR told me I hadn't submitted the form correctly."

Donnelly arched an eyebrow. "We do what we have to do."

Fenway gritted her teeth. She'd suspected that Donnelly had prevented her from hiring Celeste, but ultimately blamed herself. But no—Donnelly was the reason Celeste left.

Fenway broke the eye contact with Donnelly. Why would the sheriff be making these accusations? Maybe Donnelly knew Fenway suspected her—and this accusation was made to cast doubt on Fenway's suspicions.

"You knew the announcement about the Venn Cartel leaving the county was a ruse," Fenway said. "You thought you'd catch someone trying to take over distribution and maybe you'd catch the murderer, too. And you thought that murderer was me."

"I admit it," Donnelly said. "But all the evidence I have against you is circumstantial."

"What evidence do you have against me?"

Donnelly hesitated, and Fenway could almost see the gears turning in her head. Finally, Donnelly answered. "You admit you were at Rachel's apartment a little before midnight—dropping her off when she was drunk. Fifteen or twenty minutes later, her car runs Zellman over. The next morning, you *conveniently* state that her car wasn't in her assigned parking space when you dropped her off. But perhaps *you're* the one who took Rachel's BMW. You had access to her key, since you had to help her inside."

Fenway said nothing.

"You have an informant, don't you?" Donnelly asked.

Fenway furrowed her brow.

"A drug dealer who gives you information from time to time, right? The name *Alexander Woolford* ring a bell?"

Fenway frowned. "I've never heard that name." But hang on— she *had* heard that name. But where from?

Then it came to her: *Alexander Woolford* had been the third name on the list, arrested alongside Frank Kingman and Parker Richards.

"Maybe you know him as Zoso."

Fenway flinched.

"Yeah," Donnelly said, "I thought so."

CHAPTER TWENTY

Fenway sat in the chair across from Donnelly.

Zoso. He and Parker Richards had given Fenway information two weeks before—maybe a little longer than that—on morpheranyl. Specifically, that Cahill Warehouse Storage was involved in the storage and distribution.

She closed her eyes. What had Zoso said to her?

I don't touch that Nyllie bullshit anymore.

So at some point, he *had* touched that Nyllie bullshit.

Yep. Fenway's confidential informant—or at least a source Fenway had used occasionally—had not only sold Nyllie in the past, but had also been arrested with the man who'd disabled the cameras in the evidence room.

Frank Fantastic had also been arrested with Parker Richards, Rachel's former brother-in-law. Maybe a tenuous connection, but one that would explain Rachel still being in jail—if not for murder, assuming Donnelly suspected Fenway more than Rachel—then for something drug-related. The police had forty-eight hours to arraign Rachel. Tomorrow morning, they'd either charge her or let her go.

No risk in telling Donnelly that she was innocent. If Donnelly were behind the murders of Jericho and Zellman, or if she was simply covering it up, she'd *know* Fenway was innocent. If she'd wanted to arrest Fenway, or kill her, she'd have done so by now. There must be a reason that Fenway was still alive and—for the moment—not in jail.

Fenway opened her eyes. "I get it, Sheriff. I've been known to follow my gut. I draw some, uh, *early* conclusions. And, yeah, following the money is pretty basic."

"Wouldn't be the first time a member of law enforcement got their hand caught in the cookie jar."

Fenway shook her head adamantly. "I had nothing to do with these deaths. Dozens of people saw me when Mathis was supposed to—"

"Doesn't matter if you have alibis or not," Donnelly said. "You could have coordinated the killings through other people. I bet Zoso knows how to contact a hit man with a burner phone who takes cash."

"I'll tell you two things," Fenway said. "First of all, I didn't do this. I didn't kill Jericho, I didn't kill Deputy Zellman, and I didn't coordinate anything."

Donnelly shrugged.

"And the second thing," Fenway said, "is that you have no proof. Because I didn't do it."

Donnelly opened her mouth, then tilted her head and said nothing.

"Besides," Fenway said, despite hearing a generic lawyer's voice in her head telling her to shut up, "I was targeted too." She glared at Donnelly.

Donnelly didn't react for a moment, then leaned forward, her elbows resting on the desk. "You know as well as I do that people paint themselves as targets—with narrow escapes—to throw suspicion off themselves. Particularly people in law enforcement or service jobs. Firefighters who set fire to houses so they can 'save lives.' Nurses who mildly poison themselves to throw off suspicion from killing patients. Cops who shoot themselves, enough to bleed but not enough to cause permanent damage, so they can cover up shooting someone without provocation."

Fenway had suspected Donnelly was involved in the deaths somehow. But now, Donnelly could be behind everything. Donnelly hadn't let Rachel go, even though there was more than enough evidence to show she wasn't involved in Zellman's death—and Donnelly had even said as much in this meeting. Both Zellman and Huke directly reported to her, so Donnelly had access to their schedules, their personnel records, everything.

As sheriff, Donnelly had access to tools that ordinary people didn't. She had access to the cameras, the computers, the evidence room. Her actions would usually be tracked, but she could figure out how to hide her actions from being recorded.

But Fenway and Alvídrez had connected Frank Kingman with the theft of the drugs and the disabling of the cameras. If any connection existed between Kingman and Donnelly, Fenway would find it.

Unless Fenway was too concerned about staying out of jail—and unless Donnelly took her off this case.

Fenway couldn't risk accusing Donnelly of any of this. If Donnelly *was* guilty, and if Fenway accused her, Donnelly would arrest her for sure. At least to keep her out of the way for forty-eight hours. And in jail—well, if another prisoner were to kill a law enforcement representative like Fenway...

She was getting ahead of herself.

And it was time for her to leave.

"Well," Fenway said, rising from the chair, "at least I know you have a reason for not giving me protection."

"Sit down," Donnelly said sharply.

"No," Fenway said. "I don't report to you. You can make wild accusations all you want, but if you arrest me with nothing concrete, I'll make sure my dad's expensive lawyers get involved."

Fenway walked out of Donnelly's office, half-expecting the sheriff to follow her. Once she was down the corridor, she expected a deputy near the front door to stop her, to prevent her from leaving the building.

But Fenway was right: Donnelly *didn't* have any concrete evidence. She was surprised that Donnelly hadn't fabricated anything against her, either; had the roles been reversed and Fenway been a devious supervillain, she would have installed a believable patsy. Especially if she'd been a devious supervillain with the resources at Donnelly's disposal.

Fenway nearly forgot to look both ways before crossing the street to the coroner's suite. She walked so fast, she was almost jogging, and when she pulled the entrance door to the building, she was out of breath.

She was still a target, and if Donnelly wasn't planning to provide protection for her, she had to switch up her routine. Be in a place people wouldn't expect.

But first she had to talk with Sarah.

She paused when she was halfway down the hall so she could catch her breath, then she opened the door to the coroner's suite. Sarah was behind the reception counter.

"Hey, Sarah." Fenway stepped forward and looked up: Callahan sat at his desk, about twenty feet behind Sarah. "I asked Callahan to put a warrant application in for Judge Azurra. He ask you for help?"

Sarah stared at the screen. "No, he hasn't said more than two words to me all morning."

Ugh. Either Callahan hadn't filled out the application yet or he thought he could do it himself. Neither option was ideal.

Fenway lowered her voice. "Sarah, I need a favor. Well, maybe several favors."

Sarah looked up from her monitor. "I'm still trying to find out about Morgan Crane."

"Has he been with the county long?"

Sarah shook her head. "He's been in his current position for two weeks, but I don't know if he transferred internally or was hired from outside. His personnel file online is blocked. And he doesn't have any social media profiles—not Photoxio, not ProfLinks, nothing."

Fenway pressed her lips together. "He's such a throwback, I wouldn't be surprised if he only uses fountain pens and leather-bound notebooks instead of computers."

"Give me something else to do. I don't like running into dead ends."

Fenway nodded. "Look into me."

Sarah blinked. "What?"

"Donnelly suspects that I'm behind the murders of both Jericho and Zellman."

"What?" Sarah said indignantly.

"Keep your voice down," Fenway hissed.

Sarah glanced over her shoulder at Callahan, then turned back to Fenway and mouthed, "Him?"

Fenway leaned closer to Sarah. "He's close with Donnelly. I don't know if I can trust him. Everything I say to him could go right back to the sheriff."

As if he knew they were talking about him, Callahan stood and walked over to them. "Afternoon, Coroner," he said.

"Hi, Brian."

"I'm afraid I've got some bad news. Judge Azurra rejected the warrant application. You were right—he called it a fishing expedition."

Fenway felt a ping of annoyance; she'd asked Callahan to review the application with Sarah before he submitted it. But he had filled out the application himself.

She closed her eyes. *Focus, Fenway.* She could discuss this with him later—and more evidence had come to light, anyway. She took a deep breath and counted to ten, then exhaled. "Turns out we may not need it." There. Her voice was calm.

Callahan raised his eyebrows. "Why not?"

Fenway hesitated—but she'd already told this to Donnelly, so if Callahan ran back to her, what would it matter? "We identified the person who impersonated the Hackson Square worker."

Callahan frowned. "How?"

"Police sketch artist. Turns out a cop in Vice recognized him."

"Who is it?"

Again, information Donnelly already knew. "A guy named Frank Kingman."

Callahan's eyes were wide, his nostrils flared.

"You look surprised, Brian."

"I was trying—" Callahan shifted his weight and looked down. "I should have taken the initiative to show the sketch around. We might have identified him earlier."

This was exhausting. "Yeah, well, live and learn, Brian. Not the end of the world."

Callahan finally looked up. "Mind if we talk for a minute? Maybe in your office?"

Fenway glanced at Sarah, hoping she'd show something on her face that would let Fenway know what Callahan wanted, but Sarah pressed her lips together with the slightest shake of her head. Sarah didn't know.

Fenway suppressed a sigh. She needed to think. She had to solve the Jericho murder before Donnelly kicked her off the case—or arrested her.

"You can go wait in my office, Brian. I'll be there in a minute."

Callahan studied Fenway's face for a brief second, then nodded and walked into Fenway's office.

As soon as Callahan crossed the threshold, Sarah leaned toward Fenway. "Sheriff Donnelly honestly believes you're behind the murders?"

"It's complicated." Fenway ran a hand over her face. "It's possible Donnelly fabricated evidence. So here's the favor I need: can you run a financial check on me, too? See if there are any phantom bank accounts under my name with big payments?"

"Uh, I guess so."

"Like how Rachel had those payments she didn't know about. That's the stuff I'm looking for."

Sarah frowned. "I don't think *Donnelly* fabricated that evidence."

"Well, *someone* put money in Rachel's accounts."

Sarah nodded. "Right—into old accounts she says she didn't even know she had."

"Exactly. Unusual payments could show up in old accounts I don't know about, too." Then Fenway paused. "Hang on a second. Old accounts."

"That's what I said."

In her head, Fenway saw the three names listed on the grand theft complaint.

Names of arrested:
Frank Kingman
Parker Richards
Alexander Woolford

"Parker Richards," Fenway muttered.

"That's Dylan's brother, right?"

"Sure is."

"You want me to bring up his arrest record?"

"Email it to me," Fenway said.

"You going somewhere?"

"After I talk to Callahan, yes. I might have an answer to how drug money ended up in Rachel's account." She turned and walked into her office; Callahan was already sitting in one of Fenway's guest chairs. "You wanted to talk?"

Callahan nodded. "Can you shut the door?"

"Sure." Fenway closed the door, then stepped behind her desk.

"I wanted to apologize for my lack of judgement earlier."

Fenway sat in her desk chair. The silence stretched out for an uncomfortable moment. Finally she spoke. "For not reviewing the warrant application with Sarah like I asked?"

Callahan screwed up his mouth. "Uh, well, yeah, for that too."

"What are you referring to?"

"Going to the storage place to, uh, to get a date with a potential witness in an ongoing investigation." Callahan averted his eyes.

Hmm. She appreciated the apology, but that was unlike Brian. Had someone coached him—had he been told to apologize, even if he didn't mean it?

Maybe Lieutenant Satchel Brookline. He might not have wanted to jeopardize future security side gigs. Could be why Brookline wouldn't look Fenway in the eye when they passed in the hall a half hour before.

Fenway nodded at Callahan. How much did she want to push this? Did she want to make sure the apology was real?

No. If Callahan's apology was forced, she couldn't *make* him be sincere. She could try, perhaps, to tell him his actions would degrade the trust between the sheriff's office and the public. But if he didn't want to hear it, he wouldn't listen.

"Thanks, Brian." But that rang hollow. She leaned back and tried again. "I appreciate your apologies, but that doesn't cancel the consequences for your lack of judgment."

Callahan was quiet.

"If you'd had Sarah review that warrant application, Azurra would have granted it. You're lucky we don't need it, but between showing up late yesterday—"

"I took initiative on getting you that list of Hackson Square employees."

"Yes," Fenway said. "And you did a great job interviewing that security guard at the harbor."

"And you said I needed to wait for the right pitch."

Ah, yes, the Red Sox lecture her father had given her. "Doesn't mean I want you to go rogue. I'm all for second chances, Brian. But getting to a fourth or fifth chance, that'll be a problem."

"Understood." Callahan tightened his jaw. "So let me make this up to you. Now that you know who the Hackson Square impostor is, you want me to go with you to interview him?"

Fenway considered for a moment. Frank Kingman was on the list to talk with, certainly. He had impersonated Hackson Square employees twice now, and he hadn't fled the county after the first time, so he might still be around.

"Tell you what," Fenway said. "I have to go take care of a couple things. You and I can go find Frank Kingman as soon as I get back."

"Shouldn't we find him now?"

Fenway considered. "One thing I've learned—and maybe you've heard this too—is when you're with a suspect, always know the answers to your questions before you ask them."

"That's not always possible."

"No," Fenway said, "but I'm hoping to get some of those answers."

Callahan nodded, wide-eyed. "What can I do when you're gone?" He seemed to genuinely want to make up for his mistakes.

And even though Callahan had been a deputy for several years, this role required more independent thinking. Yes, Fenway was annoyed, and yes, maybe Callahan's missteps were worthy of write-ups, but she had made just as many mistakes on her first case. Maybe more.

"Find out where Frank Kingman is. If he has a day job, see if he showed up for work today. If he's got a significant other, get their address."

"Should I put out a BOLO on his car?"

Fenway hesitated. "I don't want to put him on notice. If he thinks no one knows who he is, he might let his guard down. Make it easier to interrogate him."

"But we should get eyes on him, right?"

Fenway pressed her lips together. "An hour shouldn't make much difference, especially if he's at a day job. Get the information I asked for." She stood. "I'm asking nicely, but I mean it."

"I still think—"

Fenway interrupted. "Brian." Her tone was sharp, a note of warning in it.

Callahan stared at her, then slumped his shoulders. "Sorry. Yes, I'll get on Frank Kingman's location right away."

CHAPTER TWENTY-ONE

FENWAY LEFT THE BUILDING, HER EYES DARTING LEFT AND RIGHT as she hurried to the parking garage.

She wanted a latte even though her pulse was racing, but she figured she could stop at a different coffee place, not the one she always went to. She rushed up the stairs to the second floor, where she'd parked her Accord, then hesitated before dropping into a crouch and looking under her car.

Again, like in her apartment parking lot, she saw no wires or other signs of a bomb. Even so, she steeled herself when she unlocked the door, and her heart raced as she started the car.

The purr of the Accord's engine let her know she hadn't blown up. She let her breath out and took out her phone, then pulled up her email. In the arrest report was Parker Richards's workplace, Il Fagiano, an Italian restaurant on the north side of Estancia that opened at five. And his last known address, the apartment Rachel had mentioned. Fenway tapped on it, popping up the Maps application.

Ten minutes later, she parked on 47th Street in front of the Majestic Arms apartment complex. An icon of a shield sat on the left side of the sign. Whoever had named the complex probably thought of a coat of arms, but *Majestic Arms* made Fenway think of two muscular, hairless forearms, one hand holding a scepter.

Parker's apartment was on the third floor, and there was no elevator. She felt a small twinge in her knee as she got to the third-floor landing. Hopefully, she'd catch Parker before he left for work—it was a few minutes past three o'clock.

She knocked on the door.

Fenway counted to five and knocked again. She opened her mouth to affect a low, powerful voice, commanding Parker to open the door.

Ah, but she'd spoken to Parker before. And you can catch more flies with honey, at least some of the time.

"Parker?" she called out in her sweetest voice. "Parker, baby, are you in?"

If Fenway's gut was correct, Parker would recognize that he knew the voice, but since they'd last spoken two weeks ago—and never in this context—he wouldn't be able to place the voice and the implication of potential romance would get him curious enough to open the door.

She heard fumbling inside, then the door swung open. Parker's look of interested curiosity turned quickly to crestfallen disappointment.

"Oh," he said, "it's you, Coroner." He looked her up and down. "I know you're probably here to bust my ass for something, but damn if you don't look good."

Fenway rolled her eyes. "You're wrong on one count. Yes, I *do* look good, but I'm here to ask you some questions about Frank Kingman, not bust your ass for anything." Well, maybe not, depending on his answers.

"You're here because Rachel's in jail."

"That's right, Parker. And your buddy Frank is in the middle of it."

Parker held his hands up, palms out. "I don't know anything about that."

Fenway stepped to the threshold of the door; not enough to come inside without invitation, but enough so that Parker couldn't slam the door shut. "I think you do, Parker. You deposited money into Dylan's old bank accounts."

Parker hesitated, then shook his head. "I didn't deposit anything."

Fenway studied his face. Maybe Parker was telling the truth, but the way he phrased his answer—*I didn't deposit anything*—made her think he did *something* with Dylan's accounts.

Fenway glared at him. "Your sister-in-law is in jail, Parker."

"You don't know what I've gone through to protect her."

"You haven't been doing a very good job, then."

Parker crossed his arms.

"A cop was murdered," Fenway continued. "And you're standing there telling me that *technically* you didn't deposit anything."

Parker said nothing.

"I've looked the other way about your drug use," Fenway began.

"I told you, I don't do that stuff anymore," Parker said quickly. "Besides, they do drug testing at work. And I'm still employed."

Fenway narrowed her eyes at him. "The Venn Cartel has *something* on you. They're blackmailing—" She stopped, running her tongue over her teeth in thought. "You didn't deposit anything. You gave the Venn Cartel Dylan's checking account information. Maybe you had an old check of his that you deposited through your banking app on your phone, but you still had the paper check in your possession. You get the bank routing number and the account number, anyone can deposit money directly into that account."

Parker averted his eyes. Was she right?

"What does the Venn Cartel have on you?" Fenway asked.

"It's not the Venn Cartel," Parker mumbled.

"Then who?"

Parker was quiet.

Fenway leaned forward. "Someone in law enforcement," Fenway said quietly. "Someone who could make your life a living hell." *Someone like Sheriff Gretchen Donnelly.* Fenway clenched her jaw.

"Please," Parker said, "just go away." He tried to push the door shut, but Fenway blocked it with her foot.

"They tried to kill me," Fenway said. "They tried to run me over, exactly like they killed Andrew Zellman."

Parker's face scrunched up; maybe he didn't know who Zellman was.

"Zellman worked in the evidence room," Fenway said. "And I think he found something he shouldn't have. They killed him for it, and they tried to kill me. So this isn't about me trying to railroad you, Parker. I'm trying to stay alive."

"I want to stay alive, too," Parker said. "Plus, how do I know you're not in on it? Tricking me into revealing information where you know what will happen to me if I talk? No thanks." He stepped forward. "I have to get to the restaurant. Are you going to let me close the door?"

Fenway stepped back and the door closed in her face.

After standing there for a moment, she went down the stairs of the apartment complex. She pulled out her burner phone and called Dez.

"Hey," Dez answered. "Sorry I couldn't take your call earlier."

"Gretchen is gunning for me. She thinks I'm behind the murders of both Andrew Zellman and Mathis Jericho."

Dez said nothing.

"You know already," Fenway said.

"I heard Donnelly's theory," Dez said. "I, uh, I had to follow up on it. But obviously I haven't found anything."

"Not obvious to me," Fenway said. "I spoke with Parker Richards, and he pretty much admitted that he gave Donnelly the banking information for Dylan's old bank account. That's how they established a money trail for Rachel. And if Donnelly is sneaky enough to frame Rachel, don't you think she's sneaky enough to plant evidence incriminating me, too?"

Dez grunted.

"Is that a yes or no?"

"Donnelly might be a lot of things," Dez said. "A terrible manager of personnel. She might be paranoid, although I am too, so I can't count that against her. But I don't think she'd stoop to planting evidence. What possible motive would she have?"

Fenway switched ears. "You know the Venn Cartel has been operating under the radar in Dominguez County for years."

"Likely true," Dez answered.

"Someone's been making sure the drug distribution stays under the radar," Fenway said. "Someone like Donnelly. And Parker Richards said someone in law enforcement made him give Dylan's bank info to them."

"Did he say it was Donnelly?"

"It was someone who could make his life a living hell." Though those had been Fenway's words, not Parker's. And Parker hadn't agreed to it so much as not responded. But if Fenway's assertion had been wrong, he would have at least reacted. Parker didn't have a good poker face.

"Doesn't have to be Donnelly," Dez pointed out. "It could be Alvídrez, or it even could be McVie."

"McVie isn't sheriff anymore."

"You said it's been happening for years, so it started on McVie's watch," Dez said. "And even though McVie hasn't been sheriff for six months, he has enough trusted people in the department where he could have—"

"No," Fenway interrupted, "you don't believe that."

"I'm just saying, you have as much reason to suspect McVie as Donnelly. But you like McVie, and you don't like Donnelly."

"That's not true," Fenway said. "Okay, it's true that I don't like Donnelly, but..." Huh. Dez was right. It didn't *have* to be Donnelly.

Maybe there was someone else in law enforcement who was pulling the strings.

"Do you have any evidence that supports Gretchen being the one behind this? Or anyone else in the sheriff's office?"

Fenway pinched the bridge of her nose in thought. It didn't have to be Donnelly. "Alvídrez," she said. "He runs Vice. He knows the drug trade better than anyone in Dominguez County law enforcement. If anyone could successfully cover up drug running, he could."

"Still not evidence, Fenway."

"Yeah, but you've made me realize I need to broaden my search." Alvídrez's team, too: Detective Jensen. Even the lieutenant in property theft—he'd know how to steal Rachel's car, probably. He'd know all about the Dokko Toccata and its ignition override.

All circumstance and conjecture.

She'd asked Piper yesterday to look into payments made to the sheriff. But Piper had found nothing. Yes, it had only been a day, but she had to broaden the scope to include more law enforcement personnel. She'd let her personal feelings about Donnelly cloud her judgement.

"Maybe you can tell Donnelly the same thing," Fenway said into the phone. "Tell her not to hyperfocus on me just because she doesn't like me."

"Yeah, I'm not telling her that," Dez said. "I won't find any evidence when I investigate you, right?"

"Not unless someone planted evidence against me."

"Don't make me look like a fool on this, Fenway."

"Same here." She cleared her throat. "We found the guy who impersonated the Hackson Square employee and got access to the evidence room. Brian and I are headed over there as soon as I track down a few more things."

Dez cackled. "Guess where Donnelly asked me to go?"

"To track down Frank Kingman."

"Ding, ding! You win first prize."

"Where?" Fenway asked.

"Veniright Software Technologies down on Augustine Boulevard."

"Just outside downtown. Will you keep me posted?"

"If I can make a call without people looking over my shoulder."

A couple of seconds of silence before Fenway spoke again. "Feels almost like we're in a spy movie, doesn't it?"

"Not even close." Dez chuckled. "But at least this job's always interesting."

"That's a curse if I ever heard one."

————

Fenway walked in the door to McVie Investigations.

Piper turned from her computer and grimaced.

"Nothing on Donnelly yet?"

"Well…" Piper hesitated. "No payments that can't be explained. Still leaves cash, but she hasn't made any bank deposits. At least none that I can find. I didn't want to go down the rabbit hole of accounts under shell companies or in the Cayman Islands."

"Right." Fenway nodded. "I think I might have been a little too laser-focused on Sheriff Donnelly."

Piper arched an eyebrow.

"I got some information that *someone* in law enforcement started the ball rolling on planting financial evidence in Rachel's account—well, in Dylan's old account, the one where you found the debit card."

"Glad to be of service," Piper asked. "Who else do you want to look at?"

"Low-hanging fruit first," Fenway replied. "The detectives in Vice would have visibility into the morpheranyl distribution. Given the right motivation, at least one of them could cover it up."

"Alvídrez too?"

Fenway thought of Alvídrez and her leaving Dos Milagros and

Fenway almost getting struck by the Dokko Toccata. He could have easily pinged someone that Fenway was coming out of the taquería. "Alvídrez too," Fenway said quietly.

"I haven't found anything on him yet, but I can keep looking." Piper turned to her computer and brought up a notepad, typing quickly. "Who else?"

"I don't know. I thought about the property theft team. Led by Lieutenant Satchel Brookline." Fenway rubbed her chin. "He was with Callahan at a private event the night Zellman was killed, though."

Piper nodded. "I can still check for payments that stick out, though."

Fenway closed her eyes. "You know, if I'm right, and someone in law enforcement was purposely looking the other way while morpheranyl was coming into the county, it started happening when McVie was sheriff."

Piper pursed her lips.

But—no. McVie didn't have the money of someone who'd been taking kickbacks from a drug cartel. He hadn't even had the money to move back to Estancia from Colorado.

"What started happening when I was sheriff?"

Fenway looked up; McVie stood in the doorway to his office. She swallowed hard. "Hi, Craig. I didn't realize you were here."

McVie nodded. "I'm getting ready to follow a client's wife home from work. See if she makes any stops along the way." He took a step forward. "What happened when I was sheriff?"

Fenway hesitated, then spoke. "Morpheranyl trafficking," she said. "From what we know, Cahill Warehouse Storage was where the Venn Cartel kept the morpheranyl until it could be packaged and shipped out."

McVie nodded. "That's why we brought on Steve Alvídrez. I wasn't too involved in the hiring process, although I did have an interview with him."

"Do you trust him?"

McVie looked at Fenway out of the corner of his eye. The look said, *I don't trust him with my girlfriend.*

Almost cute that McVie was jealous. And McVie seemed to have moved on from Fenway not telling him she was almost run over. Her apology had been sincere, and maybe it had been enough.

"I don't have any reason to think that he did anything shady," McVie said. "He busted a couple of heroin dealers. Shut down a few meth labs out near P.Q. But I can't vouch for the guy's character or anything."

Piper, meanwhile, kept typing, then spun around in her chair. "You asked about Satchel Brookline too, right?"

"Right."

"I didn't find anything in his background. But you might want to know that his credit card was used to pay for gas at a WX Fuel station off I-5 on Monday night, 11:37 PM."

Fenway nodded. "I'm not supposed to be on the Zellman case, but that would give him an alibi." And confirm Callahan's too.

Piper squinted at the screen. "About an hour-and-a-half drive from here. I suppose it's possible, if he did eighty-five or ninety all the way, that he *could* have made it to Morongo Heights and been the behind the wheel of the hit-and-run when Zellman was killed. If the time of death is at the tail end of the window."

"Would Brookline have had time to..." Fenway rubbed her chin. That timeline didn't match the witness statements, though—the loud sounds at Zellman's apartment building after midnight. Plus, Rachel's car wasn't in her parking space at that time. "When I dropped Rachel off, it was a little before, right?"

Piper shrugged. "You'd already dropped me off. I got home about eleven forty."

"Even if I took fifteen minutes to get to Rachel's," Fenway said, "the BMW was gone by then. Brookline couldn't have gone from that WX Fuel station to Rachel's apartment and stolen the BMW. He wouldn't have time."

Unless I was lying about what time I dropped off Rachel. Fenway saw why Donnelly suspected her.

"Or," Piper said, "Brookline didn't go with the others. Maybe he gave them his credit card, said gas was on him, but he didn't go."

Fenway shrugged. "I suppose there are all kinds of ways for people to establish false alibis. We could get location information from his phone."

Piper nodded. "I could do that."

"You don't work for the county. And you don't have a warrant."

"Do you want to know or not?"

Fenway *did* want to know, but if Piper found out, she couldn't use it in court. If Brookline—or any other law enforcement officer, for that matter—found out what Fenway had done, the trust would be entirely broken. Plus, if the shoe were on Donnelly's foot and she had tracked Fenway's phone, Fenway would have made official complaints until Donnelly was forced to resign.

"I don't want to find out that way."

And no judge would let Fenway go on that fishing expedition, either, especially against a fellow law enforcement officer. She'd need some real evidence.

Doesn't mean she couldn't get Callahan to prepare another warrant application, though. Good practice for him. Callahan had thought detective work was all excitement and investigative work, when sixty percent of the job was paperwork.

"Thanks, Piper," Fenway said. "Text me when you get any information."

"Will do." Piper grinned. "Put it on your tab?"

"Yes." Fenway turned to the door, reached for the handle, then stopped.

She had to clear the air with McVie. Her life *was* in danger, and she'd already apologized, but somehow it didn't feel like enough.

Fenway had had enough difficult conversations over the last few days to last her a lifetime. Grown-up manager conversations with Brian, grown-up work conversations with Donnelly, and now grown-up relationship conversations with McVie. This was exhausting.

"Craig," she said, "do you have a minute?"

"Yes."

She went into his private office, and he followed, closing the door behind him.

———

McVie walked behind the desk and looked at Fenway expectantly.

"Um," Fenway began, "it's obvious things have been weird between us since I—I didn't accept your proposal."

She stopped, and when he said nothing, she continued. "And then I screwed up by not telling you I'd had an attempt on my life."

"Oh, no," McVie said, "look, don't worry about—"

Fenway held up her hand. "I appreciate that you've moved past it, or whatever, but if the roles had been reversed, and someone had tried to kill you, and you didn't tell me?" Fenway shook her head. "I would be—well, maybe I'd be angry, but I'd be hurt. Hurt that you didn't trust me, that you wouldn't let me in, that I didn't matter to you."

McVie looked down at his desk.

She paused, then sat in the guest chair in front of McVie's desk. "I love you, and I don't think I've ever been in love before." She closed her eyes. "Ever. And it scares me."

"I know—"

Fenway's phone rang in her purse. She ignored it.

"Let me get this out, Craig." She swallowed hard. "I will screw up, because I've never been in a relationship like this before. I have trust issues. I have commitment issues. And you've got a daughter who's the most important thing in the world to you, and she's trying to break us up, and I... it's a lot. I'm trying to do the right thing."

Fenway's phone stopped ringing, and she took a deep breath

and soldiered on. "I love that you fight for Megan the way my father never fought for me. But I'm trying to navigate that. I'm trying to navigate how important I am to you, even though I come after Megan."

"This isn't a competition—"

Fenway's phone rang again.

"I know," Fenway said, digging in her purse. "I know, I know, I know. But sometimes I'm concentrating so much on being okay with where I am in your life, I forget you need to be okay with where you are in mine." She grabbed the phone: a call from Sarah. She probably had the results of Fenway's financial reporting she'd asked for earlier. Important, but it could wait a few minutes. She tapped *Send to voicemail* and returned her gaze to McVie.

He looked up, right into Fenway's eyes, and nodded.

"I meant to tell you all this in Colorado," Fenway said. "And I mean it when I say what we have is the best I've ever had." She took a deep breath. "And I don't want to lose it. But you need to understand I'm a beginner. I need to play the first few hands with the cards face up."

McVie softened his gaze and reached a hand out to her. She took it.

Fenway's phone rang again.

"Oh, for fuck's sake," Fenway said. Sarah again. She pulled her hand away and tapped *Answer.* "Hey, I'm in the middle of—"

"It's Deputy Huke," Sarah said. "Someone attacked him in the evidence room."

CHAPTER TWENTY-TWO

Fenway, with McVie in the passenger seat, pulled the Accord into a fifteen-minute visitor's spot in front of the sheriff's office and ran into the building. McVie followed a few steps behind.

She sprinted past Gretchen Donnelly's office toward the evidence room—

And there stood the sheriff.

"Coroner," Donnelly said icily.

Fenway put her hands on her hips. "You can't think I attacked Deputy Huke."

Donnelly raised her eyebrows. "I know you weren't in your office."

"Because I was in the field gathering information on the Mathis Jericho murder," Fenway said.

"Can anyone verify that?"

Fenway hesitated, but figured the truth would come out eventually anyway. "Parker Richards."

Donnelly scowled. "Dammit, Fenway, that's not the Jericho case."

"It absolutely is." Fenway folded her arms indignantly, even though Parker had much more to do with the Zellman case than the Jericho case. "A friend of his screwed with the camera footage of the day Mathis Jericho was killed. We needed to know where to find him."

"You spoke to me about Frank Fantastic already. Was he not at his last known address?"

"We wanted to know what was waiting for us," Fenway said. "I don't know anything about why he did it, if he was dangerous, what his motives might be—"

"So instead, you give his friend a heads-up? So he can warn Frank?"

Fenway paused. Had she even mentioned Frank during the conversation with Parker? She thought she had, but pushed the narrative that Parker was behind the payments to Dylan's accounts —and if she said that, Donnelly would know for sure she was investigating the Zellman murder.

Screw it. She was running the investigation into Jericho's death, not Donnelly. She balled her hands into fists. "I don't report to you."

Donnelly flinched, then immediately regained her composure. "I could bring this up in front of the city council."

"Then do it," Fenway said. "Or better yet, arrest me for attacking Huke. I've got two witnesses for the last hour, and Parker will tell you I was interviewing him."

"And did you get any information, or did you simply allow Richards to warn his friend that we were looking for him?"

Fenway cleared her throat, then decided to ignore the snarky question. "We had a lot of evidence in the evidence room for the Jericho case, and I want to make sure Deputy Huke is all right."

Donnelly stepped in front of the evidence room door, blocking it with her body. "Deputy Huke has a concussion. He's at St. Vincent's."

Fenway's eyes widened.

"It's a good thing your detective was here," Donnelly said.

"Dez?"

"Brian," Donnelly said. "The assailant didn't expect two people in the evidence room."

"Is Brian okay?"

"Just bruised his ego. The attacker pushed him out of the way."

"Did Brian see—"

"Whoever it was wore a mask."

"Where's Brian now?"

"Giving his statement," Donnelly said. "Why don't you go back to the coroner's office and meet him when he's done?"

Fenway spun on her heel and walked out, McVie following her.

"Hey," he said.

Fenway ignored him and quickened her pace.

"Hey," McVie repeated, "did Parker say that Il Fagiano did drug testing?"

Fenway looked at McVie. "What?"

"You said Parker doesn't do drugs anymore because they test at his work. Is that right?"

"That's what Parker said."

"I know the former head chef there. Il Fagiano *doesn't* do drug testing."

"Maybe they didn't when you were sheriff, but they do now." Fenway opened the door to the plaza.

McVie shook his head. "Will you slow down?"

"I have to get away from her." Fenway whirled around to face McVie and pointed over his shoulder at the sheriff's office. "*She* is the reason Huke got attacked. Donnelly thought I planned all this, and she took her eye off the ball." She scowled. "Or maybe she's the one behind everything from the beginning. Just because we haven't found a money trail doesn't mean she doesn't have one."

"I'm talking about Parker Richards right now," McVie said.

"And he said—"

"At least see if Parker has another job somewhere else that actually does drug testing. Lots of people work two jobs."

———

Fenway and McVie walked through the glass entrance doors. The maître-d' looked up from his podium. "Good evening, and welcome to Il Fagiano. Do you have a reservation?"

Wednesday night—and it was only five fifteen. What were the chances of an open table? "We don't," Fenway said.

"Not a problem, not a problem," the maître-d' said. "At least this isn't a weekend. Let me see what we have available."

"Thank you."

He turned and walked down the aisle between the leather booths.

McVie gaped at the mahogany columns and the marble floor. "I'm not sure I can afford a place like this. It's like Maxime's, only more ostentatious."

Fenway grinned. "My treat. I've wanted to see if this place was as good as it thinks it is."

"We should interview Parker and get out of here. We can go to Dos Milagros."

"If Parker's part of the waitstaff, he can't get away from us if we're paying customers."

"He can and he will, and then we'll have to stay through dinner and pay."

"Oh, come on, Craig, we've got to eat."

"We can eat somewhere that takes fifteen minutes, not two hours."

A good point.

The maître-d' reappeared. "A thirty-minute wait."

Fenway pulled out her badge. "We'll take a rain check on dinner, but I need to speak with Parker Richards."

A huff. "Mr. Richards is with customers at the moment. I'm afraid I cannot—"

"It'll only be a minute or two," Fenway said. "I can come back here with a warrant, but I'm not sure you want that. My colleague tells me there's no drug testing here, and if your waitstaff is taking—"

"Lower your voice," the maître-d' said. "Yes, you may have five minutes with Mr. Richards."

He led them into a room off the kitchen, and a moment later, he brought Parker in. "Five minutes," he hissed.

Parker glared at Fenway. "What is this?"

"You told me you have to get tested for drugs at your job."

Parker exhaled. "Yeah."

"But they don't test here. So you have another job."

Parker was quiet.

"Where they test you for drugs? What's your second job, Parker?"

Parker looked around the room, as if he were trying to escape.

"We can find out. Might take us a day or two, and we'll be pissed off, but—"

"AutoShack, okay?" Parker hissed.

"AutoShack." Fenway tilted her head. "They've got a machine that duplicates car key fobs, right?"

Parker said nothing for a moment.

"You'd get fired if anyone finds out you duplicated a key that didn't belong to the person who brought it in, right? I need a name, Parker."

Parker looked down at the floor. "Man, you're going to get me killed."

"We can put you in protective custody."

"Where I'll lose *both* my jobs," Parker said. "And I don't think you can protect me there, either."

Fenway studied Parker's face, but he kept staring at the ground, his face impassive. "Who asked you to make a duplicate of Rachel's BMW key?"

Parker pressed his lips together.

"Was it Sheriff Donnelly? Maybe Captain Alvídrez from Vice?"

Parker shook his head. "You really don't know, do you?"

"No, Parker, I don't. That's why I'm asking you."

"Arrest me if you want. I'm not getting killed over this." He took a step toward the door. "I'm getting back to my customers before I start losing tips."

———

"That was a waste of time," Fenway said, walking back to the Accord.

"No it wasn't," McVie said. "You know for certain someone in law enforcement is behind this now. And that Rachel's key was duplicated, not stolen. You have a lot more information than before."

"Doesn't narrow the suspects much," Fenway said. "Donnelly, Steve Alvídrez, Jensen or someone else in Vice?" Fenway sighed. "If I weren't me, I'd put myself on the list, too." She paused. "And we know it's someone powerful. Hell, it could be my father. Sheriff Donnelly would love that."

"Whoever it is," McVie said, "they've got Parker scared for his life. And they got him to risk his AutoShack job to copy Rachel's BMW key."

Fenway unlocked the Accord. "That doesn't get us much closer. Rachel left her keys in her purse in her office, and anyone could have gone in there to get them." They got in the car.

"True." McVie put his seat belt on. "We could go to AutoShack, see what time Parker used the machine that didn't have a customer attached to it."

Fenway started the engine. "I'm not sure that would help us. First, we know the law enforcement person is working with Frank Kingman at the very least. Maybe others in law enforcement too."

Fenway put her blinker on to pull onto the street, then stopped. "The sheriff's theory about my involvement in the murders makes a good story. There's no evidence behind it, but it has a certain, uh, narrative flow."

"And just like Donnelly doesn't have evidence for you, you don't have evidence—"

"Parker's given me a lot of information," Fenway said. "But he isn't connecting it to a name."

"Maybe Huke would recognize who hit him?" McVie said. "I assume that's how he got his concussion, anyway."

"I'm sure the sheriff's office is asking him those questions," Fenway said. "Right now, let's see if Callahan can tell us anything."

"It's past five thirty. You think he's still in the office?"

"He better be. He didn't start until after nine, and he took a lunch."

"Callahan made his statement, right?"

"Yes, but we can see if he left anything out."

McVie nodded. "And I hired him. He trusts me. Maybe he'll say something in front of me that he wouldn't in an official statement."

They got back to the coroner's office in ten minutes. Fenway pulled into a street parking space two blocks away from the parking garage, and McVie didn't even raise an eyebrow to ask why.

Fenway hurried to her building, McVie rushing to keep up with her. He followed at her heels, then quickened his pace to walk next to her. "Hey, slow down."

"I want to get this case—"

"Someone's following us. Well, probably you."

Fenway started to cast her eyes over her shoulder—

"Don't look," McVie hissed. "Well-dressed guy. Older, Black. Maybe six feet—"

"That's ADA Pondicherry's assistant, Morgan Crane. You don't know him?"

"I knew Jennifer Kim. Pondicherry was in PQ when I was sheriff. And I never met his assistant."

"Yeah, I thought he was following me earlier today, too."

McVie furrowed his brow. "Morgan Crane. And you didn't—" Then he snapped his mouth shut.

And you never mentioned that a guy was following you. That's what McVie would have said.

Just as well that he didn't say it.

"He followed me into the building, but not into my office suite," Fenway said. "He probably had business elsewhere. IT is in the building too. Maybe Pondicherry's having issues with his laptop or something."

"Maybe." McVie took his phone out, keeping one eye on the walkway ahead of him and one eye on his phone.

"Who are you texting?"

"Piper."

"Oh, you want her to look into this Morgan Crane guy, too?"

"You're casting a wide net, aren't you? Might as well add Pondicherry and Crane to the list."

"Pondicherry is on my side," Fenway said.

"Why do you say that?"

Fenway thought for a moment. The walkway ended at the building, and McVie reached out and opened the door for Fenway.

"I don't know," Fenway said quietly, as she stepped into the hallway.

McVie nodded. "Then Pondicherry goes on the list, too."

The door closed behind them and McVie leaned toward Fenway. "Crane is still following us."

Fenway nodded. "Sarah already found out Crane doesn't have a job history or any social media presence. Piper might have to dig a bit."

They opened the door to the coroner's suite.

"Craig!" Sarah said. "Good to see you!"

"You're working late."

"In the middle of an investigation, all hands on deck, right?"

"Sheriff!" Callahan said from his desk, rising to his feet. "I haven't seen you in forever."

"It's been a while," McVie said. "And it's not 'sheriff' anymore."

"Right. You're a civilian now."

"You can go home," Fenway said to Sarah.

Sarah glanced back at Callahan. "You sure?"

Fenway thrust her chin at McVie.

Sarah nodded, then leaned forward and spoke in a low voice. "There's a huge deposit in your financial records back in November."

"A hundred thousand dollars from my father," Fenway said. "He felt guilty, so he paid off my college loans."

"Oh. Yeah, that would be it."

"Anything else?"

"Not that I can find. But I'm no forensic accountant."

"Thanks for doing that, Sarah. Now, go home."

"Have a good night." She set her PC to sleep, grabbed her purse, and walked out of the coroner's suite.

As soon as the door closed behind her, McVie stepped around the counter, his big strides taking him to Callahan's desk. "Good to see you."

"Likewise."

"Listen," McVie said, "I heard you and Huke got attacked today."

Callahan shook his head. "Not me. The guy pushed me out of the way. I think he'd already hit Huke on the back of the head by the time I came up to the door."

"You have any idea if he stole anything from evidence?"

Callahan shook his head. "No, sir."

McVie nodded, then sat on the edge of Callahan's desk. "You gave your statement?"

Callahan glanced at Fenway, then back to McVie. "That's right."

"Did you see his face?"

"He had a mask on. About, uh, five-ten maybe. I think he was white, but maybe Latino. Didn't have too much skin exposed. And it happened fast—I came around the corner to the open door, and he pushed past me, knocking me to the ground. By the time I realized what happened, he'd already run out the door."

"We should have that on camera, right?" McVie asked.

Fenway was silent.

"Wait—you *don't* have that on video?" McVie said. "Why not?"

"You didn't tell him?" asked Callahan.

"No, of course not," Fenway snapped. "He's a civilian now, and you don't go around telling civilians that the cameras in your evidence room were sabotaged."

"I'm not sure I'd call it *sabotage*," Callahan said.

"Maybe I'd call it theft," Fenway said. As soon as the word *theft* was out of her mouth, she thought of Lieutenant Brookline—he investigated property theft, and this certainly fit the bill.

McVie crossed his arms. "Just in the evidence room? The cameras are still operational in other parts of the facility, though, right?"

"I don't know," Fenway answered. She looked at Callahan. "Have you heard anything?"

Callahan shook his head.

McVie dropped his hands to his side. "Okay, Brian, you know, sometimes when you're being questioned, you stick to facts. But that means you can leave out stuff you don't think is important, or things you aren't sure of. And sometimes walking—even if it's across the street from the sheriff's office to here—can help jog your memory." He paused. "Do you remember anything else? Doesn't matter how small. The color of the vinyl floor. Maybe a smell you didn't recognize. Or a sound—the guy might have made a grunt when he pushed you."

"I didn't see much of anything."

"Close your eyes," McVie encouraged. "See yourself on the floor, after you've been pushed. You open your eyes. What do you see?"

Callahan shifted his weight. "I don't know. Maybe the floor."

"What color is it?"

Callahan paused. "Beige."

"And what do you smell?"

"Uh—nothing." He shook his head. "I apologize, Sheriff. I'm embarrassed I don't remember any of this stuff."

"It's okay, Brian." McVie reached out and patted Callahan's shoulder. "Maybe it'll come back to you. But if you blocked it out, that's a reasonable stress reaction."

"I'm a cop," Callahan said. "I shouldn't have a stress reaction."

McVie chuckled. "Even cops are human. For instance, you've called me 'sheriff' twice now. And I haven't been sheriff for months."

"Sorry. Feels weird to call you 'Mr. McVie.'"

"I call you Brian. You can call me Craig."

Callahan nodded and stared straight ahead. Then, "Coroner, would you be okay if I left a little early to go see Deputy Huke? I feel terrible that he's in the hospital and it's because of me."

Fenway opened her mouth—because of him? Oh, right, Callahan had been there too, but got pushed out of the way while the assailant attacked Huke, and of course Callahan was blaming himself.

She looked at her watch. Maybe she could relent and give him a little time off. "Sure, and say hi to him from me." She paused. "Is he awake?"

"Doctors don't want him talking," Callahan said. "He doesn't remember the attack." He turned to Fenway. "You're not coming?"

"I think I should let Melissa and his friends and family be with him for tonight." Maybe Huke would remember more tomorrow. She looked at McVie. "Maybe we'll get him some flowers or something."

"Yeah," Callahan said. "Donald loves flowers. That for sure won't be a waste of money."

Fenway grinned, though a bit sadly. "Go ahead," Fenway said. "Get out of here."

Callahan reached up and clicked his monitor off.

"Maybe we'll walk you out," McVie said.

Fenway furrowed her brow. Did they need to do that? Fenway

had spent enough time looking over Callahan's shoulder on the Jericho investigation. But McVie didn't catch the questioning glance.

"Uh, sure," Callahan said. He stood. "Actually, you go ahead without me. I have to make a pit stop before I head home."

"I thought you were going to the hospital."

He clicked his tongue. "That's what I meant. It's been a weird day."

"Great," said McVie. "Come on, Fenway, let's head out."

"I should check my email—"

"We've got six o'clock reservations," McVie said. "Come on, let's go."

"I need to lock up…"

"Brian, you can lock up after us, right?" McVie winked at Callahan. "Don't want to be late for our reservation at Maxime's."

Fenway raised her eyebrows. "Uh—all right. I'm not one to refuse a nice dinner." Even if she would be the one paying for them both.

McVie hurried over to the double doors to the coroner suite, then opened it. Fenway had to rush through the door.

She turned to McVie. "This is a nice surprise."

"If you thought that was a surprise," McVie said, "wait till you hear we're not going to Maxime's."

"Oh." Fenway should have known that McVie didn't have time to make a reservation. "Then where? Dos Milagros? The new Indian place? I'll break up with you if you say All Access Burger."

"Even better," McVie said. "The evidence room."

CHAPTER TWENTY-THREE

McVie and Fenway walked out of the building toward City Hall. "We'll never be able to get in the evidence room, Craig," Fenway said. "It's locked up tight, and I know I'm the coroner and everything, but Gretchen won't let me in there without starting World War Three."

"We're not going *in* the evidence room," McVie said. "We're going *to* the evidence room."

"If I'm going to investigate the Mathis Jericho murder," Fenway said as they crossed the street, "I want to talk to this Frank Fantastic person. Now that I know Parker gave Dylan Richards' banking information to someone in law enforcement—I bet Frank is working with that same person."

"I'll tell you right now that Piper hasn't found any weird financial transactions with either Gretchen *or* Steve Alvídrez," McVie said as they reached the City Hall side of the street.

Fenway hesitated, then blurted, "I know Captain Alvídrez is into me, but I swear I haven't done anything with him. I haven't encouraged him at all."

McVie looked at Fenway. "I know that. You think I'm mad at you because another man thinks you're gorgeous?"

"I don't know that he thinks I'm *gorgeous*—"

McVie chuckled. "Yeah, trust me, he does. I know you have to work with him, and I know it puts you in a weird position, because you don't want to reject him in case he makes your work life harder." McVie glanced at Fenway as they crossed the plaza toward the sheriff's office. "If you think it'll help, I'll talk to him, but I think it's more like a crush than him actually wanting to break us up. He's rebounding from a divorce, and you're nice to him. Guys confuse that for attraction all the time."

Fenway was quiet.

"You think he's crossed the line into creepiness."

A quick intake of breath. "No, no, it's not that."

"That wasn't a question, Fenway. I can tell. You think he's crossed the line."

"I don't—"

"I didn't ask you if you wanted to testify, and I didn't ask you to prove anything to me. I'm not defending him. I'm not telling you that you 'must have misunderstood.' You think he crossed a line, and from the photographs Megan keeps sending me, I think he has, too."

"Wait—she's sent you more photos?"

"Her friends from school take pictures of the two of you together," McVie said, "And Megan forwards them to me."

Fenway's upper lip curled. "That's—"

"That's not okay," McVie said firmly. "I'm deleting them without looking at them now. But, like you said, Megan's doing what she can to break us up, and it's not like I can ground her from three states away. I'm glad I've been talking to my therapist for the last couple of weeks. Otherwise, I might react the way Megan wants me to."

"You're seeing a therapist?"

"Of course," McVie said.

"How come..."

"How come I didn't tell you?" McVie cracked a smile as they reached the sheriff's office building. "Never came up. And I couldn't figure out how to tell you without sounding like I was either bragging or complaining."

Fenway reached out and opened the door. "After you, Mr. McVie."

They stopped talking as they entered the building. McVie signed in at the front desk and spoke with the officer behind the counter for half a minute. Fenway again marveled at how easy McVie found it to talk to former co-workers, people who were barely acquaintances, even complete strangers. She took a step down the hallway toward the evidence room, and McVie caught her eye and wrapped up his conversation.

They walked down the hall. McVie had a light hand on Fenway's elbow—and turned the corner to the evidence room. Yellow police tape covered the entrance, and two deputies stood in front of the locked door—talking to Captain Steve Alvídrez.

Fenway startled. Fortunately, she and McVie had wrapped up their conversation about Alvídrez before entering the sheriff's office building. He turned his head and nodded. "Good evening, Coroner. Craig, good to see you again."

"Likewise, Steve. How's—" McVie paused, then cleared his throat. "I would ask how the investigation is going, but I'm not sheriff anymore."

Alvídrez chuckled, a hint of nervousness in his laugh. "Coroner, can I borrow you for a moment?"

Fenway glanced at McVie, who tilted his head and gave a slight nod.

"Sure," Fenway said.

Fenway followed Alvídrez. Three detectives sat in the Vice bullpen, and the light was on in Alvídrez's office. Alvídrez took a seat behind his desk and motioned for Fenway to sit in front of his desk.

Fenway leaned forward in her chair.

Alvídrez placed his hands flat on the table, then took a breath and spoke firmly but quietly. "Look, I'm really sorry if I said anything unprofessional."

"Oh."

"Yes," he continued, "I asked a few people if you and Craig were still together. I mean, if you were single, I probably would have asked you out. But you're not, so I won't. And we can still work together. We have a good working relationship, right?"

Fenway pressed her lips together. "Let's talk about this later, Captain. We've got a full-fledged attack on our evidence room—and the people who are in charge of it. We can discuss the personal—"

"I apologize, Coroner," Alvídrez said. "That's all I wanted to say. I can't deny I'm attracted to you, but I thought I was being professional."

She paused.

He ran his hand through his hair. "I know you're with Craig. And that he's back in town, and I won't do anything to, uh, make you feel...."

"Awkward and weird?" Fenway gave Alvídrez a smile. "Like now?"

"Yeah, okay," Alvídrez said. "Point taken."

"Great," Fenway said. She started rising from her seat, then paused and sat back down. "Did you see or hear anything unusual this afternoon?"

Alvídrez's forehead creased. "During Deputy Huke's attack?"

"That's right."

"No." He pursed his lips. "And I'm disappointed in myself. We're a hundred feet away from the evidence room and none of us knew anything was wrong." He tilted his head. "Wait—if you're investigating this as the coroner, is Donald Huke—"

"I'm not investigating this," Fenway said quickly. "And last I heard, Huke isn't in danger. But I can't help wondering if his attacker is the same person who tried to run me over." Or killed

Andrew Zellman, of course, but Fenway wasn't investigating that, either.

"I wish I could help," Alvídrez said. "Property theft already asked the team what we saw and heard this afternoon. We couldn't tell anything then, either."

"Thanks anyway, Captain." Fenway stood. "You have a good night."

"You too."

Fenway met Alvídrez's eyes for a split second, then turned and walked out through the Vice bullpen.

———

Fenway found McVie still in front of the evidence room.

He looked over. "Ready?"

"Yep."

They walked down the hall. "Okay," Fenway murmured into McVie's ear. "Why did you bring me over here?"

"Because," McVie said, "something doesn't add up. Masked man hits Huke over the head. Huke wouldn't let that happen without a fight."

"We don't know if he fought back or not."

"No," McVie agreed. "But it's not like Huke to turn his back on an assailant. And the cage was open, which suggests—"

"A law enforcement person," Fenway said. "You think the same person who got the payment info from Parker and who hired Frank Kingman to dress up like a Hackson Square employee knocked out Huke, pushed Callahan down, and then—then what?"

"It's the sheriff's office," McVie said. "By definition, it's crawling with cops. So how better to blend in than to remove their mask and jacket? If they stole something from evidence, they could pop it in their pocket if it was small enough."

"And if it wasn't small enough?"

"Then they'd hide it in the same place they stuck their mask and jacket." McVie shook his head. "It's not like a high school where there are lockers down every corridor, though."

Oof, this hit Fenway hard—McVie was old enough to go to high school when most kids still used lockers.

"And why didn't you tell Callahan where we were going?"

"Because," McVie said, "You suspect Gretchen, and I'm pretty sure Callahan tells Donnelly everything."

"I'm glad my paranoia has rubbed off on you," Fenway said. "If Sheriff Donnelly knew you and I were over here..."

McVie nodded. "Gretchen's office is down the hall from the evidence room. If she'd done it, she'd be able to go into her office, hide everything in her desk or a filing cabinet, and sit behind her desk like she'd been there the whole time."

"And what about Alvídrez?"

McVie considered for a moment. "He could have done it too, though not as easily."

Fenway considered this for a moment. "He'd have to walk through the Vice bullpen to get to his office. That's a lot of explaining he'd have to do."

"The captain walking through the bullpen to get to his office? No explanation needed." McVie rubbed his chin.

"He said he didn't see or hear anything when Deputy Huke was attacked." Which he'd say if he'd been the one doing the attacking, right?

"Let's look for a hiding place near *this* hall," McVie said.

Fenway pointed at a grate on the wall a foot above the baseboard. "A ventilation duct?"

McVie tilted his head. "Might as well give it a shot. And a screwdriver is easy to conceal."

Fenway bent down and tried to hand-loosen the screws on the sides of the grate. "I don't think anyone has touched these for a while."

"No harm in making sure." McVie pulled a Swiss Army knife out of his pocket and handed it to Fenway.

"And you say you're not a Boy Scout," Fenway muttered, taking the knife and opening the Phillips-head screwdriver. The screws were old, but Fenway was able to loosen both of them. The grate came off easily in her hand.

"Nothing," Fenway said.

"Might be further in," McVie suggested.

Fenway reached a hand in—

"Gloves?" McVie asked.

Fenway pulled her hand out, covered in cobwebs and dust. "I don't think there's any danger of evidence contamination. But yeah, gloves are a good idea."

She found a pair in her purse and snapped them on as they continued to look for hiding places. A small seating area on the right-hand side had no good hiding places; the end table had a small drawer, but it was empty. They walked down the corridor again— and came to the window nook.

"I've bumped into this sofa pretty much every time I've..." Fenway said. Then she tilted her head.

"This morning, the sofa was sticking out about six or eight inches into the hallway."

"Could be maintenance pushed it back. Or someone got sick of everyone running into it."

The sofa was pushed against the wall of the window nook. Not enough leg room between the end of the sofa and the window bench in front of it—no wonder people pushed it out from the wall a few more inches.

"The window bench," Fenway said. She opened the bench—only to find fifteen or twenty children's books.

"That's unexpected."

McVie shrugged. "Children are sometimes witnesses. And when you're trying to coax a six-year-old to talk about something horrific they witnessed, *The Cat in the Hat* isn't a bad first step."

"Well, there's nothing in the window bench but books." She put the last one back—

Midge Makes Marbles.

Fenway sucked in a breath. One of the few memories she had from when she was a little kid was Nathaniel Ferris reading *Midge Makes Marbles* to her. He didn't read to her very often, working late at the oil company most nights. Maybe that's why she remembered it so vividly: her father in a Red Sox jersey over a T-shirt, one of the few times he wasn't in a suit or at least a sport coat and tie. Her bedsheets were farm animals. She couldn't have been more than four.

"Fenway?" McVie said.

"Sorry." Fenway closed the window bench and barked her shin on the edge of the sofa. She grimaced, then blinked.

Was the sofa cushion on the end a quarter-inch higher than the other two?

Fenway lifted the cushion.

The ledger. Seth Cahill's ledger that kept track of all his deliveries and payments in a code that they hadn't figured out. They'd caught the killer who had nothing to do with the drug trade. But now, two more people were dead, and eighteen bags of morpheranyl were missing.

McVie looked over Fenway's shoulder. "Another book?"

"Not just a book, Craig," Fenway opened the book; the pages still looked intact. "This ledger is the schedule and the payments for all the morpheranyl going in and out of Cahill Warehouse Storage for—I don't know, years."

McVie raised his eyebrows.

"I shouldn't be telling you this," Fenway said. "Now that you're a civilian."

"But you're trying to catch a killer who's in law enforcement," McVie said softly. "And whoever it was tried to kill you."

"And I think it could be the sheriff."

"Which is why you can't go through the regular channels. I think that elbows out any ethical issues."

Fenway looked at McVie.

"And I'm a Boy Scout, remember? Even had the Swiss army knife to prove it."

Fenway scratched her scalp.

"What is it?"

"This is the ledger with all the transactions over the last couple of years. All the morpheranyl purchases, dates that Cahill picked up the drugs from the boat and brought them to his storage unit."

"If you say so."

"Whoever broke into the evidence room to take this," Fenway mused, "must have wanted to keep these dates and delivery information under wraps."

"Good thing all the evidence is digitized." McVie pressed his lips together. "Why would anyone…"

A sinking feeling in Fenway's stomach. If the video footage had been deleted, were the digitized evidence files also gone? "Someone in law enforcement is behind this," Fenway said. "And they must have known about these dates if they wanted to steal this ledger."

McVie tapped his chin. "So they must have been purposely hiding this information from other people in law enforcement."

"Right," Fenway said. "Someone in Vice who was giving the wrong location information to his co-workers. Or"—Fenway's eyes darted to McVie's—"the sheriff covering up all the dates and feeding misinformation to everyone else.".

"You still think Gretchen is behind this?"

"It's a possibility." Fenway flipped a few pages. "You know, this might not be the only ledger."

"You think Cahill Warehouse Storage has another copy?"

Fenway shook her head. "No, Tyra Cahill had no idea Seth even kept this one."

"Jericho?"

"Not what I was thinking."

"Are you going to tell me, or do I need to keep guessing?"

Fenway gave McVie a sad smile. "I don't think I can tell you."

"Right, right, I'm a civilian." McVie leaned forward. "Is that everything under the cushion?"

"I think so." Fenway set the ledger down and reached under the cushion. The only sensation was the smooth fabric of the underside. She was about to put the cushion back into place, but ran her finger along the crease where the back of the cushion met the inside corner of the sofa.

Nothing—

Wait.

The fabric felt different.

She pulled the cushion out. The back corner underneath the cushion was shrouded in shadow, but the fabric was *definitely* different; black against the navy blue. She almost didn't see it.

There was a hole in the corner of the fabric, and something made of black fabric was in the hole, sticking out a millimeter or two.

She ran her finger over the hole. Yes, this was a different fabric.

"Did you find anything?" McVie said.

"Not sure yet."

McVie came over and shined his phone's flashlight down into the hole. "Someone stuffed something in the sofa cushion."

"Sure looks like it."

McVie glanced at the phone screen, frowned, and switched the light off. "Low battery."

"It's okay," Fenway said. "I don't think I need it." The hole was large enough for her to get three fingers in, and she ran her gloved index finger over the black fabric. "Should I tear this?"

"You're getting evidence in a murder, Fenway. The county can cover the cost of new upholstery."

Fenway nodded, then ripped the hole another few inches. She snagged enough of the black fabric to pull it out gently, then held it up.

"A balaclava," McVie said.

"Something the assailant wore to disguise his identity."

"We need evidence bags. I bet Dr. Yasuda can get DNA off that if our assailant wore it."

Fenway nodded. "And if we're lucky, fingerprints from the ledger."

The alcove was between the evidence room and Vice. Close to Donnelly's office, too. Either Gretchen or Steve—or Jensen or another Vice detective—could have easily stashed both these items here and been back at their desks in less than a minute. The assailant *had* to be a cop.

"Don't get your hopes up about the fingerprints. I'd be shocked if this attack wasn't premeditated. And that usually means the assailant wore gloves."

They both continued searching the alcove, pulling the cushions off the sofa and the chair, but found nothing more.

"We still have to find a jacket." Fenway, on her hands and knees, looked under the two-inch gap under the sofa. Nothing.

"That was an educated guess, Fenway. Maybe the assailant didn't have a jacket. It *is* July."

"True enough." Fenway stood. "We should bag this up."

"You—uh, you don't have evidence bags in your purse or anything, do you?"

"There are bags—" Fenway began, then stopped. "Oh. We can't get into the evidence room." She set the balaclava and the ledger down carefully on the sofa and pulled her phone out. She considered for a moment, then took out her burner phone and called Dez.

"Is that a second phone?" McVie asked.

"Shh."

The phone rang twice, then Dez answered. "Fenway?"

"Hi, Dez. Can you get an evidence bag over to me? I'm in the hallway outside the evidence room in the sheriff's office."

A pause. "I heard the evidence room was cordoned off."

"Which is one reason I need an evidence bag—I can't get one here."

"You can't get it from some department over there? Vice is still around, I think."

"I—uh, I don't want to get it from Vice."

"Look," Dez said, "even if Steve Alvídrez has a little crush on you—"

"Oh, no," Fenway put her hand over her eyes. "Does *everyone* think that?"

"Um, no," Dez said, uncertainty in her voice. "It's probably only me. And Michi."

Fenway almost asked Dez more questions, but she shook her head. *Focus, Fenway.*

"Someone in law enforcement is behind this, Dez. Alvídrez— and for that matter, everyone in Vice—is close enough to the morpheranyl distribution to be a suspect. I'd rather not waltz in there asking for evidence bags."

"You think Alvídrez is the bad guy?"

"I don't know," Fenway said. "Look, can you get me an evidence bag or not?"

Dez exhaled loudly. "I can't. I'm at Frank Kingman's apartment in Paso Querido."

"Oh. So you're like a half-hour away."

Another pause, the sound of footsteps. Dez sounded like she was walking on concrete. "Donnelly had me get an arrest warrant," Dez said. "But he's not here. Car isn't in his parking spot, and he's not at his apartment. When I went by his work, his co-worker said he got a call and left right afterward. Family emergency."

"But you think he's skipped town."

Dez cackled. "I love your TV-cop parlance, Fenway. Never change. *Skipped town.* All you're missing are the terrible puns when you find a dead body."

"Left the jurisdiction," Fenway said with an edge in her voice.

Dez cleared her throat. "We don't know that for sure. Maybe he really had a family emergency, or maybe he's somewhere else. He could have had a friend who wanted to spend the afternoon playing video games, or he has a romantic partner who called and was in the mood."

Fenway paused. Even when she hated her job in the past, she'd never made an excuse like having a family emergency to skip out on work. She didn't believe in karma, but she certainly didn't want to play with fire.

Or maybe she was closer to McVie's Boy Scout-like behavior than she cared to admit.

"You'll look through Kingman's place, though, right?" Fenway asked. "See if he's got the Hackson Square shirts and any other evidence that might prove he was in the evidence room?"

"His laptop's gone," Dez said. "I thought maybe we could track his online usage, although he probably wasn't dumb enough to leave a trail." A noise in the background. "Hey, hold on."

Fenway waited a moment, hearing nothing but rustling fabric and muffled voices.

Dez's voice, distant. "No, only the apartment." A pause. "No—look, I don't care what you think you found, the warrant only..." More rustling. "I don't care." Dez's voice was firm. "Lock the door and step away."

Overlapping voices, the slide of fabric across the phone, then a loud exhale. "Sorry about that."

"What's going on?"

"Our warrant only covers the apartment, not the garage."

"Is there something in the garage?"

"Officially," Dez said, "we don't know if the U-Move-It van we're looking for is in the garage. We'd need another warrant for that."

"The van is in the garage?"

"It's Schrödinger's van," Dez said. "We don't know if the van is in there or not, because we don't have a warrant for the garage."

"Right, right."

"I'll tell you what we *did* find that's covered by the warrant—a phone."

"Frank's phone?"

"I don't know. Deputy Cortez found it in a desk drawer in the spare bedroom."

"Mathis Jericho's phone," Fenway said.

"What?"

"It's missing from the evidence room. I bet Kingman took it."

More rustling. "We have the phone's serial number in our system, right?"

"I sure hope so," Fenway replied. "Everyone's gone home tonight, but we can check tomorrow."

"Or I can drive in."

"The ledger, the balaclava, and now the phone," Fenway mused. "Assuming I can actually get evidence bags, where can we store them?"

"There's a safe in our building."

"Yeah, but Rondell goes home at five."

Des scoffed. "Rondell is getting overtime because the evidence room has been compromised."

"What?" Fenway said. "Rondell doesn't carry a firearm. Is he—"

"There are two deputies in there with him."

"All right." Fenway exhaled, her cheeks puffing out. She knew Donnelly was purposely keeping her out of the loop. "We'll take the evidence across the street."

"What about Sarah or Brian? Can't they bring you evidence bags?"

"I sent them home. It's past six." Fenway hesitated. "And Detective Callahan was assaulted along with Deputy Huke."

"Callahan might still be around," McVie said.

"Who's with you? McVie?" Dez asked.

"Uh—yeah."

"Fenway," Dez said sharply.

"What?"

"You've got your boyfriend—who's no longer in law enforcement—helping you with this investigation that you're about to get kicked off?"

Fenway looked up and down the hallway. No one was around except her and McVie. True, a couple of the Vice detectives were still around, but she had little choice except to stay in the hallway. She stepped to the side and lowered her voice. "We have evidence that someone in law enforcement created the fake money trail to Rachel's accounts."

Dez hesitated. "But you don't solve that problem by involving someone—"

"Someone tried to kill me," Fenway said. "Don't think of Craig like my boyfriend, think of him like my bodyguard."

Dez paused. "Don't come crying to me if your evidence gets excluded."

"He's not touching the evidence. He's just *with* me. Making sure I'm safe."

A long sigh on the other end of the phone. "Your call."

"What other options do I have, Dez? If I did this alone, you'd tell me I was stupid to go out unprotected."

"You could have asked me—"

"You're investigating me, Dez. You can't be seen walking around the sheriff's office with me, looking in ventilation ducts and under couch cushions."

Dez was silent.

"And I don't trust anyone else," Fenway said. "I trust you, and I trust McVie."

"You don't trust Sarah? You can ask her to come back to the office. I bet she'd be okay with the overtime."

"Sarah is an admin, Dez. I can ask her to run background checks, but someone's trying to run me over with a stolen car. Anything that requires hazard pay is off the table."

Dez hesitated for a moment, then spoke. "You're right, Fenway. This is a no-win situation. I don't know what I'd do in your shoes."

She paused. "You should get the evidence over to San Miguelito as soon as possible. You need to run fingerprints, right?"

"And DNA from a piece of clothing," Fenway said. "That's probably more important."

"Oh—they won't be able to send for any DNA testing until tomorrow morning."

"Right. So keeping it in the safe tonight is the right move. But obviously, this is a rush. I know DNA testing takes a week even with a rush, but if we—"

"Michi's short-staffed," Dez said. "I'm not sure a rush is possible."

"This is top priority," Fenway said. "One deputy dead, one in the hospital—"

"That's why Michi's short-staffed," Dez said. "Melissa is with Huke."

Oh, of course. Melissa de la Garza and Donald Huke had been dating since November and had moved in together. Michi didn't have a large CSI staff, and losing Melissa during a busy stretch, even for a couple of days, would be stressful.

"Maybe we can get help from another county." Fenway said.

Dez paused. "You worry about getting the evidence locked away safely tonight. I'll work on speeding up the evidence analysis." A grim chuckle. "What a mess."

"On that," Fenway said, "we agree."

CHAPTER TWENTY-FOUR

Fenway ended the call and turned to McVie.

He raised his eyebrows. "You have a second phone?"

"Yes. Look, there's no time to explain."

"I receive photos of you and Alvídrez together, and now you have a burner phone."

"It's for Dez," Fenway said.

McVie exhaled with a note of exasperation. "If I posted everything you did on Photoxio, all the commenters would tell me you're cheating on me."

"Good thing our relationship isn't being judged by the social media peanut gallery." Fenway cocked her head. "Is it?"

McVie paused, then shook his head, as if laughing at himself. "No."

"And we still need evidence bags."

"Did I hear Dez is half an hour away?"

"Right. So that leaves Brian."

"We'll have to tell him we didn't really have reservations at Maxime's." McVie grinned.

Fenway nodded. She opened her mouth—Callahan had been one of the first people she'd suspected to steal Rachel's BMW, but he'd been with Lieutenant Brookline. She didn't trust Callahan, but probably because he'd dumped Rachel. But her personal feelings about him didn't mean she couldn't rely on him in this investigation.

"Okay, right, now is not the time for jokes." McVie exhaled. "We can stay with the evidence and Brian can get us evidence bags. We've got to assume the DNA on this balaclava will tell us who the assailant was."

"If someone in law enforcement did this, it'll show a match, right?" asked Fenway. "All sheriff's office employees need to have their DNA in the database, don't they?"

"Right. We have the DNA in an elimination database so their DNA doesn't get confused at crime scenes with the actual criminals." McVie paused. "We have to program the parameters *not* to exclude the elimination database."

Fenway pulled her phone out and called Callahan. He answered on the second ring.

"Hey there, Coroner."

"Hey, Brian," Fenway said, trying to keep her tone light. "We've found some evidence over in the sheriff's office building—the hall in front of the evidence room. I know you're off duty, but they're out of evidence bags over here, and I really don't want to leave the evidence unsupervised."

"You—you didn't go out to dinner?"

"Not yet. So would you mind going back to the office and grabbing two evidence bags?"

"No problem. I'm not even out of the parking garage yet. I'll be right there."

They ended the call, and Fenway breathed a sigh of relief. That *was* probably better than carrying the evidence unprotected across the street.

"He's still here?"

"Close enough. He'll bring the bags shortly." Fenway sat on the window bench.

"Did you want to do more investigating tonight?"

Fenway turned to McVie and blinked. "I'm not going to sit still while Gretchen's trying to pin these murders on me."

"Of course not," McVie said quickly.

They were both silent for a moment, Fenway turning everything over in her head.

"Alvídrez told me property theft was investigating the evidence room break-in," Fenway mused. "Must mean Lieutenant Brookline, right? He's the only one in that department."

McVie nodded. "Right, Brookline."

"After we get the evidence put away, I'll go see him. I bet he's pulling overtime, too. Ask him if he's made any headway." Fenway looked at McVie. "You want to join me?"

"Would you like to get dinner first?"

Fenway paused. She *was* hungry, but she wouldn't be able to eat. At least not at a sit-down place.

"You've gotta eat, Fenway."

Fenway nodded. "Can you pick something up for me?"

McVie looked at Fenway for a moment.

"Brookline might not want to talk with a civilian present."

He hesitated, then nodded, and went back to his phone.

Fenway leaned back against the window and stared at the ceiling. She'd interviewed several people, she'd put at least three or four law enforcement personnel on her suspect list, and she'd collected potentially smoking-gun-type evidence. She'd done all this with Sheriff Gretchen Donnelly looking over her shoulder, and maybe even hiding evidence from her.

McVie looked up from his screen. "Are you okay?"

"No," Fenway said, trying to keep her voice even. "I'm trapped. Gretchen thinks I organized the killings and I'm probably a day away from being arrested. I'm trying to solve a murder and I'm getting no help."

"If there's DNA on that balaclava—"

She leaned forward, her elbows on her knees. "If Donnelly is behind everything," Fenway said in a low voice, "she could bury the DNA evidence. Gretchen put Rachel in jail—and I bet she moved her somewhere else. Plus, I found out Gretchen basically had her thumb on the scale to keep me from hiring Celeste. Who knows what she's capable of?" She took a deep, shuddering breath. "And I'm mad at myself for letting all that happen. If I'd been more on top of things—"

McVie sat next to Fenway on the bench and put his arm around her. "Hey, you're not alone in this," he said. "I'm here. I know the ins and outs of the sheriff's office, even if I'm not sheriff anymore. You know you can depend on me."

Fenway dropped her hands to her lap and stared at the floor. "Can I, Craig?"

He took his arm away. "Of course you can. What do you mean?"

"I mean, I—" Fenway balled her hands into fists. "I mean I don't know what I want."

"With the investigation?"

"With *us*," Fenway said through gritted teeth.

"Oh." McVie put his arm back around her. "Yeah, you're right, things have been stressful. And I know I've been..." He sighed. "I've put you in some pretty terrible positions in the last few weeks." He squeezed her upper arm. "But that doesn't mean I'll abandon you when you're in trouble. Or when you need someone with private-eye skills." He leaned into her slightly. "Or when you're hurting."

"Yeah," Fenway said. She wanted to touch the edges of her eyelashes with her fingers to see if there were tears. She hated crying in front of anyone, especially McVie. "Sometimes it doesn't feel like it."

McVie pulled away—though only a fraction of an inch. "I have your back *now*, Fenway. I can see something is bothering you. Is it about this murder, or is it—"

Fenway shook her head. "I don't know if I can tell you."

"Maybe when the investigation is over?"

Fenway tapped her foot, then looked in McVie's eyes. He wasn't pushing her; he wanted to help. He wanted to make her better. For a moment, all she wanted to do was melt in his embrace. Instead, she swallowed hard. "Maybe. Assuming I get through this investigation without getting arrested."

"If that happens—and that's a big 'if'—your dad will get the best lawyer in California for you."

Fenway nodded.

"And he'll have the best private eye in Estancia working to find exculpatory evidence."

"You're the *only* private eye in Estancia."

McVie waved his hand. "Details."

Footfalls down the hall. A moment later, Callahan appeared and set down a box of large evidence baggies.

"Okay," he said, "let's get this evidence bagged up." He pulled two latex gloves out of the opening of the box and snapped them on. "What did you find? Was it from the attack on Huke?"

Fenway nodded and stood, then walked over to the sofa. "The ledger from Seth Cahill's office." She picked it up carefully. "Get an evidence baggie," Fenway said.

"Right, right." Callahan pulled a large baggie out, opened the top, and held it out to Fenway. She dropped the ledger inside.

"And now," Fenway said, "the balaclava."

"You found a balaclava?"

"Under the sofa cushion."

Callahan held out another baggie, and Fenway dropped the balaclava inside.

Fenway exhaled—she hadn't realized how stressed she'd been with the evidence out in the open. "Now let's get this over to the safe in the other building."

"The safe?"

"The one we use—you know, it's in the equipment room Rondell Price covers." Fenway took out a pen and signed both bags.

"Oh, right." Callahan screwed up his mouth. "But Rondell only works until five."

"He's getting overtime because of the evidence room break-in."

Callahan nodded. "Great. I can take it over."

"I think I'd better do it," Fenway said. "Chain of custody."

Callahan held up the evidence bags. "Sealed and signed. Don't you still have a murder you're solving?"

"I really need—"

"Come on," Callahan said. "Let me do *something*. I let someone hit Huke on the back of the head—and I let him get away. This is least I can do."

Fenway hesitated. Callahan hadn't been an ideal employee his first two days, but when Fenway gave him clear direction and got out of his way, he'd done okay. Like with the security guard at the harbor and the spreadsheet of Hackson Square employees. She *could* insist on taking the evidence herself, but really—for such a simple task? She was being a control freak. "You're right, Brian. I have other priorities. You call me the moment you drop it off."

"Sure thing." Callahan turned and walked down the hallway.

McVie leaned toward Fenway and spoke quietly. "I'll go with him."

"Why?"

"You've got to talk with Lieutenant Brookline, remember? He might not want to talk with a civilian present."

She'd almost forgotten about going to see Brookline. "No—I mean why are you going at all?"

"Callahan hasn't worked as a detective before," McVie said. "And he reported to me for years. I can give him advice on how to..."

"Get along with me?"

"Show him what he needs to do for you to trust him."

Maybe Callahan would listen to McVie. "Fine. Meet you back in the coroner's office."

McVie turned and jogged down the hallway to catch up with Callahan.

Fenway took her gloves off. Hopefully, Lieutenant Brookline had found something in the evidence room that would blow the case open.

CHAPTER TWENTY-FIVE

Fenway went up the back stairs to the second floor. As she expected, the door was open to the Property Crimes bullpen, and Lieutenant Satchel Brookline sat at his desk. He looked up as Fenway stepped over the threshold of the door.

"Coroner Stevenson," he said.

"Evening, Lieutenant."

"You're staying late, too?"

Fenway pressed her lips together. "Yep. When one of your own gets attacked in the sheriff's office, it's all hands on deck."

Brookline glanced around the empty bullpen. "Well, some hands on deck, anyway." He looked back at Fenway. "What can I help you with?"

"You bagged up some evidence this afternoon from the evidence room."

Brookline hesitated. "With all due respect, Coroner—"

Fenway held up a hand. "Some evidence from both the Seth Cahill case and the Mathis Jericho case is missing. I know Sheriff Donnelly pulled me off the Andrew Zellman murder, but I'm still on the Jericho case, and the Cahill case is supposed to be closed."

He raised his eyebrows. "I didn't know there was any evidence missing from the Cahill case."

Fenway nodded. "The ledger Cahill kept."

Brookline frowned and smacked the table with his open palm. "Dammit. If I'd been paying closer attention—"

"What evidence was taken from the boxes from the Mathis Jericho case?"

"All the morpheranyl," Brookline said. "All eighteen bags."

Fenway shook her head. "No. That was taken before. On Monday, we think. You remember that someone pretended to be from Hackson Square?"

"Right, but he didn't take anything."

Fenway shook her head. "He took the morpheranyl bags and replaced them with lookalike bags full of cornstarch and vitamin powder."

Brookline's eyes widened. "What?"

"Captain Alvídrez took the bags of fake drugs earlier for analysis—and Deputy Huke was there, too. That's why those boxes are empty." Fenway took a few more steps toward Brookline's desk. "The bags of fake drugs should be in the lab at San Miguelito."

"Yeah, well, the sign-in sheet is one thing that's missing. That's why I didn't know about Alvídrez signing out the drugs. Or—the fake drugs."

"I signed out the evidence," Fenway said. "And it was on the clipboard, not the computer."

Brookline nodded. "After the impostor pulled down the cameras and erased the footage, we went back to paper until we could audit the computer records. If we have malware on the network, we can't trust anything the system says. It looks like some digitized files have already been deleted."

Fenway hesitated. "Anything from the Mathis Jericho case?"

"I wish we knew. We only know the size of the backup file from two weeks ago is larger than the one from yesterday."

"We still have the backup, though, right?"

"The file's been corrupted," Brookline said. "Jordan and Patrick are tearing their hair out."

Fenway paused, turning everything over in her mind. "So how did you find out the sign-in sheet was missing?"

"The attacker took the paper, but not the clipboard." Brookline narrowed his eyes at Fenway, as if he was deciding whether to trust her. Finally, he relaxed his shoulders. "We bagged up the clipboard."

"They stole the top sign-in sheet?"

Brookline shifted his weight. "We don't know. We couldn't find any sign-in sheets in the evidence room."

Fenway rubbed her forehead. If Gretchen—or Alvídrez, or someone else—was trying to frame Fenway for drug trafficking or conspiracy to commit murder, removing the sign-in sheet might throw suspicion onto her.

A buzz on her phone. Was this a message from McVie or Callahan about the evidence? She glanced at the screen—no, it was a message from Salt & Flame, asking again to fill out a survey. For such an expensive place, they sure were desperate for reviews. If only Callahan hadn't eaten at Dos Milagros the night before, they could have had a better—and cheaper meal.

Fenway blinked, frowning at her phone. She remembered her exchange with Callahan after they'd gone to the harbor.

"We're pretty close to Dos Milagros, if that works for you."

"I actually went there last night..."

He'd been to Dos Milagros on Monday night. Same night as Fenway and McVie—obviously not at the same time, but he'd been there.

Now it was time for Fenway to study Brookline's face.

"Lieutenant," Fenway said slowly, "when you and Callahan went to Fresno to work the private security gig on Monday night, when did you leave?"

Brookline knotted his brow. "A little after four. We had to get out there for setup. I know it was a little earlier than his quitting time—"

"Did you stop for dinner?"

"No, they had food for us at the fundraiser."

Fenway crossed her arms. "Brian told me he ate in town on Monday night. How is that possible if he'd left for Fresno with you?"

Brookline looked down at the ground.

"Lieutenant?"

He sighed and his shoulders slumped as he looked up. "Brian's a good guy."

She raised an eyebrow.

"But," Brookline continued, "he knows you're friends with Rachel. And he didn't want to—well, he told me he's been seeing this other girl for a few weeks."

"I knew it," Fenway muttered under her breath.

"He was out with her Monday night," Brookline said.

"Isabella Chan?"

"I don't know her name. But he was out with her pretty late. He overslept, and so he was late his second day on the job. Callahan asked me to give him an excuse to show up to work late." Brookline pursed his lips.

"So—you lied about where he was."

"Yes."

Fenway crossed her arms.

"This is a terrible excuse," Brookline said, "but it's kind of expected among cops."

"That you lie to their supervisors about where they've been?"

"That we lie to their wives and girlfriends."

"And you see me as an extension of Callahan's ex-girlfriend, and not his manager?"

Brookline looked down at the floor. "If it makes you feel any better, it's been eating at me ever since I told you."

Fenway's mouth curled into a snarl. "Well, if you're feeling guilty about it, I guess it's okay."

Brookline set his mouth into a line and stared at Fenway.

"You and Donnelly have both been lying to me." Fenway dropped her hands to her side. "You two have done everything you can to pin the murder on Rachel—and now she's set her sights on me. If that weren't enough, she's hiding Rachel somewhere."

Brookline's look of guilt changed to one of confusion. "Hiding Rachel? What are you talking about?"

"Donnelly moved Rachel out of the county jail without letting anyone know. Where did she go, Lieutenant? The women's prison in Harford?"

Brookline furrowed his brow. "What? No. Rachel hasn't even been arraigned yet. How do you know Rachel was moved?"

"She's not in the county jail. I went to talk with her this morning—first thing. Then I come back a couple hours later, and she's gone. You tell me, Lieutenant, what does that sound like to you?"

"I had no idea."

"You weren't honest about Monday night, Lieutenant. Why should I trust anything you say?" Fenway turned and strode away, then walked downstairs in a daze.

At the bottom of the stairs, her phone buzzed. This better not be another Salt & Flame marketing text—

No. A text from her father.

> Good news
>
> My one remaining contact at the sheriff's office told me an unnamed suspect was transferred from county jail to protective custody this morning
>
> Signed out at 9:41 AM
>
> Does that help?

Oh, of course. Protective custody. And the time was about ninety minutes after Fenway had seen Rachel this morning—and about thirty minutes before she went back to interview her again. That unnamed prisoner had to be Rachel.

No wonder no one knew where Rachel was. Fenway had assumed the worst about Gretchen Donnelly: that she'd moved Rachel to the women's prison without even arraigning her. But she was protecting Rachel.

She texted back her thanks to her father, hoping the short but effusive message was enough.

> Call me when you have a minute

As grateful as she was for the information, she didn't have any time to talk to her father. Fenway had been avoiding Donnelly, but now she walked right to her office.

No luck. The office was dark, the lights off, the door locked.

Fenway remembered when this was McVie's office. The room was never warm and inviting, though McVie had tried to make it as welcoming as possible.

She sighed. What was she expecting to get from Donnelly? Certainly not Rachel's location—and if Donnelly suspected her of coordinating murders, she'd never tell Fenway.

Then Fenway heard footsteps in the hallway. The sound of flats —a woman was coming closer.

And Gretchen Donnelly turned the corner.

She flinched when she saw Fenway.

"Oh, Fenway," she said. "I just got back from the hospital. Deputy Huke is expected to make a full recovery. His doctors aren't letting us ask questions yet, though."

Fenway nodded, then took a deep breath. "I think it's time for us to come clean with each other."

Donnelly stopped, switched her purse from her left shoulder to her right, and said, "I don't know what you mean."

"You think I'm involved in drug trafficking. And you also think

I'm behind the murders of Mathis Jericho and Andrew Zellman, based on a big check my dad gave me."

Donnelly took her keychain out of her purse and opened the door to her office. "Why don't you come inside and have a seat?"

Fenway nodded. "I understand why you'd come to that conclusion." Fenway stepped into the office and sat, then tapped her chin thoughtfully. "I've certainly thought my dad's been involved in a lot of shady deals. I think it's one reason we didn't get along." No reason for Donnelly to know that they'd mostly patched things up.

Donnelly took a seat behind her desk. "A check for a hundred thousand dollars doesn't sound like you don't get along."

Fenway smiled. "When people have a lot of money, they sometimes think they can buy their way into your good graces. But that's not how things work. At least not with me."

Donnelly studied Fenway's face for a moment. "You found Mathis Jericho's body."

"Yes, I did. And I discovered you moved Rachel to protective custody."

Donnelly furrowed her brow.

Fenway's shoulders dipped. "Oh, of course. Why didn't I see that before?"

"See what before?"

"You sent me that weird message—*congratulations on solving the two murders.* I thought it was odd then, and I think it's odd now."

Donnelly blinked. "Why would my text be weird?"

Fenway hesitated, then took a chance. "Because you mentioned *the two murders.* Not, 'thanks for catching the killer,' or 'great job solving the case so quickly.' *The two murders.*"

Donnelly said nothing.

"At first," Fenway said, "I wasn't sure what bothered me about it. Then I got the impression you *wanted* both murders solved—even though you knew George Pope hadn't killed Mathis Jericho."

Donnelly stiffened. "Hold on," she said, "you think *I* had something to do with the murder? And Andrew Zellman, too?"

"I thought you were essentially thanking me for covering up your involvement," Fenway said.

Donnelly scoffed. "Of course not. Where would George Pope have gotten all the morpheranyl to put around Jericho's body?"

"Well—from the garage. Or wherever the drugs were hidden in the cabin."

"And why would he have done that?"

"To throw suspicion onto the Venn Cartel," Fenway said.

Donnelly scoffed. "No way. George Pope stole the Corvette and drove to Miranda Duchy's cabin. He hid the murder weapon in her shed at her house. He was trying to implicate Miranda Duchy, not the Venn Cartel."

Fenway winced. Right. She hadn't thought of that.

"It was someone else," Donnelly continued. "Someone who knew how the Venn Cartel worked. Someone who knew what to do with the drugs."

"And you thought it was me?"

Donnelly paused. "Your father must have gotten bored in retirement. Traded his oil company in for a more exciting life, something more daring."

Fenway laughed. "My father wouldn't know the first thing about running a drug trafficking operation."

"No," Donnelly said, "but you might."

Fenway raised her eyebrows. "I might?"

"I did my research on you. I know what neighborhood in Seattle you grew up in."

Fenway barked a laugh. "You never met my mom. She would have killed me." Then she stopped and leaned forward. "And you're forgetting: I'm a target. I almost got run over."

"Like I said before, you know as well as I do that people paint themselves as targets—with narrow escapes—to throw suspicion off themselves."

Fenway shook her head. Had *she* suggested that in front of Dez,

Dez would have repeated her mantra that Fenway watched too many cop shows.

"So that's why you never broached the subject of protective custody?"

Donnelly sat back in her seat again. "You never asked about protective custody, either. Usually, people become targets, they want to stay safe. I don't even think you filed the police report."

"And that made you suspect me."

Donnelly said nothing.

Fenway cocked her head. "Oh. You suspected me *before* this."

"I thought it was a possibility."

"But you must have thought there was a *possibility* I was telling the truth. That someone would try to eliminate—" Fenway blinked.

Donnelly stared at her. "Try to what?"

"Morgan Crane," Fenway said. "You had him follow me."

The sheriff said nothing.

"You had him follow me. Half to keep me safe, half to see if I was involved in the murders. What is he? Internal affairs from another jurisdiction? U.S. Attorney's office? One of the three-letter agencies?"

"Something like that."

No wonder Sarah couldn't find anything.

Donnelly shifted in her seat. "Look at it from my perspective. You drop Rachel off, her car disappears, and you're the only one who says it wasn't in its spot when you dropped her off." Donnelly pursed her lips. "For that matter, I only have your word that you dropped her off just before midnight."

"Sarah and Piper could vouch for us, too."

"They were dropped off first."

Fenway sighed. Great. "So you have Morgan Crane tail me."

"You gave Rachel a weak alibi while looking like her bestest buddy ever." Donnelly leaned forward. "But you had all the opportunity in the world to take Rachel's car, run over Zellman, then drop the car back at Rachel's a couple blocks away, drop her keys off in her house after she passed out from drinking too much, and—"

"Why would I frame one of my best friends?"

"Drugs and money are powerful," Donnelly said.

Of course. And that's why Donnelly didn't tell Alvídrez about finding two bricks of Nyllie in Rachel's trunk: if Alvídrez had flagged that as suspicious, the killer wouldn't think they were getting away with framing Rachel.

"And," Donnelly continued, "someone sneaked into the evidence room and swapped all the morpheranyl out with a mix of cornstarch and vitamin B12."

Vitamin D, Fenway thought, but let it go.

"And Zellman called you *from the evidence room* about six hours before he was killed. He'd never called you before."

"No," Fenway said, "he hadn't."

Donnelly was quiet.

"So," Fenway said, "you still think I'm the brains behind the whole operation?"

Donnelly pursed her lips. "Now you know why I couldn't keep you on the Zellman case. Not when I suspected you."

"You suspect me for the Jericho murder too, though, right?"

Donnelly shrugged. "That explanation is fuzzier. My theory was that you covered that murder up. But I thought if I let things be, not let you know I suspected you, you'd make a mistake, let your guard down."

Fenway sat straight in the chair. "And you thought I was targeting Rachel. That's why you've moved her into protective custody."

A shadow of a smile appeared on Donnelly's lips. "For someone who's so good at solving murders, you spent a long time figuring that one out."

Fenway sat back. "So you'll let her go?"

"I still think she's a target," Donnelly said. "But I don't know who's targeting her." She folded her arms. "Now Huke *and* Callahan, too."

Callahan? Oh, right, the assailant had pushed him down getting to Huke. A little weak to say he was a target, but whatever. "You can't arrest everyone to put them into protective custody."

Donnelly shrugged. "I figured if you—uh, I mean, if the murderer—thought Rachel would still be held for the crime, she'd be safe. But I don't know what I can do about Huke and Callahan."

"What is it that made Huke a target?"

"I think Huke saw something in the evidence room. The same thing Zellman saw, and the same thing the killer thinks Rachel saw—or maybe that Zellman told him about."

"I think the killer is in law enforcement."

Donnelly shook her head. "I might think so, too, but we have literally dozens of people who have been working on the morpheranyl cases. And trying to run checks on their finances? The police union is already up my ass about ten other issues. And Dominguez County doesn't have an internal affairs department."

"Do you still consider me a suspect?"

Donnelly's cheeks puffed out as she exhaled. "No. You've convinced me—you didn't have anything to do with Andrew Zellman's death." She paused. "Or with Mathis Jericho."

That was why all her interactions with Donnelly felt off: because the sheriff was constantly on her guard, trying to catch Fenway in a misstep. Fenway had felt in her gut that Donnelly had been hiding something—but not her own involvement in a murderous conspiracy. Donnelly thought Fenway was the killer.

"Dez hasn't found anything yet," Fenway said. "Otherwise, you *would* have arrested me."

Donnelly smiled. "I know Dez is your friend—and you're her boss—but she wouldn't let you get away with murder. And she's pretty good at ferreting out liars."

Fenway's phone rang. Maybe that was Dez. Fenway took her phone out and glanced at the screen. McVie.

"Let me tell McVie I'm still in a meeting."

Donnelly shrugged.

Fenway answered the call. "Hey Craig, I'm in a meeting with Gretchen."

"Oh, okay. Did you tell her we found the balaclava and the ledger?"

Fenway blinked. "Uh, I haven't gotten to it yet."

McVie paused. "I know you don't trust her, but showing her the evidence is pretty important, isn't it? If we get fingerprints and DNA, we might find Zellman's killer. It could get Rachel released."

"Right." McVie was still a civilian; he didn't need to know Rachel was in protective custody. "Give me another ten or fifteen minutes."

A chirp came across the line.

"What was that?" Fenway asked.

"My phone's almost dead."

"I have a plug in my office."

"Callahan's taking me there now. I'll charge for a few minutes, then I can go pick up dinner for us."

"Sure."

"Do you know where you'd like—"

"Whatever kind of food you get is fine. I need to get back."

"Sure, sure. Sorry."

Fenway ended the call. "So tonight, when I arrived at the sheriff's office, I searched the hallway outside the evidence room." No need to tell Donnelly McVie was with her.

Donnelly knotted her eyebrows. "Why?"

"Because," Fenway said, "Parker Richards admitted to me that a law enforcement representative forced him to give his brother's bank information up. And that's how those payments wound up in Rachel's account. A false money trail."

"A law enforcement representative? Who was it?"

"Parker wouldn't say."

Donnelly shook her head.

"But that got me thinking," Fenway continued. "Huke would trust a law enforcement representative to get access to the evidence room. And if the stuff the assailant stole was too big to slip into a pocket, maybe the stolen evidence would be hidden somewhere in the hallway. The assailant would blend in, right? Take off their mask, shove Seth Cahill's ledger under a sofa cushion—"

Donnelly blinked. "How did you—"

"We—"

"We?"

"Uh, McVie was with me. But he didn't touch anything."

Donnelly pursed her lips.

Fenway steamrolled on. "We found Cahill's ledger—and a black balaclava—underneath the sofa cushion in the alcove about a hundred yards from the evidence room."

Donnelly stood up. "Where did you put them?"

"I gave them to Detective Callahan. He brought them to the safe on the other side—"

Donnelly grabbed her purse. "Let's go get that evidence now. I want to make sure those pieces of evidence get to San Miguelito tonight. I'll drive them myself if I have to."

"Dr. Yasuda won't be able to process—"

"We have an issue with evidence disappearing here, if you haven't noticed," Donnelly snapped. "I'm not leaving anything to chance."

"There are guards, though, right? Rondell isn't over there alone—"

"If you're right that it's a law enforcement representative," Donnelly said, "they'll be able to trick their way past Rondell and the guards. Come on. Now."

Fenway rose from the guest chair. "You're right." She had hoped to bring up Callahan's lie about seeing the other woman who wasn't Rachel, but—

Fenway stopped.

"Come on, Fenway, what are you waiting for?"

"What did you say?"

"I asked you what you were—"

"No, no," Fenway said. "Before that. A couple minutes ago. '*People paint themselves as targets—with narrow escapes—to throw suspicion off themselves.*'"

"I don't think you're a suspect anymore, okay?"

In her head, she saw the spreadsheet Callahan had showed her earlier: all the Hackson Square employees who'd left the company. Lots of names on it; they'd discussed Callahan getting a warrant for those who hadn't returned their uniforms. And Fenway had glanced at the list of names and seen blank spaces, where Callahan said he'd deleted the names of people who were in jail.

But Fenway knew a name that should have been in that spreadsheet, a name that would have jumped out at her.

And the name had been missing.

Parker Richards.

She opened her eyes. "Sheriff, call Rondell."

"We're heading over there right now."

"I think the evidence might already be gone."

"What? How?"

Fenway gritted her teeth, and everything snapped into place.

She hoped she was wrong.

CHAPTER TWENTY-SIX

"Callahan?" Donnelly said. "Are you sure?"

Fenway often walked quickly, and her five-eleven frame meant she had long legs, but she had trouble keeping up with Sheriff Donnelly. "I don't have evidence yet," Fenway said, "but if we still have the balaclava and the DNA comes back—"

Donnelly pressed her phone to her ear. "Hi, Rondell. Did Detective Callahan drop off some evidence—" She listened, then a sigh of relief. "Okay, great. And it was a ledger and—"

More listening.

Fenway's stomach dropped, and she broke into a jog. They exited the building and began crossing the plaza.

"Not a notebook," Donnelly said. "A ledger. The kind—" Quiet for a moment. "No, no. Not a wire-bound—" Quiet again. "Yes, that's a good idea. We're on our way." She paused. "And a balaclava."

Then it hit her: Callahan had never gotten the incident report from the harbor's security office about Butler's boat being broken into, either. He didn't want Fenway to see that report.

And, if Fenway was correct, Callahan wasn't dating anyone else.

He'd broken up with Rachel, yes, but not because he had another romantic entanglement.

Fenway fumbled with her phone and called McVie.

"No," Sheriff Donnelly said. "Not a mouse pad, a balaclava. Like a snow hat that goes down over your face. Okay, we'll be there in two minutes."

Donnelly ended the call and quickened her pace. "Rondell thought I was asking about a Greek pastry."

If Fenway hadn't been worried about a murderer getting away, she would have laughed.

As they crossed the street, the phone against Fenway's ear rang twice, three times, then went to voicemail, and Fenway felt sick. Had Callahan done something with McVie? She set her jaw. McVie and Callahan had been more than co-workers, they'd been friends. With McVie's prodding, Callahan had even helped move Fenway's furniture into her apartment a little over a year ago. How could he do this?

Fenway had been so anxious to get back to her conversation with Donnelly that she hadn't asked McVie about the evidence. He'd asked if Fenway had told Donnelly about the ledger and balaclava, and if there'd been any problems with it, he would have said something, right?

They got to the building, and Donnelly pulled the door handle. Locked.

Fenway pulled out her ID, held it next to the security pad, and it chirped as the door unlocked and they rushed inside.

Oh, right, McVie's phone had chirped, too. Maybe McVie's phone was dead. Or maybe it was plugged into an outlet in Fenway's office while he was out getting food for them.

They ran down the hall, past the IT office, to the equipment room. Two deputies stood in front of the entrance. Fenway hadn't met either of them before. One of them nodded at Donnelly as she and Fenway went inside. Maybe they both worked out of the Paso Querido office.

Rondell stood behind the counter. He wore a button-up Oxford shirt, not a uniform. His face was crestfallen. "I'm sorry," he said. "I didn't know what I should be looking for."

"Let's see the evidence Callahan turned in," Donnelly said.

Rondell turned to the safe next to him, about two feet square. He tapped a code on the door, and it clicked open. He pulled out two evidence bags.

The first had a red spiral-bound notebook in it. The second had a black mouse pad.

Fenway pursed her lips.

"You're sure Callahan gave you *these*?" Donnelly asked.

"I'm sure," Rondell replied.

Fenway thought of McVie. "Was anyone with him?"

Rondell shook his head.

Maybe Callahan had convinced McVie not to come with him to turn in the evidence. Of course—McVie needed to plug in his phone. That was Callahan's excuse to get McVie away from him. Then, once McVie was looking for the charger in Fenway's office, Callahan would have swapped out the ledger and balaclava with a couple of items from the supply cabinet in the coroner's suite.

Fenway stepped out of the room and turned to one of the deputies. "Callahan came here with two evidence bags?"

"That's right," she answered.

"And no one else was with him?"

Both deputies shook their heads.

"Did you see McVie?"

The other deputy's eyes widened slightly. "Sheriff McVie?"

"Former sheriff, yes."

"I didn't see anyone but Detective Callahan."

Fenway nodded. "Thanks." She stepped back into the equipment room.

"So," Donnelly said, "not the ledger and not the balaclava."

"Call Callahan," Fenway said.

"You're his boss."

"And he likes you more than he likes me."

Donnelly nodded. "Thanks, Rondell," she said. "You did nothing wrong."

"Sorry, sheriff, I've never heard of a balaclava before," he said.

"Don't worry about it."

They left the equipment room, and Donnelly tapped the screen of her phone. She put the phone on speaker and held it between them as they walked down the hall past the IT department. Fenway read the screen: *Brian Callahan, Mobile.* It went to voicemail.

Donnelly ended the call with a sigh. "Okay, Fenway, walk me through this," Donnelly said.

Fenway nodded. "Last Wednesday," Fenway said, "Dez and I interviewed Mathis Jericho at the sheriff's office. After we were done, Callahan drove Mathis Jericho back to his place of business."

"The storage place."

"Right." Fenway rubbed her forehead. "But when I went to Cahill Warehouse Storage to review the footage, the recordings had been replaced."

"But the recordings had been replaced before, right? When Cahill and Jericho were bringing drugs from the boat to the storage facility, they replaced the footage then, too."

"No," Fenway said. "They *stopped* the recording. There was *no* security footage at all. This time, someone *replaced* the footage with recordings from a while ago."

Donnelly furrowed her brow.

"We brought Jericho in because we found a little spilled Nyllie powder in his trunk. But this morning, his trunk was spotless. His whole car was. So I was looking for footage of who had taken Jericho's car to get it detailed."

"But you saw no one."

"But what I also didn't see," Fenway said, "was Callahan dropping Mathis Jericho off at his car. And he should have done that *before* the footage was replaced."

"You think Callahan never took Jericho back to his workplace?"

"It's a possibility. He might have driven him directly to Miranda Duchy's cabin, saw the Corvette there, and killed Jericho."

"Why would Callahan kill Jericho?"

"Someone in law enforcement is covering up evidence of the morpheranyl trade for the Venn Cartel. I thought it might be you."

"Me? Why did you suspect me?"

"You have the power as sheriff to coordinate everything. You control the message, you have access to the evidence room, you can hire people who look the other way and fire those who don't."

"Callahan doesn't have that power."

"Not explicitly," Fenway said, "but he can arrest people for the illegal activities he asked them to do. He can lead the investigation, bury some information, fabricate other evidence."

"Like how?"

"Like—I asked him to run a list of former Hackson Square employees. He left off the name of Rachel's former brother-in-law—"

"Parker Richards?"

"So you know him."

Donnelly nodded.

"And Parker told me he gave all of Dylan's banking information to a law enforcement representative."

"But he wouldn't say who."

Fenway shook her head. "But if Callahan left Parker's name off the list..." She stepped ahead of Donnelly, then pointed to the door to the coroner's suite. "Let's talk in here."

Hopefully, Craig would be sitting at Fenway's desk with his phone charging. They'd have to go find Callahan—but maybe Callahan would be twenty miles away by now, driving to Mexico.

Fenway reached for the door of the coroner's suite, stepping inside as she held it open behind her.

And stopped dead in her tracks.

From behind the front counter, Callahan pointed a gun straight at her.

Donnelly bumped into Fenway from behind, still in the hallway. "Fenway, what—"

Fenway twisted, bracing herself in the doorway, and shoved Donnelly backward—into the hallway and out of danger.

"Hey—" Callahan said.

Fenway leapt for the handle, pulled the door shut, and ducked.

Bang.

Callahan's shot hit the door inches above Fenway's head.

He was desperate. He'd killed before and wasn't above killing now.

Fenway turned from her crouch, holding her hands above her head. "I'm not armed," she said, as she stood slowly, leaning on the closed door behind her. She looked to her left; McVie was lying on the floor, a piece of cloth—maybe a T-shirt?—as a makeshift gag, hands cuffed behind his back, his ankles zip-tied together.

Fenway felt light-headed.

Had she let McVie go with a murderer to turn in the evidence against him? The room started spinning.

Had Callahan killed him?

Then McVie coughed, grunted through the gag, and tried to pivot himself on the carpet to look at Fenway.

She raised her head to look at Callahan: he had a cut on his cheek, dripping blood down his face, his right eye was swelling up, and his left arm hung at his side, his forearm twisted at an almost sickening angle. Broken ulna, probably.

McVie had gone down, but not without a fight.

"You can't get away from this, Brian," Fenway said. "There are armed deputies down the hall. Gretchen's getting them right now."

Callahan breathed heavily. "Both of you are hostages. They won't break the door down with you two in here."

"I don't hear an escape plan," Fenway said. She was standing all the way up now. "You may have the ledger and the balaclava, but we have witnesses. We figured out how you pressured Parker Richards to give you the banking information so you could establish the money trail to frame Rachel. How you got him to duplicate her BMW key."

"I didn't mean for her to be arrested," Callahan said. "I couldn't—Zellman ran out of his apartment, and before I knew it..." He trailed off.

Ah—the hit-and-run was because the original plan had gone out the window. Maybe Callahan planned to attack Zellman in his apartment to make it look like a burglary gone wrong. Rachel's car wasn't supposed to be a murder weapon—it was supposed to be a getaway car that couldn't be traced back to Callahan.

"And you were okay with Rachel getting arrested? The money trail you'd so neatly laid out?"

Callahan looked pained, and not just from his fractured ulna. "I didn't know Dylan's accounts would be connected to Rachel. I figured those accounts were in limbo, you know? Parker gave me access, so I could deposit the money from the cartel without any red flags."

Fenway shook her head. "You didn't think it through."

Callahan was quiet.

"And you tried to run me over." Another puzzle piece in Fenway's head snapped into place. "You took the training on the Dokko Gangz last week. That's how you knew how to steal Huke's car."

Callahan pressed his lips together.

"Your pal Brookline gave you up, too," Fenway said. "You didn't go with him on that private security gig." She shook her head. "A good story, though, breaking up with Rachel, telling Brookline you were with another girl, and counting on the bro code to make sure you had an alibi."

Oh, of course: Callahan had *never* asked Isabella Chan out. He'd used that as a cover story so Fenway wouldn't think he was at Cahill Warehouse Storage to cover his tracks.

Callahan was quiet.

"I don't know what you did with Frank Kingman," Fenway said.

"I don't think you killed him. But Dez got Mathis Jericho's phone from his apartment. We find what's on there, maybe Rachel goes free."

"Frank has enough money to go to Cabo," Callahan said. "I didn't hurt him."

"I'm glad you didn't kill Frank," Fenway said. She paused, still with her hands up. "I get it, Brian, I do. Things got away from you."

Callahan was quiet.

"What did Andrew Zellman see?" Fenway said. "Why did he call me Monday evening?"

"I—" Callahan began, then stopped.

Fenway waited. Just like McVie would. Not pressuring him.

A minute ticked by, then Callahan finally spoke. "You remember when that drunk driver totaled my car a few months ago?" Callahan asked.

Fenway stared blankly at him.

"Yeah, well, I didn't tell many people. I thought maybe Rachel would have said something." He frowned. "Anyway, I didn't have uninsured motorist coverage. And I still owed ten grand on the car."

Fenway blanched. "This was because you needed a new car?"

"How am I supposed to get to work? We're talking about my livelihood. I wasn't going to lose everything just because I didn't get the right insurance."

"That's a pricey truck, Brian. There's a difference between getting to work every day and buying the most expensive vehicle on the lot." Fenway looked Callahan in the eye. "So you killed a cop?"

"I knew you'd jump to conclusions." He tightened his jaw. "I tried to make it work with the bank. I called my parents for money. But then I got a note in my locker at work. I called a number on a burner phone and told them where Vice would be."

"And you got your money."

Callahan swallowed hard. His right hand trembled as it held the gun on Fenway.

"But it didn't stop there. Not at one job."

A pounding on the door. "Fenway?" Donnelly's voice was forceful and strong. "Brian? You need to let us in!"

"Don't open that door!" Callahan said.

"Give us a minute," Fenway said, loud enough to be heard on the other side of the door. She almost laughed at how ridiculous that sounded; like she was finishing up an email before leaving for an appointment.

Fenway stared back at Callahan. "So what's the plan, Brian?"

"I'm thinking."

"Think you can climb out the window in my office and make it to the parking garage before they catch you?" Fenway said. "Or maybe you parked on the street so you can get away more easily. Of course, Donnelly has probably already blocked your car in."

"I said I'm thinking."

"You're not thinking about getting away," Fenway said, narrowing her eyes at him. "You're thinking about how none of this is really your fault."

Silence. Only the sound of her ragged breathing. Fenway looked at McVie's body, tied up on the floor. Nothing on the counter she could use as a weapon: no scissors, no letter opener, nothing big or heavy.

"You know that bartender story?" Callahan asked.

"What bartender story?"

Callahan grimaced in pain; yes, probably a broken ulna. "A man is drinking a beer at this shithole bar when this other guy sits next to him. And the bartender pulls a baseball bat out from under the bar and tells the guy to get out. The guy's all, 'but I'm a paying customer,' but the bartender tells him he doesn't care, to get the hell out and don't come back."

Fenway nodded.

"The guy yells at the bartender, but he leaves. The first man asks what was going on. And the bartender says, 'You didn't see it, but the guy had iron crosses on, all kinds of Nazi stuff. You've gotta nip that shit in the bud immediately. They always send the nice, polite ones in first, and if they get served, they bring their friend in, and then another friend, then another few friends, and suddenly one day you look up, and holy shit, you're working at a Nazi bar.'"

Fenway said nothing, but took a small step forward.

"I needed that ten thousand dollars, and I thought that was the end of it. But then they needed me to give them another location where Vice was running a sting. I said no, but they reminded me they had a paper trail of me accepting the first payment. So I said yes, then I got another ten thousand. After that, instead of telling them where Vice was, they told me to ask around for struggling storage companies."

Fenway remembered Monday's find in Santa Anita Park. "Or look the other way when a bunch of cheap handguns came in."

Callahan ignored the interruption, but his jaw tightened. "I got twenty thousand dollars once I found Seth Cahill. Then instead of just warning them about stings, I also had to give misinformation to Vice about the drug drops." He shook his head. "Suddenly, one day I looked up, and holy shit, I was working for the Venn Cartel." Callahan's upper lip curled, but whether in self-hatred or self-pity, Fenway couldn't tell.

Fenway took a deep breath and bent her knees slightly.

"I tried to get out," Callahan continued, "but you *had* to ask me to drive Mathis back to work. And as soon as he got in the cruiser, he was asking me how we were gonna move the Nyllie from Miranda's cabin."

"So you drove up there," Fenway said. "But you didn't expect to see Seth's Corvette."

"Mathis panicked," Callahan said. "Said he had to go to the police, said he wasn't going to jail, said he'd turn everyone in. Told me I should turn on the cartel too."

"A death wish," Fenway said.

"And I—I don't know what I was thinking. A few bungee cords in the carport. I think Mathis used them to keep the Nyllie secured in his trunk. And—" Callahan swallowed hard. "And he wouldn't shut up."

Fenway nodded. The ligature marks on Jericho's neck. She'd have to ask the CSI team if they matched a bungee cord. "And you had to dispose of the body."

"I didn't have time to bury him," Callahan said, then winced in pain as he moved his left arm. He steeled himself and kept talking. "I've never done anything like that before. But the Corvette was there, and I figured, why not make it look like someone was an amateur trying to pin the murder on the cartel? You and Dez are smart enough to know that the cartel could never kill someone that way. I figured we could give up a few bricks of the Nyllie. I couldn't fit them all in the cruiser's trunk, anyway."

Fenway's mouth dropped open. "You transported drugs in the cruiser?"

Callahan grinned. "Yeah, who's gonna look there? Not when I'm on patrol. I thought this was a brilliant solution. Make it look like someone's setting the cartel up to get the investigation focused elsewhere."

"Not bad." Callahan's misdirection had worked on Fenway. Then another puzzle piece clicked into place. "But the Venn Cartel didn't want to give up eighteen bricks of Nyllie, did they?"

"Worth more money than I'd ever make in my life," Callahan said. "I helped them out of a jam and they had a couple hundred bags. But no, they wanted me to get the other eighteen bags back."

"So that's why you disabled the cameras. You worked with Parker and Frank."

"I figured with a new guy on swing shift, it'd be easy."

"Swap out the bags of Nyllie for fake drugs," Fenway said. "And since the evidence had already been processed, no one would even miss it."

Another few brilliant moves: coercing his two screw-up friends to disable the cameras, hack into the security footage, copy the key fob. If Callahan could have used his powers for good instead of evil, he might have been a stellar detective.

"But Zellman knew something was up," Fenway said.

"He knew," Callahan said, wincing in pain. "He figured out Frank wasn't really from Hackson Square. I told him Frank was fine, that we'd screwed up the paperwork, but I could see it in his eyes."

"And you thought he told Rachel about his suspicions." She paused. "And me."

He shook his head. "I didn't want to kill him."

She balled her hands into fists. "And you didn't want to frame Rachel? Or steal Huke's car? Or run me over?"

A pause. Was that a tear in the corner of Callahan's eye? "I—I didn't know what else to do."

And Callahan let the gun drop about two inches.

Fenway jumped over the counter. She smacked her shin on the edge, but she'd caught Callahan off guard. He pulled the gun up, but Fenway crashed her shoulder into his sternum.

Callahan lost his balance and fell, Fenway on top of him—

Onto his left forearm.

He screamed and dropped the gun.

A crash.

The door to the coroner's suite burst open.

Fenway pushed herself up and ground her knee into Callahan's rib cage. He still screamed in pain. "You piece of shit," she hissed at him. "You killed a cop. You tried to run me over. Then you tried to shoot me in the head. How *dare* you give me some sob story—"

Hands pulling Fenway off Callahan. Three, four, now five deputies, swarming around her. Callahan was still screaming. "Get her away from me! She's crazy!"

Yeah, Fenway thought. *I'm the crazy one.*

The hands let her go, and she took a step back, bumping into the counter, and then she was on her hands and knees next to McVie, pulling his gag down.

"Are you okay, Craig?" Oof, he'd have a nasty black eye.

He stared into Fenway's eyes. "Are *you* okay?"

"I'm mad as hell," Fenway said. "Are you hurt? Do you need—"

"I'm fine," McVie said. Then he took a deep breath and looked Fenway in the eyes. "You are a badass."

Fenway smiled, running her hand gently along the side of his face. "You knew that already."

McVie smiled, with both humor and relief, then his face crumpled. "I'm so sorry."

"For what?"

"I trusted him. I've trusted Brian for years."

"I'm the one who hired him," Fenway said.

"Yeah, but I hired him first—"

Fenway pulled McVie's face close and kissed him.

PART 4

THURSDAY

CHAPTER TWENTY-SEVEN

Fenway navigated her Accord into the harbor parking lot. After the late night she'd had, taking McVie to the hospital, giving her statement to Sheriff Donnelly, then trying to get her adrenaline to stop coursing through her veins, the alarm rang far too early. But she had to find Stephan Butler before his first whale-watching excursion of the day.

She killed the engine as her phone buzzed. A call from her father. Fenway sent it to voicemail; she'd talk to him later.

She yawned as she got out of the car and walked toward the dock where the *Ariel* was tied. Motion on the boat: Butler was already on the deck, and he startled when he saw Fenway.

"I come in peace, Mr. Butler," Fenway said.

"You'll forgive me if I don't believe you."

"Don't know if you heard, but we caught the man who killed our deputy."

"Friendly fire, from the sound of it," Butler said.

Fenway sighed. "Yes. The murderer was one of ours."

Butler thrust his chin forward. "Not only a cop. A guy who reported directly to you."

"And you knew he was the one who broke into your boat."

Butler paused. "You understand why I didn't want to tell you. Why I couldn't file a police report."

Fenway nodded. "I certainly do." She hesitated; there was no gentle way to ask this. "A ledger of some kind, right? With all the, uh, whale-watching trips you took late at night to meet Seth Cahill. You took a ledger to the safe-deposit box, and that's what Callahan broke into your boat to steal."

Butler coolly returned Fenway's stare, a hint of a smile on his face. "I don't believe I know what you're talking about."

"I don't need to see the ledger. I don't even need to make this an official inquiry." Fenway folded her arms. "If Callahan was trying to steal your ledger, though, I need to know. Otherwise, I'm barking up the wrong tree."

After a moment, Butler cleared his throat and put his hands on his hips. "You're not barking up the wrong tree."

"Thank you, Mr. Butler." Fenway turned to leave, then called out over her shoulder, "I hope you have a good season. Lot of money in these whale watching tours."

"I'll stay out of trouble, Coroner," Butler said.

Fenway cocked her head. "You know, I actually believe you."

———

Thirty minutes later, Fenway went into the coroner's suite, a large latte in her hand.

"There you are," a familiar voice said. "For a minute, I thought we were destined to talk on burner phones for the rest of our lives."

"Dez!"

Dez got up from her desk and walked over. "Now that you caught the killer, I can speak to you without fear of reprisal."

Fenway nodded. "And it looks like the detective position is open again."

Dez chuckled. "I wish I knew how to get in touch with Celeste."

"You heard about Gretchen actively blocking me from hiring her?"

"I tried to tell both of you, neither of you was behind the murders."

Fenway smiled. "We're both stubborn."

"And neither of you have yet realized that I am the all-knowing oracle of Estancia."

"It'll sink in one of these days." Fenway looked at Dez out of the corner of her eye. "If you were really the all-knowing oracle, you would have at least *suspected* Brian."

"He fooled everyone." Dez tapped her fingers on the counter. "How did you figure it out?"

"When Parker Richards told me he'd given Dylan's bank account information up, I figured it was someone who had to know Parker and Dylan were brothers—and someone who either wanted Rachel set up, or someone who framed Rachel out of convenience."

"And that person was Callahan?"

"Callahan and the Richards brothers were on the Estancia High baseball team together," Fenway said.

"That couldn't have been the only thing."

"No. But the only two people I told about Frank Kingman were Callahan, and then later, Donnelly. But after I told Brian, Kingman got a phone call at work, and he disappeared. Parker didn't want to give up the name of the law enforcement officer who could make his life hell. Then I remembered: when they got arrested together, Parker got off with a slap on the wrist, while Kingman had to serve time. Just a misdemeanor, but still—who could have vouched for Parker's character? Or convinced him to turn on his friend?"

"That's a stretch."

"I never thought of Callahan anyway, not after Lieutenant Brookline gave him an alibi. And even when Brookline told me Callahan hadn't gone to the Central Valley, he thought it was because Callahan was with another woman who wasn't Rachel—and the reason Callahan hadn't told me was because I was friends with Rachel."

"Not a bad fake alibi, as things go."

"No. And I believed it. But then Callahan left off Parker's name from a list of former Hackson Square employees. And even then, I didn't put everything together until we found out Callahan had turned in fake evidence when he was supposed to turn in the ledger and the balaclava. He knew his DNA would be on the balaclava." Fenway shook her head. "My gut failed me."

Dez nodded. "Crenshaw Auto Detailing on La Crescenta. This morning, two guys there recognized Callahan—and recognized Mathis Jericho's car. He paid in cash. Asked three times if the inside of the trunk was spotless." She paused.

Dez raised her eyebrows. "When were you planning to tell me you were going after Callahan?"

Fenway grinned. "I didn't know myself."

Dez chuckled slightly, but her eyes were downcast. She took a step back from the counter. "I remember when Brian started—this was maybe five, six years ago. He was full of energy, kind of a wide-eyed idealist."

"A wide-eyed idealist who took money from a drug cartel to feed the cops bad information." Fenway frowned. "He needed money to fix his car."

Dez looked up. "And he mowed down another cop with his ex-girlfriend's car. I mean—that's cold. I wouldn't think he'd have it in him."

"When the Venn Cartel owns you," Fenway said, "you do desperate things."

Dez nodded. "You know, I'd like to think that I'd make a different choice in the same situation. That I'd never start down the slippery slope if I had to make a choice between driving to work and taking money from a drug cartel."

"Yeah." Fenway crossed her arms and leaned forward slightly.

"I'll tell you something, Dez. When my mom was dying of cancer, if the Venn Cartel had shown up and told me to cover up evidence? And in return, they'd pay for my mom's treatment? I don't think I could've said no to that."

Dez nodded. "We all have our price."

"I guess we do."

Dez sighed. "You know Callahan won't serve much time. If any."

"He's a cop killer, Dez. There's no way—"

"For the first time, we have leverage against the Venn Cartel," Dez said. "Callahan could tell us who paid him. Who wanted the ledger."

"I basically used him to run errands two weeks ago." Fenway stared at her shoes. "If I'd been the one to take Mathis Jericho back to Cahill Warehouse Storage—"

"Then Callahan would have found another way to cover up his involvement," Dez said. "Maybe someone else would have gotten killed. Maybe you."

Fenway turned toward her office. "If I were dead, at least I wouldn't have to finish all this stupid paperwork."

———

Every step on the concrete stairs to the second floor shot pain up Fenway's right leg. Just a deep bruise on her shin that would go completely away in a couple of days. McVie had bruised ribs, but nothing broken. A black eye, too.

Fenway had to finish the enormous amount of paperwork on her laptop in the Vice bullpen, since the coroner's office was technically a crime scene. She fortunately had no awkward conversations with Captain Alvídrez, but she didn't finish until after six, and her stomach had been complaining about its emptiness since she left the sheriff's office.

Fenway got to the second-floor landing and shuffled to her

apartment. She turned the handle of her door and was greeted by the smell of Italian sausage, garlic, and fennel.

She stepped inside, and McVie was in the kitchen, stirring a pot on the stove. He looked over his shoulder—oof, the bruising around his eye was a putrid olive green now.

"Good timing," McVie said. "It'll be ready in a couple minutes."

"Smells great," Fenway said. For once, she didn't feel like Dos Milagros. "Look at me, saving your life one day, then having you cook me dinner the next. I feel like I'm in a fifties sitcom, except you're not in a hoop skirt."

"Gotta draw the line somewhere." McVie grabbed two flat bowls from the cabinet and Fenway walked into the living room to kick off her shoes. Then she looked around.

"Craig," she said carefully, "where's all your stuff?"

"Yeah," McVie said. "About that." He walked into the dining nook and set down two bowls with penne and the Italian sausage sauce. A loaf of garlic bread, a bottle of red, and two wineglasses in the middle of the table, too. This wasn't fancy; it was a quick, easy meal, but still thoughtfully put together. Fenway was grateful she had a hot meal to come home to—and McVie had obviously been busy with the boxes all day.

"Did you call your dad back?"

Fenway put her purse on the coffee table. How did McVie know that her father had wanted to talk to her? "No—I haven't had a chance yet."

McVie pulled a chair out for Fenway, and she sat. She put the napkin on her lap and looked at McVie expectantly.

"I'm moving out," McVie said.

"What? But we—"

McVie held up his hand. "I really appreciate you offering your place. Honestly, I don't know what I'd be doing without your offer. Probably be sleeping in my car in Colorado."

"But you don't have—"

"I called your father," McVie said. "I told him about my situation."

"Ah."

"He owns a bunch of apartment complexes in Dominguez County."

"Yeah, I know."

"And I asked if he had any units for rent. Turns out there's a two-bedroom available."

"Do you need to borrow money for first month's rent and the security deposit?"

McVie shook his head. "Your father is letting me slide for a month. And I'm not letting him pay for the research Piper did. Next month, I should have enough of the clients who've rehired me to cover rent and utilities."

"Well, I..." Fenway steepled her hands, then stared at her bowl of pasta. She really wanted to eat. "I don't know what to think." She picked up her fork and took a bite. She had a pang of anger at her father for not discussing this with her first—but, after all, he had tried.

"When we move in together—or when we take any step forward," McVie said, looking into Fenway's eyes, "I want it to be when we can both make a thoughtful decision. Not be forced into it by circumstances. I know you need your space. I know I've got to have a decent relationship with my daughter, and I know you don't need to see her trying to split us up." McVie paused. "And I know that this is the most serious relationship you've had, but it doesn't mean that I'm Mister Right." He picked up his fork. "Don't get me wrong. I'd like it to be me. But I don't want you feeling like you're forced into anything."

Fenway reached across the table, picked up the bottle of wine and filled both their glasses. "Where is this apartment?"

McVie chuckled. "To the only two-bedroom apartment your father had available. I picked up the keys at eleven this morning and moved most of my stuff in this afternoon."

"That was quick." Fenway cocked an eyebrow.

"The apartment's only one floor down."

Fenway paused. So if Megan visited, Fenway would see her constantly. This arrangement was barely better than the two of them sharing an apartment.

No—it *was* better. McVie knew what Fenway needed. And he'd made it happen.

She picked up McVie's wineglass and handed it to him, then picked up hers and held it up in front of her.

"Howdy, neighbor," Fenway said. "Maybe we can wait to set up your bed until tomorrow."

McVie clinked Fenway's glass. "I'll drink to that."

CAST OF CHARACTERS

- **Fenway Stevenson:** A former nurse practitioner with a master's degree in forensics, she moved to Estancia in April. Fenway has a rocky (but improving) relationship with her father. Appointed to fill out the coroner's term, she ran for election—and won. Her official four-year term started January 1.

Her family

- **Nathaniel Ferris:** The richest, most powerful man in the county, the oil magnate founded and owns Ferris Energy. After his wife took away the then eight-year-old Fenway to Seattle two decades ago, he had hardly seen or talked to Fenway in the twenty years before she came back to town. They've spent the last year rebuilding their relationship.
- **Charlotte Ferris:** The former beauty pageant winner married Nathaniel a decade ago when she was 25 and he

was 50—the weekend of Fenway's high school graduation.

Co-workers and law enforcement personnel, past and present

- **Sergeant Desirée "Dez" Roubideaux**: A detective in the coroner's office, Dez has worked for the county for over twenty years. She's a dedicated, determined investigator despite her wisecracks.
- **Craig McVie**: The former sheriff of Dominguez County, he lost the mayoral race in November. Recently divorced from Amy, he's now a private investigator. He and Fenway officially started dating after the election, and Fenway just helped him move to Colorado—a move that was quickly reversed when his job disappeared.
- **Rachel Richards**: Fenway's former assistant, she was promoted to be the county's youngest public information officer in a century.
- **Sarah Summerfield**: The coroner's assistant hired to replace Rachel. Smart and savvy.
- **Piper Patten:** Formerly in the county's IT department, this willowy redhead is a whiz at forensic accounting and data gathering. She helped Nathaniel Ferris prove his innocence in a murder case, and now works for McVie.
- **Detective Brian Callahan**: A former sheriff's deputy, he got the detective position in the coroner's office after Fenway's first choice, Deputy Celeste Salvador, accepted a job offer out of the area. He's also dating Rachel.
- **Sheriff Gretchen Donnelly:** Succeeding Craig McVie as county sheriff, she's been on the job about eight months. She and Fenway don't always see eye-to-eye on how to handle cases.

- **Melissa de la Garza:** A CSI tech from neighboring San Miguelito County, de la Garza's team is a shared forensic resource with Dominguez County.
- **Donald Huke:** An uptight, by-the-book rookie deputy in the Dominguez County Sheriff's Office, and live-in boyfriend to Melissa.
- **Captain Steve Alvídrez:** The head of the vice squad in Dominguez County.
- **Dr. Michi Yasuda:** Dez's wife is the medical examiner in San Miguelito County, whose morgue houses many victims from Dominguez County.
- **Megan McVie:** Craig's seventeen-year-old daughter with his ex-wife Amy, she moved to Colorado with her mother and still wants her parents to get back together.
- **Jordan Daniels:** The IT director for the county.
- **Peter Esparanza:** The guard at the Dominguez County vehicle impound lot.

Suspects, witnesses, and persons of interest

- **Mathis Jericho:** The maintenance and landscaping specialist for Cahill Warehouse Storage was found dead last week in a Corvette, surrounded by bags of morpheranyl.
- **Tyra Cahill:** The new owner of Cahill Warehouse Storage.
- **Isabella Chan:** An office assistant at Cahill Warehouse Storage.
- **Parker Richards:** The brother of Rachel's former husband, he likes to party and has the reputation of barely keeping his life together.
- **Frank Kingman:** A friend of Parker's who recently got out of jail on a minor misdemeanor charge.

- **Stephan Butler:** The owner/operator of a local whale-watching business who has often used the Cahill's storage facility.
- **Logan:** A harbor employee who assists with boat owners.
- **Terry:** A security guard at Estancia Harbor.
- **Zoso**: A well-connected low-level drug dealer whose penchant for the pills he uses doesn't interfere with his eyes and ears; he has helped Fenway out on a few cases in the past.

The Fenway Stevenson Mysteries
Book One: The Reluctant Coroner
Book Two: The Incumbent Coroner
Book Three: The Candidate Coroner
Book Four: The Upstaged Coroner
Book Five: The Courtroom Coroner
Novella: The Christmas Coroner
Book Six: The Watchful Coroner
Book Seven: The Accused Coroner
Novella: The Clandestine Coroner
Book Eight: The Offside Coroner
Book Nine: The Warehouse Coroner
Book Ten: The Digital Coroner
Book Eleven: The Disloyal Coroner

The Time Loop Detective
Book One: A Time for Murder

The Woodhead & Becker Mysteries

Book One: The Winterstone Murder
Book Two: The Bridegroom Murder
Book Three: The Trailer Park Murder
Book Four: The Executive Murder
Book Five: The Sweathouse Murder (coming soon)

Dez Roubideaux
Novella: Bad Weather

Collections
Books 1–3 of The Fenway Stevenson Mysteries
Books 4-6 of The Fenway Stevenson Mysteries
Books 7-9 of The Fenway Stevenson Mysteries
Fenway Stevenson: Rookie Year (Books 1-7, plus both novellas and
two novelettes)

Non-fiction
From Zero to Four Figures:
Making $1,000 a Month Self-Publishing Fiction

Sign up for *The Coroner's Report,*
Paul Austin Ardoin's fortnightly newsletter:
http://www.paulaustinardoin.com

I hope you enjoyed reading this book as much as I enjoyed writing it. If you did, I'd sincerely appreciate a review on your favorite book retailer's website, Goodreads, and BookBub. Reviews are crucial for any author, and even just a line or two can make a huge difference.

ACKNOWLEDGMENTS

Many thanks to my cover designer Ziad Ezzat of Feral Creative and my editor Dana Luco. Thanks also to my early readers, including the Wordforge Novelists group in Sacramento, Laura Shepherd, Michelle Damiani, Blair Semple, Dr. Christina Bellinger, Gavin Ralph, Angela Nurse, Charlie Lemoine, DeAnna Hart, and Rebecca Davis.

Thanks also go to Jamie Sanfelippo, who has been invaluable creating, organizing, and maintaining my author newsletter, website, reader teams, promotions, and a million other items.

To my wife and children, I'm deeply grateful for your encouragement and support.

www.ingramcontent.com/pod-product-compliance
Lightning Source LLC
Chambersburg PA
CBHW021236190726
48289CB00005B/1353